STEVE ALTEN

VARIANCE

Arkansas

Alt

Timothy Schulte, Variance Publishing, 1610 South Pine Street.
Cabot, AR 72023, (501) 843-BOOK
tpaulschulte@variancepublishing.com
ISBN: 1-935142-04-6
ISBN-13: 978-1-935142-04-1
Published by Variance LLC (USA).
www.variancepublishing.com

Library of Congress Control Number: 2009922944

Cover Design by Erik Hollander: www.hollanderdesignlab.com
Shark Image by Brandon Cole
Interior by Tom Mungovan: www.vanmungo.com
Edited by Shane Thomson: slthomson@variancepublishing.com

To personally contact the author or learn more about his novels,
go to: www.SteveAlten.com

For more information on Adopt-an-Author,
go to: www.AdoptAnAuthor.com

10 9 8 7 6 5 4 3 2 1

To my father, Lawrence Alten
for always rescuing me when I need it.

Thanks, Dad.

ACKNOWLEDGMENTS

It is with great pride and appreciation that I acknowledge those who contributed to the completion of MEG: Hell's Aquarium.

First and foremost, many thanks to my literary agent, Danny Baror of Baror International, my friend and MEG producer Belle Avery, and my terrific publicist, Trish Stevens at Ascot Media Group. Many thanks also to Joel McKuin of Colden, McKuin & Frankel.

It's an honor to work with the great people at Variance Publishing; my heartfelt gratitude to owners Tim Schulte and Jeremy Robinson, Stanley Tremblay for a great interior, and to my editor, Shane Thomson.

Special thanks to the staff at the Georgia Aquarium for their information, insight, and behind-the-scenes tour ... especially Dave Santucci, director of public relations. Thanks also to David Zelski at the Georgia Public Broadcasting for arranging the visit. My appreciation to Dr. Maria Sdorlias and her colleagues at the University of Sydney's School of Geosciences for their expertise regarding the mystery of the "undersea shelves" located in the Philippine Sea Plate as well as the contribution of their outstanding maps of the area.

A very special thanks to forensic reconstruction illustrator and commercial artist William McDonald (www.alienufoart.com) whose original artwork and extensive research breathes life into the extinct (?) sea monsters appearing in the story.

My gratitude to my talented web designer, Leisa Coffman at MontageMarketing.com and to Barbara Becker for her tireless work on the Adopt-An-Author teen reading program. Very special thanks to graphic artist supreme, Erik Hollander at HollanderDesignLab.com for another amazing cover (two actually!) and James Gelet, for his creative Internet promotions.

Last, to my wife and partner, Kim, for all her support, to my parents for always being there, my two children for putting up with dad's long hours behind closed doors, and to my readers: Thank you for your correspondence and contributions. Your comments are always a welcome treat, your input means so much, and you remain this author's greatest asset.

-----Steve Alten, Ed.D.

To personally contact the author
or learn more about his novels,
Click on www.SteveAlten.com

MEG: Hell's Aquarium is part of ADOPT-AN-AUTHOR,
a free nationwide program
for Secondary School students and teachers.
For more information, click on www.AdoptAnAuthor.com

PROLOGUE

Encompassing sixty million square miles, the Pacific Ocean is the largest and oldest body of water on our planet, and with an average depth of fourteen thousand feet, it is also the deepest, possessing some of the most biologically diverse creatures ever to inhabit the Earth.

The Pacific is all that remains of the Panthalassa, an ancient ocean that was once so vast it covered everything on our planet but the super-continent of Pangaea. Life first began in these waters 3.5 billion years ago as a single-celled organism and remained that way with very little change over the next 3 billion years. And then, 540 million years ago, life suddenly took off. From multi-cellular organisms sprang trilobites and corals, jellyfish and mollusks, sea scorpions and squids. Amid this Cambrian Explosion arose one other creature—a unique animal, tiny in size, that possessed a backbone, which separated its brain and nervous system from the rest of its organs.

The age of fish—the Devonian Era—had arrived.

The first of these vertebrates were filter feeders, possessing no jaws in which to seize prey. Because their internal skeletons were composed of cartilage, many species grew a thick armor-like, bony shield that covered their heads as a means of protection. Others developed senses that allowed them to see, taste, smell, hear, and feel within their watery environment. And then, some 80 million years after the first fish appeared, a revolutionary feature came into being—a set of biting jaws.

It would be an innovation that would lead to mass diversification, separating predator from prey, instantly reshuffling the ocean's food chain. The planet's first true hunters evolved, and with them the wolves of the sea—the sharks.

For many species of fish, the Panthalassic Ocean quickly became a dangerous place to live.

Necessity is the mother of invention, adaptation the means to survival. One hundred seventy million years after the first vertebrates hatched in the sea, a lobe-finned fish crawled out of the Panthalassa onto shore ... and gasped a breath of air. Gills would evolve into nostrils and internal lungs, ventilated by a throat-pump. Within 20 million years these new animals had colonized the land.

The age of amphibians had arrived.

Adapting to a terrestrial lifestyle demanded more evolutionary changes, propelled by the need to survive more efficiently. Limited by their need to re-hydrate and their ability to ventilate their lungs, amphibians developed a rib cage that allowed for expansion and contraction while increasing the volume of air that could be processed by the lungs. Changes in internal fertilization and the composition of the egg shell further protected the developing embryo from drying out.

Sixty million years after the first lobe-finned fish crawled out of the sea, the first reptiles were born.

More anatomical adaptations would follow. Positioning of the hip girdle gave some reptiles the ability to stand and run on their hind legs. Skull weight was reduced with the addition of new temporal openings that replaced heavy bone with tendon-like materials. These openings also served to increase the bite power of the jaws ... and a new subclass of reptile rose to prominence—the dinosaur.

By this time, Pangaea had separated into two continents—Gondwana and Laurasia. As the planet's landmasses continued to break apart and drift, the Panthalassic Ocean divided into the Atlantic and Arctic Ocean basins and, eventually, the Indian and Pacific Oceans. Changes in atmospheric and geological conditions would lead to global warming and ice age cycles, affecting the inhabitants of both land and sea. The survivors evolved into the next dominant species; the weak dead-ended into extinction.

While the dinosaurs ruled the land and air, another subclass of reptiles—the placodonts and ichthyosaurs—returned to the ocean. These were the planet's first true sea monsters; the long-necked *Elasmosaurus*; the massive-skulled *Kronosaurus*; *Shonisaurus*, a sleek, dolphin-like, fifty-foot, forty-ton *Ichthyosaurus*; and the largest beast of all—*Liopleurodon*.

Over the next 170 million years these fearsome predators would dominate the land and sea ... until one fateful day, 65 million years ago, when a seven-mile-in-diameter hunk of rock fell from the sky and, once again, everything changed.

The firestorms brought on by the asteroid strike caused a global nuclear winter of sorts by emitting caustic gasses and millions of tons of ash and soot into the atmosphere, blotting out the sun. The fires subsided, giving way to an ensuing ice age that officially ended the age of the dinosaurs, sparing only those species that could adapt to the sudden drop in temperatures.

But there were other planetary changes going on as well.

Earth's continents and ocean floors rest on a giant jigsaw puzzle of crust known as the lithosphere. Composed of fourteen massive tectonic plates and thirty-eight minor ones, the lithosphere floats over our planet's hot interior like a constantly moving glacier. These movements are driven by volcanic forces that appear along the plates' boundaries—the engine behind the planet's drifting continents.

When molten rock (magma) pushes up through the sea floor, it forces tectonic plates to spread apart, or diverge, creating valleys known as rifts. Should two or more continents collide, the result is an upheaval that creates mountain ranges. When the collision occurs underwater, the denser of the two tectonic plates slips beneath the lesser at the subduction zone, creating deep fissures, or trenches—the deepest parts of the ocean. The denser plate melts into magma, reemerging as erupting lava, which leads to the formation of island chains.

Nowhere are these volcanic interactions more evident than along a minor lithospheric plate known as the Philippine Sea Plate.

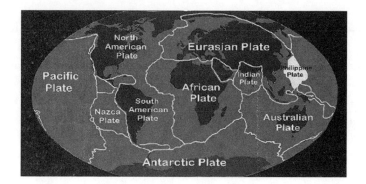

Forming the basin beneath the Philippine Sea, shaped like a diamond, the Philippine Sea Plate is unique in that it is completely surrounded by subduction zones. Bordering the plate to the east is the massive Pacific Plate, which is converging and subducting beneath its geology, forming the Mariana Trench, the deepest gorge on the planet. To the west is the Eurasian Plate, to the south the Indo-Australian Plate, and to the north the North American, Amurian, and Okhotsk plates—each tectonic border forming a deepwater trench.

With an average depth of 19,700 feet, the Philippine Sea Basin represents the most unexplored, isolated region on our planet, its tremendous pressure making it inaccessible to all but the world's deepest-diving submersibles.

Scientists have had to rely on bathymetric equipment in order to obtain any kind of significant data on this ancient geology. In the process, they had failed to discover the sea plate's true anomaly—an isolated sea, hidden deep beneath the basin's crust, that dates back to the Panthalassa. Harbored within this enclosed habitat is a thriving food chain that has sustained primitive life since the very first marine reptile returned to the ocean over 240 million years ago.

ᐁ   ᐁ   ᐁ

IT MOVES EFFORTLESSLY through depths' perpetual darkness, its albino hide casting a soft glow along the silent sea floor seven thousand feet below a tempest surface. Streamlined from the tip of its blunt bullet-shaped snout to the upper lobe of its powerful half-moon-shaped caudal fin, the fifty-eight foot, thirty-ton behemoth reigns over its habitat.

Concealed behind the barely visible gum line are hundreds of razor-sharp teeth, each edge serrated like a steak knife. The bottom teeth, totaling twenty-two, are stiletto-sharp, designed for puncturing and gripping prey. The wider upper quadrants, twenty-four in number, are powerful weapons capable of cutting and penetrating bone, sinew, and blubber. Behind the upper and lower front row are four to five additional rows of replacement teeth, folded back into the gum line like a conveyor belt. Composed of calcified cartilage, containing no blood vessels, these dentures are set in a ten-foot jaw that, instead of being fused to the skull, hangs loosely beneath the brain case. This enables the upper jaw to push forward and hyperextend open—wide enough to engulf, and crush, an adult bull elephant.

As if the size and voraciousness of its feeding orifice were not enough, nature has endowed this monster with a predatory intelligence, honed by 400 million years of evolution. Six distinct senses expose every geological feature, every current, every temperature gradient ... and every creature occupying its domain.

The predator's eyes contain a reflective layer of tissue situated behind the retina. When moving through the darkness of the depths, light is reflected off this layer, allowing the creature to see. In sunlight, the reflective plate is covered by a layer of pigment, which functions like a built-in pair of sunglasses. While black in normally pigmented members of the species, this particular male's eyes are a cataract-blue—a trait found in albinos. As large as basketballs, the sight organs reflexively roll back into the skull as the creature launches its attack on its prey, protecting the eyeball from being damaged.

Forward of the eyes, just beneath the snout, are a pair of directional nostrils so sensitive that they can detect one drop of blood or urine in a million gallons of water. The tongue and snout provide a sense of taste and touch, while two labyrinths within the skull function as ears. But it is two other receptor organs that make this predator the master of its liquid domain.

The first of these mid-to-long-range detection systems is the lateral line, a hollow tube that runs along either flank just beneath the skin. Microscopic pores open these tubes to the sea. When another animal creates a vibration or turbulence in the water, the reverberations stimulate tiny hairs within these sensory cells that alert the predator to the source of the disturbance—miles away!

Even more sensitive are the hunter's long-range receptor cells, located along the top and underside of the snout. Known as the ampullae of Lorenzini, these deep, jelly-filled pores connect to the brain by a vast tributary of cranial nerves. This "neural array" detects the faint voltage gradients and bio-electric fields produced by aquatic animals as their skin moves through the water, by the breathing action of their gills ... or by their beating hearts. So sensitive is the ampullae of Lorenzini to electrical discharges that the creature, while moving through the depths of the Philippine Sea, could locate a thin copper wire connected to two D-size batteries if it were stretched from Japan to the Chinese mainland several thousand miles away.

Carcharodon megalodon: prehistoric cousin of the modern-day great white shark. The alpha predator of all time, the Meg bears a ferocity and disposition that condemns it to a lone existence. And yet, while its numbers have dwindled over the last million years, members of the species have survived extinction by adapting—in this case by inhabiting the nutrient-rich, hydrothermally warmed waters of the Philippine Sea Plate's trenches.

❦ ❦ ❦

RINGING THE CREATURE's gray-blue right eye and football-size nostrils are a series of gruesome scars that extend down to its upper jaw line and an exposed section of gum. These wounds, along with a near-lethal bite that stole a twenty-inch chunk from its six-foot dorsal fin were inflicted by a larger rival sibling many years earlier.

To the few humans who have crossed this adult male's path and survived, the Meg is known as Scarface. To the sea creatures that lurk within its considerable range, its pale bioluminescent glow means death.

Scarface's deformed mouth twitches as the sea enters its orifice, held open in a cruel, jagged smile. Driven by hunger, the predator has abandoned its ancestral birthplace in the Mariana Trench to stakeout the Western Mariana Trough.

Rising to the surface at night, it had attacked and killed a juvenile whale shark just outside the shallows of the Palau Atoll. But before it could complete its feeding, dawn had chased it back into the depths, its nocturnal eyes still quite sensitive to direct sunlight. For six hours it had circled a thousand feet below its bleeding kill. Then, growing impatient, abandoned the whale shark to continue its westerly trek.

Scarface swims along the sea bed in water temperatures just above freezing, yet the warm-blooded goliath is not bothered by the cold. Running the length of the Megalodon's body, sandwiching its spinal column, are two thick bands of red muscle that not only empower its massive keel and tail, but act like a giant radiator, driving heat into its circulatory system—an internal thermostat operating at a full fifty degrees higher than its skin temperature.

Though it travels in depths that would crush a marine mammal, the fish, lacking an air bladder, remains impervious to water pressure. Buoyancy comes from the Megalodon's liver. Weighing more than 25,000 pounds, the organ is set internally in folded layers and contains a buoyant oil that allows for optimum maneuverability through any depth.

As it moves through its dark underworld, the Meg's ampullae of Lorenzini detect a strange object along the sea floor. Attracted by the faint electrical field, Scarface alters its course to investigate.

Its would-be-prey rests half-buried along the bottom, 12,145 feet below the surface. The rusted steel hull of the World War II Japanese destroyer teases the hungry predator, the diseased metal still producing an electrical current in the water.

Determining the object to be inedible, Scarface moves on, eventually coming to a steep rise—the Western Mariana Ridge. It ascends along the steep basalt escarpment, its ancient surface covered in thriving coral reefs. Gas bubbles percolate from the rocky formations—methane gas and hydrogen sulfide escaping from the ancient sea below.

At 7,670 feet, the ridge levels out, revealing a vast, deep sea basin, the geology of which predates the Megalodon species existence by some 200 million years.

THE GEOLOGICAL ANOMALY had formed 180 million years ago when Pangaea had broken apart, separating into Laurasia (North America, Europe, Asia, and Greenland) and Gondwanaland (Australia, Antarctica, India, and South America). The "slow rift" that had occurred between the two continental plates had created an expanding sliver of crust adjacent to modern day southern China. The stretched section of hardening magma, hundreds of miles long, had thinned and subsided underwater, creating an undersea shelf. While some of this shelf was subsequently destroyed due to other tectonic forces, the crust at the southern part of the West Philippine Basin had thickened, creating, in essence, a false bottom 7,775 feet below the surface of the Pacific Ocean, concealing the ancient subduction zone that dropped to the ocean's true depths another four miles down.

Over the next 30 million years, the magma spewed from this volcanic subduction zone gradually sealed up the shelf, isolating the habitat from the rest of the Pacific. Nutrient-filled currents insured a perpetual food chain, while the warmth provided by the region's hydrothermal vents attracted a wide variety of prehistoric life to an abyssal sea that spanned almost five thousand square miles beneath the hardened magma shelf, concealing the true depths of the Philippine Sea.

REVERBERATIONS IN THE water excite the neuromast cells located within the Meg's lateral line. Scarface alters his course, heading for the alluring current.

It is a hole in the sea floor—a black void—four hundred feet across. Warm water rises from the dark geological orifice, a tropical outflow mixed with methane gas ... and something else!

The Megalodon circles the crater-like aperture, its nostrils inhaling the enticing alien outflow, a scent-filled stew that feeds information to its brain. Scarface grows excited, his mouth opening wider, the increased flow of water causing his gills to flutter even faster, his pulse to race. The Meg's muscular keel, as wide as a sewage pipe, pumps the hunter's powerful caudal fin briskly through the water as it arches its back in an involuntary spasm, its senses on fire.

Something is rising from the hole!

The ray-finned fish is ten feet longer than Scarface and eight tons heavier. A docile giant, the juvenile plankton feeder races out of the gap into open ocean—

—unaware of the lurking Megalodon.

Scarface drives his hyperextended jaws sideways into the startled fish, burying his teeth across the filter feeder's pelvic fin, crushing its lower vertebrae.

The sixty-eight-foot Leedsichthys quivers as if shocked by 50,000 volts of electricity, its spasming torso creating a sawing action that assists the Megalodon's serrated upper teeth to cut quicker and deeper. Scarface whips his mammoth head to and fro until his prey's vertebrae snap off in his mouth, separating the tail from the torso in a cloudburst of blood.

Propelled by its heavy ray-shaped, forward pectoral fins, the prehistoric fish continues swimming up and away from the hole without its lower extremity!

His jowls full, Scarface allows his prey to escape, satisfied to continue grinding the two-thousand-pound bite of gristle and meat into swallowable pieces. Sluggish, its senses momentarily distracted, the Meg detects the presence of another creature rising from out of the hole—failing to distinguish prey from predator.

Fully aware of the circling creature, the leviathan shoots out from the hole, its imposing jaws—thirty-two feet from snout to mandible—slamming down upon the Megalodon's pelvic girdle. Dagger-shaped fangs emasculate Scarface, snapping off his twin claspers before grinding the cartilage supporting the base of the shark's thick caudal fin into mince meat.

Scarface whips his head around, his jumbled senses taking in the larger hunter as it continues rising majestically from the hole to circle the wounded Meg.

At 122 feet, the female pliosaur is longer than a blue whale and just as heavy. Behind its immense crocodile-like skull is a long, muscular torso powered by forward and rear flippers, ending at a stout tail. Incredibly agile for its size, the monster banks hard, performing a series of quick, tight loops around its adversary, ever mindful of the Meg's fearful set of jaws. Possessing a keen sense of smell, the hunter's sensory system has locked in on the steady stream of blood pouring from the Megalodon's partially severed tail. It can feel the pulsating rhythm of the shark's two-chambered heart, it can taste the hot, pungent blood pumping from the wound.

Barely able to propel himself forward, Scarface fights to stabilize himself against the circling predator's powerful current.

What happens next is as fast and furious as it is deadly.

With a colossal thrust of its powerful forward flippers, the one-hundred-ton pliosaur shoots off into the darkness. Then, with the grace of a sea lion, it banks into a 180-degree turn and, circling in from behind, strikes the floundering Megalodon with its open maw, the force like that of a charging locomotive hitting a stalled car.

A burst of bloody excrement explodes out of Scarface's mouth as its internal organs are crushed beneath 22,000 pounds per square inch of pressure. The Megalodon's stomach convulses and turns inside out, protruding from its cavernous mouth like a pinkish balloon as it regurgitates the undigested remains of its own partially swallowed meal. The shark lashes back and forth as the larger predator sets its jaws harder into its belly's yielding flesh, the pliosaur rolling its head back and forth like a crocodile to quiet its prey—the rocking motion allowing its ten-inch, spike-shaped teeth to sink deeper into the shark's albino hide.

For twenty long minutes the two titans remain interlocked, their bodies bathed in the warm outflow of the hole's rising current—the Megalodon held sideways, suspended in a vice grip as it bleeds out and drowns, its killer's fang-filled mouth clamped down in an unyielding death-hold, its locked jaw muscles tensing against its dying prey's final throes.

Finally, Scarface's once-rigid form goes flaccid, his massive cardiac muscle ceasing to pump. The pliosaur shakes the dead Megalodon back and forth several more times just to be sure, then whips its body into snake-like gyrations as it disappears back down the fissure with its young's next meal—

—leaving behind a dispersing trail of blood.

PART 1

1

Saturday

The black Lexus JX sedan is double-parked outside Gate B, the vehicle's driver, Jonas Taylor, eyeballing the airport cop who has sent him circling the airport four times already. The sixty-six-year-old paleobiologist glances at his twenty-four-year-old daughter, Danielle, curled up in the passenger seat next to him. The model-pretty blonde, who works part-time for a local NBC-TV affiliate as a news reporter and weekends emceeing shows at the Tanaka Institute, is staring at the digital clock on the dashboard, growing impatient. "Almost four thirty. If his plane doesn't get here soon, I'll miss the evening show."

"His plane just landed. Relax." Jonas taps the steering wheel to an old Neil Diamond tune on the radio. "Anyway, Olivia can always emcee the show in a pinch."

"Olivia?" Dani looks at her father as if she just swallowed turpentine. "Dad, the Saturday night show is my gig. Period. Now would you please turn off that annoying song."

"I like Neil Diamond."

"Who?"

"Come on, I'm not that old."

"Yeah, you are. Seriously, Dad, I will pay you to let me change the station."

"Fine, only no gangster rap."

"It's 'gangsta,' and get with the times. Ghetto is in. It's what we relate to."

"My mistake. I forgot your mother and I raised you as a poor black child in a gang-infested neighborhood."

The airport cop approaches the Lexus. Before he can signal Jonas to move the car, twenty-year-old David Taylor steps out of the baggage claim exit, an orange and blue University of Florida duffle bag slung over one broad shoulder. Jonas's son is wearing a gray Gator's Football tee-shirt, faded jeans, and sneakers. He is fit and tan, his brown hair long, speckled with golden highlights from being in the sun, his almond-brown eyes hidden behind dark sunglasses.

David tosses his duffle in the back seat of the Lexus and climbs in. "Sorry Plane was an hour late."

"No worries. We just got here. Right, Dani?"

"Wrong. You know dad, he had to leave an hour early." She allows David to kiss her cheek. "You look good ... Jesus, Dad, drive!"

Jonas pulls into traffic, following the signs leading to Highway 68 West.

"You look like you gained a few pounds. Lifting weights again?"

"Yes ... and no, for the last time, I am not trying out for football."

"Sure, I know. I just saw the shirt and thought—"

"It's just a shirt."

"—because the coach called our house twice last week. He lost two wide-outs to injuries in spring training. With your speed—"

"Dad, enough! My playing days ended in high school."

"Okay, okay. I just remember my playing days at Penn State ... those were the best of times."

"Please, that was half a century ago." Dani ruffles her father's thick mane of snowy-white hair. "David, what do you think of Dad's new look?"

David smiles. "It's as white as Angel's ass. It was still gray last time I saw you."

"Comes from working too closely with monsters."

"I thought you enjoyed working with Angel's pups?"

Jonas smiles at his daughter. "I was talking about you."

Dani smacks him playfully across his head. "I told him he should use that hair stuff that gets rid of the gray."

"Don't listen to her, Dad. It makes you look more intelligent. Sort of like Anderson Cooper, only a lot older."

"Good. I can use all the help I can get. David ... about this internship—"

"Dad, we talked about this."

"There are other specialties in marine biology. We just completed the Manta Ray sale with the Naval Warfare Center, thanks, in part, to your piloting demo. The Navy knows you're the best pilot we have, and the Vice Admiral mentioned they could use a good trainer."

"You know I love piloting the subs. I just like working with the Megs more. There's something about big predators—"

"You want big predators? San Diego needs a new trainer for their female orca. I could make a call—"

"Pass."

"What's wrong with orcas?"

"Nothing, if you enjoy teaching dog tricks to a whale. Angel's pups have special needs."

"Pups? Christ, you make them sound like a litter of cocker spaniels. The three runts are already larger than an adult great white, and the two sisters ... you tell him, Dani."

Dani nods, text messaging on her cell phone. "The sisters are evil. They'll be as big and nasty as their mother."

"Why do you call them 'the sisters?' Technically, all five are sisters."

"When you see them every day like Dani and I do, you'll understand. They may have shared the same womb, but the three runts look and act nothing like Bela and Lizzy." Jonas exits Highway 68, heading south on Highway 1. "How's Corrine?"

"We broke up."

Dani looks up. "Seriously? I never liked her."

"Wait," Jonas jumps in, "what was wrong with Corrine?"

"She was getting too serious."

"What's wrong with serious? Is serious so bad?"

"How's mom?"

"She's good. And don't change the subject."

"Mom's stressed out," Dani says.

"Not PETA again?"

"Worse. A thug off-shoot. They call themselves R.A.W. Stands for Return Animals to the Wild. Dad had to hire a security outfit; they were puncturing the staff's tires. I'm trying to convince my producer to let me do an exposé. These assholes don't give a damn about the Megs. They're just after the free publicity."

David says nothing, preferring to gaze out his passenger window at the Pacific Ocean peeking through the rolling hillsides.

Jonas weighs the sudden silence. "Go ahead and say it, David. 'The pen's too small. The pups are getting too big.'"

David looks at his father. "What did the State Assembly say?"

"Same as they've always said. No more expansion, at least not along the coast. They offered us six hundred acres in Bakersfield."

"Bakersfield? Why not Death Valley?"

"There may be another option. Mac and I have a meeting on Monday with Emaar Properties out of the United Arab Emirates. Rumor has it they're constructing some kind of new, state-of-the-art aquarium and hotel in Dubai."

"I heard about that. The place is supposed to be incredible, ten times the size of the Georgia Aquarium. You think they want one of the pups?"

Jonas nods. "I'd bet the house on it."

❦ ❦ ❦

The Lexus heads south on Cabrillo Highway, exiting onto Sand Dunes Drive. David stares at the ocean, mesmerized by its crashing surf, marveling at the differences between Monterey's rough Pacific and Florida's calmer Atlantic, where he has spent the last three summers interning at the Harbor Branch Oceanographic Institution in Fort Pierce, completing field work in order to earn his bachelor's degree in marine biology. Up ahead he sees the familiar concrete and steel bowl, the arena's ocean-access canal running out to meet the deeper ocean waters like a submerged pier.

The Tanaka Institute and Lagoon: home to the most dangerous creatures in the planet's history.

❦ ❦ ❦

Built by David's maternal grandfather, Masao Tanaka, more than thirty-five years ago, the lagoon had originally been designed to function as a field laboratory to study cetacean behavior. Each year, tens of thousands of whales migrated south from the Bering Sea along California's coast, searching for shallow, protected harbors in which to birth their calves. The Tanaka Lagoon, essentially a man-made lake with an ocean-access canal, was thought to be the perfect birthing place for pregnant females who were struggling to make it down to Baja.

Masao had mortgaged his family's future to build the facility, but when rising costs had depleted those funds, he had been forced to seek help from the Japanese Marine Science Technology Center. JAMSTEC was more interested in creating an early-warning, earthquake detection system off the Japanese coast, and Masao held the patents on UNIS—a new Unmanned Nautical Information Submersible. In exchange for funding his whale lagoon, Masao accepted a high-risk contract with JAMSTEC to deploy twenty-five UNIS robots seven miles below the Western Pacific along the seismically active sea floor of the Mariana Trench.

To complete the mission, Masao's son, D.J., had to escort each UNIS to the bottom using an Abyss Glider, a one-man, deep-sea submersible resembling an acrylic torpedo with wings. It would take months to deploy the robots, but once the system was up and running the network worked like a charm. And then, one after another, the drones stopped transmitting data. JAMSTEC froze funding on the whale lagoon, insisting Masao fix the problem. To do that required retrieving one of the damaged UNIS robots—a two-submersible job—but Masao refused to allow his other pilot—his daughter, Terry—to make the dive with her younger brother. Instead, he turned to an old friend for help.

Before he became a paleobiologist, Jonas Taylor had been the best deep-sea submersible pilot ever to wear the Navy uniform … until his last dive in these very waters seven years earlier. Working in a three-man submersible below 33,000 feet, Jonas had suddenly panicked, launching the Navy's vessel into a rapid emergency ascent. The duress of the maneuver had caused a malfunction in the cabin's pressurization system and the two scientists on board died. Jonas, the only survivor, claimed he had performed the risky ascent after being confronted by "an enormous, ghost-white shark with a head bigger than the entire sub!"

The Navy diagnosed their prized argonaut with psychosis of the deep. His naval career over, his confidence shot, Jonas set out to prove to the world that he was not crazy, that the unexplored 1,550-mile-long gorge was indeed inhabited by *Carcharodon megalodon*—a sixty-foot, prehistoric version of a great white shark, an ancient predator long thought extinct.

Masao cared little about Jonas's bizarre theories. What he needed was a second deep-sea pilot to accompany his son on a salvage operation. Forced to confront his fears, Jonas accepted the mission, but only because he was convinced he could recover an unfossilized white Megalodon tooth—proof that the creatures were still alive.

What he found was a nightmare that would haunt him the rest of his days.

Jonas Taylor was right: The deepwater's of the Mariana Trench contained an array of undiscovered life forms comprising part of an ancient food chain dependent on chemicals originating from hydrothermal vents. These volcanic pumps created a tropical bottom layer capped off a mile above the sea floor by an insulating silty plume of debris. For tens of millions of years, this isolated habitat had been a haven for prehistoric sea life, its deadly pressures discouraging man from venturing into its forbidden depths.

After an hour's descent in suffocating darkness, Jonas and D.J.'s one-man subs managed to penetrate the hydrothermal plume and were soon tracking down one of the damaged UNIS robots. The titanium shell had been crushed, but what Jonas had taken to be a white tooth was merely the severed arm of an albino starfish. Feeling the fool, he assisted D.J. in digging out the half-buried seismic device.

But the vibrations created by the sub's robotic arms reverberated sound waves throughout the underwater canyon, attracting a forty-five-foot male Megalodon! D.J. was attacked and killed when his sub imploded, while the Meg became hopelessly entangled in the sub's retrieval cable. As the surface ship unwittingly hauled the entrapped beast topside, an even larger Meg—a pregnant female—showed up and attacked its struggling mate, following its gushing trail of blood topside.

Because of Man's intrusion into the abyss, history's most dangerous predatory species had been released from its 100,000-year purgatory.

The Tanaka Institute was charged with the task of hunting down the female. Their goal: to quarantine the monster within the whale lagoon. Jonas was eventually forced to kill the Meg, but one of the female's surviving pups was captured and raised in Masao's cetacean facility.

COME SEE ANGEL: THE ANGEL OF DEATH
TWO SHOWS DAILY
ALWAYS YOUR MONEY'S WORTH!

Over the years, Angel had grown into a seventy-four-foot-long, seventy-thousand-pound monster, her presence attracting millions of visitors. Jonas and Terry were married. And then, one day, Angel broke through the giant steel doors of her canal and escaped, making her way across the Pacific to the Mariana Trench, returning to her species' ancient habitat to mate.

Two decades later, the creature would find its way back home to California waters to birth a second litter of pups in the man-made lagoon.

Masao died tragically in the interim, but Angel's return gave his institute a new lease on life. With help from the state of California, the Tanaka Lagoon once again became the most popular tourist attraction in the world.

But success is fleeting, bringing its own innate set of problems. Running an aquarium as large as "Angel's Lair" required an extensive staff: marine biologists and animal husbandry specialists to care for the Meg as well as her new pups; an environmental team charged with maintaining the lagoon and the new Meg Pen; and administrators and public relations staff, security and food handlers. Working with a fully mature, fifty-one-ton Megalodon and her five offspring created its own unique challenges, where any mistake could be a fatal one.

▽ ▽ ▽

THE LEXUS TURNS right onto Masao Tanaka Way, a private drive that leads to the aquarium's grounds. Jonas pulls around three lines of cars seeking entrance

17

into the facility, turning down an access road for the … *blocked* staff lot!

Several dozen protestors wearing Army fatigues were carrying signs in blood-red paint that read: FREE THE SHARKS; MEG-A-TORTURERS; and MONEY + EXPLOITATION = CRUELTY. Recognizing Jonas's car, the picketers swarm in, hurling raw eggs and insults. Bodies press against the windows, rocking the sedan, threatening to roll it over.

A thin Hispanic woman in her late thirties, wearing a red tee-shirt featuring dead, finless sharks lying on a pier, presses her bra-less chest against David's window as she yells an expletive-filled diatribe about slaughtering the shark population.

"What is wrong with these people? The Institute isn't about killing sharks. We *protect* them!"

"All I know is that these assholes are making me late!" Danielle leans over and honks the car horn, alerting a team of security guards. Armed with tasers, they rush out of their booth, scattering the crowd.

Jonas rolls down his window to speak with the head of security. "I thought these bozos were told they had to stay outside the main entrance."

"Yes, sir. The cops have already been here twice. They issued citations. Even hauled a few of them off. But they just pay the bail money and are back out here in a couple of hours. Local TV crew was out here earlier. I think it just encourages them. Maybe you ought to sic Angel on 'em, huh?"

Dani leans over her father. "What TV station? It wasn't Channel 5, was it?"

Jonas cuts her off. "Don't taser anyone—" he winks "—at least not while the film crews are around." He seals his window and drives on to the staff lot, recently enclosed with chain-link fence.

Despite the presence of the protestors, the adjacent public parking lot is packed with cars for the evening show.

Dani runs ahead to the Lower Level gate to get ready, while David follows his father through the staff entrance into the administration building. They take the elevator up to the third floor then follow the main corridor to Terry Taylor's office.

David's mother sits behind her desk, speaking on the phone. She waves and smiles at her son, signaling, "One minute."

Jonas taps David on the shoulder, ushering him to the bay windows. He raises the Venetian blinds to reveal the lagoon and its surrounding arena, the bleachers packed with people of all ages. Dusk is settling over the Pacific, bathing the western horizon in shades of gold and magenta. With the sun fading fast, three light towers posted along the stadium perimeter slowly come to life, their bright beacons illuminating the azure-green, windswept waters of the main tank—a three-quarter-mile-long, eighty-foot-deep artificial lake running north and south along the coast. Connecting this man-made body of water to the Pacific is a perpendicular channel located at the midpoint of the lagoon's western border. Consisting of two concrete sea walls running parallel to each other, the canal extends across the beachhead behind the facility like a highway off-ramp before it submerges a thousand feet into the Pacific, ending fifty yards short of the Monterey Bay Canyon drop-off. Only a pair of mammoth underwater doors made of reinforced steel prevent the lagoon's star attraction from escaping to the open sea.

David's eyes search the main tank. The lagoon is empty, its lone occupant preferring the depths of the canal and its steady rush of ocean current. Craning his neck, he looks to the northern end of the bowl to see a new section of bleachers still under construction.

☙ ☙ ☙

FIVE YEARS AGO, the stadium's original northern bleachers had been removed to expand the facility, allowing for the construction of a brand-new, state-of-the-art, sixty-million-gallon, saltwater aquarium. Dubbed the "Meg Pen," the rectangular tank, along with its medical pool became home to Angel's five female pups. Though designed as a separate habitat, the pen was technically connected to the larger lagoon via a twenty-foot, submerged concrete tunnel, the doors of which always remained sealed on both ends to protect the pups from their overly aggressive parent.

Situated on a boom truck anchored close to the Meg Pen is the *Jellyfish*, a maintenance submersible featuring a twenty-two-foot-in-diameter, four-inch-thick spherical hull made of clear acrylic too wide for Angel and her aggressive brood to wrap their jaws around.

Two stories below the Meg Pen's main deck is the largest underwater viewing window in the world. Thirty-two feet tall by eighty-five feet wide, composed of four-foot-thick, clear acrylic glass and buttressed by seven-foot-thick concrete pillars, the Meg Pen Gallery was quickly rivaling Angel's Lair as the most popular attraction at the Institute.

Beside its smaller medical holding tank, the Meg Pen could be divided in half by a retractable, rubber-coated, titanium chain-link fence set on tracks. The intent was to give the facility's staff the option of segregating one or more of the pups ...

should the need ever arise. With each passing day, that need seemed to be gaining a new sense of urgency.

THE STANDING-ROOM-only crowd of 15,596 cheer as three men in orange staff jump suits wheel a headless, skinned steer carcass toward the large, steel A-frame that stands poised at the southern end of Angel's tank. Teddy Badaut, a French-Portuguese marine biologist, instructs his two "guest feeders" on how to prepare Angel's meal. Tucked within fatty pockets of the 225-pound side of beef are pouches of vitamins and mineral supplements. Using digestible plastic ties, Teddy and his two assistants attach the A-frame's four-inch-thick steel chain to the carcass's rib cage before swabbing the meat down with mop-fulls of fresh blood as the sound of voodoo drums simultaneously flow out of the arena's sound system and thump through the lagoon's underwater speakers.

Danielle Taylor, the show's emcee, waves to the crowd as she approaches the southern end of the bowl and the more expensive seats. Her podium is located behind the A-frame, close enough for the nauseating scent of raw meat from the star attraction's prepared meal to wash over her. "Ladies and gentlemen, boys and girls ... welcome to the Tanaka Institute."

∇ ∇ ∇

HOVERING IN THE deepest part of the ocean-access canal, her snout rubbed raw from her ampullae of Lorenzini's attraction to the electrical discharges emitted by the porous steel doors, is the twenty-seven-year-old female Megalodon known as Angel. The predator—pure white—inherited her albino features from an ancestral line that had inhabited the eternally dark recesses of the Mariana Trench over the last quarter of a million years.

Basketball-size pores perforating the the steel doors channel a steady current into the Meg's nostrils and open mouth, enabling her to breathe without exerting much energy. Upwards of a thousand gallons of seawater flow through her body every minute, providing oxygen to be processed by her gills while conveying a sensory picture of the environment just outside her realm. Angel can taste whale urine drifting from a passing pod of humpbacks three miles away and can feel the reverberations of their exertions. She can hear the annoying whine of speedboats and whale watchers. Farther to the south, she senses the electrical pitter-patter of heartbeats—a family from New Jersey wading in the shallows off scenic Carmel.

And then, like a wave of white noise, the underwater cacophony of bass drums overwhelms Angel's sensory orchestra, sending the sensitive neuro-cells along her lateral line into spasms. Her routine disrupted, the Meg bashes her triangular snout against the gate several times and then circles, heading back into the lagoon to register her annoyance.

∇ ∇ ∇

A GREAT ROAR rises from the crowd seated in the western bleachers, the cheers spreading throughout the rest of the bowl as a slow-moving wake, six feet high, rolls majestically into the main tank, the submerged creature's sheer girth pulling a river of current.

A cold Pacific wind whips through the open-air arena. Visitors adjust their collars against the sudden chill. Parents zip their children's jackets and bundle their infants in souvenir blankets while they wait impatiently for the main attraction to surface. To the purists among them, simply bearing witness to *Carcharodon megalodon* circling the bottom of the tank is worth the price of admission. Here was a living, breathing prehistoric monster everyone believed extinct—a giant great white shark that had ruled the planet's oceans over most of the last 30 million years.

Turn back the clock a mere 100,000 years and you would find Angel's predecessors stalking whales along this very coastline. Why these apex predators ever disappeared remains a mystery. How a sub-species managed to survive in the abyss is a paradox of evolution. To the millions who have seen her, the big female's presence in modern man's world seems nothing short of a minor miracle. But to some locals and experts alike, the Megalodon and her five maturing pups represent the potential revival of a dangerous species that many feel is better off left extinct.

Angel remains deep, moving along the bottom of the lagoon in a perpetual figure-eight pattern. Reaching the northern end of the tank, she circles back to the south, rushing head-first into her own oncoming current.

The sudden surge invigorates her gills while momentarily muting the annoying underwater acoustics—stimulating a cause-and-effect response.

🦷 🦷 🦷

DANIELLE TAYLOR'S BLUE eyes focus upon the approaching wake, its height rising noticeably as its speed increases. Crossing the length of the lagoon, Angel abruptly circles back again to the north, one swell running into the next—

—the sudden displacement of sea causing the water level in the far end of the tank to drop precipitously.

Something's wrong. She's moving way too fast.

Dani grips her microphone, uncertain what to do. "Ladies and gentlemen … Angel, Mother Nature's own angel of death!"

The side of beef is swung into place over the southern end of the tank. Blood drips from the chain, falling thirty feet to the surface. Patrons steady their camcorders and cell phone cameras, waiting for the money shot, while up in his mother's velvet perch, David watches, spellbound, his heart pounding in his chest. "Something's setting her off. Dad, the swell—it's rising higher than the sea wall!"

"Sweet Jesus." Jonas grabs the walkie-talkie from its charger on his wife's desk. "Dani, get out of there. Clear the deck! Dani, can you hear me? Dani!"

🦷 🦷 🦷

DANIELLE TAYLOR'S EARPIECE is tucked snugly inside her shirt collar; she can hear nothing but the echo of cheers and groans as the Meg races around the oval tank like a mad bull. The lagoon is essentially a giant bathtub, the female's moving mass creating an ever-increasing ebb and flow that lifts a mountainous swell at one end of the tank, a retreating valley at the other, the inertia building, each swell growing exponentially higher until ...

Dani backs away from her perch beneath the A-frame, falling, stumbling over the concrete base as an eighteen-foot wall of water rolls out of the tank, its towering crest blocking the arena lights from her view.

Sound disappears, followed by an intense ocean roar as Danielle Taylor is lifted off her feet and launched backwards over the suddenly submerged deck, her head striking the concrete riser in the second row. The wave pounds the south bleachers and blasts skyward, drenching the audience twenty rows up with bone-chilling water and foam before its backwash, an eight-foot, retreating torrent, rolls back into the lagoon, dragging the Institute's two guest handlers with it.

Submerged beneath the wave, Andy Murch, a staff photographer at *Shark Diver* magazine, claws at the concrete sea wall, his left hand somehow maintaining its grip on painted cinder-block as he fights and kicks like mad against the powerful current, trying to outlast the wave before it sweeps him into the lagoon. Just as the water level recedes, he's struck by the floundering figure of the second guest handler, twenty-one-year-old Jason Francis, a varsity soccer player at USC.

The crowd gasps as the two men surface in the south end of Angel's Lair.

ᐁ ᐁ ᐁ

HAVING HEARD HIS best friend yellin g to Dani over the walkie-talkie, James "Mac" Mackriedes races out of his office in the new Meg Pen annex and out onto the lagoon's main deck, confronted by chaos.

Two men in orange handler jump suits are floundering in the water.

Drenched fans in the lower southern bowl seats are climbing over people in the upper rows to get to higher ground—

—while in the main tank, Angel is riding a two-story swell that could easily wash her over the five-foot sea wall and twenty feet of decking—all that separates the lagoon's waters from the Meg Pen.

Mac holds his breath, watching as the albino creature submerges a split second before the wave crashes against the sea wall, the wall of water rolling across the northern deck and into the Meg Pen.

Hurrying to an equipment closet, Mac grabs a rescue ring and rope from a hook—

—while on the far side of the arena, Jonas exits the eastern stairwell. Slogging through ankle-deep water, he searches for his daughter.

Three stories up, his wife shouts commands to him over the walkie-talkie, "Jonas, I see her! She's in Section D, in one of the front rows!"

Jonas rushes to Dani. Cradling his unconscious daughter in his arms, he looks up, bracing his legs against the aluminum bleacher in front of him as another swell—this one even higher than the last—breaches the lagoon sea wall. Pinching Dani's nose while maintaining mouth-to-mouth, Jonas breathes air into his oldest child's lungs as the wave crashes atop the concrete deck and submerges them.

He holds on, closing his eyes as the surge threatens to rip him from his refuge.

Finally, the wave recedes, dissipating across the deck and returning the evening light.

Jonas struggles to his feet. Dani is breathing, but her head is bleeding badly. He yells into his radio for an ambulance before carrying Dani out of the southern end of the arena, racing to get out of the bowl before the next swell arrives.

Terry drops the walkie-talkie and dials 911 on her office phone.

David grabs the radio, changing frequencies. "Dr. Stelzer, it's David! Angel's going berserk! Shut off the acoustics, now!"

ᐯ   ᐯ   ᐯ

MAC EMERGES FROM the equipment room with a life ring and a hundred feet of towline, his eyes searching the lagoon's chaotic waters for the two missing men.

Jason and Andy are being dragged toward the center of the tank, struggling to tread water in a tumultuous sea, unable to reach the eastern wall as the water level beneath them suddenly drops from its eighty-foot depth to a mere forty-five, while at the northern end of the tank, Angel is knifing beneath the surface, catching up to a thirty-foot wall of water rolling towards the Meg Pen!

The crowd gasps as the wave washes over the northern sea wall into the juvenile's tank, beaching Angel as it recedes. Caught by surprise, the fifty-one-ton shark flounders like a giant eel along the flooded deck until she manages to slide back inside the lagoon.

Shaking its head, the stunned creature draws in mouthfuls of sea to breathe—

—as the reverberations in her brain suddenly cease.

The predator calms. She zigs, then zags, regaining her senses, which immediately lock onto the heartbeats of the two life forms that have entered her domain.

Mac runs along the eastern sea wall to get a closer shot at the two men. The crowd noise beckons him to turn around.

The white dorsal fin rises like a sail as the Megalodon heads for the southern end of the tank!

Christ, she sees them.

Andy and Jason see the telltale dorsal fin, too … just before it disappears beneath another rolling mountain of water. They start swimming toward Mac, who throws the life ring at them, the nylon rope feeding out sixty feet.

Jason is closest to the ring. The college senior lunges for it and holds on for dear life, hooking his elbow around the doughnut-shaped flotation device. Mac tows him in, guiding the ring towards the second man.

Andy swims for Jason and the rope, missing both as he's lifted by the approaching swell and washed away.

Hand over hand Mac takes up the slack, staff members rushing in to help, their combined effort propelling the USC student-athlete rapidly along the surface of the water… like bait on a hook.

Gliding just beneath the surface, Angel rolls sideways onto her left flank, her primordial senses locked in on the fleeing intruder. Her mouth opens, exposing a band of pink gum line and rows of seven-inch teeth.

A bizarre sensation rushes through Jason Bruce Francis's mind as his body suddenly becomes lighter. Maintaining his grip on the flotation device, he bounces along the surface before going airborne, his body lifted over the sea wall and let down onto the flooded deck—

—while back in the tank, everything below his waist is devoured and swallowed.

Lying on the ground, going into shock, a relieved Jason stares up at Mac and smiles. "Man, that was a close one, huh?" he says … as a tide of blood drains from the dead man's face and out his open chest cavity onto the deck.

Back in the lagoon, Andy Murch is lifted over the southern sea wall by the dying fifteen-foot swell and tossed sideways into the fourth row of seats. Barely conscious, he wraps his arms around the aluminum bleacher and holds on until the wave recedes over his head, and the evening sky returns its breath of cold night air.

Angel hovers near the bottom of the lagoon. Her appetite teased by the morsel of food still caught in her teeth, she circles back into the southern end of the tank and rises. The emotionally spent crowd lets out a collective gasp as the monster's enormous head and upper torso rise surreally out of the water. The Megalodon's upper jaw hyperextends as it opens, its retracting gum line, stained red with Jason Francis's remains, exposing a murderous upper row of triangular teeth that snatches the swaying side of beef like a steel bear trap striking a wild pig. Screams ripple through the arena as Angel whips her garage-size head back and forth on the iron support chain until she rips the entire carcass loose.

The A-frame snaps back on its base as the 102,000-pound predator falls sideways into the water, soaking the already-frazzled crowd in the lower bowl seats once more.

The audience swoons. A few applaud, then are silenced by the sheer horror of what they have just witnessed.

COME SEE ANGEL: THE ANGEL OF DEATH
TWO SHOWS DAILY
ALWAYS YOUR MONEY'S WORTH!

2

Community Hospital of the Monterey Peninsula
Monterey, California

Saturday night

Terry Taylor sits alone in the hospital administrator's private office, away from the waiting room's prying eyes and the plasma TV screen's never-ending regurgitation of the evening's events. Though she will be celebrating her fiftieth birthday in the coming weeks, the daughter and only surviving child of the late Masao Tanaka could be mistaken for thirty-nine, her long, onyx hair containing only a few scattered threads of gray, the skin around her almond eyes still smooth. On the outside she remains quite the beauty—

—while on the inside, she is aging rapidly. Stress has taken its toll on her nerves, her right arm and right leg prone to bouts of shaking. She saw a neurologist, who ran up a nice medical bill before deciding it could be the onset of Parkinson's or "maybe something else; we'll keep an eye on it."

Doctors ... what do they know? Most of them are just "practicing" medicine, diagnosing out of habit, basing their remedies on what expenses insurance will cover, not what is actually needed. But that's what you get when your entire medical system is regulated by a for-profit industry and subsidized by pharmaceutical companies that give away free trips to Cancun like they're lollipops. "Here, Mrs. Taylor, take these pills twice a day for three weeks and we'll see how it affects you. Abdominal cramps? Hair loss? Double vision? No problem, we'll just try another prescription until we get it right. Liver damage? Hell, that we can replace—"

Terry chases the persona her therapist has dubbed "Angry Annie" out of her head, her mind yielding to "Manager Mary."

Call your publicist ... have her issue a public statement. No, better you do that in person. Look them in the eye ... let them know that no words can begin to express your sorrow.

It won't make much of a difference. In the end they'll still come after us with guns blazing. Call the lawyers. Make sure those waivers were worth the expense ... God, how could this have happened? Poor kid. He was a senior in college ... David's age. It could have been David ... it could have been—

—D.J.

The thought of her long-deceased brother sets her right leg to quiver.

D.J. … How long has he been gone? Twenty-four years? Is that even possible?

She replays the college student's death in her mind's eye. *Is that how D.J. died in the Mariana Trench? Devoured by that male Meg?*

She chokes down the bile running up the back of her throat.

Stop it! Just stop! Falling apart helps no one. This was unpredictable … like a car accident … or a lightning strike. Bad things sometimes happen. You can't make sense of it! … Focus on the to-do list before the insanity hits you like a tsunami wave. Express your grief in public, then step back and let the lawyers deal with the repercussions … call a mandatory staff meeting on Monday … readdress the question of safety. Watch their morale—

"Mrs. Taylor?"

—prep them for the worst. If you think those animal rights assassins were nasty before, you haven't seen anything yet—

"Mrs. Taylor? Are you okay?"

She looks up at the doctor, settling her quivering right arm with her free hand. "Me? Fine. My daughter … how is she? Did you finish the tests?"

"She's resting. Basilar skull fractures are rare, more common with race car drivers during sudden speed accidents. It's what killed Dale Earnhardt. Anyway, Dani's MRIs were negative for blood clots in the brain. But she did suffer a bad concussion and trauma to the rib cage; so we'll be keeping her in intensive care just as a precaution. You can go back and see her now. Your husband's already there waiting for you."

Terry follows the specialist through the intensive care unit to one of eight stations separated by a blue curtain. Jonas is seated by Dani's bed, while their daughter sleeps, her injured body hooked up to IVs and monitors.

He greets his wife with a hug. "You okay? Never mind. Dumb question."

"Don't say anything in public. Let the professionals do their jobs."

"I wasn't even thinking about the Institute. Terry, Dani could have been killed … and David—"

"Not now, Jonas."

"No, now is when it needs to be done! Our son has pushed and prodded and coaxed us into letting him work with these monsters since he was fourteen. Well, guess what … Come Monday he'll be entering the kill zone, and I just think the two of us need to stop this insanity before—"

"Shh, that's enough! For Dani's sake, no more arguing." Jonas stares at his daughter. He checks his watch. "It's late. Dani's in good hands. We should go."

"You go. I'm staying."

"Then I'm staying, too."

"No. You need to find David. I sent him to look after Mac. Trish said he wasn't handling the boy's death very well. She's afraid he might drink."

▽ ▽ ▽

A VELVET NIGHT sky hovers like a glistening cathedral over the imposing presence of the Pacific, each silent swell rolling through the darkness unabated until it crashes in a dull roar that echoes across the deserted shoreline. The arena is empty, too—save for four armed security guards and two lone figures seated high up in the western bleachers.

Mac lays his head back on the cool aluminum bench, allowing the ocean's pulse to soothe his rattled nerves. "Okay, kid, I'll concede the point. What I saw in 'Nam was probably a helluva lot worse, but when you're in a war your brain's wired differently. Watching the life flow out of that boy ... this one'll haunt me the rest of my days."

David nods. "Turk's Bar and Grill is still open. Wanna get pasted?"

"You testing me?"

"Sort of."

"Don't play head games with your Godfather, kid. If I was going to drink I'd be drunk by now." He rubs the stress from his eyes. "Trish send you after me?"

"No."

"You're a lousy liar."

"Okay, but she was worried."

A dull, metallic *thud* echoes across the arena but goes unnoticed.

"Tell my wife I called my sponsor, and I'll get to an AA meeting later this week."

"Maybe you should tell her."

"I will. Eventually."

"You scared of her?"

"Hell, yes. Trish is a good woman, but she'd leave me in a New York minute if I fell off the wagon. Can't let that happen."

"You love her that much, huh?"

"Nah. I've just gotten used to three square meals a day and clean underwear."

David smiles, then abruptly sits up as his ears register another *thud*, this one followed by heavy splashing. "Angel?" He leans out over the western rail, his

29

eyes tracing the nearly submerged walls of the canal until the concrete border disappears a hundred yards away into the black Pacific. Somewhere out there, lurking beneath the dark surface, is a force of Nature that no longer wishes to be penned.

From his vantage point, David is still too far from the ocean-end of the channel to see Angel's soft, bioluminescent glow.

More splashing, followed by heavy reverberating wallops.

Mac stands. "That's coming from the Meg Pen. Come on!"

David follows him down the bleachers to the main deck and past the northern end of the lagoon and over a concrete bridge to the Meg Pen's main tank—an open pool that descends three stories below the deck to the main gallery.

Ⴥ Ⴥ Ⴥ

THERE ARE FIVE of them—all females—their names decreed by public opinion on a website contest that took place six weeks after they were born. The three "runts," each now over twenty-five feet and five tons, had been designated Angelica, Mary Kate, and Ashley. The latter two names had been selected following an Internet campaign to name this pair of identical runts, who refused to feed during their first month, after the famous child actors-turned-models. Being good sports, the Olsen twins showed up at the naming ceremony and even fed their namesakes ... albeit from a safe distance.

The remaining two sisters seemed to have been born from a different litter. At forty-six feet and twenty-one tons each, they were nearly twice the size of their three smaller siblings and far more vicious.

Elizabeth, or Lizzy for short, was pure albino like her mother. The voting public (swayed by various European blogs) had named her after Elizabeth Bathroy, the worst serial killer in Slovak history. In 1610, the infamous "Countess of Blood" had been charged with the torture and deaths of hundreds—mostly young girls. Her cold savagery seemed to match the personality of the stark-white juvenile, who often took a calculated second position to her more ferocious twin, Belle.

Belle, affectionately referred to by the staff as "Bela the Dark Overlord," was the only Megalodon offspring born with pigmentation. Though her head was pure-white, the rest of her dorsal surface was a dark charcoal-gray from her dorsal fin to the upper lobe of her tail, giving her a rather bizarre, sinister appearance. Named after Belle Gunness, the infamous "Black Widow" who teased and killed fourteen of her suitors back in 1908, Belle was the brawn to Lizzy's brains, an aggressive predator who often had to be separated from the pack before feeding time.

It is not feeding time, but the pen is in turmoil.

▽   ▽   ▽

DR. JONATHAN STELZER, the Institute's director of marine biology, is frantically calling out orders by the iron rail that surrounds the illuminated azure aquarium as workers attempt to close the titanium gate behind Mary Kate and Ashley, the two panicked Meg pups swimming in tight circles along the near side of the tank. On the opposite end of the aquarium, sub pilot Steven Moretti is climbing inside the *Jellyfish*, the acrylic sphere-shaped submersible rigged to its truck boom. The head of animal husbandry seals the hatch, tugs on his lucky turquoise baseball hat, and gives the thumbs up.

Moments later, the sub is swung over the tank and quickly lowered into the water, remaining tethered on its cable leash.

Mac sees Dr. Stelzer and hurries over to him. "Jon? What the hell—"

"The sisters!" Stelzer points to the far end of the tank where a three-foot, ivory caudal fin cuts erratically back and forth along the surface, shadowed closely by a far larger pale dorsal fin. "Lizzy has Angelica by the pectoral fin, and she won't let go."

David sees a dark shadow shoot past them underwater on a collision course for the two albino creatures. "Belle ... she's attacking!"

The lead-gray caudal fin lashes a great, arcing swath of water through the air as Belle strikes the runt, Angelica.

Moretti submerges the *Jellyfish* in time to witness the underwater assault. Lizzy is on Angelica's right flank, her jaws firmly secured around Angelica's pectoral fin. The bite is not meant to inflict damage but to control the smaller Meg; still, blood flows freely from the savage wound—

—exciting Belle! The dark-backed Megalodon glides beneath the *Jellyfish* and attacks Angelica's exposed left flank, tearing into the runt's thick, white hide with her sharp, juvenile teeth.

Moretti activates the "predator prod" as he races in after the darker Meg. Protruding from different angles along the spherical hull, the six steel lances pack 5,000 volts of electricity—more than enough to ward off the aggressive sisters. Striking Belle along her pelvic fin, he chases the dark predator away.

Angelica's gushing flank is now enshrouded in a bloody haze. Descending the sub beneath the wounded runt, Moretti attempts to strike Lizzy with one of the prods—

—while above the tank, a hoisting crane rolls along a pair of tracks embedded in the concrete deck. The steel expanse stretches across the width of the Meg Pen. A heavy-duty cargo net is being readied atop the yellow beam, fifty feet above the surface.

After several attempts, Moretti finally manages to jolt the albino sister. The ghostly brute reluctantly releases its death-grip on its smaller sibling—

—as Belle charges the *Jellyfish*, only to be stung herself from a different protruding lance. The dark-backed Megalodon quickly circles along the eastern divide of the tank, falling in formation below her albino twin.

Moretti speaks quickly into his headset, "Angelica's free! Drop the net!"

The cargo net is released. Moretti uses the sub's robotic claw to position it in place over the wounded runt. Angelica is swimming erratically, her right pectoral fin enveloped in crimson clouds of blood. Maneuvering the submersible along Angelica's left flank, Moretti powers down the predator prod lest he accidently strike the injured Meg. Glancing down at his sonar, he tracks the two larger Megs—

—who are swooping in from behind! Swiveling around in his pilot's chair, Moretti catches sight of the siblings charging him head-on, their heads appearing as large as his entire sub. Quickly, he reactivates the prods, the sisters' ampullae of Lorenzini instantly detecting the electrical impulse. The creatures veer off at the last second, spinning the *Jellyfish* like a top in their wake.

Moretti pumps his foot pedals, using bow thrusters to steady his vessel. *Smart fish.* The pilot wipes beads of sweat from his forehead then swivels around to face Angelica, the creature caught head-first in the cargo net. Activating the submersible's two robotic appendages, he secures the netting around the runt's abdomen.

The maneuver elicits a reflexive slap from Angelica's caudal fin. The injured predator arches its back in pain as it attempts to swim away, succeeding in only pushing herself deeper into the entanglement.

"Jon, she's secure, but watch her abdomen. I think Bela struck her there pretty good."

Above the tank, a pair of winches activate, retrieving the cargo net and its 10,470-pound catch. Gently, Angelica's body rises out of the water, her wounded twenty-five-foot torso twisting and flexing like a snake.

Dr. Stelzer makes his way to the holding tank—a circular shallow pool used as a "Meg ER." His medical assistant, Fran Rizzuto, prepares a half dozen syringes, filling each ten-inch steel spike with a chemical synthesis of Tricaine Methanesulfonate—a powerful anesthesia designed to calm the fish and reduce injuries. Then, she screws the last syringe into the business end of its fifteen-foot reach pole. "Six syringes, each packing 5,000 milligrams of MS-222 should be enough to put her under while we scan her injuries."

Angelica thrashes in the cargo net, thirty feet above the Meg Pen. Fran, now wearing a safety harness, climbs the steep steps built inside the right column of the crane, each powerful thrash of the Megalodon's torso threatening to toss the native New Yorker into the aquarium. Taking no chances, she clips her harness onto one of the numerous eye-bolts fastened beneath the crane's steel expanse beam.

Dr. Stelzer hands her the first reach pole. Leaning out, she stabs the syringe into Angelica's flank just below the gill slits, injecting the elixir directly into the wounded creature's blood stream. She passes the reach pole back to Dr. Stelzer, who exchanges the used syringe for a new one.

On the opposite side of the tank, the tethered *Jellyfish* is raised out of the water by a winch and crane built into the back end of a truck.

Two more injections and Angelica calms down. Fran turns to Dr. Stelzer. "She's good to go. I suggest we wait until the X-rays before we inject her again."

David joins Dr. Stelzer and Mac. "What started all this? Were they fighting over food?"

"We'll have to look at the videotape. But no, we weren't feeding them. The sisters suddenly swarmed Angelica without any—"

Fran screams.

David, Mac, and Dr. Stelzer turn in time to see Belle leap out of the aquarium, her open mouth hyperextended for a split second before her jaws slam shut around upon Angelica's exposed abdomen! For several frozen seconds the 42,000 pound monster simply hangs vertically, suspended above the water by its teeth, while the semi-tranquilized Angelica spasms in the cargo net, blood gushing from her mortal wounds directly into Belle's open mouth.

The knife-sharp serrated edges of the dark-backed Megalodon's teeth rip through the thick hide and crush the organs of her prey before falling back into the aquarium's illuminated azure waters—

—Angelica's innards pouring from the ten-foot-wide gaping hole in her belly like an exploding piñata.

3

Tanaka Oceanographic Institute
Monterey, California

Monday

David steps off the elevator, entering the third floor administrative wing of the Institute, when he runs into the office manager—a petite blue-eyed blonde in her early forties.

Patricia Mackreides greets David with a hug. "Thanks for looking out for Mac."

"Not a problem. Guy's been looking out for me since I was in diapers."

The mention of diapers causes Trish to tear-up and blush.

"Hey? You okay?"

She beams a smile. "Don't tell Mac."

"Tell Mac what?"

"That I'm pregnant."

"Holy shit!"

"Shh!"

"Is it Mac's? Kidding ... I'm just ... oh, man, you have got to videotape the moment you tell him. Does anyone else know?"

"No. I just found out this morning."

"Trish, this is so cool. When are you going to tell him?"

"Tonight." She glances over at the conference room as the double doors are closed. "You'd better get inside before they start. And not a word about this to anyone."

"I promise." He gives her a gentle hug then crosses the corridor and enters the chamber.

▽ ▽ ▽

THE ROOM IS packed with the Institute's department heads and key staff, everyone seated around the immense mahogany table. Joining them are Thomas Cubit, senior partner with the law offices of Cubit and Cubit, and Kayla Cicala, the company's publicist. David finds a seat at the perimeter of the room, bypassing the empty chair at the head of the conference table reserved for his mother.

Jonas taps his water glass with his wedding ring, signaling for quiet. "Let's get started. Quick update: Terry's with Dani. The doctor says she'll be fine. She should be coming home within the next few days."

Several staff members applaud.

"That, unfortunately, is the extent of the good news. The bad news, well, bad doesn't begin to describe it. As you know, Jason Francis, one of our winners in the Feed Angel contest, died tragically during Saturday night's performance. Kayla?"

Kayla Cicala holds up a press release. "We're placing full-page ads in all the local papers, extending our condolences to the victim's family. Terry has asked the Francises's lawyer for permission to meet with the family. I've already fielded offers to discuss what happened in public with the four major network morning shows—"

"—which you'll graciously decline." Thomas Cubit, a forty-seven-year-old, Irish-Catholic attorney from Philadelphia, refers to his legal pad of notes. "No one is to address the media. No one is to make any statements unless I approve them first. The Francis family wasted no time in hiring a big legal firm out of San Francisco, and they don't need any more bullets in their chambers. In addition to the Taylors, they'll want depositions from Mac, Ted Badaut, Dr. Stelzer, and ... who is Andrew Murch?"

"He was the second contest winner," Jonas answers, "the one who survived. Tom, how liable are we?"

"We have a signed, binding waiver agreement, but they have fifteen thousand witnesses to make a case of severe negligence. The game plan at this juncture is for everyone to stay away from the media while we settle out of court as quickly as possible. At the same time, you need to shut things down until you can make the changes necessary to prevent this type of accident from happening again."

"That's right. Accident ... it was an accident, not negligence!" Ted Badaut, the French-Portuguese Meg handler is racked with emotion and more than a little defensive. "Jonas, I have always fed Angel the same way, every day, for the last four years. This is not my fault, nothing like this has ever happened!"

"Ted, calm down—"

"What am I supposed to say to these lawyers? They will try to blame me for this boy's death."

"No one's accusing you. Mr. Cubit and his staff will prepare you for the deposition and be with you the entire time. We're a family. We stick together."

"And what are we supposed to say to the press when they ask us about Angelica?" Virgil Carmen, the Institute's assistant director of husbandry, stands up at the back of the room to be heard. "Do we tell them the Meg Pen is too small for five maturing adolescents? That we've been warning you for months now that the two sisters were getting testy?"

Jonas feels the weight of the room suddenly squeezing in on him. "What would you have us do, Virgil? Sell one of the pups to an aquarium that's even smaller than the Meg Pen? Or maybe we should release Angelica into the lagoon like some of those wacko bloggers suggested, allowing Angel to play a quick game of cat and mouse for the cameras? I suppose we could always allow the PETA radicals to have their way and release the three runts into the Monterey Bay Sanctuary. That might work. Or better yet, why not free the sisters? That would spice things up real good."

Jonas glances at his son. "Your warnings were on the money. No one ever disagreed with you. We just didn't have a feasible option on the table ... and we still don't; although I'm working on one as we speak. So, for now, if someone in the media asks, you tell them to direct their barbs at me. Got it?"

Virgil clenches his teeth and nods, his anger seething.

Tom Cubit clears his throat. "With all due respect to the dead fish, the more immediate concern is to the family of the deceased human and the viewing public that we hope will continue to keep this institute in business."

"No worries there," says Christopher Eckardt, the aquarium's director of sales and marketing. "Since the Saturday show, our phones have been ringing off the hook. The website's jammed, too. Everyone wants tickets. You could raise prices sixty percent and you'd still have lines just to get into the nose-bleed section ... sorry, no pun intended."

"Safety's the main concern," Jonas says. "Do we build a plexiglass retaining wall around the main tank? Do we close the lower bowl? How do we prevent Angel from going berserk again?"

"It was the drums."

All eyes turn to David, who is leaning back in his chair against the far wall. "The underwater acoustics irritated her. She didn't enter the lagoon to feed; she came in to show you who's boss."

Side discussions break out, the staff's reaction mixed.

Jonas taps his glass again for quiet. "David, Angel was conditioned to respond to those acoustics. I trained her myself. If we can't regulate her feeding times, she'll remain in the canal underwater and we'll have no show."

"Then use a different stimulus. Re-train her."

Teddy Badault shakes his head emphatically. "She's too set in her ways. She is too old to learn anything new."

"That's ridiculous," David retorts. "Two summers ago I worked with a guy in Gainesville who specializes in shark behavior. He told me the Navy recruited him to train sharks as stealth spies in order to follow enemy vessels. Angel's smarter than any of the sharks he worked with, and just as capable."

"I agree." Jonas nods. "Call him. He's hired."

"We don't need him. He taught me everything I need to know. I can set up a light grid along the canal doors and—"

"No! Let the experts handle this."

"He's never worked with Angel or her pups. I have!"

"Dropping a side of beef into a tank is far different than what your friend will be doing."

"What do you think I've been doing at the University of Florida? Grooming seals? I'm a marine biologist—"

"Not yet, you're not!"

The conference room quiets, the staff uncomfortable, caught in the middle of this sudden battle of wills.

Jonas stares down his son. "Don't fight me on this, David. I still call the shots around here. Make the call."

"Fine." David stands to leave. "You know something? Maybe Ted's right. Maybe Angel is too old and set in her ways to learn something new. But she's not the only one."

The angry twenty-year-old stalks out of the conference room—

—passing Sadia Kleffner, Jonas's long-time assistant. "Jonas, sorry to interrupt, but your guests have arrived. Mac took them downstairs to the main gallery."

THE MEG PEN'S massive main gallery features an underwater viewing window that reaches three stories high and runs the entire width of the aquarium. Visitors can stroll the promenade, or just sit back and relax in one of two thousand cushioned chairs that make up row after row of theater-style seating surrounding the subterranean arena housing Angel's voracious offspring.

There are ten members of the Dubai entourage: four businessmen wearing the traditional, ankle-length white *dishdasha* and matching *gutra* head cloth; a fifth in a gray suit and tie that matches his neatly-trimmed beard; four armed security guards in black suits; and a videographer equipped with an expensive high-definition camera and tripod. The men stand before the viewing window of the 60-million-gallon tank, pointing and rattling off exclamations in Arabic as Belle and Lizzy swim past the four-foot-thick acrylic glass, each sister the size of a double-decker bus.

Mac intercepts Jonas, pulling him aside. "Quick! What do you know about Dubai?"

"It's part of the United Arab Emirates, and it has lots of oil. What else should I know?"

"Some basics wouldn't hurt."

"Okay, give me the basics."

"First, unlike the rest of the greedy wackos in the Middle East, the UAE's royals actually invest oil profits back into their country's infrastructure. Dubai's the largest emirate—a modern metropolis that is spending billions to create a thriving entertainment industry."

"Mac, I already know those basics. Tell me who the players are."

"See the short Arab in the white pajamas, standing next to the guy in the suit?"

Jonas glances over Mac's shoulder at the stout man with the thick, black goatee and uni-brow with eyes cold and black, like a shark's. "The guy with the big Joe Torre nose?"

"Bingo. His name's Fiesal bin Rashidi. He's first cousin to the crown prince. Big-time billionaire, the prince. Word is bin Rashidi's behind this whole trip. The taller guy is Abdullah something-or-other. He's the CEO of Emaar Properties, the construction firm that partnered with the Dubai government to build the world's tallest tower, the most expensive hotel, the largest marina—"

"He's the Donald Trump of Dubai. Got it."

"The clean-shaven dude over there is some kind of scientist, and the other egghead, Ibrahim something, runs a big aquarium in Abdullah's hotel."

"What about the man in the gray business suit?"

"Him, I'm not sure. He hasn't said a word. Probably head of security."

"Have they picked out their fish yet?"

"Not yet, but Bela put on quite a show earlier. Ashley swam a little too close to the titanium fence and the Dark Overlord started ramming the gate. Put the fear of Allah in a couple of those guards. One of them actually reached for his Glock. One other thing: Bin Rashidi wants to see the Manta Rays. He made it clear the submersibles have to be part of the package."

"What do they need them for?"

"He didn't say, and I didn't ask. Come on, I'll introduce you to our new friends. Just don't ask me to repeat any of their names."

Mac leads Jonas to the four businessmen in *dishdashi*, who are whispering, their eyes locked onto the aquarium. "Gentlemen, this is Dr. Jonas Taylor, the CEO of the Tanaka Institute and our resident Megalodon internist."

Jonas shoots his friend a chastising look.

Fiesal bin Rashidi claps his hands, a broad smile on his face. "Incredible. Absolutely incredible. I've seen the footage on television, of course, but to stand in the presence of such magnificent creatures ... incredible! The big one ... Angel ... when can we see her, please?"

"Maybe later, if we can coax her back into the lagoon. She tends to stay in the canal."

One of the Arab businessmen steps forward to shake Jonas's hand. "Dr. Taylor, my name is Ibrahim Al Hashemi. I am Executive Director of the Dubai Mall Aquarium. Please tell me, how do you trust these animals will not attempt to break through the glass?"

"Well, mister ... uh, Ibrahim, the glass is actually layered acrylic designed with tiny micro-fibers that carry an electrical charge running through it. While the charge isn't powerful enough to shock the Megs, it creates an electrical field that upsets the creatures' sensory organs located beneath their snouts, persuading them to steer clear of direct contact with the window. If you were interested in purchasing one of the pups for your mall aquarium, we'd have to refit your tank with—"

"That won't be necessary, Dr. Taylor. The Dubai Mall is stocked to capacity."

"Well ... okay then. Perhaps—"

"—perhaps there is a more private place we can discuss our business?" Fiesal bin Rashidi interrupts.

Jonas and Mac sit across the conference table from the five Dubai businessmen, their security detail posted outside the private office, the videographer with them.

Fiesal bin Rashidi begins his presentation. "Dr. Taylor, I don't know how many Arab countries you have visited or what your opinion of the Middle East might be, but I can assure you, Dubai is the exception to the rule. We are one of seven emirates that make up the United Arab Emirates, possessing its largest population and second largest landmass. Under the leadership of the late Sheikh Zayed, the UAE's oil revenues were reinvested in the people and the economy, and we have worked extremely hard to transform our country into a westernized trading hub. More ambitious is our plan to make Dubai a world-class resort. We have the world's finest marina, the world's only seven-star hotel, the finest entertainment facilities. We sponsor golf tournaments and attract business conventions; we host major events like the Dubai Land Cup and the Desert Classic; and yet most Westerners will never consider vacationing in our country because of the stigma associated with terrorism and the Middle East."

Jonas smiles. "Well, at least it hasn't stopped Haliburton from moving its headquarters there."

Mac kicks him under the table.

Bin Rashidi's smile remains frozen. "Thank you for demonstrating my point."

"My apologies. And you're right, there'd have to be something pretty special in Dubai to get me to fly halfway around the world to see it—I don't care how tall your buildings are."

"On that point we agree. We can also agree that very few people would ever travel to Dubai from North or South America to see a Megalodon when they could simply visit your facility here in California ... even if they do risk being eaten."

Mac winces. "Pick up your jock strap, Jonas, you've just been schooled."

Jonas ignores his friend. "Point taken. So why the visit?"

Bin Rashidi nods to Ibrahim Al Hashemi. From his briefcase, the Dubai Mall Aquarium director hands him several brochures. "You are correct, of course, in that we have traveled here to arrange the purchase of two of the Megalodon juveniles, but not for the Mall Aquarium."

The director passes out copies of an elaborate, glossy-color brochure, featuring maps and lists of attractions on par with Disney World.

"Dubai Land: an innovative series of projects designed to make Dubai the tourism, leisure, and entertainment capital of the region. Phase I, completed several years ago, includes water parks and roller coaster rides, global villages, space and science worlds, petting zoos, safaris—virtually every entertainment venue that we could offer has been offered.

"Phase II has only recently begun, centered around a brand-new aquatic theme park featuring the largest viewing aquariums ever conceived, including twelve 80-million-gallon tanks that exceed the capacity of your own Meg Pen. Monorails running throughout the park will connect the facility with a dozen first-class hotels and restaurants, while two high-speed rails will transport visitors to and from Dubai's new international airport. But the facility itself is not what will attract tourists the world-over; it is what we plan to stock the big tanks with that will make the resort the entertainment Mecca of not only the region ... but the world!"

Al Hashemi hands bin Rashidi a large manila envelope. From it he removes a dozen sketches, laying each rendering out on the table-top, one by one: "*Kronosaurus.* A carnivore I believe you crossed paths with several decades ago in the Mariana Trench. *Thalassomedon,* a plesiosaur with a twenty-foot-long neck. *Shonisaurus sikanniensis,* a species of *Ichthyosaurus* that measured seventy-five feet from its dolphin-like nose to the tip of its tail. *Dunkleosteus,* a heavily armored, prehistoric fish possessing two long, bony blades that could crush titanium. *Mososaurus,* a fifty-foot, crocodile-like brute that dominated the Cretaceous seas. And finally the king—*Liopleurodon ferox*—the largest and most vicious animal to inhabit the planet, save, perhaps, for *Megalodon.* Although, *Liopleurodon* was bigger and faster. There are more nightmares of nature on our wish list, but these are the predators that will draw the biggest crowds."

Mac smiles broadly. "Well, hell, since it's a wish list, how about King Kong or the Loch Ness Monster? Unless this is one of those special effects deals—"

Jonas stares at the free-hand drawings, the blood rushing from his face. He knows the artist responsible—an ichthyologist whose brilliance led him to a break-thru discovery, a rival who considered Jonas a disgrace to the paleo-community, a man whose unbridled ego ultimately led to his own self-destruction: Dr. Michael Maren. He died when a deadly plan he had conceived for Jonas and Mac backfired the last time their paths crossed.

Jonas recalls his last conversation with Maren five years ago aboard the biologist's yacht, just before Jonas had been tossed into the Philippine Sea as bait for the male Megalodon known as Scarface.

"The Mariana Trench is nothing, Taylor. The real ancient marine sanctuary is located along the Philippine Sea Plate. The area is a paleobiologist's goldmine. At least four major submarine canyons feed nutrients into this valley, creating a habitat that has sustained primitive life since the very first marine reptiles returned to the sea over a hundred million years ago.

"I've discovered species long believed extinct and evidence of creatures we never knew existed, all endowed by Nature to adapt to the pressures of the deep: prehistoric sponges with immune systems that could potentially cure cancer; jawless fishes with bony armor plating; undiscovered ray-finned life forms; ichthyosaurs and pliosaurs possessing gills, giant sea turtles with teeth that could tear open a small truck. This labyrinth of the deep is a lost world just waiting to be explored, and the ruler of these primal waters is Carcharodon megalodon.*"*

"Congratulations, Maren, you've made an incredible discovery. But why lure a Meg to the surface?"

"The male? I came across him about five years ago. He was in pretty bad shape. In fact, he was close to death, having recently lost a territorial dispute with another Megalodon. We weighted down sea lion carcasses loaded with medicines and fed him in nineteen thousand feet of water. Took us seven months of gradually raising the lures to get Scarface to finally surface."

"Scarface?"

"My assistant, Allison, named him. His face was raked by tooth marks. Over the years we've managed to tag him with several homing devices. As you can see, he's doing quite well now. I estimate he's gained at least ten tons since our first encounter."

"And me? Why am I here?"

"Because I despise you. You're not a scientist, Taylor. You never were. Yet for years, you pretended to be one, giving ridiculous lectures about these magnificent predators, how they avoided extinction, how they might be alive in the Mariana Trench. Tell me, 'Professor' Taylor, when you became an overnight sensation, did your new-found celebrity serve anyone but that ego of yours? And those sold-out shows at the Tanaka Lagoon ... did any percentage of the gate ever find its way back to the science you so flaunted all those years?

"It takes money to explore the abyss, and the abyss needs exploring; for there are life forms down there that may harbor cures for diseases ... discoveries just waiting to happen. You had the means, you had the world's attention, you could have spear-headed the movement. Instead, you destroyed it. Angel's escape and eventual return to the abyss chased away dozens of potential investors ... major universities, pharma-ceutical companies ... scientists, like myself, who could have opened the realm to real exploration."

"So you dared the devil up from his purgatory just to raise money?"

"Scarface is far from the devil. In fact, it turns out Megalodon isn't even the meanest fish on the block. Many years ago, my first drone crossed paths with a real monster of the deep, a creature that was at least one hundred twenty feet long and weighed seventy-five to one hundred tons. The beast had jaws that could snatch a fully grown Megalodon. It destroyed my drone and has been eluding me for eight years. But it's down there, perhaps the last of its kind, and with the proper funding and equip-ment, I'll find it."

"I assure you, Mr. Mackreides, these are not animatronic creations nor some digitally created, celluloid beasts. The creatures we've targeted for our aquarium are extant. They still exist."

"Excuse us for just a moment, gentlemen." Jonas grabs his friend by the elbow, leading him out of his office. The security detail allows them to pass, watching as they head down the third floor corridor. "Mac, this is Michael Maren's work. I'm sure of it!"

"Maren? Christ ... still, that doesn't make it real. The Institute spent two years exploring the Philippine Sea. Other than a few benign encounters with Scarface, the expedition found nothing."

"Maybe we were looking in the wrong place."

"And somehow the Arabs found the right one?"

"Those drawings were Maren's. Somehow, they've gotten access to his research."

"Research isn't proof. As for Maren, that blowhard was nothing more than a psychopath with a big vocabulary and an axe to grind."

"He managed to tag Scarface."

"And you tagged Angel's mother. It doesn't make you Jonas Salk. Mention Maren and my Spidey sense starts tingling. I say we sell them the sisters, offer to validate their parking, then we walk away from whatever wacky proposal they have tucked up their pajama sleeves."

"Agreed."

They return to Jonas's office and the Dubai consortium. "Gentlemen, since Angel's pups were born, the Institute's been searching for suitable aquatic facilities that can meet the needs of an adult Megalodon. If your aquarium can meet those needs, and it certainly looks impressive on paper, then we can begin making the arrangements."

Bin Rashidi's black eyes narrow, but his smile never wavers. "So the man who discovered the existence of not one, but two prehistoric predators in the Mariana Trench refuses to believe other extinct species might also exist?"

Jonas shrugs. "The ocean's a big place. Less than one percent of its depths have been explored. If these creatures exist, I hope you find them."

Bin Rashidi opens a second manila envelope, removing seven color photos. "Tell me, Dr. Taylor, do you recognize this particular species of fish?"

The crown prince's cousin lays out the eleven by fourteen inch photographs of an immense, ray-finned fish. The multiple angle shots were taken on an unidentified beach, the creature long dead. Its dark gray flesh is marred with bite marks from other predators, its lower extremity completely missing. Despite this fact, the head and upper torso are longer than the flatbed truck that appears in two of the photos.

Mac grabs the last photo. "Damn. What'd you fellas use as bait? An elephant?"

"It's not a carnivore, Mac. Believe it or not, it's a filter feeder. Alfred Leeds discovered the species' fossils back in the nineteenth century, so naturally, he named it a Leed's fish."

"Its correct scientific name is *Leedsichthys*," Al Hashimi says. "With its lower section intact, this fish would have been seventy feet long, making it an immature adult. The mature adults reached ninety feet. It was the largest fish that ever lived, and it lived in the Late Jurassic, more than 150 million years ago."

4

David Taylor sits behind his mother's desk, the phone pressed to his ear. He has been on hold nearly ten minutes, his already agitated blood pressure now a rolling boil. Gazing out the bay windows at the empty arena below, he watches Teddy Badault and his team lower a side of blood-drenched beef into the lagoon from the steel A-frame, each worker wearing a safety harness attached by cable to a concrete pillar supporting the southern bleachers.

For the next eight minutes the crew bobs the hunk of meat in and out of the water without a response from their intended diner. David is about to hang up and join them when a familiar voice comes on the phone.

"Ricardo Rosalez. Is this my lawyer?"

"Lawyer? No, man, it's David ... David Taylor."

"David? How the hell are you, man? How'd you find me?"

"I called Sandra, and she gave me this number. Where are you, anyway?"

"Man, I'm in the brig, charged with assault."

"Assault? You? No way, man. What the hell happened?"

"Couple of Marines and I were in a bar. There was a guy there who kept slapping this woman around. I told him he better stop, so he wheeled back and punched her. Broke her jaw. Me and my buddies, we beat the holy hell out of him."

"Good! They should give you a medal."

"Not this time, Bro. The woman was a prostitute. Turns out the guy abusing her was the deputy JAG officer's favorite nephew. His uncle's looking through my personnel file to see if he can build a case to have me court-martialed."

"That's f'd up, man."

"Screw 'em. My lawyer's dealing with it. Let 'em discharge me. If it was my daughter, I'd want someone stepping in to protect her. I don't care how she earned her living."

"How is your daughter? Alex, right?"

"Alekzandra Francisca Yesca Rosalez ... and she's great. So what's up with you? Why the call?"

"The Institute wants to hire you to train Angel. We need to get her to respond to a new feeding stimulus."

"Wow. Wish I could help you, amigo, but I'm officially unavailable. Besides, for a monster like Angel, you'll want the best, and that's the guy who taught me. His name's Nichols, Dr. Brent Nichols. Degrees in marine biology and ecology from Jacksonville State with a doctorate in molecular systems and evolution from South Florida. I met him years ago at the Dauphin Island Sea Lab in Mobile, Alabama. Guy's a real shark fanatic. Discovery Channel uses him on all their specials. I'll ask Sandra to e-mail you his contact info."

"Thanks, man. And don't let the discharge get to you. The Navy did the same thing to my old man thirty years ago. In the end, he proved them wrong, too."

∇ ∇ ∇

THOMAS CUBIT FINISHES reading the newly edited version of the Dubai Aquarium's non-disclosure agreement. Finally satisfied, he hands a copy to Jonas and one to Mac, indicating where to sign.

"Thanks, Tom. Glad you were around."

"Just make sure you don't sign anything else unless I approve it ... especially if fine print's in Arabic." Cubit offers Jonas a playful backhand smack to the chest and leaves.

Mac hands his signed NDA to Jonas. "There you go, pal. Now we can *officially* step in whatever pile of doo-doo your new friends have in mind." He follows Jonas back to the conference table where bin Rashidi's people have laid out a series of maps of the Philippine Sea. The man in the gray business suit remains off to one side, disinterested.

Bin Rashidi introduces the clean-shaven associate in a *dishdasha* who has yet to speak. "Gentlemen, this is Dr. Ahmad al-Muzani, head of the Geology Science Department at United Arab Emirates University. Eighteen months ago, Dr. al-Muzani was asked to review research data provided to us by Miss Allison Petrucci, former assistant to the late Dr. Michael Maren. This data—Dr. Maren's legacy—included never-before-seen gravity and bathymetric charts of the Philippine Sea along with a detailed computer journal and sonar signatures supplied from a series of remotely operated vehicles. The volume of research compiled by Dr. Maren would put Darwin's *Origin of the Species* to shame. In a word, the man was a genius—"

"That fat prick was a murderer, responsible for the deaths of half a dozen people," Mac states with contempt. "He'd step on his own mother's throat if he thought it would get him on the cover of *National Geographic*. If it wasn't for Jonas, he'd have killed even more innocent people and would have probably gotten away with it."

The businessmen never flinch. Bin Rashidi offers a conciliatory nod. "When the aquarium opens, the families of the deceased will receive a most generous compensation. May I continue?"

Mac exhales. "Yeah, do whatever. It's J.T.'s show. I'm just wall covering."

Bin Rashidi nods to Dr. al-Muzani, who refers to the first chart—a satellite map of the Philippine Sea. "The tectonic forces that created the Philippine Sea are most unusual. As you can see from this map, volcanic islands form the four borders of the sea, revealing the effects of the tectonic plate's subduction zones below. To the west is Taiwan and the Philippine Islands; to the north, Japan; to the east, the Marianas; and to the south, Palau."

The geologist rolls out a second map—a bathymetric chart of the Philippine Sea Plate and the surrounding lithosphere. Jonas notices the signature at the bottom: M. Maren.

"Now we can better understand and appreciate the Philippine Sea Plate for what it really is—a marginal basin plate, completely surrounded by subduction zones and as many as six different tectonic plates. To the east, we have the massive Pacific Plate, subducting into the Mariana Trench, along with the Indo-Australian Plate to the south. To the west is the Eurasian Continental Plate, the northern boundary consisting of three smaller plates: the North American, the Okhotsk, and the Amurian Plate. The northern tip of the Philippine Plate ends at the Izu Peninsula where the Okhotsk Plate meets at Mount Fuji.

"Each of these subduction zones created a deep sea trench, where we find some of the deepest locations on the planet. Dr. Taylor, of course, is familiar with the Mariana Trench, running some 1,550 miles in length, but the Philippine Trench is nearly as deep, stretching just over 700 nautical miles to the east of the Philippine Islands. Completing the diamond-shaped basin are the Yap, the Ryukyu and Izu-Bonin Trenches ... every gorge seismically active, representing some of the oldest-known sea floors on the planet."

PHILIPPINE SEA PLATE

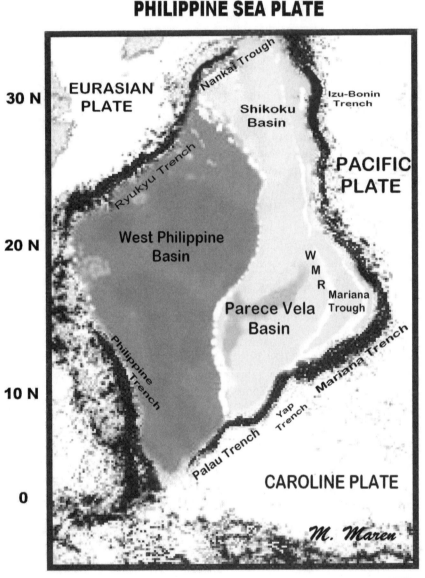

"Dr. Maren's focus was not on the trenches that border the Philippine Sea Plate, but the unusual contours and anomalies of the basin itself. From this map it is clear that the sea floor is actually divided into four distinct basins. Moving from east to west from the Mariana Trench we have the Mariana Trough, a narrow basin that leads to the Western Mariana Ridge. From here the sea floor widens considerably, with the Shikoku Basin to the north, the Parece Vela to the south, and then farther to the west, the massive West Philippine Basin. For hundreds of millions of years the sea floor has been slowly gobbled up to the west by the Eurasian Plate, while it expands to the east atop the subducting Pacific Plate. And yet the basin we are looking at is not representative of the true sea floor. It is, in effect, a geological anomaly."

Jonas can feel his heart racing with adrenaline.

"The first clues that led Dr. Maren to discover the true nature of what lies beneath the Philippine Sea began with a comprehensive study of the Shikoku and Parece Vela Basins back in 1979. Two geologists, Drs. Mrozowski and Hayes, found irregular oceanic crust and magnetic anomalies along these eastern basins. More recently, researchers at the University of Sydney reported anomalies in the basement sediment of the Parece Vela Basin."

"What sort of anomalies?" Jonas asks.

"Geological age discrepancies. Big ones. While the northern section of the east basin, the Shikoku, is less than 30 million years old, and basalts dredged from the Parece Vela Basinreveal geochemical characteristics that date back to the Early Cretaceous period, approximately 150 million years ago. We now believe the floor of the Parece Vela is actually part of an ancient sea shelf that formed as far back as 275 million years when two continental plates rifted apart, the magma creating a crust that eventually stretched east before colliding with the Western Mariana Ridge, approximately 7,000 feet below the surface. This remains a working theory, mind you, but it is supported by Dr. Maren's overwhelming evidence. More important is what Maren discovered hidden beneath the basin … a vast ancient sea that has remained isolated from the Pacific for hundreds of millions of years!"

"Whoa, slow down a minute." Mac stares at the bathymetric chart of the three basins that make up the Philippine Sea Plate. "Let's pretend I'm a fifth grader. What I think you're telling me is that this sea floor here," he points to the Parece Vela Basin, "isn't the real sea floor, that it's just a shelf, a ceiling of volcanic rock, located thousands of feet above the real sea floor. And beneath that shelf is an ancient sea, isolated from the Pacific, that I'm guessing Maren believed harbors life from what? You said a coupla' hundred million years ago?"

"Or perhaps as far back as the Devonian Age."

"Devonian, huh?" Mac glances at Jonas. "Exactly how far back is that, Mr. Peabody?"

"About 320 million years."

"Oh. Is that all?"

Dr. Al Hashemi smiles. "It's incredibly exciting, don't you agree? A lost world, preserving the most dangerous life forms ever to have existed."

Mac looks at the geologist and shrugs. "I'm just a working stiff, pal. The shelf and the ancient sea ... sure, that I can believe. But these other monsters? I mean, granted, Jonas did find a Megalodon population inhabiting the Mariana Trench—"

"—along with a subspecies of *Kronosaurus*," adds bin Rashidi.

Jonas turns his attention back to the bathymetric chart. "Megalodon only disappeared between ten and a hundred thousand years ago. The *Kronosaurus* ... I always considered their survival more of a fluke of nature, sort of like the *Coelacanth*. But these species?"

"Look at the common variables," Al Hashemi says. "Survival over eons of time is a matter of adaptation combined with circumstantial luck. There have been several mass extinctions that wiped out land and sea creatures alike since the Devonian Age. For any species to survive that long would require a vast isolated habitat possessing a perpetually replenishing food chain. This particular area, which Dr. Maren called the Panthalassa Sea, is contained beneath a five-thousand-square-mile geological ceiling, isolating and protecting its inhabitants from sudden environmental changes resulting from volcanism, asteroid strikes, ice ages. If the *Coelacanth* managed to defy the odds in the isolated deep waters off the coast of Africa, then—"

"The *Coelacanth* is a fish," Jonas snaps. "Half the creatures on your wish list began life as air-breathing marine reptiles. Living in the sea is one thing; living beneath it is another. At some juncture they would have had to evolve gills—"

"—just as the kronosaurs you encountered in the Mariana Trench managed to do," Ibrahim Al Hashemi retorts. "Considering that the first land creatures were once fish like the *Coelacanth*, reacquiring gills over the last several hundred million years would probably not be a big leap up the evolutionary ladder."

"What about the food supply down there?" Mac asks.

"The entire region is volcanically active," answers Dr. Al Hashemi. "We believe there are vast hydrothermal vent fields down there, using chemosynthesis as a basis to sustain a thriving, diverse food chain."

"There is also evidence of high levels of methane gas," offers Dr. al-Muzani. "Dr. Maren's notes indicate the western section of the Panthalassa Sea may contain more than a thousand square miles of cold seeps."

A harsh glance from bin Rashidi tempers the geologist's excitement.

"Cold seeps?" Jonas ponders this new information. "Yes, that would make sense. Cold seeps emit methane and hydrogen sulfide at a slower and far more dependable rate than hydrothermal vents. We've discovered huge abyssal communities supported by cold seeps, with prokaryotes—chemo-autotrophic bacteria—processing abundant amounts of chemical energy. Exactly how much methane gas did Maren indicate he discovered down there?"

The geologist looks to bin Rashidi for help.

The cousin of the crown prince waves the matter off. "Impossible to say. But the sonar signatures Maren left behind provide evidence of a variety of life occurring in several different locations beneath the Parece Vela Basin. His notes and drawings go far to theorize what these creatures might be."

Mac looks again at the chart. "If this ridge ceiling is sealed like you say, how did your genius manage to get his remotely operated vehicles down inside this ancient sea?"

"He discovered a hole in the basin ... here." The Dubai geologist points out a red dot located in the southwest section of the basin. "This access point became Maren's base of operations ... and ours."

"Thank you, Dr. al Muzani, that will be all." Bin Rashidi once again assumes control of the discussion. "Based on Dr. Maren's findings, along with the recent evidence of the dead Leeds' fish, the crown prince has generously committed a billion dollars to fund the new Dubai Aquarium and Resort and stock it with these amazing remnants of the prehistoric age. Dr. Taylor, in addition to purchasing two of your Megalodon juveniles, the crown prince has asked me to employ the services of both you and your staff, as well as purchase a dozen of your institute's new Manta Ray submersibles, which we would use to help lure and capture life forms inhabiting this ancient sea. Your field expertise would be invaluable, Dr. Taylor. You and your associate would be extremely well paid for your services."

Jonas and Mac look at one another ... and break into hysterical fits of laughter.

Bin Rashidi's smile disappears.

Mac wipes tears from his eyes. "Oh, baby, that was worth the price of admission."

Jonas clears his throat. "Forgive me, but after everything we've been through, there's not enough oil in Dubai to convince us to return to that hell hole, especially on a venture having anything to do with Michael Maren."

"Five million dollars each, gentlemen. Think it through."

"The old deal or no deal, huh?" Mac fights to control his smile. "Tell you what, toss in a luxury box at Pac Bell Field and a peace treaty between the Israelis and Hamas, and we'll pack our bags for the Philippine Sea."

"Mac, enough."

"I offer you the opportunity of a lifetime and you mock me?" Bin Rashidi signals to his entourage. The four men in *dishdashi* stand as one to leave—

—until the Arab in the gray business suit speaks to bin Rashidi quietly in Arabic.

Bin Rashidi's demeanor changes. "Dr. Taylor ... my colleague requests a moment with you ... alone. Please, it would be most appreciated."

"Of course. Again, my apologies."

The four men in *dishdashi* exit the room. Jonas nods to Mac, who follows them out, closing the office door behind him.

Jonas turns to the man in the gray suit. "Your Highness, it's a pleasure."

The crown prince smiles with his eyes. "You knew?"

"I recognized you from your photos." Jonas pulls out a thick file from his desk drawer and holds up several State Department photos of the crown prince. "I always like to know who I'm dealing with before any business meeting. Masao taught me that years ago."

"A wise man. So? As one businessman to another, tell me your opinion in regard to our little venture. Is it feasible, or am I wasting my time and money?"

"Is it feasible? If the creatures Maren claims to have found really exist, then sure, anything's feasible. What's puzzling is why you would need my help."

"You were the one who captured Angel's mother twenty-five years ago with nothing more than a net and a harpoon. Who better to lead the expedition?"

"For starters, anyone younger. If you haven't noticed, I passed my prime long ago; moreover, I did my time in hell chasing sea monsters. Besides, you and I both know you're not really after these creatures. You're after the methane."

The crown prince's eye lose their sparkle.

"Yeah, I know about that, too." Jonas leans back in his chair. "Philippine basin's loaded with gas hydrates. Estimates of the Nankai Trough alone exceed 27 trillion cubic meters. The Japanese are already drilling for the stuff, pinpointing locations using Bottom Simulating Reflectors. Maren probably bribed an official for the sediment data.

"No offense, Your Highness, but I've traveled down this road before. Twenty years ago, Benedict Singer stole the Institute from Masao in order to gain access to manganese deposits located in the Mariana Trench. The way I figure it, teaming your expedition with our institute buys you the same kind of credibility and backdoor access. Hell, if it works for you go for it; the world certainly needs to get off the fossil fuel needle. But other than selling you two of Angel's pups and a few of our submersibles, my family and I won't be a part of your little methane venture. And there's no wiggle room in my answer."

"Fair enough. But you are wrong about the aquarium. While it is true the hydrates would subsidize the venture, the aquarium stands on its own virtue. Attracting tourists to my country remains my primary objective, and a new resort featuring such aquatic attractions would certainly accomplish that. The main tanks are already complete, and two refitted oil tankers are on their way to the Philippine Sea as we speak to locate these creatures and capture as many of them as we can. What harm would it do for you to supervise such a venture aboard the lead vessel?"

"Again, Your Highness, you have my final answer. As for the sale of the Meg pups—"

"Mr. bin Rashidi will negotiate the terms and conditions of the two surviving runts."

"Mary Kate and Ashley? Really? I thought for sure you'd want the sisters."

"While they are, by far, the more impressive specimens, they are too vicious, making them unpredictable. I may be a risk taker, Dr. Taylor, but I am not a gambler. You have given me your answer, and I must respect your wishes. However, before I leave, I really would like to see Angel. And of course, those wonderful submersibles of yours."

"I'll have my son show you the subs. As for Angel, unfortunately, Your Highness, she is also unpredictable. But we'll do our best to coax her out of the canal."

"I would be most grateful."

5

R.A.W. Headquarters
San Francisco, California

Tuesday

The organization's address is listed in a tri-level house overlooking San Francisco Bay. The floors are bamboo, the main rooms naturally lit by bay windows and block glass. Airy and open, the dwelling is one that would attract most local artists—if they could afford it.

Thirty-two-year-old Jessica Jean Tompson feeds her two dogs, Daisy and Duke, while her cat, Sawyer, purrs on the counter, craving attention. Grabbing her coffee in one hand, the cat in the other, she heads upstairs to the third floor loft—headquarters of her foundation: Release Animals to the Wild. Sliding into her ergomatic chair, she pulls her brownish-red hair into a tight bun, exposing the underlying purple-dyed locks, then turns her attention to the video already cued up on her laptop.

The opening footage, supplied by her partner's mole inside the Tanaka Institute, had been filmed using the Meg Pen's mounted underwater cameras. The sequence features a pale object thrashing underwater, moving in and out of focus. She advances the video, pausing as a dark blur moves into the frame. *Not much here, you can't really tell what's going on.* She fast-forwards the tape again, hitting PLAY as the camera angle shifts to a surface shot. Taken at night, filmed using a hand-held camcorder, the wobbly footage clearly shows the wounded Megalodon being lifted out of the tank in a cargo net. For a full minute it hangs from the steel crane's expanse beam, its thrashes subsiding as a female trainer stabs at it with a reach pole.

Cruel bastards. Jess sips her coffee—

—choking down the last bitter swallow as the lead-backed Meg suddenly leaps into the frame from below and clamps its hideous jaws upon its netted sibling's exposed belly in a sickening, horrifying bite! Jessica's eyes widen, her heart pounding from caffeine and adrenaline, as Bela remains suspended out of the water by her teeth, her twenty-ton girth obliging her serrated fangs to tear a massive chunk out of the smaller Meg's stomach. Innards pour from the eviscerated wound like a waterfall, the sight causing the animal activist to gag.

54

She reaches for her cell phone, speed-dialing a number, her eyes refusing to leave the computer screen. "Sara, have you seen this?"

"Only four times." Sara Toms, R.A.W.'s co-founder, is a former Airborne surveillance instructor with the United States Air Force with a hit-the-ground-swinging attitude. "Mike McCormick's editing it down to three minutes. It'll be on our website by noon Eastern Time. I haven't been this primed for battle since Michael Vick decided to buy himself a bunch of dogs. My 'Deep Throat' did good, didn't he?"

"He did great. What about the Lost Boys?"

"Still too early to reach them, and honestly, we don't need them protesting today. This video pushes us into the major leagues. Morning shows, evening news ... we're there."

"What about that last bit, the one with the Meg's guts falling out ... you think it's too gory for prime time TV?"

"Probably, but they'll air it anyway, especially after a million people an hour start downloading it from our site. Jess, you concentrate on donations; let me play Rambo on this. I don't want PETA stealing our glory ... or our sponsors."

"It's your baby, Sara. Run with it."

The line goes dead.

Jessica Tompson rewinds the footage, replaying the attack again, a smile creasing her face. *By tonight we'll be the major story on every network and cable news program. By tomorrow morning we'll be global. God, I live for these days ...*

She pauses her stream of thought only to toss Sawyer off her desk when the purring cat blocks her view of the screen.

Tanaka Oceanographic Institute

David Taylor follows Dr. Jonathan Stelzer into the staff locker room. The Institute's top marine biologist converses as he dresses in a pair of protective orange coveralls, matching rubber boots, rubber apron, and thick, double-layer rubber gloves. "Necropsy is an important phase in your development as a marine biologist, David. Analyzing the threat of a disease in an aquarium can prevent an epidemic that could wipe out your entire ecosystem. Morbidity and mortality must be examined."

"No argument. But Angelica didn't die of a disease."

"It doesn't matter. Her demise offers us a rare opportunity to delve into the internal workings of a predator species we still know very little about."

David tugs on his own pair of heavy rubber boots. "Can we really make accurate conclusions when most of Angelica's guts fell out?"

"There's still plenty of internal organs left in place. Again, knowledge is a hands-on experience, and we don't get many opportunities like this in our line of work. Ready?"

"Yes, sir." David adjusts his face shield in place and follows Dr. Stelzer out of the locker room—

—into a refrigerated warehouse. The dead female Megalodon has been placed belly-up, propped slightly on its left side to prevent the remains of its insides from falling out of a jagged wound the size of a Jacuzzi. Heavy plastic sheets cover the concrete floor, bright portable lights illuminate the carcass. Dissection tools have been laid out across the tops of three large tables located by the creature's head. This "surgical" equipment includes a variety of chainsaws, handsaws, vacuum hoses, hunting knifes, machetes, rakes, hooks, and a stack of clean towels. A fourth table—a portable lab—holds beakers, test tubes, blood sampling kits, and a dozen sterilized, plastic vacuum packs. Two electric, heavy-duty Toyota forklifts are parked off to one side, their steel prongs wrapped in plastic.

The necropsy team has already assembled, everyone dressed in similar protective attire. Steven Moretti, director of husbandry, is using a metal rake to retract Angelica's upper lip and gums, allowing Dr. Stelzer's assistant, Fran Rizzuto, to snap a few photos of the wide front row of teeth. Moretti's assistant, Virgil Carmen, uses an acetylene torch to mark areas of incision along the remains of the dead Meg's devastated ventral surface.

Dr. Stelzer observes his crew then walks to a dry-erase board. "Gentlemen— and Frannie—if you could join us, please." He picks up a blue marker and draws a rough sketch of the dead Megalodon. "Moretti, I want you and Virgil to begin with the skull. Remove Angelica's right eye and place it in formalin before starting on the upper and lower jaws. You'll need to cut here—" he references the diagram "—to remove the jaws to allow us access to her gill arches. Every tooth, including those folded back into the interior gum line, will be removed from the jaw, then laid out on a board and numbered, measured, and photographed, as they're worth a small fortune. And please don't get any ideas; there are security cameras recording every procedure.

"Fran, you and David will assist me in taking tissue samples of the major organs. Heart, liver, intestines, gonads, and swim bladder ... at least what's left of them. Remember, all toxicology samples must be frozen and stored immediately. Anything that appears abnormal gets documented, cut, placed in formalin, and tagged. Keep an eye out for lesions. We'll work for two hours then break for twenty minutes and reevaluate. Questions? ... No? ... Then let's get started."

The two teams head for the equipment tables. Steven Moretti grabs a hunting knife to excise Angelica's eye, his assistant filling a Tupperware bowl with formalin—a strong-scented liquid disinfectant that will help preserve the visual sensory organ.

Dr. Stelzer points to the sixteen-inch chainsaw. "David, that's your tool for today. Fran, grab a machete and a handsaw."

The biologist selects a metal rake then leads them to the massive bite mark located along Angelica's stomach. "Bela did quite a job on her. We lost her stomach, spleen, and most of her intestines. We'll access her heart after Moretti and Virgil remove the gills; so, for now, our primary target will be the gonads. David, very carefully, I want you to make an incision from the edge of the bite mark to the anal fin, making sure you only slice into the hide. Fran, as he cuts with the chainsaw, we'll use the rake and machete to retract the Meg's skin, exposing the internal organs."

David sets the chain saw on the floor and gives the pull-starter a yank, starting the engine. Avoiding Angelica's enormous wing-like pectoral fins, he moves to the edge of the jagged bite mark and sets the whirring blade against the rancid bite wound.

The chain saw spits out blood and shards of alabaster-pink skin.

Dr. Stelzer sets the teeth of his rake against the splitting four-inch-thick skin, pulling the upper flap back while Fran hacks at the connective tissue with her machete. David continues his cut, pausing five minutes later at the anal fin, an equilateral triangle of flesh harboring the female Megalodon's cloaca.

"Good enough, stop there." Dr. Stelzer climbs over the carcass. "Now, make a transverse incision here." He traces an invisible crosswise line over the Meg's lower belly.

David makes the incision. Using their tools, Fran and Stelzer pull back the ten-foot flaps of skin created by the cut, exposing the dead Meg's ovaries and right and left oviducts.

The smell is overpowering.

Using a handsaw, Dr. Stelzer slices open the ovary, revealing hundreds of clear eggs, each the size of a tennis ball. Fran hands him a plastic ladle and opens a specimen bag. One by one, Stelzer scoops out twenty eggs, then seals up the bag.

"Set these aside, Fran. We'll look at them later. Let's see how the guys are doing."

Moretti and Virgil have removed Angelica's eye and retina, bagging it in formalin. Using ladders and chainsaws, they are hard at work cutting around the juvenile's six-foot jaws. It will take another hour before the incisions are complete, allowing Moretti to yank the jaws free from the Meg's mouth using cables rigged to the forklift.

V V V

THE SUN IS just setting over the Pacific by the time David emerges from the locker room. The muscles in his shoulders, lower back, and arms ache, and despite two showers, he still reeks of formaldehyde. He steps out onto the main deck of the lagoon, allowing gusts of cold wind to blow in his face and long brown hair.

His eyes search the lagoon. The surface waters of the concrete bathtub are choppy with whitecaps, but there is no sign of its seventy-four-foot, fifty-one-ton resident.

Looking to his left, David spots Teddy Badault and his team working in the southern end of the arena by the A-frame, using a long chain to dunk a slab of raw beef from the steel tower as if it were a church belfry.

David jogs over. "Any luck?"

Ted shoots him a disgusted look. "Not a bite in forty-five minutes. Your father's guests are growing impatient."

Seated midway up the southern bleachers are the visitors from Dubai.

"Wait here. I have an idea." David heads for the equipment room. The metal door is unlocked, and he enters.

Inside the large rectangular storage space are shelves filled with flotation devices, reach poles, lengths of steel chain, hooks, and an assortment of underwater lights. He quickly finds what he is looking for—a metal vibrator roughly the size of a coconut.

David powers-on the device. Nothing.

He checks the batteries, replaces them with eight new D cells, and tries it again.

The thumper reverberates in his hands like a giant artificial heart.

Leaving the equipment room, he returns to the A-frame. "Ted, pull the carcass out of the water. I want to try something."

The trainer signals to his two assistants, who swing the water-laden side of beef out of the lagoon and onto the deck.

Using his pocket knife, David slices a deep slit into a section of fatty tissue then shoves the thumper inside, powering it on high. "Try it now, only don't bob the meat. Just let it float along the surface."

The assistants hoist the carcass up over the sea wall and back into the lagoon. The side of beef floats just below the surface, the meat vibrating rapidly in the water.

Several minutes pass.

A harsh wind kicks up, whistling through the near-empty bleachers.

"*Al Abyad! Al Abyad!*" One of the men in *dishdashi* is on his feet, pointing at the canal entrance as a ten-foot wake pushes majestically into the lagoon, the ghostly form fully submerged, the killer remaining deep.

"*Al Abyad! Al Abayad!*"

Ted Badault and his men instinctively back away from the sea wall as the great fish slowly approaches the thumping bait.

David never moves. He has watched Angel feed a thousand times. He knows her every approach, revealing her every mood. *She's hungry, but in no hurry. She'll circle first, just to be sure. Maybe take a nip, then circle again ... until she goes deep and comes up from below ...*

The alabaster dorsal fin, streaked with scars, cuts the surface like a triangular periscope as Angel rises. An eddy forms as the pale behemoth circles the bait twice. Then, with a sudden slap of her caudal fin, the huntress launches herself at the side of beef, waves cascading over the sea wall as she steals a quick bite before tossing her prey aside.

The Dubai delegation is on their feet, their videographer filming. For several long minutes they simply stare at the water, the lull allowing their fluttering hearts to calm as the creature remains out of sight. *Is it over? Have they waited so patiently for so long, just to be teased?*

Small waves lap at the sea wall. Somewhere close by, a metal bracket clinks against a naked flagpole, its hollow cadence set to the wind. The Pacific thunders in the distance. Monterey grays as a storm front moves in from the west.

There are no warnings, no telltale fin, no tsunami-like wake. Death simply rises from the aqua-green depths as if drawn to the heavens. The triangular head, as large as a garbage truck, yawns open to form an encompassing cavern of teeth. The carcass—and several hundred gallons of sea—are siphoned, crushed, and swallowed in one all-consuming bite, pink froth squeezing out of the sides of the clenching jaws as the albino goddess continues to rise clear out of the lagoon.

The half-moon tail curls as it flicks air. The broad, almost barrel-shaped back, arches. For one gravity-defying split second the most prolific hunter ever to stalk the planet is airborne, its 102,000-pound girth blotting out the opposite end of the arena—

—until the laws of physics return and the monster plunges through the sea, its mass not so much sinking as opening a great hole in the water from whence it is swallowed.

The *craaack* of mass striking water echoes across the empty arena, followed by a geyser of sea that shoots four stories high. The Dubai entourage remains awestruck, their mouths hanging open, their minds struggling to grapple with what their eyes have just witnessed—

—save for Fiesal bin Rashidi, who is staring at David Branden Taylor. The twenty-year-old had never so much as flinched. Poised three feet from the heaving sea, Jonas's young prodigy remains unafraid, totally within his element.

6

Wednesday

Terry Taylor closes her eyes as the woman applying make-up touches up her dark circles. Hovering behind her is Kayla Cicala. The publicist had arranged this morning's live interview as a means of presenting the Tanaka Institute's side against the mounting tide of public opinion that is being stirred by members of the radical PETA affiliate, R.A.W.

The station's producer enters the room. "Terry? Keith Auton. I'll be coordinating things on our side. Have you ever done a satellite interview before?"

"No."

"It can be a little disorienting. You'll be looking into the camera while one of the hosts at *Good Morning America* speaks with you through an earpiece. He can see you. You just can't see him." The producer scans his notes. "I see they have Frank Youngblood scheduled to do the interview."

"Frank's straightforward but fair," Kayla says, checking Terry's make-up. "Blot the lipstick. You don't need it, and it sends the wrong message."

An intern pokes her head inside the doorway. "They want her on the set."

Kayla gives Terry a smile and two thumbs up. "You'll do great."

The studio is cold, the lights hot and bright, the cameras a bit intimidating. The set features a backdrop of the San Francisco skyline. A sound man attaches a microphone to Terry's blouse collar, instructing her to snake the wire down her shirt. He pins the remote's battery pack to the back of her skirt then hands her an earpiece.

She hooks it in place behind her right ear, eavesdropping on a cross-conversation among producers in New York.

"Hi, Terry. Can you hear me?"

"Yes." She looks at the large studio camera, its lifeless glass lens pointed directly at her. Someone has taped a "Happy Face" above the lens, providing her with a point of reference.

"Terry, this is Frank Youngblood. Thanks so much for agreeing to do the show. How's your daughter?"

"Fine. Better. She gets out of the hospital today."

"Great. Stand by."

Terry sits back in the upholstered chair, each breath slow and deliberate, her racing pulse gradually slowing.

"Thirty seconds." The red light above the camera blinks on. Theme music plays in her ear ...

"... and we're back. For the last four years the Tanaka Institute and Aquarium has rivaled Disney World's popularity, attracting tens of millions to its seaside arena to visit Angel: The Angel of Death. Last Saturday, visitors watched in horror as two volunteers were swept into the lagoon, one of the men—an undergrad at USC—devoured by the seventy-four-foot Megalodon. Less than twenty-four hours later, one of Angel's offspring attacked and killed a smaller pup inside the aquarium known as the Meg Pen. With us here this morning, live, via satellite from our ABC affiliate in San Francisco, is Terry Tanaka-Taylor, CEO of the Tanaka Institute. Terry, good to have you with us."

"Good morning." The bright lights cause her eyes to water. She forces herself to focus on the yellow Happy Face.

"Let's start with the incident on Saturday. Packed audience, visitors of all ages ... what do you say to the fifteen thousand people who witnessed this horrible death?"

"There's not much anyone can say. It was a tragic accident. Unfortunately, on rare occasions, these things can happen. Whether it's in an aquarium or zoo or circus, we're dealing with wild animals. Years ago, Roy Horn was mauled by one of his white tigers. Sometimes, despite every precaution, the unthinkable happens. Our thoughts and prayers go out to the family and friends of the young man who died."

"Looking at the footage ... it seems like it could have been worse. Massive waves were rolling out of the lagoon, pummeling frightened visitors. Parents were clutching their children. Panic ensued. Several people, including your own daughter, were taken to the hospital."

"It was a bad day for all of us."

"Where do you go from here?"

"Changes are underway to make the pavilion seats less exposed. New precautions are being implemented regarding feeding regimens. Safety has always been a priority at the Institute, and that will continue."

"What about safety for your animals? Members of Release Animals back to the Wild have accused the Institute of keeping far too many Megalodons in the Meg Pen, that conditions are unsafe, and things will only get worse."

"The Meg Pen was constructed before Angel birthed her pups. We were expecting a litter of two, not five. Angelica's death was an unfortunate incident. I do not classify it as an accident, because the species is predatory, and attacks among rival predators happen all the time in the wild. The male that fathered these pups was himself killed by Angel following insemination. The radical group that has been stalking myself, my family, and our staff for two years now is more concerned with acquiring donations than the actual safety of these animals, whose ferocious nature prevents us from ever releasing them back into the wild."

"Can the Meg Pen be expanded?"

"No. We've petitioned the governor several times and have been turned down. However, my husband is making arrangements with another aquarium to transport two of the remaining four juveniles to another facility."

"Really? And where might that be?"

"I cannot say ... at least not until the deal has been finalized."

"You realize there are groups, comprised of family members of those killed by these Megs, that are calling for the extermination of the species. What do you say to them?"

"These are wild animals. Unlike humans, they kill only to feed, and humans are not part of their natural diet. By studying them we can add to our growing body of scientific knowledge and can learn to protect all sharks and the sanctity of the ocean's food chains. It serves no purpose other than revenge to slaughter Angel or her offspring. My family first crossed paths with these amazing creatures twenty-five years ago. My younger brother, D.J., died when he was attacked by Angel's mother. He was about the same age as the young man who was killed on Saturday. My initial reaction was revenge. I wanted to hunt down and kill the shark, but my father refused; he knew it was wrong and that my brother would never have agreed to such an inhumane act."

"So ... in that regard, you share the same beliefs as the members of R.A.W."

"No. R.A.W. is an extremist group. Their leaders espouse animal rights only as an excuse to draw public attention and monetary contributions. We're an aquarium—an educational facility. We believe in protecting our aquatic species, not harming them."

"And yet R.A.W. was right about the Meg Pen being too small."

"Animals sometimes die in captivity, Frank. Years ago, despite every precaution, one of the whale sharks at the Georgia Aquarium contracted an infection and died. Some people protested, calling the habitat cruel. But while these whale sharks were being slaughtered by the hundreds in Taiwan and other Asian countries nobody seemed to protest that fact. Orca and sea lions are dying off—a result of the effects of global warming. The media ignores that story, preferring instead to cover the death of one whale shark or one Megalodon. The more sensational the better. The reality is aquariums offer a practical means of understanding and studying these sea creatures while protecting them from the onslaught of man. Hopefully we can prevent another species from becoming extinct."

"Does that mean you intend to breed Megalodons?"

Terry smiles. "God, no. Even if we wanted to, the juveniles are all females."

"Finally, as someone who lost a brother to one of these predators, what do you say to the family of the young man who was killed?"

Terry pauses. "I would say that sometimes bad things happen to wonderful people. Cancer, war, traffic accidents ... these tragic losses affect us all. My heart is heavy with your pain. From my own loss I can tell you that you will never get over it; but I pray, in time, that you will learn to live with it."

Tanaka Oceanographic Institute
Monterey, California

The creature is dark brown on top with a white belly, its body nine feet long, not counting its four-foot tail. Its wingspan extends eighteen feet.

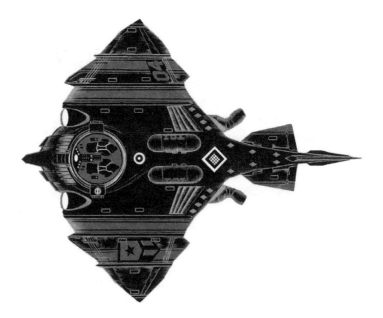

The crown prince follows David Taylor down into the dry dock located at the end of a concrete pier outside the southern bleachers. Suspended above the ocean by a pair of hydraulic arms, the two-man submersible resembles *Manta birostris*, the giant manta ray.

The prince taps the sub's outer hull with his knuckles. "This is metal?"

"Layered acrylic," David says. "Gives it positive buoyancy. There's a second shell inside, a spherical escape pod that can withstand nineteen thousand pounds per square inch of water pressure. The old Abyss Gliders used similar technologies, only they ran like a torpedo. The *Mantas* actually glide hydrodynamically through the water." He kneels by the tail assembly and points. "Twin props. Silent and fast. With the current she can approach forty knots, or barrel roll into a 360-degree loop. Flying these puppies is better than sex."

"You have piloted this vessel before?"

"Only all the time. I've even trained some of the Navy guys. It was my demo that got us a contract with the Pentagon. You should have seen them kissing my father's ass. Man, he was loving it. Of course, their suped-up version will be bigger, loaded with all sorts of gadgets and weapons, but ours will still be faster. Wanna go for a spin?"

The crown prince's eyes widen. "A ride? Yes, please. Are you allowed to take it without clearance?"

"My father asked me to show you the sub. Best way to see it is to take it for a test drive." David points to the four armed security guards. "The gorillas have to stay here."

The prince converses with his men. They do not appear pleased.

"The captain wishes to know if the ride will be dangerous."

"Nah, I'll go easy." David lifts a concealed panel roughly the size of a gas tank cover positioned in the Manta Ray's port-side wing. Inside is a circular lever and two indicator lights: one green, one red. The green light is on. Reaching inside the compartment, David turns the lever ninety degrees clockwise. The red light turns on—

—activating the outer hatch of the spherical escape pod, the upper twenty percent of which protrudes from the dorsal surface of the Manta Ray behind its two exterior headlights, shaped like eyes. With a hiss of hydraulics, the dark-tinted acrylic top pops open, allowing them access into the cockpit.

There are two low-slung, leather bucket seats inside, each set before dual, high-tech steering wheels and an operational system equipped with a radio and sonar. "Most of the actual steering is done using your feet," David explains, climbing down into the command hub. "Left and right foot pedals operate the port and starboard engines. If you want to go left, you press down with the right pedal which guns the starboard prop. So everything works opposite. Joysticks control your pitch and yaw. Pull back to raise the nose; push down to descend."

The crown prince climbs down into the co-pilot's seat on the starboard side, assisted by his security detail. He can see the entire cockpit is actually a Lexan sphere that sits low inside the Manta Ray's body. "Both of us are required to pilot the vessel?"

"No, just one. Port controls are the primary. Your side is strictly backup. So? Ready to go?"

The crown prince catches a deep breath. "Yes."

David reaches for a circular lever on the dashboard, identical to the one embedded in the outside wing. He gives it a quarter-turn counterclockwise and closes the hatch, rotating it into position above their heads before sinking a half inch into a titanium band that wraps around the diameter of the escape pod. With a *click* the hatch locks into place, the panel light switching from red to green, indicating a perfect seal.

David opens a padded compartment situated between the two seats. Inside is a small remote control. He presses LOWER—

—activating the dry dock arms, which immerse the sub into the awaiting Pacific.

The crown prince, just under 5 feet 10 inches, strains to peer out of the tinted hatch.

"Reach along the side of your seat," David instructs. "You'll find a series of control switches that will raise and adjust your seat. There's barf bags in the glove box, just in case you need 'em."

"Will I need them?"

David smiles. "Buckle up!" He presses RELEASE on the remote, freeing the Manta Ray from its docking clamps. The flat-winged submersible is immediately buffeted by the incoming sea. Pushing down gently on the pedals with both feet, David propels them forward—

—the sleek craft leaping ahead, gliding effortlessly between a row of concrete pilings before accelerating into the majestic-blue underworld.

The crown prince holds on, almost giddy. "This is ... fantastic!"

"You ain't seen nothin' yet."

David pushes the twin joysticks forward, diving the vessel toward the sea floor. The depth gauge drops from 35 feet to 80 feet in seconds then levels out. For several moments they soar above a flat sandy terrain—

—which suddenly drops away into a deep gorge that plunges into blackness.

David hits another switch, activating the night glass—an optical feature that transforms the sphere's treated acrylic surface into night vision glass. The crown prince reflexively grabs for the handles of his seat as he stares below into a gray-green, three-dimensional abyss, the trench highlighted with jagged cuts that slice into the widening aperture of geology like giant fingers. "Amazing. What is this?"

"Monterey Bay Submarine Canyon. It's just over a mile deep here, but it widens out and descends to about twelve thousand feet a bit farther out. The chasm walls are sheer vertical rock faces with some real nasty currents, so we have to be careful."

They soar through a ravine, surrounded by rock. The depth gauge drops below 700 feet.

The prince breaks out in a cold sweat, struggling to breath. "Please ... I would prefer the shallows."

David glances at his guest, who appears pale in the olive green light. He adjusts the cabin temperature, blasting him with cool air as he pulls back on the joysticks, ascending to 130 feet. "You okay?"

"Better. I never realized I was so claustrophobic."

"Happens to almost everyone. I once took a jet fighter pilot for a ride. The moment we dived into the canyon the guy wigged out. Guess he realized if something went wrong he couldn't parachute to safety."

"Please ... you are not helping."

"Okay, okay. We'll move back into the shallows in a minute, I just want to show you something really cool."

They remain above the lip of the chasm, which winds around to the north, then narrows slightly as it turns back to the east.

"By the way, Your Highness, back at the lagoon ... what was it your men were chanting at Angel?"

"*Al Abyad*. The white. Albino creatures have a special place in our culture."

"Then I'm guessing you enjoyed seeing Angel up close and in the flesh?"

"I loved it. She is death personified—a vision that rattles the soul."

"She's all that, alright." David slows the sub to a crawl, the Pacific waves rolling in at their back, the surface seventy feet above their heads. Ahead, appearing out of the gray-blue murk, looms something massive. They venture closer, the prince's heart beating faster as the object materializes in the haze—

—a set of steel double doors.

"Just thought you might like to meet Al Abyad up close."

The crown prince grips his seat, going white-knuckled. "No! You will take us away from here!"

"Easy, Your Highness. I rattle my soul like this all the time."

The submersible closes to within fifty feet, the basketball-size pores of the giant doors now visible, revealing a soft white glow—

—as the sea awakens with sound ... a deep metallic *whump*. The reverberation registers in their bones as the albino monster on the opposite side of the barrier makes its presence known.

Sweat pours from the prince's face. He gasps for breath, his limbs quivering. "I command you to take us away from here! Do it now! That's an order!"

"Order? You want fries with that order? This is America—"

Whump! ... Whump! Whump!

The crown prince reaches inside the glove box, his fingers groping for a sick bag. He opens it, then quickly shoves it over his nose and mouth and breathes into it, hyperventilating.

"Alright, alright. Hold your cookies." Fighting a mischievous grin, David accelerates directly at the double doors—

Whump! Whump!

—banking hard to the south at the last second. Leveling out, he races to the surface, the sea above their heads turning to blue sky as the winged sub bounces over the wave tops doing thirty knots. Fifteen seconds later he eases his feet off the twin accelerators, allowing the Manta Ray to settle back into the water, the pier appearing on their left.

David guides the vessel carefully between the two rows of concrete pilings then hits GRIP on the remote control, activating the docking clamps.

A minute later the submersible is rising out of the water.

David turns to his guest, attempting to make peace. "Seriously, dude, you were never in any danger. Angel can't get out. And even if she could, she could never catch us. So ... we cool?"

The hatch pops open. The crown prince tosses the barf bag aside and climbs out, speaking rapidly to his guards.

David looks up ... at the business end of four assault weapons.

One of the guards, a big man weighing over 280 pounds, reaches into the cockpit and grabs David by his collar, lifting him bodily out of the sub and dropping him to the deck on his knees. The captain of the guard pushes the big man aside, chambers a round, and aims the barrel of his Glock 19 inches from David's left eye.

David's heart pounds in his throat. Part of him knows the man will not pull the trigger, but this is the crown prince, a member of the royal family and U.S. ally possessing diplomatic immunity. *What was that stupid expression of Mac's? Accidents happen in the best of families. So, when in doubt ... pull out.*

The crown prince rattles off another order. The captain holsters his weapon then leads his security detail out of the dry dock, leaving the two men alone.

"You had your fun, yes? Now I have had mine. So, David ... are we cool?"

David stands, his limbs still shaking. "Yeah, man ... we're cool."

"Good. Because you have many talents, and I have many needs. Has your father told you anything about our new facility in Dubai?"

"Only that you'll be purchasing Mary Kate and Ashley."

"Indeed. The facility has the best of everything and will be run by some of the top marine biologists and animal specialists in the world. But your experience with Angel places you far above their level of expertise. I'm offering you a job, David. I want you to return to Dubai with me to inspect the facility then oversee the acclimation of the two Megs into their new habitat. We will take care of all your expenses, including lodging and travel."

"Why me? Dr. Stelzer's the expert—or Fran Rizzuto or my father. I haven't even graduated from Florida yet."

"Degrees are merely pieces of paper. What you possess is practical knowledge and a comfort level that can only be acquired through years of interaction with these creatures. I am spending a small ransom on this purchase; the fish offer me nothing in return if they die after being moved."

"How long will you need me for? I have to be back in school August twenty-seventh."

"The entire summer. With an option to remain if you like what we have to offer."

"The summer, huh? How much money are we talking?"

"Fifty thousand for overseeing the two Megs until your school starts, with an additional twenty-five thousand for training a team of submersible pilots to operate a small fleet of Manta Rays. How many of these subs do you have in stock? A dozen?"

"More like four. And one's in the shop being repaired. But are you sure my father agreed to sell you the subs?"

"It will be negotiated into the purchase price for the two juvenile Megs."

"Why do you need them?"

"I need them, David, because I want them. So then? Seventy-five thousand dollars for a summer of fun in Dubai. What is your answer?"

"As long as I can leave no later than August twenty-fourth, you have yourself a deal." David shakes the prince's hand, his thoughts shifting from buying a new sports car to how he's going to break the news to his mother.

7

Retired United States Air Force pilot Jerry L. Bobo II stands before the two MLST (Megalodon Life Support Transits), dwarfed by the sheer size of the rectangular objects now situated on the lagoon loading dock. "Mac, exactly how big are these things?"

"Thirty-one feet high, sixty-two feet long, fifteen feet wide ... that's including the motorized carts they'll sit on when we drive them into the cargo hold."

"And these will be filled with water?"

"And one heavily medicated Megalodon. Each. We were thinking of having the Arabs lease one of Boeing's Dreamlifters—the converted 747-400s they were using to ship components of their 787s."

"The Dreamliner's are big enough, but the cargo hold isn't pressurized. Unless you want your monsters arriving dead-on-arrival, we're looking at a C-5 Galaxy."

"You think the Pentagon would let us use one?"

"No. But they might allow the crown prince." Jerry walks halfway around the container. "I'm no shark expert, but how do you plan on keeping your fish breathing in a steel box for a twelve- to fifteen-hour flight?"

"First, these contraptions aren't steel. They're acrylic. Six inches thick. You can't have any metal in the tank; it upsets the Meg's senses. As far as breathing, these MLST are rigged with built-in head currents similar in design to the ones used to train Olympic swimmers. It's sort of like being on an underwater tread mill. The Meg has to swim to breathe. This allows them to swim in a stationary position."

"You said the fish will be medicated?"

"With oxygen and Tricaine Methanesulfonate. They'll be acclimated to the mlsts days before we move them. We calculated a combined weight of the two tanks at 275,000 pounds."

"How many in your flight party?"

"Seven. Four marine biologists and three engineers."

"With the cargo weight—" Jerry Bobo makes a few quick calculations "—it's seven thousand nautical miles and change from San Francisco to Dubai International. That puts us about seven hundred miles short on fuel. Looks like we're stopping over in London."

Mac frowns. "It's a major hassle to add an additional stop. Customs can be a bitch; everyone and their mother wants to see what's in the hold. Plus, it's more added stress on Mary Kate and Ashley."

"Well, I suppose we can arrange to refuel in-flight, but it'll cost you."

"Won't cost me a dime, pal, it's all on the crown prince."

V   V   V

"Dad, what's your problem?" David pushes himself away from the conference table in disgust. "This is a great opportunity. Why do you want to blow it for me?"

Jonas rubs the tension from the back of his neck. "I'm not trying to ruin your life, David, but I worry. Your mother worries. It's what parents do. Keeping these monsters penned, allowing you and Dani to work with them ... it's like playing with fire. And this whole Dubai venture ... it just doesn't feel right to me."

"Seventy-five grand for keeping an eye on the two runts and training a bunch of submersible pilots doesn't feel right to you? Dad, come on. I'd practically do this for free!"

"If you're just training these pilots in Dubai, I don't have a problem. If it's something else—"

"What else? Tell me what you're afraid of."

Jonas debates on what he should reveal to his son. *Tell him about Maren's discovery and he'll jump at the chance to go. There'll be no stopping him.*

"Dad."

"Okay. I'll sell the crown prince the Manta Rays as agreed, but only under one condition—that you promise me you'll remain in Dubai for the summer."

"Where else would I go?"

"David, I can't go into details, but one of the reasons the crown prince came here was to recruit me to help them capture different deepwater species for their aquarium."

"What kind of species?" David's eyes widen. "Wait. I know. They wanted your help to capture a kronosaur! That's it, isn't it? Dad, no worries. I'd never go down to the Mariana Trench—not after what you and mom went through. No way."

"Then promise me you'll stay in Dubai."

"You have my word."

"And you'll be careful with the runts?"

"Dad—"

"I worry, David. You've got that cocky swagger that leads to mistakes. I had it, your mother had it, and it contributed to your Uncle D.J.'s death. If anything ever happened to you … well—"

"Dad, I'm not D.J. And I'm not out to prove something to the world. I'm a marine biologist, and I love what I do. Please, for once, just let me do it!"

Jonas stares at his son, his heart swollen with pride. *Wasn't it yesterday when I held my newborn son in my arms? Coached his little league team? Taught him how to scuba? To pilot a mini-sub? Where did all those years go?*

"Dad?"

"Better make sure your passport's in order. The prince leaves in the morning."

David pumps his fists and gives his father a quick hug before dashing out of his office … leaving Jonas to wonder how he's going to explain this to his wife.

🦷 🦷 🦷

THE TAXI CAB turns into Masao Tanaka Way, inching its way through a throng of protestors. The lone passenger stretched out in the backseat shakes his head in amazement. *A million people a day are starving to death or dying of AIDS, and these assholes have their underwear knotted in a ball because one big shark was killed by another bigger shark.*

The cab double parks as close as it can to the main entrance. Brent Nichols struggles to pull his heavy-set, 6 foot 3 inch, 290-pound frame out of the cramped backseat and waits for the driver to unload the two metal trunks on wheels. The scientist pays the cabby, grabs a trunk handle in each thick palm, and trudges toward the nearest set of glass doors.

A sign reads: CLOSED FOR RENOVATION.

A security guard approaches. "We're closed, big fella. Can't you read?"

"Far better than you, my friend. Does that walkie-talkie work?"

"Yeah."

"Then do us both a favor and let Mr. David Taylor know his shark trainer has arrived."

∇ ∇ ∇

"Ricardo told me you were the best," David says, leading the marine biologist down an access corridor to the main gallery.

"Were? I *am* the best, kid, and don't let this spare tire fool you. In the water I'm a seal. Okay, maybe a sea elephant." Dr. Nichols wipes sweat from his reddish-brown goatee. "I'm a field scientist by nature; not much escapes my eye. After I graduated with my masters, the Sea Lab in Mobile hired me to condition their aquatic animals to feed. Using flashes of light, we were able to teach lemon sharks to congregate in assigned areas of their tanks, segregating the population to ensure they were all being properly fed. Amazingly, sharks were able to learn these tasks ten times faster than cats or rabbits."

"And that led you to be recruited by the Pentagon?"

"DARPA, actually. The Defense Advanced Research Projects Agency. They're the evil Frankensteins who dream up our future weapons systems. Some pencil pusher decided sharks would make great spies. Of course, using animals to complete military missions is nothing new; the Navy's been using dolphins and sea lions for decades to patrol harbors and locate sea mines. When it comes to stealth and spying, sharks provide far more advantages than marine mammals."

"Only they're not as smart."

"Not true, my friend, not true. If you look at the relationship between brain size and body weight, sharks are right up there with mammals."

"Body weight, huh? Tell me, Dr. Nichols, what do you think of these geniuses?" David pushes open the double metal doors at the end of the corridor—

—revealing the main gallery tank and the two sisters cruising the aquarium in formation—Lizzy on top and Belle below, slightly behind her albino sibling.

"Good God ..."

"Elizabeth's the albino. Bela's the dark one. There are two smaller albinos in the hospital pen. We're readying them for transfer to another facility."

"And you expect me to train these monsters?"

"Heck, no. These are the juvees. We want you to train their mother."

8

San Francisco International Airport
San Francisco, California

The private Boeing 747 jumbo jet sits in the hangar, being readied for its flight to Dubai. David leans back against the hood of his father's Lexus, watching Jonas "instruct" the four crewmen on how best to load the three huge crates containing the Manta Ray submersibles into the belly of the plane.

His mother declined making the trip to the airport, saving her final salvo of guilt for when her son was packing.

"Why go, David? Anything you can do in Dubai you can do here."

"It's just for the summer, Mom."

"No. I think you're hoping it's more than that. I think you see this as an opportunity to step out of your father's shadow."

"You couldn't be further from the truth."

"Your father ... for many years, he allowed the creatures to define him. And your grandfather, Masao, he fell into the same trap. Don't make the same mistake, David."

"Mom, it's cool."

She sat on the edge of his bed, saying nothing, her long onyx hair hiding her face.

"Mom, what's wrong?"

"I don't know."

"You're not going to put the kibosh on my whole trip by giving me the old 'bad karma' deal, are you? You've been pulling that shit on me and Dani for years."

For a moment he thought she was laughing, until he realized she was crying. That freaked him out.

But his mother could be like that, conjuring up her Asian harbingers of doom whenever her family stepped out of her comfort zone. In many ways David knew she was right, that by working at the Institute he would always be "Jonas Taylor's kid" no matter what he developed in the lab or came up with in the field. Dubai represented a fresh start, a place he could earn his oats.

In the end, she relented, preferring to send him off with positive energy.

For his father, there would be hell to pay.

"Take this." Jonas hands his son a thick envelope.

"Dad, it's okay. I have plenty of money. Plus, all my expenses are covered."

"Just do your old man a favor and take it."

"Thanks." David hugs his father. "I'll call you from Dubai. Make sure you check your e-mail; I'll be downloading photos of the aquarium."

"Have a good time. Just remember our deal."

"I know, I know. And sorry about Mom. Guess you won't be getting any tonight, huh?"

Jonas smiles. "Get your ass on the plane."

⋅ 🦷 🦷 🦷

DAVID BOARDS THE jet, an Arabic woman leading him down a circular staircase to the lower level. "His Royal Highness occupies the upper level, but I think we can make you quite comfortable. Can I get you something to eat or drink?"

"No, I'm fine."

Six rows of first-class seats are located up front, followed by a cherry-wood conference table, several private work stations, bathrooms, a dining area, and, in back, a home theater complete with padded lounge chairs and a fifty-two-inch screen.

"Nice."

"You got that, brother. All we need now are some babes." A leather recliner spins around, revealing a big chested, broad shouldered man in his late twenties with a shaved head and six-inch devil's goatee. He's wearing cargo shorts and a Chicago Cubs baseball jersey, his thick forearms covered in tattoos—Spiderman, the Marine Corps eagle, the United States flag and the University of Arizona mascot—the words "pain don't hurt" inked around his neck.

"Jonas Junior. Name's Jason Montgomery, but you can call me Monty. All my buds do." He never stops to take a breath. "So, dude, how's it feel to work with monsters? Must be pretty cool, huh? Ever get nightmares?"

"Sometimes. And it's David, not Jonas Junior. David Taylor."

"Hey, David Taylor, did you know Coca Cola was originally green?"

"I'm sorry?"

"I wouldn't have drank it. Hey ... do you have dogs? I read the cost of raising a medium-size dog is sixty-five hundred dollars a year. Glad I have two pipsqueaks. Of course, two small dogs probably equals a medium-size dog. What do you think?"

"I think you'd better lay off the caffeine or the coke. Seriously, dude, are you amped?"

"Amped? No way, not me. On my mother's life, I don't do drugs. Well, actually, I do do drugs, just not *that* kind of drugs, you know … narcotics, space blasting, free-basing, on the pine, doin' the line—"

"Dude, you're mental."

"Yes. Exactly. Thank you, Sigmund. I am mental, only I wasn't born that way. Served in the Marine Recons as a corpsman combat medic. Got hit with a grenade in Baghdad. Almost blew off my right shoulder. Funny, I don't remember seeing that part in the recruitment DVD. After the doctors put me back together again, the shrinks told me I had post-traumatic stress and bi-polarism. Double the pleasure, double the flavor, right? Ah, it's all good."

"What are you doing here?"

"I'm here to learn from you, brother. I used to be a pretty damn good pilot."

"You piloted submersibles?"

"Choppers. That was before my brain got bounced. My former brother-in-law … he works for a guy who knows a guy who does business with some company in Dubai City. You know the deal. Next thing you know, I get a call at 2 a.m. telling me to pack a bag. What the hell, right? If I make the cut, I'm set for the next ten years. If not, it still beats disability."

"What cut? What are you talking about?"

"Six submersible pilots." David turns as two more men enter the cabin: the first, a tall athlete with a military crew cut and Thai complexion; the second, a short Canadian built more like a wrestler.

"Sean Dustman, United States Navy."

"David Taylor." David shakes the taller man's hand. "Sorry, I'm a little lost. Did you say six pilots were recruited?"

"Actually, I heard fourteen were recruited to fill six positions—plus two alternates. Each of us gets ten grand to complete your training and a hundred large, plus bonuses, if we make the grade."

"The grade? What exactly is the mission?"

"No one knows." The Canadian steps in between them offering a thick paw of a hand, his piercing gray-blue eyes reminding David of Angel's cold eyes. "Hugo Boutin, Garde côtière canadienne. Canadian Coast Guard. No offense, eh, but you seem too young to be a submersible pilot, let alone a trainer."

Monty slaps David across his shoulder blades. "Hey, frenchy, a little respect. This here's Jonas Taylor's kid. *The* Jonas Taylor. I'll bet our boy here was practically weaned in subs. Hell, he's probably more comfortable with a joystick in his hand than his own pecker."

"Is that true? Are you more comfortable with a joystick in your hand?"

The three men turn in unison, staring at the stunning, blue-eyed woman seated at the conference table. She's in her mid-twenties, her brunette hair long and wavy, tinged with red highlights, her features resembling those of a young Stefanie Powers. She's wearing white shorts and a navy hooded sweatshirt, the name *K. Szeifert* embroidered in white beneath a Scripps Aquarium insignia. Her long, tan legs reveal the calves of a sprinter. A pair of flip flops dangle from her bare feet, which are propped up on the polished wood table top.

Monty squints his eyes to read her sweatshirt. "K. Szeif ... Szerf?"

"It's pronounced 'See-furt.' Kaylie Szeifert."

Monty grins. "I never met a female sub pilot, at least none that looked like you."

"Yeah, well, maybe there's a reason for that, scruffy."

Sean Dustman circles the conference table, eyeing her like a hawk. "U-Cal, San Diego, right?"

"Good memory."

"We met at the Birch Aquarium. You were interning at Scripps. Did we ... you know?"

"Honey, if you have to ask, it didn't happen."

Monty bellows a Santa Claus laugh. "I'm in love."

"Get over it. I'm here to make the cut, and I don't take prisoners. And before any of you start prejudging me because of my 'X' chromosomes, I spent the last two summers working at Hawkes Ocean Technologies helping them test their new Deep Rover submersibles. So I'm pretty comfortable with a joystick in my hand, too."

"I bet you are," Monty mumbles.

The stewardess reenters the cabin. "The captain has received clearance to proceed to the runway. For takeoff and landing we ask that you find a seat in one of these first six rows. Once we're airborne the captain will give the signal that it's okay to move around the cabin."

Kaylie heads forward, selecting a window seat on the left side of the cabin. Sean points to the aisle seat next to him, but she waves him off. "You had your chance, sailor boy."

"Easy, girl. Before you crucify me, you should know that I rated one of the top three sub pilots in the Navy. If you really want to make the cut, I could show you a few pointers."

"In that case, I'd rather speak to the teacher." She pats the seat for David. "Join me?"

David's pulse pounds in his neck. As he slides into the leather chair, he casually cups his hand over his mouth, doing a quick breath check. "I'm David."

"Yeah, I know."

Monty ducks into the window seat directly behind Kaylie. He leans in between David and the girl, offering an air sickness bag. "Feeling queasy? I know I am."

David's eyes flash a warning. "Behave yourself, or you won't make it through orientation."

"Ouch." He sits back, staring out the window.

A genuine smile creases Kaylie's face, accentuating her high cheekbones. "Feeling your oats. I like that. Let them step on you once and soon they'll be using you like a doormat."

"Are you speaking from experience?"

"Hell, yes. My mom and dad ... they worked double shifts at Walmart for as long as I can remember just to save money for my college fund. Me? I wanted to join the Armed Forces and would have gladly gone Navy had the recruiting officer given me any sign of hope that one day I could pilot a sub. 'Subs are not for women,' he said. Can you believe that? Damn old boys network. Thank God Graham Hawkes's people didn't think like that."

"So how did you get invited to this gig? I thought the Arabs weren't exactly into the whole women's lib deal."

"Some bigwig—Fiesal bin Rashidi—contacted one of the engineers at Hawkes looking for their best available pilots. I wasn't the best, but I was available. It didn't hurt that I've been interning at the Scripps Aquarium."

"And you have no idea what this mission is about?"

"They said it's being sponsored by the firm building a new aquarium in Dubai. I'm guessing it has to do with netting species for their exhibits, which is very cool, don't you think?"

"Sure."

She smiles. "Why are you looking at me like that?"

"How old are you?"

"Twenty-four. How old are you?"

"About the same."

"Liar. I bet you aren't even twenty-one."

"Yeah, I am ... next month."

She takes his hand in hers. "I need you, David. I need you to make me the best damn submersible pilot in the group. Life's been kickin' my butt for a long time, but I'm the kind of person who kicks it right back. Getting this job is very important to me. So I need you to do me a favor."

"Yeah. Anything."

"Don't fall in love with me."

She instinctively squeezes his hand tighter as the jumbo jet accelerates down the runway, then tilts into the sky, leaving San Francisco behind. Heading west, it banks over the ocean, then briefly follows the coastline south past Monterey before turning east.

David lays his head back in the cushioned leather seat, staring at Kaylie until she releases his hand.

"Sorry," she says. "I'm a nervous flyer. But I'm totally at home in the water."

"What's the deepest you've ever been?"

"In a submersible? Twelve hundred feet. Twice."

Monty pokes his head in between their seats. "Wow, that's really deep. Still, I bet that's not as deep as these Arabs want us to go. Am I right, Junior?"

"I wouldn't know."

"You wouldn't know?" Monty wiggles his index finger at David. "Beep, beep, beep, beep, beep—"

"What are you doing?"

"That's my bullshit detector. Your old man did the Mariana Trench more than a few times. That's thirty-six thousand feet, as deep as it gets. How deep have you gone, Junior? I mean, in a sub."

"Close to twelve thousand."

"Twelve hundred, meet twelve thousand. Good thing it's a long flight, huh?"

"Ignore him, Kaylie. It's not about how deep you go; it's about keeping your head, controlling your fear. My first night dive freaked me out, and that was in two hundred feet of water. Piloting a submersible means maintaining your focus. Something you may want to work on, Monty."

"Good advice, teach. I think we can see where your focus is being maintained. May I?" He plucks a stray hair from the back of David's head.

"Ow! What the hell?"

"They say intelligent people have more copper and zinc in their hair than the rest of us non-achievers. I'll get back to you."

Monty leans back in his seat, reclines the chair to its maximum setting, and closes his eyes.

9

From his vantage in the northern bleachers, Brent Nichols can see everything: the two pure-white runts now occupying the shallow medical pool, their much larger siblings circling in the Meg Pen, and, in the deepest part of the man-made channel, an occasional froth of water and thunder of pummeled steel marking the location of the juveniles' temperamental parent.

For the last two hours, a team of marine biologists and Meg husbandry experts have been monitoring Mary Kate's and Ashley's vital signs, the two predators having been moved into the medical pool earlier in the day. Approximately the size of a baseball infield, the medical pool is only fifteen feet deep and has been divided into two rectangular sections barely twice the Megs' girth. The tight quarters force the pair of twenty-five-foot sharks to swim against an artificially created current, conditioning them for their fifteen-hour trip to Dubai. To reduce the stress induced by having to swim in close quarters, the water in the tank is being filtered with moderate doses of Tricaine Methanesulfonate. Today's session had been scheduled for three hours, at which time the two runts were to be returned to their half of the Meg Pen and observed.

Belle and Lizzy had forced those plans to be changed.

As a field scientist, Brent Nichols has spent hundreds of hours in the water observing sharks, including bull sharks, a species driven by high levels of testosterone. But even those killers couldn't hold a candle to the ferocity of the two big Meg juveniles known as the sisters.

Moments after the second runt had been hoisted from its tank, the lead-backed sister, Belle, began ramming the fence that divided the Meg Pen. Fearsome, with no regard to injury, the creature seemed to attack the barrier with a pent-up rage that Brent Nichols had never witnessed in the wild. After fifteen minutes, the powerful blows began tearing the rubberized titanium barrier clear off its reinforced frame, forcing trainers and maintenance crews to hastily winch the fence out of the water or risk losing it altogether.

And yet as ferocious as Bela the Dark was, it was her albino sister, Lizzy, that really spooked Dr. Nichols. For every time Belle ceased her relentless attack on the fence, her counterpart would strike it herself with one solitary resounding blow, as if egging her sibling on. Having observed the ritual for several hours,

Dr. Nichols was convinced it was Lizzy who wanted the barrier removed, and the clever predator knew how to get her brutish sibling to carry out the task.

A cooperative, well-defined relationship exists between the two sisters, Dr. Nichols wrote in his journal. *The albino is the clear instigator, with the darker Meg functioning as her assassin. Even when they swim in formation, it is Lizzy on top, Belle riding below, being towed in her wake.*

Dr. Nichols looks up from his notes in time to see Jonas Taylor approaching from the eastern pavilion. "So? Learn much?"

"Enough to fill two legal pads, but merely the tip of the iceberg. I'm disappointed Angel won't leave the canal. But, I've made some fascinating observations regarding the two litters of juveniles."

"Two litters? Sorry, Doc, but these Megs were all birthed live from one litter."

"They might have been birthed at the same moment in time, Taylor, but these juvenile Megs come from two different litters, fertilized by two different males."

Jonas feels the blood rush from his face. "Different males? Christ, how many of these monsters are out there? Unless Scarface ..."

"Scarface?"

"Another male I crossed paths with around the same time Angel returned to the lagoon with that big bull. The two males were Angel's offspring from her first litter. A field sample taken from Scarface a few years ago matched the DNA of his deceased bigger brother."

"Let's be sure. If it wasn't Scarface, then there could be another adult male out there somewhere. The runt that died last week, Angelica ... did your biologist perform a necropsy?"

"Yes."

"Perfect. We'll compare Angelica's DNA with the DNA of the two males from Angel's first litter. If the samples match, the runt's father was Scarface. If not, there may be another big male out there somewhere. I'll also need tissue samples from one of the sisters."

Jonas exhales a groan.

"Is that a problem?"

"Ever pull an alligator's tooth when it was still conscious? That would be easy compared to this."

∇ ∇ ∇

VIRGIL CARMEN BRUSHES strands of black hair from his face as he steadies himself along the Meg Pen rail, his "spearing" arm slightly constricted by the fluorescent orange harness around his waist. Adjusting the ten-foot reach pole, the assistant director of animal husbandry stares at the water while Moretti continues to drag the seventy-five-pound morsel of beef along the surface, hoping to lure one of the sisters topside.

Belle and Lizzy remain wary, circling thirty feet below.

Moretti turns to Jonas and his heavyset companion. "No good, J.T. They're on to this game. If you really want the sample, I'll need the *Jellyfish*."

∇ ∇ ∇

VIRGIL SCREWS THE back end of a two-inch-diameter, eight-foot-long steel pipe to its mount along the outside of the *Jellyfish* submersible. The business end of the spear—a four-inch-long hollow point—is designed to puncture the Meg's hide and quickly retract, slicing off and capturing a pencil-thin sample of tissue while simultaneously cauterizing the wound. *Underwater camera's rolling ... if I can get a tight shot of Moretti jabbing one of the sisters with this spear ... that would make Sara happy. Maybe she'd get me a job working for R.A.W. Anything's better than this deal.*

Virgil tests the spring-loaded assembly several times then signals to his boss, who is already inside the acrylic, sphere-shaped vessel.

Moretti returns the thumbs-up and adjusts his headset over his lucky turquoise baseball cap and speaks into his radio. "Ready here, Chris."

Parked next to the *Jellyfish*, anchored to outriggers in one of four reinforced-concrete, rectangular pits located around the Meg Pen, is the Institute's 70-ton Link-Belt hydraulic truck crane. Designed for heavy lifting, the truck possesses a three-stage, 109-foot telescopic boom that supports ten lines, each able to lift 14,000 pounds. The boom is connected to a Rotex gear mounted beneath the operator's cab, enabling the load to be moved left or right as well as up and down.

"Roger that. Stand by, Moretti." Crane operator Christopher Baird enters the pre-programmed weight of the *Jellyfish* (7,800 pounds) and the maximum height he will be raising the submersible (17 feet), along with the angle of the lift and the radius of the boom into the crane's on-board computer. The system is designed to warn the operator if the load limitations are exceeded.

Earlier that morning, Baird had engaged three of the ten spools of sixty-five-foot-long, heavy lifting cable to individually transport Mary Kate and Ashley from the Meg Pen into the medical pool, allowing for plenty of backup capacity without overtaxing the truck's crankshaft, which is needed to torque the load. For the *Jellyfish*, Baird reduces the boom setting to two cables, 28,000 pounds being more than enough torque to lower and raise the submersible into and out of the Meg Pen.

Baird, a former corporal at the Southern State Correctional Facility in Springfield, Vermont, had switched careers four years earlier to get away from the daily stress of working in close contact with "pathological killers." He often wonders if he has jumped from the frying pan into the fire.

"Buckle up, Moretti, it's time to take a dip."

There are two joysticks in the cab, one on either side of Baird's seat. One controls forward and aft movements, the other left to right. Foot pedals extend and retract the boom while regulating the hydraulic pressure used to move the crane. Baird pulls back on the right joystick, engaging the hydraulic pump—

—raising the *Jellyfish* off the concrete deck, and swings it over the Meg Pen. Seconds later, the acrylic sphere is lowered into the water, the two spools of cable playing out, allowing the tethered submersible to head for the bottom of the tank.

Sensing a disturbance in their domain, Lizzy breaks off her circular swimming pattern to investigate.

Moretti activates the predator prod as he searches the aquarium. The two Megs are huddled together along the far tank wall, remaining a healthy distance from the six steel lances that project from different angles along the submersible's hull.

Fifteen minutes pass. Still no change.

This is crazy ... they're five times faster than the sub and a million times more agile. I could be down here a week and still not come close. "*Jellyfish* to Base: Virgil, they're playing cat and mouse. I'm going to shut off the current to the prods and see if that'll lure them in."

"Roger that, *Jellyfish*. Be careful."

Knowing the two Megalodons' senses can detect the electrical field coming from the predator prods, Moretti shuts down the voltage lever, cutting the current. Though risky, it's not altogether dangerous, the sheer size of the sub's spherical hull, too large to be bitten, offering more than ample protection.

Reaching for the "gun" mounted to his dashboard, Moretti slips his index finger inside the trigger mechanism of the tissue sampler and waits.

As anticipated, Bela breaks off first, coming straight at him—

—turning away at the last moment before he can stab the twenty-one-ton fish.

Still cautious, are we? Moretti glances at his sonar, verifying Lizzy's position, the albino continuing her slow, steady pattern around the circumference of the Meg Pen.

He watches as the freakish-looking Bela moves through the tank in agitated S patterns as she readies her second bullrush. Arching her back as she turns, the juvenile monster veers straight for the sub.

Moretti maneuvers the *Jellyfish*, changing a direct hit into a harmless deflecting blow, simultaneously pulling the trigger as she passes. The tip of the sampling spear juts out several feet from its spring-loaded assembly, striking the Meg on her left flank in a puff of blood.

"Got you!"

Belle swats the *Jellyfish* hard with her caudal fin—

—as the white glow appears at Moretti's back! The submersible is smashed from behind, driven forward at heart-stopping speed. The pilot fights to regain controls as he swivels 180 degrees in his pilot's chair to see—

—Lizzy's eight-foot-wide, hyperextended mouth open, now pressing against the aft end of the sphere as she plows it ahead toward the far tank window, the two cables feeding out rapidly!

Metal screeches as the lines catch at sixty-five feet, the sudden jolt short-circuiting the predator prod in a shower of sparks. The aquarium's four-foot-thick, acrylic viewing window looms a mere twenty feet away ... and Lizzy is still pushing the sub!

Moretti's heart flutters as he grips the controls. "Base, she's trying to ram the sub against the aquarium window! I can't break free!"

▽ ▽ ▽

Topside, Christopher Baird is closing in on panic mode. His computer screen is flashing red warning lights, his cab reverberating beneath him as if caught in a magnitude-7 earthquake—

—his left outrigger, a three-foot-wide, hydraulic stabilizer leg located along the side of the truck, threatening to collapse. If it goes, Baird knows there will be nothing preventing the truck from being dragged sideways into the Meg Pen.

"Crane to base! I'm losing the—"

With an ear-piercing *screech* of metal, the stabilizer closest to the tank bends then collapses beneath the right side of the truck with a bone-jarring *whump*—

—the truck crane's chassis, which had been elevated above the concrete pad by its pair of stabilizers, smashing hard into the ground!

"Dammit!" Baird falls sideways, the cab now tilting thirty degrees, the aqua-blue surface of the Meg Pen suddenly appearing six feet below!

Whump!

Baird bites his tongue as the remaining stabilizer collapses, dropping the truck's chassis on its eight wheels, jamming the drive axle and differential that he had been using to control the cables and telescopic crane. The former correctional officer reflexively presses both feet against the foot pedals controlling the boom as the massive truck, freed from its stability platform and devoid of brakes, jack-knifes sideways as it is dragged, inch by inch, closer to the edge of the tank.

Jonas is the first to reach Baird, who has unbuckled his harness to evacuate the cab. "Where are you going?!"

"Anywhere but here!"

"What about the *Jellyfish*?"

"Nothing I can do. We lost the outriggers. I need the wheels free to engage the crankshaft."

"There's no way to retract the sub?"

The truck lurches again, its right front bumper slamming into the aquarium's guardrail. Two feet of concrete deck is all that separates the right front tire from the water.

Baird leaps off the back of the truck and races for the driver's cab. He yanks open the door, retrieving a two-pound, single-edge axe from beneath the driver's seat. "We've got about thirty seconds to sever two cables before your fish drags this entire truck into the water!"

Jonas follows Baird onto the back of the boom, which houses the ten spools of cable. He begins hacking at the two steel lines feeding out to the crane with the hand axe—

—as the truck is jerked forward once more, metal screaming as the guardrail is pried loose from its mounts and the right-front truck tire slides off the deck into the water, the front end of the chassis collapsing halfway onto its front axle.

Baird continues hacking at the unyielding cables—

—until the truck's rear end begins raising off the deck. "She's all yours!" He hands Jonas the axe then jumps down off the back of the teetering flatbed.

Jonas holds on as the truck's reinforced front bumper tastes sea water and an immense dark shadow swims by. Belle's dorsal fin is so close he could almost hit it with a swipe of the axe.

He hacks at the cables, desperate to prevent the seventy-ton truck from slipping over the edge. His mind leaps forward, imaging the suddenly submerged vehicle plummeting three stories through the water, its engine block crushing the aquarium's concrete floor before falling backwards and bursting through the acrylic viewing window, flooding the gallery with 60 million gallons of sea water.

He strikes the cable again and again as the truck screeches beneath him, teetering between the deck and water.

"Jonas! Move!"

He looks up at the tall silhouette.

Mac guns the chain saw, waiting for his best friend to leap out of the way before he sets the whirring teeth to the cables—

—chewing through the steel in seconds, snapping both lines!

The tension released, the truck's elevated rear end drops back onto the concrete deck with a resounding *thud*—

—freeing the *Jellyfish,* which is instantly propelled forward by the 42,000-pound Megalodon.

Steven Moretti lets out a scream, shutting his eyes as the acrylic sphere is rammed against the aquarium window. A hairline fracture materializes in the submersible's four-inch-thin hull, followed seconds later by a pencil-thin spray of chilly seawater.

The pilot opens his eyes. He looks up, his nerves trembling as two massive shadows pass overhead—

—the sisters circling their wounded prey ... waiting ... patiently.

10

Dubai Land Central International Airport
Dubai, United Arab Emirates

Located in southern Dubai, only twenty-four miles from the original Dubai Airport, Jebel Ali International is an aerotropolis—the largest and most ambitious airport project ever conceived. Designed around six major runways, the $82 billion complex is home to hotels and shopping malls, sixteen cargo terminals, over 100,000 parking spaces, and a high-speed express rail designed to whisk upwards of 120 million passengers a year to their destinations within the UAE.

David Taylor stretches in his seat as the 747 taxis across one of the runways to a private hangar reserved for the royal family. For the twenty-year-old undergrad, the twelve-hour flight had been an invigorating, and exhausting first date. He and Kaylie had talked non-stop for the first four hours—he, hoping to impress her—she, wanting to know about his family, his experiences with the Megs, and especially his father's dives to the Mariana Trench. David had been vague on this last topic. Information about Benedict Singer's exploits in the Mariana Trench had never been made public, nor had the discovery of kronosaurs inhabiting the isolated gorge.

Instead, David had changed the subject to his own piloting experiences aboard the Manta Rays. This last topic had drawn a crowd, causing Kaylie to excuse herself to enjoy the buffet spread. David had forced himself to continue on without her for another five minutes before abruptly ending the conversation.

He was hopelessly smitten, but swimming upstream. In his mind, Kaylie was clearly out of his league: a grad student with far more experience, an intoxicating beauty who could have anyone she wanted, her interest in him purely professional.

He didn't care.

▽   ▽   ▽

THE 747 SLOWS to a halt, the stewardess instructing the five submersible pilots to wait until the crown prince has de-planed. Ten minutes later, they follow her up the stairs and out the main exit of the jumbo jet where two stretch limousines are waiting—one flying the royal flag and the other loaded down with their luggage.

Fiesal bin Rashidi exits the jet and joins them. "So? I trust your flight was enjoyable? As you will soon learn, Dubai is a land that caters to its guests. You will be staying in one of the five-star luxury hotels inside the new theme park. Room service is open twenty-four hours; order anything and everything you wish. By tomorrow morning the rest of your party will arrive, and we will begin your training. David will be instructing you on how to operate the Manta Rays, but there are other things to learn as well, with other instructors. Besides, we will need David to tend to Afra' and Zahra' when they arrive."

David looks confused. "Who're they?"

"The Meg juveniles. Afra' and Zahra' are Arabic for 'white.' You didn't think we would continue to call them Mary Kate and Ashley?"

"No, of course not. I never liked those names anyway. It was sort of an Internet gag."

"Your initial training will last two weeks, at which time a team of eight will be selected from the twenty-three pilot candidates we have invited. David will remain at the aquarium for the rest of the summer, while those selected will proceed with the mission at hand."

"And exactly what is that mission?" Sean Dustman asks.

"The mission is to capture aquatic specimens for the aquarium."

"Yes, but what kind of aquatic specimens?"

"Earn your place on the team, and you will know. Have an enjoyable night, but try to get some rest. Orientation begins tomorrow morning."

A chauffeur opens the rear door of the limousine bearing the royal flag. Bin Rashidi climbs in and the vehicle drives off.

"I suppose we're on our own." Hugo climbs in the backseat of the second limo, followed by Sean and Monty.

David holds the door open for Kaylie. "Thanks, but you go ahead. I like the window."

"It's yours." He squeezes in beside Monty, giving her plenty of room.

Monty places a tattooed hand on David's inner thigh. "You didn't hold the door open for me, Junior. I'm getting jealous."

"Shut up."

"Hugo, are you jealous? How about you, Sean?"

"It doesn't bother me, as long as all of us get treated fairly in the end."

"That's what I'm afraid of ... getting it in the end. Right up the old dirt road. The Bunghole Express. Hey, Kaylie, did you know the first couple to be shown in bed together on prime time TV were Fred and Wilma Flintstone? Makes you wonder why they sing, 'we'll have a gay old time.' You think Fred was a transvestite?"

"I think you need to take your Lithium."

∇ ∇ ∇

THE LIMO PROCEEDS down a private road, past a security checkpoint, and out one of the main avenues to a gleaming, tinted-glass terminal, the street lined with Canary date palms. The vehicle stops to take on a passenger: a strawberry-blonde woman in her forties, dressed in an ivory business suit. She climbs in the front seat then lowers the glass partition separating the driver from the five passengers.

"Hi, I'm Caree Crossman. I'll be your chaperone during your stay in Dubai City. Let's see ... you're obviously Kaylie, and you must be David ... tattoos is Monty, Sean's our sailor ... and wait, don't tell me ... huge ... Hugh? Wait, Hugo! How'd I do?"

Monty applauds. "Better'n a trained seal."

For the next ninety minutes they take a driving tour of Dubai City, Caree pointing out unique places of interest, from the massive indoor skiing center to the towering high-rise office buildings and impressive luxury hotels—tinted-glass structures whose gargantuan steel frames twist into the cloudless, blue heavens— their pavements granite, their lobbies adorned in white marble.

The limousine heads east on Jumeirah Road, the sparkling azure waters of the Persian Gulf on their left. Caree points ahead. "In the distance you can see our famous landmark hotel, the Burj al-Arab, which translates to the Tower of the Arabs. Considered by many to be the world's first seven-star hotel, the Burj al-Arab is the second tallest building in Dubai and rests on an artificial island constructed of sand and silt laid over two hundred thirty, forty-meter-long concrete pilings. The hotel was built to resemble the sail of a *dhow*, which is a type of Arabian vessel. Two wings spread in a V to create a giant mast, while the space between them serves as a massive atrium. I'd be happy to take you over when we have more time. It really is a must-see attraction."

They continue following the coastline, past man-made islands laid out like giant mosaic tiles, to the Dubai Marina. "The marina is Dubai's version of the French Riviera. The complex was developed by Emaar Properties, the same firm building our new aquarium. When completed, it will feature several hundred high-rise buildings as well as a dozen super-tall skyscrapers with heights that exceed one thousand feet."

"Quite the sprawl," Monty says. "Capitalism meets the Roman Empire in the ultimate tourist trap."

Carree flashes a false smile. "The UAE is a progressive country, Mr. Montgomery, with rulers who care."

"Rulers who care ... but far from a democracy, and barely an ally. Tell me, Caree Crossman, do the grandiose buildings and primped golf courses make it easier to forget that you're simply a tolerated guest to a bunch of chauvinistic autocrats who cater to the nouveau riche while censoring their own people? Do you ever lose sleep over the reality that the only reason you, a woman, got this tasty little job is because your hubby's probably some oil V.P. who plays polo with one of the royal tribe?"

Caree's smile fades.

David turns to face Monty. "Dude, what is your problem?"

"My problem, Junior, is how easily barrels of oil trump human rights, how we're willing to look the other way as long as we get our taste."

"What are you talking about?"

"I'm talking about those shipping containers lining the docks we just passed, the ones marked for the Islamic Republic of Iran. Guess it's okay for the White House to send me and my buds over to Iraq four times in five years to get our brains blown out by Islamic radicals, but when it comes to money, they're ready to sign our port security over to the UAE—the devil's own well-paid advocate."

"Dubai's government's different," Caree retorts, her enthusiasm waning.

Monty rolls his eyes. "Sure they are. And you know this because they sign your paycheck with Happy Faces?"

"If you have such a problem, why are you even here?"

"Rock and a hard place, Caree Crossman. See, while my government gleefully subsidizes your hubby's oil business, it draws a line in the sand when it comes to covering veteran's medical expenses. By their definition, I'm too able to be disabled, even though I'm too disabled to work. So much for supporting the troops, huh? Wish I could work for Parker Brothers. Did you know they print more money for Monopoly than the U.S. Treasury?"

"Just ignore him, Caree," Sean advises. "Our tattooed friend will be going home in a few weeks anyway."

"That's not your decision!" David snaps. He takes a deep breath of cold air blowing out the vent, the long travel suddenly wearing on his nerves. "It's been a long day. Think we could just skip the rest of the tour? I'd just as soon get to the hotel and sleep."

Kaylie and the others nod in agreement.

Leaving the coastline, the limousine heads south, passing Zabeel Palace—residence of the ruling Al Maktoum family. Entering Dubai Land, they detour through Dubai Sports City, a complex set on a 50-million-square-foot spread. Four stadiums are under construction, along with The Dunes, an 18-hole championship golf course designed by Ernie Els.

Ten minutes later, they turn onto a six-lane highway bordered by palm trees and "Jurassic" lakes and arrive at the grand entrance of Dubai Land's new aquarium.

It is a city unto itself, though still very much under construction. A heavy lifting crane swings a prefabricated section of monorail track into place. Earth movers level ground across from a visitor's center. A dozen hotels rise along the periphery of the complex, connected by monorail, each skyscraper exceeding fifty stories. Temporary signs written in Arabic and English direct deliveries to the main attractions, hotels, and a luxury golf residential community called Monster's Cove.

At the very center of the resort is the aquarium complex—a glass and steel structure that looks like it was designed by Frank Lloyd Wright. A dozen two-hundred-foot-high, gold-plated "shark fins" surround the facility, set in place like hours on a watch face, each dorsal fin aligned in turn with a hotel towering along the periphery.

Kaylie and David look at one another, beyond impressed.

Monty whistles. "Gotta hand it to the A-rabs ... they sure do gluttony good."

Careee ignores the comment. "Besides the aquarium and hotels, there are three monorail systems, twenty-two five-star restaurants, a residential complex, an international school, a world-class medical facility, a well-being and lifestyle country club, and a retail mall with aquatic-life themes. And everything should be up and running for opening day in thirteen months."

The limo follows a brick-paved winding road that leads to a sixty-story Hyatt. The hotel's fifth-story atrium is shaped like the bony jaws of *Dunkleosteus*. The monorail track runs through the ancient marine predator's open fangs along the outer face of the building.

Caree hands out envelopes with room keys inside. "Everyone gets a suite on the thirty-sixth floor. The staff will bring up your belongings. Exercise and fitness center is on Level Three, outdoor pool and tennis on Two. The monorail is on Level Five. Be at the station tomorrow morning at ten o'clock; a car will arrive to take you to the aquarium for your orientation."

David and his entourage exit the limousine, blasted immediately by the dry desert heat.

They enter the hotel, the interior's thermostat set forty degrees cooler than outdoors. The lobby is magnificent, the room floors situated around an open atrium that rises clear up to its tinted glass roof. Tropical plants, palm trees, and waterfalls mix with painted murals of a prehistoric ocean. A neon blue sign reads: WELCOME TO THE DEVONIAN ... MANAGED BY HYATT. Poised one hundred feet above their heads, spanning the fifth floor, is a clear acrylic skywalk that runs through a reproduction skeleton of a giant *Dunkleosteus.* The creature's bony body surrounds the bridge, ending at its armored head, which empties out to the monorail station along the exterior of the hotel.

Glass elevators running along the inside of the atrium whisk them up to the thirty-sixth floor. David takes out his room card key: 3605. He turns to his left. Kaylie is keying in the suite next door.

She waves. "See you in the morning."

"Yeah. Maybe we could—" She enters her suite and shuts the door, cutting him off.

David has to slide his room key several times before the magnetic strip turns the light panel green and unlocks his door, letting him inside.

"Wow."

The suite is enormous, the floors polished marble, the furnishings luxurious. Floor to ceiling bay windows reveal a breathtaking view of Dubai, clear to a golden sunset setting over the Persian Gulf. A wraparound, sectional leather sofa faces a sixty-five-inch, plasma-screen TV. A small conference table and matching chairs occupy the dining area, the kitchen equipped with a sub-zero, built-in refrigerator.

A marble landing and double doors lead into the master bedroom. The bathroom done in onyx marble, with a double shower and whirlpool tub. A balcony looks out to the Persian Gulf.

Kicking off his shoes, David grabs the room service menu and lies back on the king-size bed.

"Yeah, I suppose I could force myself to get used to this ..."

Tanaka Oceanographic Institute
Monterey, California

Steven Moretti releases the safety harnesses keeping him strapped in his command chair as water rises up to his waist. His body shivers from the cold. His fingers tug strands of his brown curly hair in an attempt to awaken him from the madness.

The *Jellyfish* is stranded at the bottom of the Meg Pen's aquarium seventy feet from the surface. The radio is dead, the sphere is taking on water at the rate of an inch a minute ... but it is not drowning that the pilot fears most.

Glancing up, he sees the sinister silhouette still circling just below the surface, refusing to allow him to abandon the sub.

What the hell are those guys doing up there? They have to know I've lost power. Maybe they don't know about the leak.

Moretti stares at the steady flow of water pushing its way through the crack in the acrylic hull. Each breath becomes more labored, each thought more frantic. He forces himself to focus on his wife, Mary, and the light of his life, their beautiful daughter, Annie. Memories flash before his mind's eye: the trips with Annie to the fossil sites in New England ... fishing with family and friends in Cape Cod ... *catch and release ... catch and release ... no need to keep 'em, Annie. Just reel 'em in and let 'em go.*

Moretti turns, his eyes drawn to movement as Bela the Dark Lord circles along the bottom, her snake-like movements becoming rigid, her back arching as she suddenly veers toward the *Jellyfish* and attacks!

Whump!

The forty-foot juvenile strikes the acrylic sphere like a sports utility vehicle plowing into a Volkswagen Beetle, the collision chipping the points off two of Belle's lower teeth while flinging Moretti out of his chair, face-first into the control panel. The *Jellyfish* rolls awkwardly along the bottom and resettles.

Moretti blows blood from his nostrils, the impact with the console having broken his nose. He watches tiny droplets of blood disperse in the water by his sternum.

Lizzy's shadow passes overhead.

Moretti shivers as his mind fights against being pushed over the precipice of sanity. *Five minutes, ten tops. Assume the worst, assume they can't get to you in time ... what are your options? Unseal the hatch ... wait until Bela makes her next pass, then swim to the surface like a bat out of hell. Ten second ascent, another five to make it to the side—*

He glances up again at the albino's circling silhouette. *Look at her. She's waiting for me … like she knows there's only one way out. Think you're so clever, do you fish? Well, screw you, bitch! I'd rather stay inside and drown than let you eat me!*

His limbs convulse in fear as the water rises to his throat …

∇ ∇ ∇

JONAS TAYLOR'S HANDS tremble as he fastens the clasps of the bulky smell suit—a porous wetsuit filled with a network of pressurized tubing. Virgil hands him the bottle of putrescene—a red chemical dye developed by the Navy that contains a powerful scent, which, once jettisoned, reeks like rotting fish. Pull the chord and the putrescene shoots out of the wetsuit's pores.

The hoist crane's steel expanse beam rolls into place above the Meg Pen and the disabled *Jellyfish* submersible. Fran Rizzuto is working by the crane's steel staircase, releasing cable from the spool of a portable hydraulic winch.

Virgil clips the free end of the cable to the back of Jonas's canvass harness. "Doc, no kidding around, but this is the most fucked up thing I've ever seen anyone attempt."

"Not a whole lot of choices." Jonas struggles to seal the suit's pump over the open bottle of putrescene. "Is Mac ready?"

"There." Virgil points across the tank to another Manta Ray dangling in its harness from the truck crane. Ted Badault and his crew have just replaced the sub's damaged starboard propulsion unit. The Frenchman calls over Virgil's walkie-talkie, "We're ready here!"

Virgil struggles to secure an eighty-pound weight belt around Jonas's waist, while Fran hands him a pony bottle of air connected to a face mask with a built-in radio transmitter.

"Okay, darlin', here's the drill: Belle's circling the *Jellyfish* every forty seconds, but she's not the problem … it's Lizzy. She refuses to stray from the surface. Steven's only got a few more minutes of air, so we have to be quick. As you make your way out to the jump-off spot, you'll see the pulley we attached to an eye-bolt beneath the beam. I'll follow you out and detach your cable and loop it through the pulley. As soon as Mac gets the sisters' attention, you jump.

"Dr. Stelzer's in the gallery; he'll be in your ear the whole time. You're not wearing an air tank and you're loaded with weights, so you'll go down like an anchor, figure five seconds tops. You need to locate one of the free ends of the truck crane's two cables. As soon as you have one, yell out, purge the smell suit, drop the weight belt, and I'll hoist you out of the water like you had a jet pack strapped to your ass. I'm leaving you one hundred and thirty feet of slack, that's fifty to the water, seventy to get to the sub, and ten feet just in case."

"Is that enough?"

"Trust me, darlin',' you'll wish it was less once you're in the tank. Seriously, J.T., you've only got one shot at this. So, whatever you do, do not drop the cable."

"Understood." Jonas ascends the steps leading up to the crane's expansion beam, Fran pushing him from behind. His muscles feel like lead, his body trembling from adrenaline and fear and the additional hundred pounds of equipment he's shouldering. He straps the mask and pony bottle of air to his face then speaks into its communicator. "Jon, can you hear me?"

"Loud and clear," says Dr. Stelzer, who is positioned in the main gallery, three stories below. "Tell me when you're in position."

Reaching the top of the fifty-foot-high crane, Jonas carefully steps out onto its four-foot-wide steel expanse beam, refusing to look down at the albino creature circling below. *Move slow, stay low, don't let Lizzy see you.* He breathes in slowly, his mask fogging … then clearing, fogging … then clearing, his jumbled nerves causing his limbs to shake. Thirty feet out, he reaches the jump-off point marked with gray duct taped X.

Jonas sits down on the edge of the beam, allowing Fran to detach the cable from his harness. Lying flat on the beam, she feeds the line through the pulley before reattaching the cable to his harness, making sure everything feeds cleanly.

"You're good to go, J.T. Remember, don't drop the cable."

He watches her retreat and speaks into his headpiece. "Jon, I'm set here. Mac, can you hear me?"

"Loud and clear, Dr. Crazy."

"Mac … nothing even close. At the first sign of trouble, you launch the Manta Ray out of the tank."

"Define trouble. Trouble to me is the occasional bout of constipation … *that* particular trouble I don't have at the moment."

"If you have any doubts—"

"I'll handle my end, Cochise. You just get your ass back up on that beam with Moretti's cable."

Mac is strapped into the Manta Ray's cockpit, his sub suspended ten-feet above the Meg Pen's eastern wall. Scanning the aquarium, he searches for the lead-gray back of the always-dangerous Belle. He spots her moving deep, heading for the northern end of the tank.

Mac starts the sub's engines—

—signaling Baird, who's back in the boom's cab, to release the Manta Ray into the aquarium. The harness releases cleanly, the sub belly-flopping in the water, twin engines pumping.

The disturbance immediately registers with Lizzy. The albino creature abandons her post above the downed *Jellyfish* and moves off to investigate.

"Now, Jonas! Jump!"

God help me. Securing his mask to his face with both hands, Jonas steps off the steel expanse beam—

—plummeting three, stomach-churning stories—

—plunging feet-first into the water! He drops like a lead brick, the speed of his descent through the toxic blue world scaring the hell out of him, his eardrums popping as if squeezed in a vise. With the mask over his entire face he cannot even pinch his nose to depressurize.

His feet strike the hard surface of the *Jellyfish's* damaged hull, the sudden impact spraining his ankle, his knees collapsing into his chest, driving the wind from his lungs. His legs sprawl overhead as he slides down the side of the sphere on his buttocks, tumbling to the bottom of the tank in a heap.

▼ ▼ ▼

KEEPING BOTH FOOT pedals to the floorboard, Mac grips the two joysticks in both hands, his palms sweaty as he accelerates the sub toward the bottom—

—cut off immediately by Belle. The dark Meg's mouth spasms open, offering a potentially fatal reflexive bite—

—that barely misses. Mac releases his right foot and jams both joysticks to starboard, veering away from Belle, registering a blur of white as the other sister charges in from above!

Mac banks hard to port, the Manta Ray's smooth belly scraping the bottom of the tank before leveling out and soaring past Lizzy's open jowls, doing twenty knots.

▼ ▼ ▼

MORETTI IS TREADING water, the frightened pilot down to his last six inches of air space. Having felt Jonas's impact with the hull, he grabs a breath and ducks underwater, pressing his face to the interior glass, and watches his employer and friend struggle to stand on the bottom. *Crazy mother ... what the hell does he think he's doing?*

▼ ▼ ▼

THE BLUE WORLD spins as Jonas wheezes into his mask, his wobbly legs fighting to stay upright against a swirling artificial current. *Twenty seconds ... come on, asshole, what the hell are you doing?! Grab the line and get the hell out of here!*

"Jonas, it's Jon! Can you hear me?"

"Yeah." He turns to see Dr. Stelzer staring at him from behind the gallery window, the biologist's smallish frame made gigantic by the four-foot-thick acrylic glass.

"By your left knee ... the cable!"

Jonas looks down. Sees the cable. Reaches awkwardly for it, everything spinning ... and misses it.

"Oh, Jesus ... no!"

Stelzer's voice inflection hits him like a jolt of electricity. Regaining his senses, he reaches down and snags the snake-like cable in his right fist—

—as his eyes lock onto the albino predator's reflection in the acrylic window before him!

"Now! Pull me up!" Jonas releases the eighty-pound weight belt with his left hand—

—as Fran's right palm slams the winch's lever into REVERSE, the spool reeling in cable, dragging Jonas away from the bottom, away from the *Jellyfish*—

—and into the direct path of the charging ivory-white beast! Lizzy cocks her head to one side, her mouth hyper-extending open to take her prey in one bite—

—as Jonas's left hand rips the release cord of his smell suit, igniting five hundred tiny explosions of putrescene that envelop his quickly rising body in a cloud of red dye.

Lizzy veers away, the sudden smell of death overwhelming.

Jonas clutches the steel cable as he rockets to the surface—

—passing the Manta Ray, now engaged in rolling figure-eights, the maniacal Belle in pursuit, her snout banging into the sub's tail-like antenna, unable to catch the swifter creature heading straight for the southern wall of the tank.

"Aw, hell!" Mac jams both feet to the floor while yanking back hard on the joysticks, the sub racing for the surface—

—and launching clear out of the tank! The Manta Ray's belly skims the four-foot guardrail surrounding the Meg Pen and hurtles over twelve feet of deck before landing hard on the brick pavers, the impact jarring Mac's back teeth loose. The submersible skids and spins another eight feet—

—before flipping wing-first over the edge of the lagoon's northern sea wall, plunging into the deep Pacific-blue waters of Angel's lair.

❦ ❦ ❦

SUDDENLY AIRBORNE, JONAS is hauled upwards like a marionette on a string, his back driven into the beam's pulley with such force he is nearly knocked out from the impact. For a long moment he simply dangles fifty feet over the Meg Pen, the *Jellyfish* cable held loosely in his right fist, his body pinned against the steel beam—unable to move.

Woozy, he watches the two sisters surface, their broad backs circling below like some perverse, animated *yin yang* symbol—

—until the dark one abruptly goes deep.

The image of Angelica's demise hits him like a bucket of ice water. "Fran, get me down! Wait! Not down! Just a few feet of slack ... only a few feet!"

Fran's hand quivers above the winch's control board. *Just a little tap! Tap it and reverse!* She hits FORWARD then STOP—

—releasing sixteen feet of cable!

Belle leaps out of the tank, seawater rolling away from her opening jaws—

—as Fran quickly reverses the winch, yanking Jonas back to the beam. The leaping Megalodon bites down on crisp Monterey air, eight feet below Jonas Taylor, who has managed to wrap his legs and arms tight around the beam in a bear hug, breathless—

—as Belle's twenty-one-ton girth plunges back into the aquarium, barely missing the half-inch steel cable still dangling from Jonas's hand.

The beam shakes as Fran races to him. Fishing knife in hand, she cuts loose the canvass straps of his harness and drags him to his feet. Together, they hurry back across the length of beam, the cable trailing.

❦ ❦ ❦

MAC OPENS HIS eyes, feeling disoriented. *I'm still in the water? What the hell?* His eyes widen as he suddenly realizes the azure Meg Pen is now a telltale, deep Pacific blue. *Sweet baby Jesus ... from the frying pan into the fire!*

Shaking loose the cobwebs in his brain, he jams both feet to the floorboard, sending the sub spinning in a tight circle.

"Broke the damn prop!"

Blip ... blip ... blip ... blip ...

He looks down at his on-board sonar, his pulse beating in time with the blips. Something immense is moving from the canal into the lagoon ... heading right for him!

Angel ...

▽   ▽   ▽

BRENT NICHOLS HUSTLES his burly frame from the far end of the Meg Pen to the western bleachers bordering the canal, his breath taken away as he stares at the water, staggered by the sheer size of the ancient predator rising from the depths. Angel's back is as wide as a three-lane highway. Her sheer-white hide lights up the surrounding sea with the luminescence of an iceberg. Unlike the frenzied movements of its offspring, the adult Megalodon glides slowly, in total command of its domain. Moving just beneath the surface, the shark displaces a river of current behind the sweeping strokes of its towering caudal fin.

The triangular head rises, drawing a gasp from Dr. Nichols. The blunt conical snout snorts an gurgling draft of sea and air as the powerful tail lashes back and forth, slapping frothy, six-foot waves over the northern sea wall, soaking the scientist's feet.

Then, Dr. Nichols sees it—the flat, brown object that he realizes is the submersible, the craft lurching along the surface in an awkward circle like a wounded fish, its floundering movements attracting the monster.

Sensing the object, Angel circles slowly, merely investigating at first, until her head suddenly lunges sideways, her open jaws biting water as she makes a reflexive attempt to snag the wounded prey.

Compensating for the damaged starboard propeller, Mac barely manages to avoid Angel's "bump and taste," as he rolls the submersible past the Megalodon's fluttering gill slits. He descends beneath an enormous pectoral fin that passes over his vessel like the wing of a jetliner, the Manta Ray nearly sideswiped by the thrashing caudal fin.

Past the ghostly behemoth, attempting to coax speed from his crippled vessel, Mac dives the sub and heads west toward the canal entrance. Twelve knots ... fifteen ... *I'll need at least thirty to clear the barbed wire above the submerged doors. Please be high tide!*

He registers the sudden change in current—knows it is Angel turning in pursuit. *Don't look back! Focus on being hydrodynamic ... keep your wings level while you ease*

100

your foot down on the left pedal … compensate with the right joystick …

He hits twenty knots as he exits the lagoon and enters the canal, the concrete barriers on either side, his feverish mind white-hot as his hands and feet adjust the sub's pitch and yaw against the head-current coming at him from beyond the porous doors.

Twenty-two knots.

Gotta push it … risk the roll for more speed! Get deeper … forty feet at least, or you'll never clear the coils …

He sees the doors looming up ahead, his mind adjusting on the fly, calculating speed and distance, estimating when to begin his rapid ascent.

Not yet … not yet … now!

Mac floors the one working prop as he heaves back hard on the joysticks, pulling the Manta Ray into a steep climb, doing twenty-six knots. The sub breaches, skims the eight-foot-high coils of barbed wire anchored in place above the submerged canal doors, and barrel rolls as it splashes down on the other side of the canal into open ocean.

Angel is right behind him, and with a tremendous thrust of her caudal fin, the albino beast launches its head and upper torso out of the sea—

—her airborne belly snagging barbed wire. The heavy coils stretch and twist around Angel's pectoral fins, pinning her belly-first against the submerged upper portion of the underwater doors. For a heart-stopping moment, the monster's head and gills remain clear out of the water, her upper torso fighting for equilibrium.

Mac surfaces the sub and watches, his pulse pounding, his left foot poised above the accelerator, ready to flee. "Fall back … damn you! Stop thrashing and fall back inside!"

Gasping a suffocating mouthful of air, the Megalodon panics. It writhes and twists, its tail churning great swaths in the canal, but the beached seventy-four-foot-long prehistoric shark cannot generate enough forward momentum to get free of its perch. And the creature possesses no reverse gear.

The wave catches Mac by surprise, nearly flipping him over as it lifts and propels the Manta Ray back toward the trapped beast. Slamming his foot down on the pedal, Mac accelerates farther out to sea—

—as the incoming swell strikes Angel, lifting her up and over the steel doors, and pushes her back into the confines of the man-made canal.

V V V

THE FLOODED *JELLYFISH* is hoisted slowly out of the tank, the truck crane's lone cable barely enough to handle the additional ballast. Water pours out from the cracked hull as the sphere is set down upon the concrete deck. Virgil is first to scale the vessel, jamming a crowbar into the wheel of the topside hatch as other staff members join him to wrench loose the seal.

Somewhere up the coastal highway, an ambulance siren welcomes the night.

Somewhere out to sea, a pregnant humpback continues her journey south, never realizing that fate and several fortunate inches have just spared her life and that of her unborn calf.

But fate is not always fortunate. Inches not always enough.

Wrapped in a wool blanket, seated somewhere in the vacant stands, Jonas Taylor watches in silence as members of his staff drag the lifeless body of Steven Moretti from its watery tomb.

11

David Taylor lies in bed, staring at the digital clock.

4:46 a.m.

Despite the million-dollar view and the five-star room service, the king-size bed and more down pillows than he could ever use, he has had a restless night. Though exhausted from the long flight, it had taken him several hours to fall asleep, his mind refusing to cease its endless conversations. He had nodded off around ten, but was back up an hour later, struggling to breathe, the air far drier than he was used to. He had downed several bottles of water and returned to bed, only to awaken an hour later to use the bathroom. And so it had gone for the rest of the night and well into morning.

4:47 a.m.

"This is crazy! I can't sleep. My body's still on California time." He kicks off the covers, leaps out of bed, and ruffles through his suitcase for his workout clothes. A quick search of the snack basket yields a protein bar. He wolfs it down, chases it with an orange juice, then pockets his room key and leaves the suite, heading for the elevators.

He takes the lift down to Level Three, the entire floor dedicated to a health and fitness club. The exercise room is empty, just the way he likes it. He inspects the weight training equipment, formulates a routine in his head, then warms up with fifteen minutes on the stationary bike before setting to work.

David is lying at a thirty-degree angle on a decline bench, finishing his third set of dumbbell presses when Kaylie suddenly steps into his view, the girl looking down on him.

"Morning, glory. Need a spot?"

"No ... I'm good." He continues pressing the weight, beads of sweat pouring down his face, his exhausted arms shaking as he looks up past Kaylie's spandex pants, her bare midriff, and six-pack abs. She smiles, peering down at him between her twin peaks, held back by a matching spandex top. Finally he drops the weights onto the rubber exercise floor and pulls himself up into a sitting position.

She tosses him a clean towel from a stack. "How'd you sleep?"

"Not so good. My room needs a humidifier or something."

"I couldn't sleep either. You should have come over."

"Really?"

"Sure. We could have watched movies together. I brought a bunch of DVDs from home."

"DVDs ... right." He watches her stretch her hamstrings. "You look like you workout a lot."

"I'm training for a triathlon; I did four last year. My best time was three hours seven minutes. My goal is to break two fifty."

"That's pretty good. I don't think I could even finish."

"Sure you could. You look like you're in shape." She selects a treadmill from a row of three and starts running. "You get better as you go ... figure out how to pace yourself. Dumbest thing I ever did ... was not lubing up. Leg cramps are nothing compared to chafing ... my nipples were raw."

"Yeah. That's gotta suck."

"So ... what are you training for?"

"Me? Football. I played in high school. Wide receiver. Made all-state twice. Used to be a sprinter too. Hundred and two hundred meters. Florida coach asked me to come out. Figured I'd give it a shot."

"That's great."

He watches her run another moment then heads off to work his lats, keeping an eye her reflection in the mirror. *Football ... good comeback ... idiot! Practice starts in three weeks and you don't even own a playbook, let alone a prayer. When's the last time you even ran a wind sprint?*

He works his bis and tris, finishes with three sets of concentration curls then debates working his legs. *Nah ... save 'em for tomorrow.* He looks over at Kaylie, who is still running strong. He contemplates doing a mile on the treadmill, but he's never liked running on machines, preferring the outdoors.

"I'm going outside for a run. Catch you later."

"I've got twenty more minutes ... then I'm in the pool. Come and find me ... we'll do breakfast together."

"Okay, great." He towels off and waves, nearly walking into the wall as he leaves the fitness room.

⩔　⩔　⩔

THE SUN IS just coming up as he exits the lobby and heads outside, the desert morning air far cooler than he expected. *Sprints or a two-mile run? ... Screw the sprints. I'm not really trying out for football.* He stretches his quads and hams then starts jogging at an easy pace, following a pedestrian trail that leads in the direction of the aquarium.

He jogs through a small park, passing several construction sites, the night shift just getting off work, yielding to day workers in hard hats drinking coffee. Dubai's population numbers just over a million, yet more than eighty percent of the people are expatriates, most hailing from Asia. Almost all of the workers he sees fits the demographic.

The trail connects to Avenue D, a pedestrian roadway lined with recently transplanted Canary date palms and the concrete block and wood frames of what will eventually be retail kiosks. The roadway intersects with a circular drive—future home to restaurants, eateries, and an open bazaar. Beyond the drive is an enormous man-made lake that harbors the twelve towering shark fins.

At the center of the lake is the aquarium.

Six futuristic acrylic glass and steel walkways arch gracefully over the lake, connecting the circular drive to the aquarium. The aquatic complex itself resembles something out of Oz's Emerald City—a tinted green glass pyramid structure surrounded by interlocking triangular trusses that jut out from every possible angle.

David is drenched in sweat, his knees sore from running on concrete, and his blood sugar low, but having come this far he decides to take a quick look around before returning to the hotel. He sprints up the walkway then slows to admire the architectural details of the aquarium as he jogs down the other side to a third-story pavilion.

There are three public entrances, none of which is open. He is about to begin the journey back when he sees the tractor trailer.

It is moving slowly up an access road on the street level, located forty feet beneath the pavilion. A double-wide eighteen wheeler, it is hauling an enormous railcar (sixty feet long, thirty feet wide, and fifteen feet high) chained to its flatbed. The load is being escorted by a detail of park officials in golf carts, technicians in white lab coats, and a handful of heavily armed military police riding shotgun.

As David watches, something causes the MPs to suddenly jump down off the truck and aim their weapons at the container. The vehicle stops, the technicians immediately scaling the flatbed. Water spills out from a series of air spaces located along the roof. The container is being rocked from within! Then David hears it—a dull, heavy *thudding* sound—something pounding on metal from within.

They're transporting a live specimen ... something big!

A short, dishwater-blonde woman in her mid-fifties rushes over, followed by a tall man—six foot six—in his early thirties. Probably her assistant. The assistant scales the outside of the container then lowers a hose into the air vent, siphoning out a water sample. The woman quickly tests the sample as the pounding increases.

She converses briefly with her lanky assistant then moves to the front end of the railcar where she opens the valve on one of a series of seven-foot-tall, yellow aluminum tanks, waits thirty seconds, before shutting it off again.

After a few moments the pounding ceases.

The woman speaks over a walkie-talkie, and the truck restarts, moving beneath the aquarium complex and out of David's view.

He hurdles the pavilion's guardrail and slides down a steep grassy slope to the facility's receiving area. Remaining concealed, he peeks around the corner of a concrete pillar.

The woman is yelling orders to the technicians in lab coats, who are frantically unchaining the railcar from the flatbed. Overhead, a crane designed to lift heavy cargo containers moves into position along tracks embedded in the loading dock's ceiling. Workers secure the crane's lifting arms into position around the railcar, which is then slowly offloaded from the flatbed and lowered into position on rails built into the concrete foundation.

Aluminum doors are raised, allowing a small railcar engine to exit the complex. As it backs into position, the engine's coupler mates with the railcar container's boot-lift connector. Moments later, the sixty-foot load is towed into the aquarium's infrastructure and out of sight.

⍦ ⍦ ⍦

BY THE TIME David returns to the hotel, the morning sun has moved off the horizon, bringing with it a taste of the desert heat to come. He entertains thoughts of showering, but instead heads for the pool.

Kaylie, the lone swimmer, is doing laps. A few maintenance people linger on the pool deck, setting up chairs and stealing glances at her physique. David peels off his sneakers and jumps into the water, wearing his sweaty socks, shirt, and shorts.

The cool water revitalizes him. He rinses out his mouth then takes off his shirt and socks, ringing them out before tossing them on the closest chair. *Okay ... laundry's done.*

"Hey!" Kaylie swims over, removing her goggles. She's wearing a red one-piece *Speedo*. "I've been waiting for you to get back. I didn't want to get out of the pool with all these workers staring at me; they give me the creeps. How was your run?"

"Good."

"Where'd you go?"

"Nowhere special."

"Liar. You went to the aquarium, didn't you? So? How's it look?"

"Great. Beautiful ... at least from the outside. Not like there's much to see."

She stares at him, reading his expression. "Why are you acting so weird, then? Did you see something?"

"Like what?"

"You tell me."

He looks around, making sure they're alone. "They were moving a huge crate into the aquarium, and something was inside. I could hear it banging around."

"Wow. What do you think it was?"

"I don't know. A whale maybe? Whatever it was, it was big. Spooked the hell out of the guards."

"Cool. Maybe we'll get a peek of it later."

"Maybe. But don't say anything, Kaylie. Let's keep it between us."

"Okay." She moves closer. Touches his chest and a pale, six-inch scar that contrasts with his tan skin, running from his left pectoralis to his deltoid. "That's sexy. How'd you get that?"

"High school. Mary Alaina Edwards. She broke my heart then ripped it right out of my chest like a Mayan priest making a sacrificial offering to the gods."

"An interesting visual."

"It's all true. She warned me not to fall in love with her, but I couldn't help it."

Kaylie leans in and kisses him gently on the lips. "I'm a free spirit, David. I don't want to be tied down."

"Tied down? Me either. I've never been into that whole S and M thing."

"Shut up." She slides her arm around his neck and kisses him again, this time with passion—

—neither one of them realizing that, six stories up, someone is watching.

12

The Crown & Anchor
Monterey, California

The British Pub is located in the center of Old Downtown Monterey, just a short walk from Cannery Row. The floors are a dark mahogany, the posts and matching walls decorated with artifacts from vintage sailing ships. It is the kind of place one ducks inside to get out of the weather then remains for hours nursing a draft beer or three with new friends.

At one in the morning, it is a place to escape.

Patrick Duncan is forty, a devoted father who has been raising his teenage daughters alone since the day his ex-wife left them, deciding she preferred a lover of the same sex. Burned out by twelve years of bad relationships, he has taken a week's vacation from his job as a business analyst to find himself in Monterey.

Patrick has been sitting at the bar for two hours conversing with Vicky Lynn Loehr, a high school marine science teacher from Jacksonville, Florida. Vicky is a self-professed shark nut who made the pilgrimage to Monterey a week earlier to see Angel and her juvenile pups. With the Tanaka Institute closed indefinitely, she has been spending countless hours wandering the Pacific coastline, renewing her love affair with the sea. She has never gone home with any man she met in a bar, but Patrick is a good listener, and life is too short.

These thoughts are echoed by the white-haired gentleman seated alone in a corner booth. He has not touched his clam chowder, even though he hasn't eaten since breakfast. He is not deserving of food. He is not deserving of company. Or pity.

Six hours ago he watched a friend die. The death was as horrible as it was meaningless, made worse by the fact that it was *his* fault. *What was so damn important about collecting a DNA sample? Did you really need to know the genetic history of that litter of monsters? Like the information's going to alter the marine sciences as we know it ...*

What do I say to his wife and daughter? How can I even face them? I'm so sorry, Mary, I know I destroyed your family today, but if it's any consolation, my life is ruined, too.

What about my own wife and daughter? How do I justify my actions to them? Terry's been pushing me to sell the Institute for years ... she's already on the verge of a nervous breakdown. My family deserves better than to watch me jump in the Meg

Pen like live bait. And what about Mac? I asked him to put his life on the line. How can I face him again, or his wife?

Jonas stares at his reflection in a picture frame. The white hair. The slumped figure ...

The Rolling Stones were right: What a drag it is getting old. Not that it ever affected them. Maybe I should sell the Institute and take up the guitar ...

He glances over to another booth, occupied by two regulars: Maxine Davis and Lillie Burris. Maxine is in her nineties, Lillie in her eighties. Active seniors living in the same mobile home park. Happy. Content. Stress-free.

Sure ... it's not like they killed anyone today.

Mac enters the pub. He approaches Don Ruetenik, who is watching highlights of the Cleveland Indians-Detroit Tigers game on ESPN. The bartender, in his late sixties, never bothers to look up. "He's in the corner, occupying space and time. I'm kicking him out in ten minutes. You want some chowder?"

"Put it in a cup with a rusty razor blade."

Mac nods at the couple seated at the bar then saunters over to Jonas's booth. "Hey, did you hear the one about the dyslexic guy who walked into a bra?"

No response.

Mac slides in across from him. "So what's next, Evel?"

Jonas looks up. "What'd you call me?"

"Evel Knievel. For your next stunt, I think you should try to jump the Meg Pen on a motorcycle, wrapped in a ton of bratwurst."

"Not now, Mac."

"Jonas, I'm sorry about Steven. He was a good man, and he's going to be missed. I also know there's nothing anyone's going to say to stop those self-absorbed feelings of guilt from churning in that snowy-white head of yours, but this one was not your fault."

"How do you figure?"

"A: Moretti knew the risks since the day he first signed on to join our little zoo. He was well paid, he was good at his job, and for what it's worth, he enjoyed it. B: You had no choice. Even if we hadn't severed the crane's cable, Moretti would have been stuck in the tank with Belle and Lizzy. C: Steven could have fled the *Jellyfish* at any time, but he wouldn't risk it. You, on the other hand, jumped into the tank to save him in what has to be the ballsiest, dumbest fucking move since the first doofus strapped a set of wings to his arms and jumped off a cliff, believing he could fly."

"You came in a close second. I told you to leap out of the tank if things got hairy. I didn't think you'd be stupid enough to land in Angel's lagoon."

"Hey, I can't let you have all of the fun."

Jonas smirks. "Two old dickheads, huh?"

"Got that right, amigo ... although I've been feeling a bit more spry of late."

"You have been smiling a lot more. I just assumed it was a new laxative. So what's up?"

"Apparently my sperm count." Mac beams a wide smile. "Trish is pregnant."

Jonas's face lights up. "No way! Wow! How long have you known?"

"Not long. To be honest, I've sort of been in shock."

"That's the best damn news I've heard in years." Jonas gives him a two-arm bear hug—

—as Don Ruetenik approaches with a bowl of home-made New England Clam Chowder. "Hey, enough of that. This ain't that kind of bar." He places the bowl of hot soup in front of Mac. "Eat fast. I'm closing."

"You put the rusty razor blades in it like I asked?"

"I'm out of razor blades, so I doused it with rat poison." The bartender sticks his index finger in Jonas's soup. "Wasted a perfectly good bowl of chowder. What the hell's wrong with you?"

"I'd tell you, but you're closing. Hey, congratulate Mac; he's going to be a daddy."

Ruetenik looks at Mac, half grinning. "Sure it ain't the UPS guy's kid?"

"Could be your soup? Maybe it put a little hitch in my giddy-up."

"Not according to *my* wife." Ruetenik collects Jonas's bowl and shuffles off to the kitchen.

Jonas punches Mac in the arm. "Asshole! What the hell were you doing risking your life today with a baby on the way?"

"You have kids! What were you doing?"

"It's my business."

"Last I checked, I owned twenty-five percent."

"That's not what I meant, and you know it. You need to be more careful now; you're not exactly a spring chicken."

"Look who's talking, gramps. You're the poster boy for the geriatric society ... hobbling around on two bad knees ... jumping into shark tanks like you're some *Die Hard* action hero. Face it, I'm a stud compared to you."

"Okay, so we're both assholes."

"Agreed. But unless you're suddenly planning on retiring, don't even think about putting me out to pasture."

"Fine."

"Good! Now let's talk business. We've got major problems, not the least of which is that our star attraction has become camera shy. What do we do about that?"

Jonas looks at his friend. "We close off the canal, seal up the lagoon."

Mac is about to respond when Don Ruetenik returns with Jonas's bowl of soup, now steaming-hot. "Nuked it in the microwave. No charge. We close in five, ladies."

Mac waits for the bartender to leave. "Sealing off the lagoon presents some major engineering challenges, not the least of which is the fact that the canal's vented doors allow us to use the ocean as a filtration system. Seal the canal and we'd have to add more filters, more ozone contact chambers ... all the devices we use to keep the Meg Pen clean."

"I know."

"Okay, assuming you add the plumbing, how do you plan on overhauling the lagoon with Angel still in it?"

"We'd have to prefabricate a barrier. Once it's in place, we drain the canal and reinforce the new wall. Angel would have to be drugged, of course. I have a few ideas how it could be done, but I want to run them by Dr. Nichols. Have you seen him?"

"The shark trainer? Yeah. He took the DNA sample Steven managed to get from Belle and disappeared."

"Probably in the lab." Jonas takes out his cell phone, powers it on, then dials a number.

"Lab. Stelzer."

"Jon, it's Jonas. What are you still doing there?"

"Jonas, where the hell have you been? We've been trying to reach you all night. Never mind, just come down to the lab. Dr. Nichols has discovered something extraordinary."

13

David Taylor finishes blow-drying his hair then pokes his head in the bedroom to check the time: 9:34 a.m.

His heart pounds with excitement, his mind continuously replaying the scene at the pool. Kaylie had entwined her body around his, the two of them touching and teasing one another until things had gotten a little too hot for being out in public. Gathering their belongings, they rode up together in the glass elevator, only to discover it was already 9:10 a.m., the monorail set to pick everyone up at ten.

"I have to shower. Come by my suite at nine forty-five, and we'll ride down in the elevator together."

She had kissed him good-bye, long and passionate.

He can still taste her on his lips.

David leaves the bathroom, re-checking the time on the bedside clock: 9:37. *What to wear?*

He empties his suitcase on top of his bed, rooting through the pile of wrinkled clothing. *Jeans? Too hot, and too tight to train in the Manta Ray's cramped cockpit. Go with either the Florida sweat suit or the cargo shorts and a baggy tee-shirt.*

He opts for the shorts.

Thirty seconds later he's dressed, tying his damp cross-trainers when someone knocks at his door.

It's Kaylie. She's dressed in shorts, tee-shirt, and a blouse, her hair still wet. She pushes him back inside his room, pressing her lips and body against his. "Sorry ... am I early?"

"Early's good. I like early." He runs his hand beneath her blouse, attempting to reach beneath the tee-shirt.

She stops him. "Not now. Maybe tonight ... if you're good."

"I'm always good." He readjusts his cargo shorts then grabs his room key and follows her out to the elevator. They ride down to Level Five ... holding hands.

The elevator opens to an acrylic bridge that spans the atrium, the clear walkway running through the anatomy of the recreated and greatly enlarged skeletal model of *Dunkleosteus*. Crossing the bridge, they look down through the monster's pelvic girdle to the lobby five floors below.

Kaylie pauses at the animal's gill slits, gazing at the bones of its smallish pectoral fins. "What was this thing called again? The Paleozoic era was never my specialty."

"It's pronounced dunk-lee-OWE-stee-us. It was the nightmare of the Devonian seas, a placoderm, meaning it was an armored prehistoric fish. This model exaggerates its size; it only grew to be thirty feet or so, but it was fearsome. Instead of teeth, it had these bony blades that could crush anything. They say its bite was more powerful than a *T. rex* or Meg bite."

They proceed through the skeleton's thickly armored neck and head then out the mouth, stepping outside the automated glass door to the monorail platform.

Waiting in the depot, congregating in small packs, are the other pilot candidates—twenty-one in all. They are older than David by an average of twenty years—all men, save for one woman in her early fifties. Everyone looks fit and trim, many sporting military-style crew-cuts.

Kaylie mumbles, "Looks like an Army PX just let out."

One of the soldier-types, a 6 foot 2 inch specimen in his early forties, leaves his group to introduce himself. "You're the Taylor kid, right? Brian Suits, captain, United States Naval Warfare Center, retired. Appreciate you being here." He turns to Kaylie. "You must be Szeifert. You're experience with Graham Hawkes should give you an edge over most of these other recruits, half of which have never set foot in a submersible."

Kaylie looks him over. "Are you a sub pilot?"

"Head instructor."

David feels the blood rush from his face. "You're in charge? I thought I—"

"You'll assist. You're primary responsibility is to care for your two sharks. You didn't think bin Rashidi was about to put a twenty-year-old in charge of this mission, did you?"

"No ... I just thought—"

"—that you're familiarity with the Manta Ray qualified you as an instructor? Sure it does ... if this was a resort in the Bahamas. You've been pleasure diving, kid. Ever maneuver in a thirty-knot current? Or find your way out of a debris storm three miles down in zero visibility?"

"I can handle it."

"With proper training, I'm sure you could. But that's not why the prince had bin Rashidi hire you. You're a fish-keeper first, a demo pilot second. We clear?"

"Am I supposed to salute you?"

Captain Suits forces a grin. "Excuse us a moment, Szeifert." He waits until Kaylie leaves. "Listen, hotshot, before I went Navy, I was Psy Ops—that's Psychological Operations. Spent eighteen months learning Arabic in heavy immersion training. In Iraq, I headed over forty cordon and search missions while living among the Arabs, Kurds, and the Yizidis, a relatively unknown tribe that has roots in the Middle East deeper than most Arabs. My relationship with the locals meant I knew what the insurgents were up to before they did. After I was wounded, I earned my stripes extracting information from enemy combatants for Military Intel ... and I was real good at my job.

"Now, the way I see it, you're a college student here for the summer, at the end of which you collect a nice paycheck and go back to Florida to finish out your senior year. Me? I'm here to accomplish a mission for bin Rashidi, a man who doesn't screw around. Neither do I. So, be a good boy and toe the company line, but don't cross it, or I'll squish you like a June bug. Understood?"

David feels beads of sweat trickle down his armpits. "Understood."

In the distance, a high-speed monorail, painted white with navy trim, makes its way silently around the track.

Brian Suits checks his clipboard. "I'm missing a man ... Montgomery, Jason. He's in Suite 3612. Get him."

"Yes, sir." David heads back through the *Dunkleosteus* walkway to the elevators then takes the lift back up to the thirty-sixth floor. Cursing to himself, he knocks loudly on the double doors of Suite 3612. "Monty, let's go! Monty, you in there?" He bangs again.

After a few seconds Monty opens the door, still wearing the clothes he had on yesterday. His eyes look vacant.

"Dude, what's with you? You're going to miss the first day of training."

Monty walks back to the sofa and sits.

"Hey! Did you hear me? The monorail's waiting."

The vacant eyes roll up to David. "You surprise me. I had you pegged for the shallow rich kid."

"Yeah, well, coming after you wasn't exactly my idea. Some ex-navy hard-ass sent me to find you. You look like shit. Did you even sleep?"

"Sleep? I'm not sure. I can't remember." He lies down again. "Guess my doctor was right ... I thought I could handle things."

"Handle what? We haven't even started yet."

"Did I take my lithium? Can't remember..."

"Lithium? Why do you need—"

114

"Ever play football, Junior?"

"Yeah."

"Ever have your bell rung?"

"A concussion? Sure ... once, I think."

"Multiply that by a hundred and you'll know what an IED feels like. Brain damage is the gift that keeps on giving. It never heals, it just keeps pushing you slowly into the abyss. Dementia, memory loss ... suicide. Some days you lose the will to stand. Today's one of those days. Go on without me."

"Did you eat?"

"What?"

"I said, have you eaten anything?"

Monty's eyes stare at the heavy drapes covering his bay windows. "Eat? I can't remember."

David opens the mini-refrigerator. "You haven't touched anything in here, and haven't changed your clothes. Between the jet lag and your blood sugar, you've bottomed out. Here, drink this juice."

Monty drains an orange juice.

"Better?"

"A little. You'll make someone a fine wife."

"Shut up." David shoves a handful of nutritional snacks into Monty's jacket pocket, grabs another orange juice, and guides him toward the door.

"You're wasting your time, you know. I'll never make the grade. Hell, I'd be lucky just to make it through training."

"You're a war vet. Leave it to me; I'll get you through training."

"Thanks, brother."

"Just don't sit next to me on the monorail. You reek."

Monty follows him out the door and onto the awaiting elevator, gulping down a handful of trail mix nuts and raisins. "Hey, ru rang rat rhick ret?"

"Try swallowing."

"Sorry. Just asking if you did that chick last night."

"No."

"You will."

The monorail is waiting at the station. An Arabic conductor is using his body to block the platform gates from closing, triggering a relay which prevents the automatic doors from sealing and restarting the monorail.

Brian Suits is standing next to the conductor with his clipboard. "Montgomery, J. Consider this your one and only warning. Show up late to my training again and you'll be thumbing it home."

"Aye, aye, sir."

The captain gives David and Monty a dirty look as they enter the car.

The doors seal with a *hiss*, the straddle-type monorail, developed by Hitachi, moving effortlessly along its track, its velocity approaching seventy miles an hour. Monty finds a vacant row away from the others, emptying his pockets of snacks across one of the seats next to him.

Still feeling a bit emasculated, David passes up the open seat next to Kaylie and opts for a window seat in the next row.

The monorail shoots past two more hotel stations then banks and slows as it approaches the aquarium. They reach the station moments later, the train's doors opening with another hydraulic *hiss*, breaking the seal.

An Egyptian man in his early thirties is standing by the gate. He's wearing a sports coat and tie, his jet-black hair slicked back, a scar over his right eyebrow. "Welcome, welcome! My name is Magued Wadie Ramsis Haroun. I know that is a lot to remember, so just call me Magued. I am assistant director of the aquarium, and this morning I will be giving you a behind-the-scenes tour before you begin your submersible training with Captain Suits. If you will please follow me."

Magued leads them inside through the automated entry doors and past a security and ticket checkpoint into the main lobby— the very center of the emerald glass pyramid. An open, three-lane-wide circular stairwell winds down two more stories, while above, the interior of the aluminum-trussed steel pyramid rises another seven stories.

"This is the fifth floor mezzanine—the Temple of the Gods. There are three main levels open to the public. Level Three, the Queen's Chamber, functions as our ground floor and handles foot traffic entering from the park. Level Four, just below us, is the King's Chamber; it features our food court and gift shops. This level, Level Five, accommodates hotel guests using our monorail system. From the three mezzanines, visitors can access any of our twelve main galleries."

The entrances to the main galleries are set along each of the pyramid's interior four walls, three to a side. The assistant director bypasses the three galleries on the east wall labeled T-1, T-3, and T-5, and proceeds through a tunnel on the south side designated T-4. The opening is wide enough to admit a bus, its ceiling and walls created out of fake rocks made from fiberglass. Magued leads them past several empty, twelve-foot-wide by ten-foot-high aquarium tanks, pausing at the last one.

Backlit in black-purple lighting, it is a scene right out of the Mariana abyss.

Steaming currents of soot-clouded mineral water pump out of squat man-made volcanic stacks that feed several blooms of six-foot-long tube worms, their swaying stalks ghostly-white, their tips blood-red.

"These are *Lamellibrachia luymesi*, the only tube worms ever kept alive in captivity. The black smokers are not hydrothermal vents, but a cold water methane seep similar to those found in the Western Pacific and off New Zealand's eastern coast. The cold seep pumps out methane and hydrogen sulfide which nourishes chemoautotropic bacteria. The bacteria in turn feed large communities of tiny, independent organisms known as extremophiles. The bacteria, which we call prokaryotes, process methane and sulfides through chemosynthesis to create chemical energy. Higher organisms, such as these tube worms, feed on this energy.

"Unlike hydrothermal vents, which release superheated mineral water into the depths, cold seeps are far more stable, pumping methane and other hydrogen-rich fluids at a far slower rate. This steady, more reliable pace actually increases the life-span of those creatures inhabiting the seeps. We now believe tubeworms, such as these, can live in excess of 250 years."

David stares at the tubeworm colony, losing himself in their ancient dance, performed in the swirling currents.

"Hey!" Kaylie tugs him by his elbow. "What's wrong with you?"

"Nothing."

"Forget about Captain Crewcut. Come on!"

They catch up with the rest of the group, the tunnel emptying into an enormous gallery, its large acrylic window half the size of the Meg Pen.

The vast blue world before them is occupied by dozens of giant jellyfish, each longer than seven feet and as wide around as a sumo wrestler. Luminescent white, with crimson-red bands and bright white tentacles, the alien-looking behemoths move through the tank like massive globs in a house-size lava lamp.

"We call this our zen gallery," Magued says proudly. "The creatures are called *Echizen kurage*, more commonly known as Nomura jellyfish. Each weighs in excess of four hundred and fifty pounds. As beautiful as they are to look at, they have become a terrible nuisance to Japanese fisherman, as they clog their nets. The tentacles yield a painful sting, but they are not toxic to humans."

Magued allows the group a few minutes then continues the tour through a winding tunnel that opens to a titanic aquarium that occupies Levels Three, Four, and Five as well as two more open stories above their heads. Small octagon-shaped devices, each the size of a man's fist, are spaced at ten-foot intervals along the inside of the aquarium's bay windows. Large enough to accommodate a blue whale, the tank appears empty. Nevertheless, it is incredible to behold.

"This is aquarium T-4, one of twelve oceanic habitats we've built within the complex. The acrylic glass panels are composed of six layers that have been chemically bonded and heat treated on site to 185 degrees Fahrenheit. The process takes over a month to complete. The tank itself holds 80 million gallons of water, a full 20 million more than the Tanaka Institute's Meg Pen, which had been tops in the world."

David points to one of the small, eight-sided devices spaced along the interior facing. "Excuse me, but what are these?"

"Part of the life-support system."

"What do they do?"

The Egyptian smiles. "I'm not at liberty to say. Now, if you'll follow me, I'll show you how we keep these amazing habitats functioning."

Magued heads for a door marked T-4: RESTRICTED. He swipes his identification badge, and the hydraulic door hisses open, revealing an interior corridor. They turn right down a main hallway, an avenue of filtration pipes running along the high ceiling. A stairwell leads them up three flights to Level Eight. They pass through another set of security doors marked T-4, and into a gymnasium-size arena housing the aquarium's deck, surrounding a pool of water as large as a small lake.

Banks of ultraviolet lights are aimed at areas of the tank where coral blooms have taken root. A horizontal gantry, similar to the crane at the Meg Pen, spans the width of the tank. The group follows Magued onto its ten-foot-high steel bridge.

Looking down through the crystal clear waters, David can see the large gallery window and notes how the rock formations have been strategically situated to enhance the visitor's view.

"Gives one a different perspective, doesn't it," Magued says. "Each tank operates like a sophisticated, giant saltwater swimming pool. The water that fills our exhibits originates from the Persian Gulf, but it must be cleansed of all impurities, including salt, before we allow it to enter the system. The process actually begins at a desalination plant at the Persian Gulf, where salt water is filtered. The fresh water is then pumped through miles of pipe into the man-made reservoir that surrounds this complex. The reservoir serves as a backup and drainage area. Before this fresh water is used in any of our aquariums, it must be conditioned and processed.

"The first stop is a series of foam fractioners, which eliminate organic compounds like oil and protein from the water. From there, huge sand filters remove particles and provide an optimum environment for the growth of bacteria, which is used to consume the specimen's waste products. Heat and cold exchangers regulate water temperatures, while a de-nitrication filter uses natural processes to remove ammonia from the water. Again, these animals are defecating in their habitats, so the water must be filtered twenty-four hours a day, seven days a week.

"The water then passes through an ozone contact chamber which disinfects and decolorizes, while a de-airation tower agitates the water to remove excess dissolved gases. Now that the water is properly treated, we add back salt and minerals using a product called "instant ocean." Again, the levels of minerals and salinity within each tank are regulated based upon the animal's natural habitat.

"If you look below, you'll see a series of large grates located throughout the tank. In addition to keeping the water filtered, balanced, and clean, we've installed currents within each tank. The ocean, of course, has currents, and we've found that aquatic animals prefer to swim with and against them. We've positioned them to channel the animals past our viewing gallery, which adds to the spectacle.

"Any questions? No? Then follow me, and I'll give you a quick look at our filtration devices and current machines."

Magued leads the group off the gantry to a filtration room.

Monty taps David on the shoulder. He points to the far end of the tank at a giant coil of steel mesh. The mesh, set in grooves situated around the deck gutters, can be unraveled from its massive spool in a manner similar to that of a baseball infield tarmac. When rolled in place, the grating will cover the entire surface of the aquarium.

"What do you suppose that's for?"

"I imagine to keep the staff from falling in the tank. Maybe this aquarium is designated to hold one of the two Meg pups."

"No, that would be T-2 and T-10."

"And how would you possibly know that?" Kaylie asks, annoyed.

"Rule of thumb."

"Excuse me?"

"You never heard of the rule of thumb? See, back in the 1400s, England ruled that a man could legally beat his woman with a stick, as long as the stick was no thicker than his thumb. Ergo, we have the rule of thumb. Not sure if the law applies to new girlfriends, but—"

"What the hell does any of this have to do with the two Meg tanks?"

"Nothing, really, except my own rule of thumb is to never make assumptions unless provided with proof positive ... proof positive, in this case, being this diagram." Monty unfolds a hand-written floor map of the aquarium, galleries T-2 and T-10 marked in Arabic. "See? Those words translate to *abayad akht* ... white sister. I suspect Magued means your sharks, unless he's having Hillary Clinton over for dinner."

David grabs the floor plan, using his back to shield it from the others, who are filing into the filtration room. "Where did you get this?"

"It sort of fell out of our Egyptian director's back pocket as he was bending over to tie his shoe."

"Jesus, Monty. I hope Captain Ball-buster didn't see you swipe this."

"Leave him be," Kaylie says. "He's nothing but a common thief."

"I resent that. There's nothing common about me."

"Shh! Knock it off!" David quickly examines the floor plan. "There's something else here, marked in gallery T-1. Monty, can you read this?"

Monty squints at the hand-scrawled Arabic: كامسآل ءوس. It means ... bad fish."

14

It is after two in the morning by the time Jonas and Mac return to the Institute.

The research lab is located in the basement of the new Meg Pen wing—an air-locked chamber covering three thousand square feet, not counting its two-hundred-foot walk-in freezer. There are six work stations equipped with aluminum tables, fresh and salt water sinks, and high-speed computers, each linked to high-capacity duplex laser printers, a format plotter, slide scanner, and an image analyzer. Another work table spans the length of the entire back wall, its table top littered with beakers and test tubes, petri dishes, refrigerated centrifuges, fluorometers, spectrophotometers, pH meters, and both inverted and compound microscopes equipped with cameras and Nomarski optics.

Seated between Dr. Stelzer and Dr. Nichols along the back wall is a husky Caucasian man with brown-black hair and a matching goatee, trimmed close. He's peering through a microscope, making notes on a legal pad.

Dr. Nichols greets Jonas and Mac as they enter the heavily air conditioned chamber. "Jonas, my sincerest condolences regarding the death of your sub pilot. If I had known—"

"Why am I here?"

"You're here because we've discovered something important ... as fascinating as it is frightening."

Mac points. "Who's the new guy?"

"A colleague of mine, Dr. Jesse Brown. Dr. Brown's a forensic scientist. I hope you don't mind me asking him here, but what we found ... it's way over my head. Better I let Dr. Brown explain it ... he's the expert."

Jesse David Brown looks up from his microscope, his glasses fogging. He wipes them, using his tie. "Dr. Taylor, heard you had a rough day. Hope I'm not adding to it."

"I'll let you know after I've heard what you have to say."

"At the request of Dr. Nichols, I've spent the better part of the last six hours analyzing DNA samples taken from the Megalodon you call Angel, her deceased runt, the runt's big sister, and the two potential fathers. Before I explain the results, it's important that you understand the process. Essentially what we're

121

doing is creating a nuclear DNA profile. Be it prehistoric shark or human, each of us receives half our DNA from our mother and half from our father, this is set at conception and does not change over time, except when cancerous cells are involved. No two individuals, other than identical siblings, have the same DNA profile.

"In humans, DNA is the same throughout the body ... be it hair roots, skin cells, or white blood cells. Reproductive cells all have the same DNA profile. We don't use red blood cells as they don't have a nucleus. Now, I'm not a marine biologist, nor am I a Megalodon expert, but I think it's safe to assume that the DNA rules that apply to humans and other species also apply to your monsters.

"Forensically, we're evaluating sixteen Short Tandem Repeats, or STRs in the nuclear DNA. STRs, are short sequences of DNA, normally two to five base pairs in length, that are repeated numerous times in a head-tail manner throughout the genome. For instance—" Dr. Brown points to his computer screen "—in this sixteen base pair sequence of 'tagatagatagataga' we have four head-tail copies of the tetramer 'taga,' a sequence that demonstrates sufficient commonality among individuals, making them—

Jonas yawns, cutting him off. "Sorry. No disrespect, but it's late, and my brain's not functioning well at the moment."

"Then I'll cut to the chase. When it comes to determining if a specific male Megalodon conceived either the dead runt or its bigger sibling, we're pretty conservative with our cutoff, 99.9% being the minimum value for stating that the male is most likely the biological father. If it's 99.89%, then the male is definitely *not* the father."

"That's pretty scary," says Mac, stretching out on an aluminum table. "Having once been accused of fathering a child to a certain Filipino woman back in my heydays on Guam, I would have had a heart attack if you told me there was a 99.89% chance that little Rafael Herrera carried Mackreides blood."

Dr. Brown smiles. "It may not seem like a big difference, but in the world of DNA, it's day and night. The reality is, we share a lot of DNA with a lot of different things. Almost 60% of our DNA is shared with a bacteria. We share 98% with chimps. A recent study found we share 154 genes with mice, dogs, and, believe it or not, elephant sharks. It's only the slightest percentile that makes us unique."

"That's what I told Concepción, but she wouldn't listen. Hell, the woman had fourteen kids ... she was playing the lottery."

Jonas clears his throat. "Doc, the Megs?"

"Right. Let's begin with the big sibling, Belle. My tests reveal a 99.9999% chance or higher in favor of an inclusion, meaning the big male was definitely Belle's father. As for the runt, Angelica, the shark DNA profile is 98.7% for both the big male and the Meg you call Scarface. Absolutely no match. Zero."

Jonas squeezes the bridge of his nose. "Which means there's another male out there."

"No, there's not," Dr. Nichols states, his eyes widening. "This is the fascinating and really scary part. Tell him, Jesse."

"The three runts—Angelica, Mary Kate, and Ashley—were not conceived by a male Megalodon. Angel's eggs were fertilized ... by Angel."

Jonas feels queasy. "You lost me. Did you just say Angel conceived the three runts herself ... that there was no father?"

"Precisely."

"That's not all, J.T.," Dr. Stelzer adds. "I checked the eggs we removed from Angelica. The runt's eggs were fertilized as well."

Jonas finds an empty chair and sits, his mind attempting to grasp the information at hand. "How is any of this possible? I mean, you're looking at a guy who grew up questioning the whole immaculate conception deal with the Virgin Mary, but this?"

"Sex-free reproduction in the animal kingdom is far from unprecedented," says Dr. Brown, defogging his glasses again with his tie. "We know of more than five hundred different species that reproduce without sex. Take the common greenfly. Every summer the females give birth to exact replicas of themselves, sex never entering the equation. Another example is the whiptail lizard, found in the southwestern United States. There are no known male whiptail lizards in existence, the entire species is made entirely of females that lay eggs which hatch as females genetically identical to their mother."

"Several examples of asexual, or parthenogenesis have now been documented in sharks," Dr. Nichols adds. "The first case was in Florida Bay a few years back when a hammerhead shark gave birth without mating. At first, scientists thought someone had dropped the pup in the tank as a hoax, but after testing its DNA they determined it was a genetic duplicate of its mother—with no paternal genes. Same thing happened with a blacktip reef shark a few years later. Man has been decimating the ocean's shark populations ... perhaps nature found a way to counteract some of the effects."

"Yes, but aren't these fatherless offspring weaker?"

"Not at all. Granted, the two siblings—Belle and Lizzy—are far bigger specimens than the three runts. But I think it's safe to say that in years to come, the runts will grow to be just as large as their mother. After all, they are Angel's genetic duplicate."

"Wonderful," Jonas whispers. "Just what we need."

"I don't get it," Mac says. "Are you saying male Megs are on the outs?"

"It's very possible. For a moment, forget the fact that sex is pleasurable and remains, at least for now, the most common way in which humans reproduce. I say most common, because there are, of course, other ways to impregnate a female, including Invitro fertilization. For now, accept the fact that sex and reproduction are two entirely different things. By definition, sex is two cells fusing to become one, while reproduction is one cell dividing to become two. When it comes down to the survival of a species, reproduction is far more important than sex.

"I'll give you an example. Let's take Angel's mother, whom we'll call Momma Meg, and Angel's deceased runt, the Virgin Angelica. Momma Meg, living in the nutritionally challenged depths of the Mariana Trench, relies on the conventional, and quite restricted, method of conceiving baby Megs through sex. Her grandchild, the Virgin Angelica, living in a habitat with plenty of food, reproduces without sex, her eggs released pre-inseminated during ovulation. Let's say Momma Meg has four pups—two males and two females. A generation later, her two females have identical litters—again, two males and two females. Meanwhile, the Virgin Angelica, having no need for males, has produced four female pups. In turn, each of her four daughters have four daughters of their own. After only two generations, Momma Meg is responsible for eight new pups, four females and four males.

"Our Virgin Angelica, on the other hand, has produced all females, which have yielded a total of twenty pups. In the next generation, those twenty females can potentially produce another eighty female pups for a running total of one hundred Megs, while old Momma Meg, still relying on sex with males, can yield a maximum of only thirty-two pups, assuming, of course, each of these females can, in turn, link up with a suitable male partner. Let's face it, gentlemen, when it comes to the survival of a species, males are dead-end products. Not only can't we reproduce, but we also consume a lot of food."

Mac smiles. "Some of us more than others, eh Doc?"

"Let's not forget," adds Dr. Stelzer, ignoring Mac's comment, "that with *Carcharodon megalodon*, it's the females that are bigger, nastier, and far more dominant than males. Angel actually hunted down and killed her mate to establish dominance in her territory."

"Maybe it was revenge," says Mac, only half-joking. "I saw video of the insemination; Angel wasn't exactly having a good time."

"Regardless," Dr. Brown states, "the point here is that sex is clearly an inefficient method of reproduction. With their numbers dwindling close to extinction, it makes perfect sense that Megalodon would eventually evolve to sex-free reproduction. For all we know, it could have been the species' adaptation back to surface waters that triggered the event."

Dr. Stelzer nods in agreement. "Now you know why we wanted to speak with you. If Angelica was pregnant, then there's a good chance the two surviving runts you just sold to the Dubai Aquarium are pregnant too—or will be very soon. They're en route as we speak."

Jonas feels his blood pressure simmer. "Jon, what the hell are you talking about? The runts weren't scheduled to leave for another week."

"Jonas, what choice did we have? Belle destroyed the Meg Pen gate, and the medical pool is far too small to keep the runts another week. Terry agreed it was safer to move them now."

"Terry?"

"We tried to reach you. When we couldn't—"

"Okay, fine, you did the right thing." Jonas forces himself to think. *David's in Dubai if you need him to monitor the runts ...* "What about Belle and Lizzy? Is there any way to tell if their eggs are fertile?"

Mac shakes his head. "After what happened today, I don't think you want to go there. My advice: Assume the worst and you won't be disappointed."

Dr. Stelzer isn't through. "Since we're examining worst-case scenarios, there's one more we need to consider: It's highly possible that Angel is also pregnant."

Jonas and Mac groan.

"No ... no ... think about it! She hasn't fed in weeks. She even regurgitated the snack David managed to get in her. Her behavior's been erratic. She's certainly put on weight. And we know she's already reproduced one litter of pups without sex. It's been four years ... I'm telling you, she could be pregnant."

For a moment, no one says a thing, the enormity of the statement simply hanging in the air.

Finally, it is Jonas that speaks, his right hand trembling noticeably. "This is insane. We cannot allow the most dangerous predator in the history of the planet to make a comeback. Agreed?"

Mac and the three scientists nod in unison.

"Okay, then. Keeping in mind the PETA crazies are watching our every move, how do we stop the insanity?"

"Not a whole lot of options," Dr. Nichols replies. "You either find a means to sterilize the five remaining females ... or you kill them."

15

The classroom consists of twenty-three chairs with table attachments set up along aquarium T-7s topside deck. Suspended five feet above the water, swaying within a canvass harness attached to the arm of a small hydraulic crane, is one of the Manta Ray submersibles.

The trainees, all wearing wetsuits, gather around the wide, flat sub. Brian Suits allows the unzipped top half of his wetsuit to hang around his waist, exposing his muscular upper torso and battle scars as he points out a few of the water craft's features.

"... radio antenna located in the tail assembly. Twin directional propulsion units, 350 horsepower each. The outer hull is acrylic. The interior pod is Lexan, capable of withstanding pressures exceeding even that of the Mariana Trench. Over the next six days, each of you will log twenty hours as both pilot and co-pilot, as well as five hours a day in your rooms practicing on simulators. At the end of this week of intensive training we'll begin a series of field tests which will determine who our final candidates will be. Those chosen six, along with two alternates, will be flown out to our fleet in the Pacific where operations have been underway for several months. Questions?"

Hugo raises a thick arm, constricted by the wetsuit. "You said six days. I was told we would have two full weeks of training."

"Change of plans. Because we only have three Manta Rays available, I decided to make cuts a week early. I'd rather give our finalists the extra week to log hours on location in the open ocean before the mission's first official dive."

The captain motions for David to step forward. "This is David Taylor. David has probably logged more time aboard these subs than any person alive. While pleasure diving is a far cry from what I'll be training you to do, I've asked David to give us a quick demonstration of the sub's basic capabilities."

Brian Suits presses a switch on the side of the hydraulic winch, lowering the submersible into the water. He pulls David aside. "Just a few laps. Give us a barrel roll, maybe a figure eight or two."

"Basically a pleasure dive. Got it." David steps out onto the starboard wing, then down into the open cockpit. He buckles the shoulder straps in extra tight and seals the pod—

—stealing a glance at the expansion bridge now situated fifteen feet over the center of the tank. *Pleasure dive, huh? Pleasure this, Captain Dingus.*

David starts the sub's twin propellers, quickly maneuvering the Manta Ray into a shallow dive. He descends to forty feet then slowly increases his speed as he circles counter-clockwise around the immense tank, getting a feel for his tight surroundings. He executes a tight barrel roll then banks into a semi-hard, ninety-degree turn, flying past the huge expanse of window located along the northern end of the aquarium. Turning again, he rolls into a sweeping figure eight as he moves into the center of the tank.

Brian Suits activates his radio. "Well done, David. A few bursts of speed along the surface and bring it on home."

Ascending quickly, David jams both feet to the pedals, the Manta Ray breaking the surface doing forty knots. Eyeballing the crowd, he shoots across the length of the tank in seconds. Then, nearing the classroom he drops his port-side wing as he jams his right foot down on the accelerator, pulling a full G as he drives the sub into a hard 180-degree surface turn—

—unleashing an arching spray of water that soaks the trainees and their pissed-off head instructor.

David shuts off the radio as he descends to seventy feet, accelerating along the bottom at thirty knots before he runs out of tank. He eases up and banks into a sweeping 180 along the far end of the tank, feeling the adrenaline butterflies in his stomach.

Pleasure cruise my ass!

Accelerating out of the turn, he levels out along the bottom, then yanks back hard on both joysticks, launching his craft topside at a steep sixty-degree angle.

The Manta Ray leaps out of the water and continues rising—

—easily clearing the suspension bridge ... coming within ten feet of the duct pipes running along the top of the aquarium's ceiling!

Gravity quickly intervenes. David leans forward, coaxing the nose of the sub downward as he free falls twenty-three feet, punching nose-assembly-first back into the water.

The jolt knocks him woozy. Heart pounding, he submerges the vehicle, circles the tank one last time at ten knots (gathering a few precious seconds to regain his composure) then surfaces the sub, guiding it back into its harness.

The cockpit opens and David climbs out, greeted by a smattering of applause—and severe looks from Brian Suits, whose clipboard is dripping wet.

Reaching into his wetsuit, David pulls out a dollar bill from the lining, and casually hands it to the Navy captain. "Park it in the shade, will you? Us pleasure divers hate climbing into a hot cockpit."

❦ ❦ ❦

SEATED IN THE shadows along the opposite end of the aquarium are two figures. One is Fiesal bin Rashidi, the other a petite brunette in her early thirties. The Boston native wears no make-up and bites her nails, more to keep them short than out of habit.

"So, my dear ... what do you think?"

"Brash and cocky ... just like his father." Allison Petrucci, Michael Maren's former assistant and fiancé, smiles. "He's perfect."

16

Virgil Carmen fidgets on the violet sofa, the uncomfortable cushions unyielding, the armrest set at an awkward height. As if that were not annoying enough, there is no air conditioning in the loft, and the purple-haired woman's cat keeps climbing on his lap, pawing at his groin as if giving him some kind of feline lap-dance.

He stands, dumping the cat to join the two women at the computer. "So, Sara? Did I do good?"

With her blonde hair and green eyes, R.A.W. co-founder Sara Toms possesses a classic girl-next-door look—until one sees her arms and back, which are covered in military tattoos. The former AWAC airborne surveillance instructor pauses the playback of the video-cam footage taken yesterday at the Meg Pen. "Virgil, this is great stuff ... if our organization were filming an action movie. Where's the cruelty you promised us?"

"Are you kidding? My boss drowned!"

"She means cruelty to the animals." Jessica Tompson clicks off the program. "None of this is useful to our cause. If anything, it only reinforces Taylor's point of not releasing the Megs back into the wild."

"Agreed." Sara spins around in her chair to face Virgil. "What I was hoping for was footage of the two runts who were confined to the Med Pool. That's the kind of cruelty that gets us air time."

Virgil suddenly feels naked. "The runts ... I totally forgot. I meant to call you—"

"What happened? Was there another accident?"

"The runts are gone."

Sara grabs his wrist, a Celtic cross visible on her right arm. "What do you mean they're gone?"

"Jonas sold them to another aquarium."

"Another aquarium?" Sara grips his arm tighter. "Virgil, which aquarium? Was it San Diego?"

"I don't know. They kept it quiet. But there were a bunch of Arabs hanging around all last week. I'm guessing they're the ones who bought Mary Kate and Ashley."

"Dammit!" Jessica turns to her partner. "Sara, what am I supposed to do?

I've got three private donors lined up—big donors! This diffuses the whole situation."

Sara releases Virgil. "Take it easy. We pull back and refocus our attention on Angel."

Jessica shakes her head. "Angel is way too big and way too scary. Even the most radical animal lover won't take a public stance to set her free."

"Then we focus on the two sisters. The Meg Pen's still too small to hold two adult Megs; let's make the push to release them now, while they're still pups and can adapt to the wild."

"You want to release Bela and Lizzy?" Virgil shakes his head. "I don't think you want those two predators roaming free."

"Elsa was a predator," Jessica retorts. "Should they have denied her the right to live free?"

"Who the hell's Elsa?"

"Go rent *Born Free*. You'll cry your eyes out."

"Do it later. We have other priorities." Sara removes an envelope from her purse. She hands it to Virgil then leads him down the stairs. "I'm paying you, but you owe me big time. Look through the Institute's archives. Find me footage of the two sisters ramming their heads against a tank wall, shots of them fighting over food ... any erratic behavior that demonstrates how inadequate in size the Meg Pen really is."

"Yeah ... I can do that. How soon do you want it?"

She opens the front door. "Yesterday works for me."

Dubai Land
Dubai, United Arab Emirates

David opens his eyes. He is lying on the wraparound leather couch in his suite. Sitting up, he looks out the bay windows. The sun has already set, the Persian Gulf's distant horizon alive with a twinkling night life. He checks the wall clock: 8:43 p.m.

Must've really dozed off. Kaylie has to be back from training by now ... wonder why she didn't come by?

He uses the toilet, brushes his teeth, then pockets his room key and exits the suite, heading for Kaylie's door.

She answers on the third knock, dressed in baggy sweat pants and a tee-shirt. She looks tired, the lust from twelve hours earlier completely gone.

"Hey. When did you get back?"

She breaks eye contact. "A few hours ago."

"Long day, huh? Are you hungry? I thought we could order up some dinner."

"I already ate."

"Oh ... kay. Want some company? We could rent a movie."

"I don't think so. I have studying to do and—"

"Kaylie, did I do something wrong?"

Her blue eyes flash anger. "Why did you have to show up Brian like that?"

Brian? "I wasn't—Kaylie, the guy's an asshole. He's on an ego trip. I know more about those Manta Rays than—"

"He's on an ego trip? What about you? You think the rest of us were impressed by that little stunt? Yes, David, you certainly know how to pilot a submersible better than the rest of us, but Brian's still heading this mission, not you!"

"I was hired as a trainer. He's been dissing me from the moment we met."

"You want respect, try earning it. Most of the trainees are ex-military. They've been in combat. They're not going to listen to some cocky, twenty-year-old college student. The maneuvers we'll be doing, the depths will be working in ... it's dangerous stuff. Maybe not to you, but to us—to me."

"So where does that leave us?"

"I'm sorry. Like I told you, I didn't come to Dubai looking for a boyfriend. I need the job."

"So that's it? This morning meant nothing?"

"It was impulsive. I'm sorry if I misled you. I think it's best if we just stayed friends."

She closes the door quietly, ending the conversation.

Friends? Friends! "Sure! Maybe we'll catch a camel race ... do lunch!" David kicks the door and storms off, his emotions caught in a maelstrom. Keying open his suite, he throws the key against the wall and paces the living room, cursing aloud, wishing he could somehow undo the entire day. "All you had to do was keep your mouth shut and everything would have been fine. But nooooo, you had to be a bigshot, didn't you? You had to show him up!"

He flops down on the leather sofa, pounding the cushions with both fists until his anger's spent.

Okay, asshole, now what? Think Suits'll accept an apology? Doubtful. He'll have you scrubbing toilets with your toothbrush before he let's you back into his training. Better to let him cool off a day. The two runts arrive in the morning. That'll help. Keep your mind on your business and your ego in check, and maybe things'll work themselves out.

Maybe.

David picks up the room service menu, leafs through its thick pages, then tosses it aside, too upset with himself to eat.

Go for a walk ... clear your head.

Locating the room key, he pockets it and leaves. He presses the elevator DOWN button then glances across the hall to Suite 3612.

He debates internally, then ignores the arriving elevator and knocks on the double doors. After a few moments Monty answers, dressed in Army fatigues and white sweat socks. "Junior? You look pissed. Either someone broke your heart, or you've got a raging case of blue balls."

"Both."

"Hah! Come on in. You can watch me crash and burn another submersible."

The Manta Ray simulator is set up on the Persian rug in front of the big plasma TV screen. The system, which consists of two foot pedals and two joysticks, is attached to a collapsible graphite frame. A control box is wired into the simulator and television.

Monty sits inside the contraption and pushes RESET.

The blank TV screen changes to a realistic ocean surface setting, the sky blue, the sea tranquil. "This is the beginner setting. I've yet to dive a hundred feet without losing control and dive-bombing like a pelican into the sea floor."

David watches as Monty surface dives, descending at an awkward angle. "Drop your starboard wing! Now ease back on the port-side pedal. Port-side! Left!"

"I know port from starboard! I just can't get the feel!"

The underwater image barrel rolls into a dizzying dive before smashing into a coral reef.

Monty lays his head back against the sofa in disgust. "Face it, I suck. It's like trying to lick your elbow."

David bends his arm, attempting the maneuver, his tongue coming up eight inches short.

"Should've seen me in the aquarium today after you left. Everyone got ten minutes in the sub. Me? I went down like an anchor. Captain Courageous had to take over or we'd still be lying on the bottom."

"I can help you."

"I doubt that."

"At least let me try. What else am I going to do tonight?"

"She really did a number on you, huh?"

"It was my fault. I screwed up this morning by showing off."

"Yeah, you did. Jumped on the hook like a horny blowfish."

"Yeah. Huh? Wait. What are you talking about?"

"Wake up, Junior. He baited you. These Psy Ops guys are all about head games. I'll bet my nutsack they moved that crane dead center of the tank just so you'd be tempted to jump it. Hell, I knew you'd go for it the moment you gunned the engines. But the dollar tip ... that was inspired. I laughed my ass off."

"He baited me?" David sits on the coffee table, his thoughts racing. "Am I really that stupid?"

"Stupid's a relative thing. To a Psy Ops officer, you're easier to read than a billboard."

"Why bait me? What do they want?"

"Not a clue. But be wary; they know you like the girl. If I'm bin Rashidi, I'm recruiting her just for that purpose. Hard to blame any man from jumping on that hook."

"Ahh, God-dammit!" David grabs a throw pillow and flings it across the living room. "Am I that shallow?"

"I believe the medical term is pussy-whipped."

"What now? What should I do?"

"I recommend heavy masturbation."

"I'm being serious."

"You really want my advice? Whatever your twenty-year-old instincts tell you to do, do the opposite. Next time they push you, don't push back. That'll force them to come to you at some point with whatever proposal they have in mind."

"Don't push back? Yeah, that makes sense. What about Kaylie?"

"I already gave you that advice. Look, it's not her fault. Maybe she's a helluva pilot. Who knows? More likely she's a tool. Don't feel bad; it's simply the way these arrogant assholes operate. They have more money than they can spend, so they amuse themselves by playing Allah."

"Screw 'em! We should quit!"

"Good idea. You quit. I need the money. When you're disabled and poor, pride takes a backseat to putting food on the table. Right now, I just need to make it through training."

"Then I better teach your poor, disabled ass how to fly. Here, give me a hand." David moves to the large plasma TV, lifting one end of its frame off its support hooks, Monty lifting the other end. "What are we doing? Pawn shop?"

"Set it on the coffee table."

They lower the TV, balancing it on its six-inch-wide frame. David repositions the simulator so the big screen is directly in front of the trainee.

"There. That should give you a more realistic view. Have a seat."

Monty sits down on the simulator cushion. "Not sure how this helps."

"Just watch and learn." David kicks off his shoes then scoots up close behind Monty, placing his longer legs next to his, his stocking feet atop Monty's shoes. His hands rest on top of the war vet's hands, which are poised around the two joysticks.

"Hey now …"

"This is how my dad taught me to get the feel."

"If you ask me, it feels a little too much like *Brokeback Mountain*. Do you have to spoon me from behind? In your present state of mind you're liable to—"

"Shut up and pay attention. Unlace your sneakers and tie them around my feet."

"Now you're scaring me." Monty complies, re-lacing his shoes, binding his feet atop David's.

David restarts the simulator. The image on-screen returns again to the surface, only this time the view encompasses Monty's entire visual perspective.

"Hey … that really does make a difference."

"Let me control the joysticks and pedals. Just keep your hands and feet over mine so you can feel how I maneuver the sub. Ready? Here we go."

David descends in a long shallow dive, keeping the view before them on an even keel.

"Okay, left pedal down, right leg up, joysticks compensate like so. Feel how the wings catch the water instead of slicing through?"

Monty grins, his limbs shaking with adrenaline. "Yeah, I can feel it now. Sort of like a bird."

"We shift back the other way, compensating with speed until the wings re-catch the sea. Now back again as we change to a steeper angle of descent, always keeping an eye on our sonar. The green blip is us, geology outlined in red, life forms in blue. Sonar AUTO sets distances according to visibility, but you can set it to MANUAL and adjust it as you see fit. Again. Left pedal down, right foot up. Adjust the pitch and yaw. Then right pedal down, left foot up. Feel the pattern? It's just a matter of getting the coordination."

"Yeah, I can feel it now!"

"Now we add speed. Speeds places torque on the wings, allowing us to make rapid turns. Ready? We turn and lean … "

The view moves into a dizzying 180-degree turn.

135

♥ ♥ ♥

IT IS JUST after midnight when David leaves Monty's suite. He heads down the hall, pausing at Kaylie's door, debating whether to offer her the same instruction he gave to Monty.

No, let it go. Tomorrow she'll see Monty piloting the sub like a pro and she'll be practically begging you for help. Order room service, rent a movie, get some sleep.

He continues on to his own room and keys open the suite—

—shocked to find Fiesal bin Rashidi and Brian Suits seated at the conference table.

The Arab smiles. "There he is, our young rebel. Still, a pilot with potential, don't you think, Captain?"

"Mustangs are useless unless they can be bridled. He'll never be a team player. Let him go. I don't need him."

Are they baiting me? "Look, I was out of line this morning. I apologize."

Brian Suits raises an eyebrow. "Humility from a Taylor? I don't buy it."

"I apologized. What else do you want from me?"

"Nothing. You're going home."

David's flesh prickles with alarm. "You're letting me go? What about the Megs?"

"The staff can handle them."

"Give me another chance! Let me prove to you I can train these pilots. You should see Monty. I worked with him all night."

"I don't give a—"

Bin Rashidi turns to the captain, speaking to him rapidly in Arabic.

Brian Suits argues, then relents. "Mr. bin Rashidi thinks you deserve another chance. I don't agree, but he's the boss. Grab Candidate Montgomery and be in the lobby in ten minutes."

"You mean now? Where are we going?"

"You'll know when we get there."

♥ ♥ ♥

THE PENINSULA IS situated on the Persian Gulf—a half million acres of leveled ground with no avenues or habitats, just several dozen waterside projects in the beginning stages of development.

A ten minute drive over sandy roads brings them to the bridge.

When completed in two years, the structure will be eight lanes of concrete and steel that will connect Dubai with its neighboring emirate. For now, the bridge is an elevated expanse of construction, an island of support beams and rebar that stretches from its inception point two thousand feet inland to concrete pilings that abruptly end a quarter mile out in the swirling, heavily trafficked waters of the Gulf.

Construction crews are working under powerful lights. Towering cranes are moving expanse beams into place. Barges, located a half mile out to sea, are pounding new pilings into the Gulf bedrock.

Bin Rashidi's limo is flagged to a stop by a police officer. An exchange with the driver and they are allowed to proceed to the shoreline.

Red and blue lights revolve atop police cars. An ambulance is parked off to the side next to a massive pick-up truck. Resting in the rear cargo bed is one of the Manta Rays.

Brian Suits exits the back of the limo, followed by David and Monty. Bin Rashidi remains in the car. The captain points to the end of the bridge a half mile away. "They lost a man tonight. Chinese, in his late thirties. Had a wife and kids. They want the body back."

"Geez ..."

"All this construction has churned up the bottom. Visibility's near zero. Currents are some of the worst in the region. The worker was weighted down with a riveting gun and assorted tools. He went in where the two causeways divide, so you got a little break. Locate the body, and we'll send down the divers."

David and Monty look at one another.

"You two have a problem with the mission?"

"Not at all." Monty smiles nervously. "I was just wondering why we're doing it in the middle of the night."

"Because the sun's not up." The captain's eyes flash anger. "The worker went in less than two hours ago."

"I see. And he'll be less dead if we fish him out now, as opposed to six hours from now, when we can actually see him?"

"Candidate, you'll be operating in less than two hundred feet of water, as opposed to the seven-thousand-foot depths required for the aquarium's mission. If two hundred feet scares you, I suggest you resign now and saves us the time in cutting you later."

"We're good to go, Captain," David interjects.

Ten minutes later the sub is in waist-deep water, six workers positioned along its wings, keeping it steady against the incoming tide. David and Monty, both wearing wetsuits, wade out, hoisting themselves into the open cockpit.

Brian Suits approaches as they strap in. "Activate your homing signal, Taylor, just in case we lose you."

"Yes, sir." David lowers the Lexan top and locks it into place, sealing them within the emergency pod. He offers a thumbs-up then accelerates forward, keeping the sub along the surface.

Monty grips the dashboard in front of him as they bounce along the chop, cutting across open water on an intercept course with the uncompleted bridge. "They're testing you. You know that, right?"

"I know. You nervous?"

"After four deployments in Iraq? Please. This is Disneyworld."

They reach the last pilings, the night reverberating with the sound of heavy machinery. David descends, enveloping the submersible in brown, murky space, the sub's exterior lights illuminating a swath of brown, flaky particles.

"Man, he wasn't kidding about the zero visibility. Monty, grab those head-phones and listen in on sonar. Go active and listen for a return ping that registers the bottom, or anything else in our path."

Monty flips a toggle switch on the sonar controls, pinging their surroundings with sound waves. "It's hard to hear anything. Sounds like I'm in a toilet bowl. Is that it?"

David steals a quick glance. "Those are pilings. The sub's diving on a forty-degree plane. You have to chart objects based on the horizon in yellow or you'll never know up from down. What's our depth?"

"Depth ... depth ... uh, one hundred thirty-seven feet. One forty—"

Crunnnnnch!

The Manta Ray heaves hard to starboard as David overcompensates for the sudden port-side impact. "I told you to watch the sonar!"

"I am watching! I just don't know what the hell I'm watching for!"

David slows the sub to a crawl. The ship's exterior lights illuminate a cement mixer, barely visible along the bottom.

"Guess we've arrived."

"How can you tell?"

"Cement mixers don't float." David guides them along a parallel course to the bridge, remaining a good twenty feet from the unseen pilings. "This sucks. I can't see shit."

"Funny. All I see is shit. This is a fool's errand, you know. We might as well be searching for Jimmy Hoffa. In fact, I think we just—"

—the port-side wing suddenly heaves up and over their heads, the current flipping the Manta Ray upside-down, driving the craft into a jungle of unseen concrete bridge supports. The unrelenting river of muck pushes them deeper. David is unsure how to react, afraid to muster the propulsion necessary to roll the sub right-side up lest he end up burying them nose-first in the mud.

As quickly as the thought passes they are slammed sideways, the Manta Ray's port-side wing driven into the muddy bottom, the vessel pushed backwards until its belly is bashed against an immovable object, wedged in by the current.

For several terrifying moments they say nothing, suspended sideways and nearly upside down in the cockpit, David below Monty, both men held in their seats by their harnesses.

The current rocks the sub like a brown churning snowstorm.

"Monty, you alright?"

"Can't breathe! Gonna be sick."

"No! Don't be sick!" David strains to reach the temperature controls, blasting them both with waves of cold air. "Better?"

"No." Monty leans forward and retches, the vomit barely missing David as it splatters the sonar controls with chunks of tortillas and refried beans.

"Ugh!" David pulls his wetsuit collar up over his nose, gaging at the overpowering stench. "What is wrong with you?"

Monty spits out remnants. "I'm hanging upside down, being buried alive in a mud storm. Do something quick before I really wig out."

Pressing down on his right foot, David eases back on the left joystick, rocking the sub forward as he fights to level them out, and succeeding, only to smash the sub nose-first into a concrete piling.

"What the hell was that?"

"A piling! I can't see where the hell we are. Your damn dinner's covering my sonar!"

Monty wipes it clean with his rubber sleeve. "Here! Take the headphones and get us topside!"

"I can't. We're somewhere beneath the bridge. Sonar can't distinguish the muddy current from the pilings."

"Then jettison the chassis, the escape pod will float us to the surface."

"No way. Even if I did, we'd still be lucky to make it out alive."

Monty begins hyperventilating. "David, I've never been claustrophobic, but I'm not doing real well in my skin right now. Do something soon, or I'm gone."

"Shut up and let me think!" David peers outside, his lights reflecting the mud

139

blizzard, his depth gauge steady at 139 feet. He shuts off the lights, casting them in pitch darkness, the orange glow of the controls all that is visible.

David can hear Monty's labored breaths. The claustrophobia becomes contagious, the smell in the cockpit nauseating, tempting him to pop open the cockpit and simply wash their lives into oblivion—

—and then his eyes adjust and he can see out the night vision glass, discerning a faint pattern before him.

Gently, he presses down with both feet, adjusting his course to starboard, the current still pushing him to port. No matter, the Manta Ray is moving forward, slipping between two sets of pilings one row at a time, the current increasing, forcing him to adjust his pitch. *Keep your nose down, don't let it flip you over again ...*

And then they're free!

David punches both feet to the pedals and ascends in a long arching turn—

—plowing the sub upside down into the muddy sea floor!

The suddenness of the unexpected impact releases waves of panic. David struggles to breathe, his body bathed in sweat. He rips open the wetsuit zipper, fighting to reason.

Asshole, you were upside down! You never checked your horizon!

"Monty? Dude, you alright?"

Jason Montgomery hangs suspended from his harness, unconscious.

Okay ... remember what dad always told you to do when you're in trouble ... stop and think! Take a breath and analyze the situation. You're buried upside down in mud. Pull up on the joysticks and you go deeper. Push down and—

David taps the right foot pedal and pushes down on his joysticks, rolling the sub right-side up. He checks the sonar again, verifies he's indeed right-side up and level, then he slowly ascends the sub.

Seconds later, he is rewarded by a tapestry of stars and a symphony of construction noises, and, looking around, is surprised to find they are on the opposite side of the bridge from where they started. Remaining on the surface, he accelerates around the structure then races back to shore, nudging Monty awake.

"You okay?"

Monty nods, grateful to be on the surface. "I've had worse first dates. Did you find the Chinese guy?"

"Yeah. He's on his way back to Beijing by way of the EAC."

"EAC?"

"Eastern Australian Current. It was a joke. The corpse can rot on the bottom for all I care."

David beaches the craft then pops the cockpit, the brisk fresh air invigorating. They climb out, washing off as Captain Suits watches from the shoreline, observing everything.

"Sorry, Captain. We looked everywhere, but we couldn't find the body."

"There was no body. This was a test to see if you could navigate in zero visibility under difficult circumstances. I was tracking you the entire time and you failed miserably, hotshot. You and your protégé here couldn't coordinate your tasks or find your way in a hundred feet of water. If this had been the abyss, you'd be dead. Maybe now you know what I mean by pleasure cruising."

He's right. Guess I'm the real asshole. David looks up at the crew-cut veteran with a newfound respect. "I owe you an apology. I became disoriented and panicked. It won't happen again ... sir."

Brian Suits nods. "The two of you stink like a Mexican banquet. Get your asses in the back of the pick-up truck. You can ride back to the aquarium with the sub."

They head for the vehicle, the staff positioning the Manta Ray in the cab.

"Taylor!"

"Yes, sir?"

"Be at training at ten o'clock sharp. And so help me God, if you ever challenge me again, I'll rip your head off and shit down your neck."

17

Jonas and Terry Taylor sit together at one end of the conference table, watching the short young man with the white-blonde hair unpack his briefcase and carefully lay out three thick manila folders.

"Mr. and Mrs. Taylor, my name is Adam Wooten. I'm the underwriter the insurance company has assigned to these pending claims."

"You seem kind of young," Jonas remarks.

"Yes, sir. Anyway, the insurance company has given me the task of determining if the recent deaths suffered at the Institute are covered under your workers' compensation policy. If we look at the first claim—"

"By young, I meant inexperienced," Jonas continues. "There's a lot at stake. I just want to make sure you have the same qualifications as Earl Fischl. Earl sold us our policy five years ago and kept close tabs on our business. If Earl said we were covered, we were covered. A real shame he had to move back to Ottawa— something about starting up a web-game company. Good man, Earl ... not that you're not. It's just that—"

"With all due respect to my predecessor, it's my responsibility to determine if the risks associated with your organization have exceeded the insurance company's responsibilities. You may feel I'm too young, you may not agree with my decisions, but I assure you, those decisions will stand."

Jonas is about to respond when Terry grips his arm. "Jonas, let the man finish before you rake him over the coals." She smiles. "Go on, Mr. Wooten."

"Uh, yes. Thank you." The underwriter opens the first folder. "Now, in regards to the drowning of Mr. Moretti, I've determined the claim is covered by your workers' compensation policy."

Jonas nods to his wife.

"As for the college student who was ... eaten, Mr. Francis was a volunteer, and he did sign a waiver form which covered accidental death or dismemberment. After careful consideration, I've determined the deceased's death would fall under your General Liability Umbrella policy. We'll cover the settlement with the family, as well as the defense costs."

Jonas's squeezes his wife's hand beneath the table. "You're doing a helluva job, son. And hey, if you ever want to bring your family down to see one of the shows—"

"I'm not quite done. The insurance company will cover the losses, but we will not be renewing your policy. I'm giving you a thirty-day notice."

Terry releases her husband's hand. "You're canceling our policy? Do you know how much your premiums have cost us over the years? Cancel us now and we can't reopen."

Wooten packs his files into his briefcase. "I'm sorry."

"Sorry? You're putting us out of business, and all you have to say is sorry?"

"Terry, take it easy—"

"Before this accident, we had zero claims. Not even a burn from someone spilling their coffee. Still, we paid you millions of dollars and—"

"Ma'am, you have my sympathies, but these animals are simply too dangerous to continue to insure under present circumstances. Mr. Moretti's death could have been worse. You almost lost a truck crane and its driver. Had that vehicle fallen in the aquarium, the losses would have been catastrophic. Then there's Angel. I'm not convinced those steel doors can hold her much longer."

"Now you're an engineer?"

"No, ma'am, but I've had three engineers look at the structural loads. If that monster escaped again, well, she could bankrupt both our businesses."

"Nonsense! You're just like the rest of the damn insurance companies; you'll keep a policy active until the holder actually needs it, then you run for the hills when it's time to collect. It's all about the profit margin."

"No, Mrs. Taylor. It's about the risk. Penning a fifty-ton monster that eats people in an aquarium that seats fifteen thousand potential meals is risky business. Since there's no way to actually control the shark—"

"What if there was?" Jonas motions his wife to sit. "What if I told you I have a team of scientists who, at this very moment, are designing a neural implant that will allow us to control Angel's behavior."

"A neural implant?" Adam Wooten stops packing his briefcase. "You mean ... like in her brain?"

"You got it."

"Well, I don't know. Has it been tested?"

"Absolutely. Same design as the device created by the Pentagon. They've been using neural implants to turn sharks into stealth spies for years. A series of electrodes would be embedded directly into Angel's brain. Using a radio signal from a laptop, we'll be able to stimulate the Meg's directional olfactory center, causing her to move in any direction we desire. Better yet, the implant allows us to monitor her central and autonomic nervous system. We can tell when Angel is agitated and even calm her down by tapping into her sleep functions."

The insurance underwriter takes out a legal pad. Terry and Jonas wait while he jots down notes and takes out a pocket calculator. "If you can prove this device actually works, then I'd be willing to renew your policy at an adjusted premium."

Terry's expression darkens. "What kind of increase are we talking about?"

"Twenty percent."

"You little shit, I should feed you to Angel myself!"

"Terry, easy." Jonas smiles at the insurance agent, who has gone deathly pale. "Adam, if we're removing the risk, then why would you raise our premiums?"

"Premiums always go up after claims are made—"

"—unless the risk is reduced. Not only have we reduced our juvy population by sixty percent, but we now have a means of keeping our big girl calm. That's significant progress on any slide rule, wouldn't you say?"

"Well ... yes."

"Forget him, Jonas." Terry says. "At what we've been paying in premiums, I bet one of his competitors would bend over backwards to get our business."

"Fine, okay. No raise in premiums, if the device actually works."

"Surgery's scheduled at the end of the week. I'll call you when we're ready for a demonstration. Meanwhile, the policy remains intact. Agreed?"

"Agreed. For now. But I'll be here when you reopen." Adam Wooten gathers his belongings. He hastily shakes Jonas's hand, avoiding Terry's burning eyes, and exits the conference room.

Jonas turns back to his wife. "That went well, don't you think?"

"I think you're insane, that's what I think. How the hell are you going to implant an electronic device inside Angel's brain?"

"I don't know. Carefully?"

⩔   ⩔   ⩔

DR. BRENT NICHOLS finishes downloading the animation program into the computer work station then turns the monitor to face the Taylors, Mac, Fran Rizzuto and Dr. Stelzer. "Okay, I know this seems like *Mission Impossible*, but keep in mind I've performed more than a dozen of these operations on hammerheads and nurse sharks, and working on a specimen the size of Angel is actually easier in many ways."

Mac scoffs. "Easier almost ate me a few days ago. Nothing about this monster ever goes easy."

"I was referring to the actual surgery. A hammerhead's brain is the size of two fingers; Angel's brain is the size of a man. Once we complete the incisions, we're in and out in twenty to thirty minutes tops."

"And where exactly is this surgery going to take place," Terry asks.

"That's the best part. The entire procedure will be done remotely, from right here in the lab. All we have to do is attach a benthic chamber equipped with a da Vinci surgical unit to Angel's skull. Here, let me show you."

Dr. Nichols types in a few commands, starting the animation program.

A computer graphic featuring an overhead view of the canal appears on screen. Angel is situated just inside the channel's porous steel doors, a boat anchored outside the underwater barrier. Animated workers lower a series of hoses to divers, who swim them down to the doors.

"Step One will be to sedate our patient. This will be accomplished by pumping high doses of tricaine methanesulfonate from the boat directly into the canal by way of the door's pores. Angel will ingest the anesthetic and slowly lose consciousness. Once asleep, she should drift to the bottom of the canal where the combination of her enormous pectoral fins and the close confines of the canal should keep her propped fairly upright. Divers will then insert a tube into her mouth, pumping in sea water and more anesthetic so she can breathe."

Dr. Nichols pauses, allowing the animation to catch up with his presentation.

"Step Two is the actual surgery. The benthic chamber shown here is a six-by-eight-foot-wide, self-contained surgical chamber that will be weighted down and sunk, then bolted in position atop Angel's head. Once it's sealed in place, the chamber will be pumped free of water and Dr. Stelzer and I will perform the procedure, using robotics."

He opens a cardboard box, removing a Y-shaped device about the size of a violin from its Styrofoam protective casing. Electrodes protrude from all sides of the pliable, wafer-thin implant. "This is the neurotransmitter. It's actually a fairly simple device, essentially a series of electrodes and microprocessors that receive their instructions from a laptop. The program's signals are sent by way of a radio signal to an antenna that will be attached to Angel's dorsal fin. The antenna relays the signal to the Megalodon's brain, stimulating the sensory areas desired. Stimulate the right side of her olfactory center and she moves right. The left and she goes left. Sharks don't reason; they're conditioned to respond to any sensory stimulus. It's a phantom sensation, but she can't tell the difference."

Mac examines the device. "I get it. You're turning Angel into a Pavlov dog. Is that it, Doc?"

"More or less. But DARPA's advances have gone far beyond the olfactory center. For instance, we've learned that a shark's ampullae of Lorenzini uses the earth's magnetic field like a compass. It's no doubt how Angel found her way back to the lagoon after being gone for so many years. If she ever escaped again, we could use this device to lead her right back to the lagoon without her even knowing it."

"Let's go back to the antenna," Jonas says. "I assume that's not being attached remotely."

"No. The job requires two divers." Dr. Nichols offers a nervous smile. "I was hoping you and your friend here could take care of that little chore while Dr. Stelzer and I are operating."

Mac exhales. "So let me get this straight: While you and Jon here are playing with joysticks and sipping piña coladas, Jonas and I will be scuba diving inside the canal, bolting a transmitter onto you-know-who's dorsal fin."

"Second dorsal fin, actually. The primary dorsal's too thick to get through. But no worries, Angel will be completely sedated. It'll be no more dangerous than changing a tire."

"Changing a tire. Right. While the car's doing sixty miles an hour."

Dubai Land
Dubai, United Arab Emirates

David is alone in the cockpit, lost in a black sea so vast it has no up or down, no beginning or end. He jams the foot pedals to the floor, yet nothing happens. He works the joysticks and gets no response. The powerless sub continues to drift sideways in the ceaseless current, the emptiness of the void shrinking his existence, the cockpit closing in, his air supply diminishing. Fear brings with it paralysis, his limbs become numb. As powerless as the sub.

Breathe ... can't breathe!

Death's icy fingers tingle his flesh even as its soothing weight sinks him deeper into the abyss.

Sleep ... mustn't sleep. Sleep and you won't wake up ...
So tired ... don't fight it ... just sleep ...
No!

The instinct to survive battles the paralysis, his strength of will shaking his body, forcing a single finger to flex, the effort draining yet encouraging. Over and again, flex the finger, circulate the blood, now move the hand! Smash it, roll it, feel the pain. Pain is sobering. Pain is life! Now the arm. Beat it against the lifeless leg. Wake the limb, keep smashing it until the pain is solid—

—until it awakens you.

Wake up, David! Wake up and breathe!

☗ ☗ ☗

"Ahhhhhhhh!"

David's face rolls off the suffocating, goose-down pillow, gasping a life-giving breath. His left arm is numb and asleep, his right, tingling with pins and needles. For several moments he just lies in bed and breathes, staring at the ceiling, exhausted and shaken—

—until he realizes someone is knocking on his door.

He rolls off the bed, staggering into the living room. The sun is barely up, but he has no right to be, not after last night—a night that ended mere hours ago. It was after five a.m. when his head had finally hit the pillow, his exhausted body sinking like lead sand.

Another knock. More urgent.

"Alright, I'm coming!" David yanks open the door, his irritation rising.

It is a tall man, the one he had seen days ago, the one assisting the woman orchestrating the transportation of the giant crate. He's wearing jeans and a white lab coat, a black tee-shirt peeking through, the words *Sicilian Taurus* embroidered across his barrel chest. "Dr. Becker needs you now. Get dressed and come with me!"

"Who the hell is Dr. Becker?"

"Barbara Becker. Director of marine biology." The big man shoves David back inside. "Get your clothes. We have to hurry!"

"Why? What's the rush?"

"The runts have arrived. We have them in the tanks, but they're dying."

☗ ☗ ☗

THE CAR IS waiting for them outside the lobby. The lanky assistant climbs in back, David scooting in after him, and the vehicle accelerates away before he slams the door shut.

"When did they get here?"

"Twenty minutes ago. The biologists from your institute, they knew something was wrong on the cargo plane. I'm Michael Eason. Dr. Becker recruited me from Scripps. Did you know your father's a legend there?"

David's retort is stifled as he grabs for the door handle, the car making a sharp right turn before the driver slams on its brakes.

"Come on!" Eason climbs out from the back seat, David right behind him, and the two of them jog past the aquarium's loading dock and down a covered path that leads to a secured entrance way. The tall biologist swipes his magnetic security card, causing the locks to open. He pushes the gate back and they enter.

The hydraulic hum of generators fills a basement corridor lined with pipes. They hurry down a double-wide avenue, passing alcoves numbered T-7, T-5, T-3 on the left, and T-6 and T-4 on the right. They stop at the T-2 service elevator, which opens immediately, and transports them up to the seventh floor.

The lift doors open, revealing the deck of the 80-million-gallon tank. Dr. Becker is supervising her team of six, three members of the Tanaka Institute among them. The fifty-year-old dishwater blonde sees David and signals him over to the side of the tank.

"I'm Barbara Becker. The Megs arrived in shock. This one swam half a length and sank."

David looks down into the crystal clear water. Lying on the bottom, seventy feet below the surface, is the Megalodon runt known as Ashley. A team of divers is manipulating the twenty-five-foot shark into a canvass harness. The bridle is attached to cables that rise out of the tank to a motorized cart located on a circular track suspended from the ceiling.

Dr. Becker's walkie-talkie squawks to life. "She's in. Start the winch!"

Becker signals to an assistant, who activates the motorized cart. The device starts up, retracting cable as it drags the ten-thousand-pound juvenile Meg along its circular route at two knots.

One of the institute's scientists, an intimidating bald-headed man with a braided goatee, approaches David. "Steve Akehurst. We worked together a few years back."

"I remember. What happened?"

"Bad luck is what happened. Belle and Lizzy forced us to transport the runts before they became acclimated to swimming in tight quarters. Six hours into the ride Mary Kate's vitals bottomed out, Ashley's an hour later. We shot 'em up with enough adrenaline to jump-start a truck, but their swimming remained erratic. At one point I had to climb inside the MLST with Ashley and jam a water jet into her mouth just to keep her breathing."

Barbara Becker shouts into her walkie-talkie, "Is she responding?"

"Gills are moving, but not on their own. Vitals haven't changed. Pulse still hovering around twenty beats a minute. No movement from her caudal fin. She's dying."

"Increase the speed to five knots." Dr. Becker turns to David and Dr. Akehurst. "If you two have any bright ideas, now would be the time to share them."

"We can't give her any more meds or she'll O.D.," Akehurst says. "Only thing you can do is keep water circulating through her gills and hope she comes out of it."

"Mr. Taylor?"

"Shock her system."

"How?"

"Defibrillators. As many as you can get. We put her in the ER pool, then flip her over on her back, inducing sleep. Then we shock the shit out of her until the arrhythmia's terminated and her body reestablishes its natural pacemaker."

"Akehurst?"

"It's never been done, but with two of them in shock its worth a try, at least on one runt."

Dr. Becker takes out her cell phone. "This is Becker. Contact the medical center. I need as many defibrillators as they have loaded into an ambulance, along with a tech who knows what the hell he's doing, and bring them to T-2's upper deck ASAP!"

☙ ☙ ☙

THE LISTLESS, FIVE-TON albino shark is dragged into the shallow medical pool located at the far end of the aquarium. Six scuba divers emerge from the tank with her, quickly detaching the harness cables, then re-hooking the left cables to the right side of the harness.

"Go!"

The cable retracts, the harness twisting, flipping the juvenile predator onto her back with a walloping splash. She sinks, belly up, to the bottom of the twelve-foot pool as divers and medical staff set into motion around her like a pit crew.

The medical pool is drained so that Ashley's belly remains above the waterline.

A padded rubber hose is placed carefully into the Meg's open mouth, sending a stream of foamy salt water gushing into her orifice and out her gill slits, allowing her to breathe.

Six pairs of defibrillator paddles are laid in place along the creature's chest cavity just above the pectoral fins and weighted down by dive belts. Wires from the paddles stretch across the deck to emergency carts stacked with the defibrillator power packs.

Miguel Maximiliano Franco, a cardiologist from Argentina, finishes charging the devices. "This has to be done simultaneously. I need four more hands."

Dr. Becker turns to David. "You and Dr. Akehurst, give Dr. Franco a hand. Michael, I want you monitoring the Meg's vitals. Everyone else, clear the pool. Make sure no one's standing in water."

The divers exit the ER pool, retreating to a dry landing.

Dr. Franco assigns David and Dr. Akehurst two defibrillator power switches, taking the last two himself. "Alright, gentlemen, I'm going to say: 'One, two, three.' On 'three' we flip the switch. Everyone clear?"

"Flip it on three. Got it."

"Divers clear. Personnel clear." The Medical tech looks at Dr. Becker, who nods. "Here we go. One ... two ... three!"

Waves of electricity jolt the ten-thousand-pound creature, sending ripples down its stark white abdomen, causing its pectoral fins and tail to jump as the paddles leapfrog off its chest.

"Got a beat ... shit. Lost it! Hit her again on my count. One ... two ... three!"

The Megalodon spasms, her tail curling up reflexively.

"Got a beat ... pulse is stronger, but it's still fading to 123 ... 117 ... 113. We've got to roll her back over!"

"Flood the medical pool!" Dr. Becker orders.

The pumps kick in, raising the water level, the Megalodon with it. Divers jump back into the pool, positioning themselves along the deck-side of the unconscious predator, close to her left pectoral fin. As the harness cables snap to attention, the men push, their combined efforts succeeding in rolling the twenty-five-foot shark right-side up.

Ashley greets her rescuers with a slap of her caudal fin.

"Ninety-three ... ninety-four ... pulse holding steady!" Michael Eason sits on the edge of the deck close to the Meg's gray-blue eye. "Her eye just rolled forward; I think she's coming out of it!"

David high-five's Dr. Akehurst then turns to the ER pool, his smile instantly fading. "Look out!"

Her central nervous system coursing with adrenaline, Ashley lurches her enormous head sideways, her telltale snout rising in a primordial bite reflex—

—snatching the nearest prey—Michael Eason—who is frozen like a deer in headlights, the scream caught in his throat as the Meg's teeth sink deeper into his chest cavity, puncturing his lungs as his ribcage splits into bone fragments and his spinal column is pulverized.

A fountain of blood spouts out of the dead man's mouth—

—scattering the divers as they scramble out of the medical pool for safety!

Still gripping her squirming prey in her mouth, Ashley whips her tail, sending great arching swashes of water in every direction, the action propelling her girth over the edge of the shallow med pool and into the main aquarium.

Meg circles underwater, becoming acquainted with the confines of her new home, oblivious to the shrieks and catcalls of her human audience. Every pass or two she shakes the bleeding corpse in her jaws like a dog shakes an old towel. Finally, she bites down through the yielding flesh and swallows Michael Eason's torso, the arms and legs falling away.

Barbara Becker collapses to her knees on the wet deck tiles, her chest convulsing in sobs. Her staff—in shock themselves—leave her alone, until one brave soul approaches with a walkie-talkie.

"Dr. Becker, are you there? Dr. Becker, it's Dr. Jivani in T-10."

She takes the communication device, fighting to regain her composure. "Go ahead, Karim."

"I'm sorry, Dr. Becker. We tried everything. The Megalodon juvenile … it's dead."

18

The morning is overcast and gray, the air a chilly fifty-six degrees. Virgil Carmen stands just inside the open cabin in the stern of the forty-two-foot dive boat, trying not to appear nervous to the two men in wetsuits who are checking their scuba equipment on the tank racks.

Fran Rizzuto is with the boat captain in the flybridge, her walkie-talkie positioned on her jacket close to her right shoulder, her cell phone in her left breast pocket. The boat is moving south along the coast at fifteen knots, the empty arena on the eastern horizon, the rectangular outline of barbed wire that marks the canal just coming into view.

"Easy, Captain, nice and easy. Let's not agitate her any more than we have to."

The captain pulls back on the twin throttles, dropping his speed to three knots as he approaches the canal.

Virgil covers his nose as plumes of blue exhaust kick up from the twin 385-horsepower Cat engines. Swells lift and drop the boat, pushing them ever closer to the barbed wire coil barrier less than ninety feet away.

The captain reverses his engines, backing them toward the gated underwater entrance.

Beyond the barbed wire, a resounding *slap* echoes across the surface—a warning from the agitated predator's caudal fin.

Virgil's heart races. Sweat pours down both sides of his face.

Sixty feet ... fifty! That's close enough!

"Weigh anchor." Fran's voice startles him. He watches as the anchor line feeds out over the side, securing their position just outside the submerged steel doors.

The engines are silenced. Waves lap at the swaying fiberglass hull.

A deep *boom,* like distant thunder, rattles his bones.

The two divers look at one another. Ed Hendricks smiles nervously at his companion, Carlos Salinas. "She's just letting us know we're uninvited guests."

"I hope she doesn't like Mexican food."

Fran climbs down from the flybridge. "You boys ready? Let's check your communicators."

The two men secure their full-face dive masks to their heads. "Testing. Can you read us?"

Fran adjusts the volume on the walkie-talkie. "Loud and clear. Virgil, start the pump."

Bolted to the floor of the dive cabin is a hydraulic pump with an eight-inch intake hose and matching outflow, all connected to a seventy-five-pound slurry feed bucket. Virgil slips a gas mask over his face as he empties a fifty-pound bag of Finquel MS-222 into the bucket. He adds water to the white powdery anesthetic, mixes the elixir with an oar, then starts the machine.

The two divers secure their air tanks and buoyancy control vests, adjust their weight belts, then carry their fins down to the swim platform. Sitting on the edge, they slip their feet into their fins, the rolling Pacific rocking them from side to side.

Fran unwinds slack from the rubber outflow hose and walks it out to the divers. With a thumbs-up, the two men ease themselves into the water and submerge, dragging the length of hose with them.

Ed Hendricks, big and muscular, sucks in shallow breaths as he kicks toward the steel barrier looming thirty feet ahead. Married with a teenage daughter getting ready to graduate from high school, Hendricks is an experienced diver who has open dived with great whites off the coast of South Africa. He has never feared the water, until now.

The two divers level out at sixty feet then slowly begin swimming to the barrier, their hearts racing faster as the doors loom into view. Twenty feet away, Hendricks can see through the array of pores ventilating the face of the algae-covered steel doors, the Pacific blue peeking through—

—suddenly brightening to an ivory white!

"Jesus, Mary and Joseph!" Carlos's voice rattles in his ears as Angel rises into view from behind the massive barrier, her presence causing both divers to hover in their tracks.

"Ed ... I can't do this!"

"Stay calm."

"I can't!"

"Carlos, she can feel your pulse racing. She can sense everything. Slow and easy movements. Pass me the hose, and I'll do the dirty work. Frannie, can you hear me?"

"Yes, Ed."

"Start the anesthetic."

A twenty-second delay, then the hose jumps to life, becoming rigid as a milky-white substance pours out from its open end.

Securing the hose beneath his right armpit, gripping it tightly with both hands, Ed swims to the door, aiming for a line of holes close to Angel's mouth.

Whump!

The resounding wallop seems to penetrate to his bones. Hendricks kicks harder, his muscles like lead as he reaches the door, its surface slick with seaweed. Each vent hole varies in size, from basketball-size pores to the occasional oval hole, large enough for a man's shoulders to squeeze through.

Avoiding the larger holes, he peeks through a smaller orifice—

—as a white blur bashes against the steel facing to his left, an SUV-size snout momentarily widening the six-inch gap between the two sealed doors.

The brain-rattling impact nearly sends Hendricks into shock! In a state of panic, he releases the hose and swims away—

—colliding with Carlos. "Easy, amigo."

"D—Damn, she's big!"

Carlos pulls up slack on the hose until he retrieves its gushing end. "We'll do this together, okay?"

"Okay."

They swim the hose back to the door, shoving the free end into one of the holes.

Angel presses her snout against the enclosure, the seventy-four-foot shark enraged at the presence of the two seal-like creatures. Moving back and forth along the door, the caged animal rubs her nose raw against the algae-coated steel panels—

—her nostrils suddenly inhaling an alien, pungent scent. Her movements slow, her jaws going slack as the incoming current pushes a steady stream of the alluring chemical into her open mouth.

The pounding slows, then stops.

Angel hovers in sixty feet of water, her snout pressed against the doors. Her caudal fin slows, churning the sea in long, heavy strokes.

Then the tail stops moving, and the big female sinks.

The two divers descend with her, relocating the hose as they follow her to the bottom. She lands upright on her pectoral fins, her head remaining poised against the steel door eighty-seven feet below the surface, her lighter tail reaching up into the shallows at a thirty-degree angle.

"She's out! Stand by!" Ed locates the nearest large, oval pore and peeks in at the sleeping behemoth. His confidence returning, he unhooks his BCD vest and pushes it through the hole, following his air tank inside the canal.

Carlos feeds him the tube through another pore. Ed pulls the slack through then gently swims toward the cavernous mouth, now hanging open like a jagged crevice in a mountainside. Slowly. Carefully, he eases the gushing hose inside the slack jaw between two lower side teeth, his pulse pounding.

Hendricks remains by the mouth an excruciating forty seconds longer until the milky-white substance begins bleeding out of the Megalodon's fluttering gill slits.

Leaving the hose in place, he swims forward to Angel's eye—

—which has rolled back into the skull, only the bloodshot white sclera showing. *Thank you, God.* "One fifty-ton monster, sleeping like a lamb. Hey, Frannie, you tell Jonas I want a raise!"

▼ ▼ ▼

JONAS HEARS THE message in his ear as he, Mac, and six staff members lower his daughter's twenty-one-foot, fifteen-hundred-pound sports utility ski boat from its portable winch onto a skiff that angles from the lagoon's eastern sea wall down into the water. Resting in the speedboat's open bow is the benthic surgical chamber: a domed, clear-acrylic, rectangular affair the approximate size of two coffins positioned side by side. Next to the device, lying on one of the seats is a porous canvass tool bag containing the components for the Meg's relay antenna.

Fran's voice squawks over Jonas's earpiece, "J.T., the patient's ready."

"On our way." Jonas and Mac climb into the speed boat, chosen for its 250-horsepower EFI outboard, capable of hitting speeds of up to 70 miles an hour.

Mac guns the engine and they're off, the boat racing across the lagoon into the canal, both men wearing wetsuits and scuba gear.

The boat slows as they approach the barbed wire barrier. Mac cuts the engine, allowing them to drift, the two men looking over the side at the pale object resting off the bottom.

Mac looks around. "Potential problem: We can't drop anchor and we can't let the boat drift while we're down there."

Jonas nods. "Okay. You stay with the boat. I can handle this myself."

"Agreed."

"Agreed? Really? No argument?"

"Hey, if you say you can handle it, you can handle it. Who am I to question your ability?"

Both men jump in their seats as a diver surfaces close by. Hendricks yells at them through his mask's communication device. "Get that goddam surgical thing-a-ma-jig in the water now, before I shit my wetsuit!"

Jonas straps his dive mask and flippers on then quietly lowers himself over the side. Mac hands him his tool bag, waits until Jonas has secured it around his waist, and then eases the acrylic chamber overboard into the two divers' hands.

The contraption is open along the bottom, its sides outfitted with a thick, pliable rubber housing and snag bolts and its clear, domed interior supporting three, pencil-thin cameras along with a series of retractable robotic surgical arms, one of which is gripping the neural implant. Attached to one end of the rectangular housing is a small hydraulic pump.

The weight of the object causes it to flip over as it sinks. Jonas and Hendricks each grab an end, guiding it down sixty-seven feet—

—moving it into place atop the sleeping Megalodon's massive skull.

▼ ▼ ▼

LESS THAN A mile away, images from the chamber's three exterior cameras appear over three computer screens located in the Tanaka Institute's lab. Dr. Jonathan Stelzer monitors the images, while Dr. Brent Nichols sits at the primary control station of the da Vinci Surgical System, both hands resting in two hand controls fitted with finger-hole sleeves. Leaning forward, he looks through a three-dimensional view-master that allows him to zoom in or pull back on any of the surgical chamber's three cameras.

"Gentlemen, can you hear me?"

"Go ahead," Jonas replies, tension in his voice.

"There are two bumps located atop the Meg's skull, the supraorbital crests. Position the chamber so it rests dead-center of these two processes, with the front end located approximately six feet behind the tip of the snout."

"Did you have to say dead-center?"

"Sorry."

"Okay, we're in position."

"Excellent. Lock her down."

Jonas and Hendricks press down on the chamber so its rubber housing is squeezed securely against Angel's thick albino hide. Snag bolts, made of bio-degradable plastic, puncture the skin, drawing whiffs of blood as they draw the chamber in tighter, ensuring a watertight seal.

"You sure she can't feel this?"

"Absolutely sure. Mr. Hendricks, start draining the chamber. Jonas, you have your own work to do."

Jonas offers Hendricks a thumbs-up before swimming past the gills and dorsal fin, ascending along Angel's torso toward the immense half-moon-shaped tail, now angled toward the surface.

Ed Hendricks activates the hydraulic pump, which quickly drains the acrylic chamber. A few seconds pass, then he watches in amazement as one of the surgical arms jumps to life, a whirring, ten-inch buzz saw that extends down from the appendage, its teeth carving a razor-thin, longitudinal incision deep into the alabaster hide—

—while a second surgical device, equipped with a tiny camera and light, rinses off the bleeding wound with saltwater. The buzz saw completes the sixty-inch cut then realigns itself, beginning a second incision six feet away, parallel to the first.

Ⅴ　Ⅴ　Ⅴ

AIDED BY THE current, Jonas glides past the towering dorsal fin. Then, kicking hard, he ascends another twenty feet before arriving at the Megalodon's powerful caudal keel. The secondary dorsal fin is located just forward of the muscular tail section—an equilateral triangle of flesh the size of a small child. Straddling Angel's back, Jonas removes the antenna from his tool bag. The cylinder, approximately three feet long, is attached to an eight-inch-square, rubber faceplate, its four holes holding four plastic screws. Jonas fishes out his underwater drill, clips it to his weight belt, then lines the faceplate up against the surface of the small dorsal fin. Pressing the Phillips' head screw bit to the first screw head, he squeezes the trigger.

But instead of puncturing the skin, the screw chews into the thick hide, twisting the tough muscle—

—the pain causing the half-moon-shaped tail to suddenly flick!

Jonas stops the drill, his heart beating so hard in his chest that he fears he's about to go into cardiac arrest. "Hey, Dr. Nichols ... small problem here."

"I'm a little busy, Jonas. Can you handle it?"

"Yeah, sure. Sorry to disturb you, but Angel's reacting to the faceplate."

"Define reacting?"

"Her tail's flicking. The screw twisted up under her skin when I used the drill. She can feel it, and she doesn't like it. Suggestions?"

"Don't use the drill. Use a screwdriver."

Jonas searches his tool bag, his limbs quivering. "Don't have one. Mac?"

"Stand by, I can see your air bubbles. I'll toss one overboard."

∇ ∇ ∇

VIRGIL CARMEN WATCHES as the slurry bucket drains the last of the chalky anesthetic into the hydraulic pump. Returning to the supply rack, he retrieves another fifty-pound bag of tricaine methanesulfonate, shocked to discover it's the last bag on the shelf.

"Hey, Fran. I'm on the last bag of Finquel."

Fran Rizzuto climbs down from her perch. "That's impossible. We brought twice the dosage needed. How could you be out?"

"How can I be out?" Virgil tears open the last bag and dumps the powder into the slurry bucket. "Maybe someone miscalculated."

Fran searches the shelves then goes below, dragging out another large bag, this one marked QS.

"Quinaldine sulfate? Frannie, are you crazy? She'll be a terror when she comes out of i ... *if* she comes out of it."

"Mix it with diazepam."

"I didn't bring any."

"Dammit!" She turns her back on him, calling into her radio. "Dr. Nichols, how much longer?"

∇ ∇ ∇

"DON'T BOTHER ME, I'm operating!" His face pressed against the viewfinder, Brent Nichols remotely manipulates the buzz saw, completing a transverse incision, which connects the first two parallel cuts. Switching to a robotic forceps, he carefully grips the edge of the excised skin and pulls the six-inch-thick flap towards the Megalodon's snout, Dr. Selby assisting with a second clamp to roll back the fifty-two-inch-long, ninety-pound section of skin and muscle. Armed with a scalpel, Dr. Nichols shears away the remaining connective tissue as he exposes a smooth layer of cartilage.

"Dr. Selby, secure the skin flap while I slice through her skull."

It takes the biologist another few minutes to surgically remove a two-inch-thick section of cartilage. Adjusting his camera angle, Dr. Nichols pans out, revealing the inner workings of the creature's brain.

"Magnificent ..."

Unlike a human, the Megalodon's brain is long and thin, spread out across the cranial cavity like an inverted Y with the extensions reaching out to the nostrils and olfactory bulbs, as well as a labyrinth of nerve cells located in the snout.

Dr. Nichols stares at the anatomical design in awe.

Stelzer nudges him. "They're running out of anesthetic."

"Right." Switching controls, he manipulates the robotic appendage gripping the neural implant, positioning the device so that it rests atop the brain's Y junction. One eighteen-inch-long, wire-thin electrode at a time, he connects the device to various surfaces of the brain.

▽ ▽ ▽

Fran Rizzuto and Virgil Carmen stare at the empty slurry bucket.

"That's not good."

"No shit. Keep pumping water." Fran speaks into her radio, "Jonas, how much longer?"

▽ ▽ ▽

"Stand by, Fran." The packet of screwdrivers, attached to the fishing line, is being pushed inland by the current. Jonas swims out to it, tearing it from its barbed hook—

—slicing open his right thumb in the process. He curses as blood trickles from the open wound. Pinching the cut, he kicks hard against the incoming ocean current just to get back to the base of the tail.

Mac's voice chirps over his ear piece. "Jonas, did you get the screwdrivers?"

"I got them, and a nasty cut from your damn hook."

"Thank me later. I just got off the radio with the guys who tag great whites in Baja. They advise that you line up the faceplate then drill four pilot holes with the quarter-inch bit. Use the bolts and nuts in your tool bag. They say it's far less invasive than a screw."

"Okay. Thanks." Jonas reaches into his tool bag. Retrieving a bit, he locks it in the drill, and lining up the faceplate, he drills a quarter-inch hole through the secondary dorsal fin, his eyes never leaving Angel's tail.

No movement.

Breathing a sigh of relief, he quickly drills two more holes, then slowly removes the screw twisted into the flesh and re-drills that hole as well. Feeling into the tool bag, he locates four ten-inch plastic bolts and four matching nuts. One by one, he inserts the bolts and tightens the nuts down against the opposite side of the fin by hand.

▼ ▼ ▼

BRENT NICHOLS WIPES sweat from his forehead as he sits back, admiring his handy work. "All electrodes connected. Preparing to close. Wish we could test this thing first. We always tested them with the hammerheads and nurse sharks."

"Brent, this isn't a frickin' nurse shark! We've got divers in the water—"

"Okay, okay. Ready with the clamp." Using the forceps, he assists Dr. Stelzer in adhering the severed section of upper skull in place with glue. Satisfied the cartilage will hold and mend, the two marine biologists proceed to roll the heavy section of skin back in place. Dr. Nichols then begins the arduous task of suturing the incisions—

—while Jonathan Stelzer injects the surgical area with a combination of anti-inflammatories and antibiotics.

▼ ▼ ▼

ED HENDRICKS IS positioned above the surgical chamber, witnessing a robotic appendage stitch a bleeding flap of skin using a fourteen-inch titanium needle. The sutures are made from Megalodon intestine taken from Angelica's remains.

"Ed, how much longer?"

"I don't know, Frannie. They're suturing the incisions now. Five, maybe six minutes, plus another two to flood the chamber and release the device. Carlos, what's happening at your end?"

▼ ▼ ▼

PERSPIRATION IS POURING down Carlos Salinas's face, creating a small pool inside his face mask as he keeps the saltwater feeder tube in place between Angel's slack jaws. "Man, it's been at least fifteen minutes since I saw white stuff coming out of the monster's gills."

"Any sign she's coming out of it?"

"How the hell should I know? Do I look like a vet?"

"Check her eyes."

"Her eyes. Yeah." Leaving the tube wedged between two lower teeth, Carlos swims forward to check on the Meg's left eye.

The blue-gray pupil has rolled back in place—

—staring at him!

Carlos's voice deserts him as his throat constricts in primal fear, his limbs refusing to move though his mind is screaming at them to do so.

Angel sees what appears in her blurry vision as a juvenile sea elephant. She continues to breathe water without exerting herself, the veil cloaking her senses slowly clearing, yet not quite enough to awaken her muscles.

The realization that he is still alive breaks Carlos's momentary paralysis. He kicks his fins, propelling himself past the Megalodon's open mouth to the steel door in seconds flat—

—his wake causing the saltwater hose to slip from out of Angel's mouth.

Forgetting to remove his BCD vest and air tank, Carlos forces his way through the shoulder-width hole, wheezing breaths from his mask as he attempts to shout a warning to Ed Hendricks. "She's ... awake! Get out ... she's—"

▽ ▽ ▽

"WHAT DID YOU say?" Hendricks looks up in time to see Carlos disappearing through a slime-covered hole in the door. His heart racing, the diver abandons his post and swims like mad for the barrier.

With the jet stream no longer delivering water into Angel's mouth, the Megalodon's gills stop fluttering. Seconds pass without a breath, triggering an internal alarm. The creature's core temperature suddenly jumps, releasing a burst of adrenaline that causes the thick red muscles running the length of her back to spasm—

—tossing Jonas from his mount as he finishes tightening the antenna's last bolt.

"She's awake! Carlos, Ed, get the hell out of there!"

Jonas swims for the surface—

—only to be swatted aside by the thirty-foot caudal fin.

The Megalodon propels itself forward, ramming a mouthful of seawater into her gills—

—just as Ed Hendricks reaches the door.

The diver can feel the gargantuan presence bearing down on him. In a state of panic, he tries to ram his shoulders and air tank through a steel hole that is far too small. He kicks and squirms, the slick algae allowing him to twist his way through to his waist—

—just as Angel's snout bashes into the barrier, her open mouth slamming down upon the base of his air tank and through both his legs! The punctured gas cylinder explodes—

—propelling him through the hole and out the other side in a burst of air bubbles and blood.

Forty feet from the surface, Carlos's eardrums register. He turns around, long enough to see his friend sinking toward the bottom in a cloud of blood. Instinct blotting out fear, he releases air from his BCD vest, and plunges after his friend's body. He grabs Ed's arm, still full of life, and over-inflates his vest and rockets to the surface.

Angel shakes her mammoth head, the collision with the steel barrier causing her numbed ampullae of Lorenzini to tingle. For several moments she hovers by the door, her nostrils still registering acidic scents from the anesthetic, unaware that the remains of Ed Hendricks's severed legs are caught in her upper front teeth like a pair of human cigars.

Blood rises from the amputated appendages, diverting into her inhaling nostrils like smoke. The scent revives the Meg. Banking slowly along the steel doors she turns, heading back toward the canal entrance—

—her lateral line detecting an intruder.

V V V

Mac cranks the speed boat in tight circles as he yells frantically into his face mask, "Jonas, where the hell are you! Jonas—"

"Forty feet beneath you! Stop moving the damn boat!"

"I have to move the boat! Drop your weight belt and get the hell up here. Your girl's awake!"

Jonas releases his weight belt, kicking hard for the surface—

—as Angel rises directly beneath him like an ivory dirigible!

"Mac, she's coming up right behind me! There's no way I can get in the boat that quick!"

"Don't! Grab the rope!" Mac tosses the water ski rope behind the boat. "Say when!"

Jonas kicks for the red and white wooden handle bobbing above his head along the surface ... grabs it!

"Go!"

Mac jams the throttle down, the bow kicking out of the water as the 250-horsepower engine launches the speed boat ahead—

—nearly yanking Jonas's arms out of their sockets as he's dragged across the surface, losing his face mask and tool belt in the process.

Angel's eyes roll back in her head, momentarily blinding her as she bites down upon her prey—

—her sluggish jaws clamping down on empty sea. Detecting the boat, she levels out to give chase, her muscles, still feeling the affects of the anesthetic, struggling to move.

Jonas rolls onto his back, propping his feet and fins in the air as he's whipped and bounced over the speed boat's wake doing thirty knots.

Mac glances over his shoulder, relieved to see that his friend is still there, and the Meg is still back at the canal doors. He throttles down, afraid of going too fast, lest he lose Jonas. "Hold on, pal, we'll be on dry land in a second."

Jonas grits his teeth as the boat races into the lagoon, then veers for the floating ramp—

—driving straight over the angled Astroturf surface, its fiberglass hull skidding across the concrete deck.

Jonas's butt slides across the ramp at fifteen knots. Releasing the rope, he curls himself up in a ball and rolls to a dead stop in front of a concession stand. For a long moment he just lies on the blessed dry deck, analyzing his injuries. *Scuffed elbows ... knee hurts like hell ... not too bad.* "Mac?"

Mac sits up in the speedboat's bow. The two men look at one another and suddenly convulse in wild laughter, the joy of still being alive making them giddy. "J.T., we have got to stop doing this shit."

"Agreed. Maybe we can sell Amway?"

"I was actually thinking about opening a strip club for seniors."

"Early bird specials. I like it."

"Jonas? It's Fran—"

"Fran, we're okay—"

"We need an ambulance—make it a chopper! Ed lost both legs. He's bleeding out. We'll be at the dock in two minutes!"

Jonas sits up. The dive boat races past the canal as a white dorsal fin slips beneath the waves. *I hate you, Angel ... I really hate you.*

19

The shadow moves through a black sea illuminated olive-green by the night vision glass.

"There!" Kaylie Szeifert points out the Manta Ray's cockpit to starboard. "Bring us in closer, so I can shoot the net."

"I can't see it." Sean Dustman, seated to Kaylie's left behind the primary control station jams his left foot too hard on the port-side propeller, sending the submersible into a dizzying clockwise barrel roll.

Registering the current, the 530-pound green sea turtle flaps its forward flippers and disappears into the darkness.

Brian Suit's voice crackles over the radio. "Two minute warning, Sub One. You're score stands at minus twenty-five."

Kaylie grabs the dashboard as Dustman overcompensates with the starboard prop, spinning them upside down. "Sean, give me the damn controls!"

"Just do your job, and I'll do mine!"

Her eyes search the sonar array as she listens to the pinging sea over her headphones. For the last week the submersible pilot candidates have been prowling the Persian Gulf's coastal waters at night, netting sea turtles, each captured specimen worth positive points, each missed opportunity penalized. Tonight is the last round of open water training before tomorrow's cuts, and Kaylie's rank is a dismal eleventh, a good forty points below the final position of the eight candidates who will be selected to go on the mission.

Sean Dustman ranks a well-deserved seventeenth.

"Found him! Come about to course two-seven-zero, depth seventy feet."

Dustman launches the Manta Ray into a rapid, dizzying descent, dropping them a hundred feet below the turtle and two hundred feet to the west.

"You overshot! Sean, watch the reef! Pull up!"

"I got it! I got it!" The former Naval officer pulls back on both joysticks and levels out, barely avoiding a head-on collision with a bed of coral.

The radio crackles. "Alright you two, time's up. Surface and dock, and do not dive anywhere near the Iranian oil tanker. Its mass will suck you right off the bottom into its keel. Szeifert?"

"Yes, sir. Understood." She tracks the massive object moving due east on her sonar, losing herself in a cacophony of sound coming from the tanker's twin screws.

Minutes later, they are being hauled out of the water up the slanted stern ramp of the *Dubai Land II*, a 196-foot, 280-ton fishing trawler. Deck lights blot out the night sky, replaced by three Arab technicians, who secure the Manta Ray onto its motorized chassis.

The cockpit hatch unlocks then is raised, releasing a spray of seawater outside the seal. Kaylie climbs out, her skin-tight wetsuit drawing looks from the other pilots and crewmen as she heads forward, her anger seething. She crosses the main deck, passing beneath the enormous canary-yellow stern gantry and the twenty-thousand-gallon acrylic tank holding nine recently captured sea turtles. The animals will be taken back to the aquarium to be part of an outdoor exhibit.

Kaylie locates Brian Suits on the upper deck as he exits the wheelhouse.

"Sir, may I speak with you?"

"Can it wait, Szeifert? I'm in the middle of tallying scores."

"Now, sir. Please."

He sees the rage in her eyes. "Two minutes."

"Respectfully, sir, my scores are not reflective of my abilities. I've been consistently paired with the lower third of the class, most of whom barely know port from starboard. I was lucky to survive my last dive, let alone score any points."

"Candidate pairings were randomly selected, Szeifert. You know that."

"Yes, sir, with the objective of determining the top thirty percent of the class. Piloting? Okay, I admit I need some work, but when it comes to co-piloting and running sonar, only Peter Geier's logged better scores. Individually, I'm easily in the top five, but these random pairings have consistently placed me with pilots who have no idea what they're doing, or have attitudes about taking directions from a woman. They've killed my overall score."

"Maybe that's true, but tonight's our last night of trials. What would you suggest I do?"

"Give me one last chance at making the grade, one last run with a decent pilot."

"With who? Every other candidate has completed their scores. None of the top eight would dare jeopardize their position to accommodate your request."

She scans the deck. Spots David standing alone in the bow by the anchor windlass. "Give me one run with David. Let me show you what I can do."

"David's a trainer."

"And I'm your best co-pilot. Let me prove it."

The former Psy Ops officer stares at the passing Iranian oil tanker, thinking. After a minute he takes out his radio. "Mr. Bellin, are any of the Manta Rays charged?"

"No, sir. But Sub Two's got enough juice for a twenty minute run."

Kaylie's eyebrows raise, her expression pleading.

"Grab Taylor. I want you in the water in four minutes."

"Yes, sir!"

ᐯ   ᐯ   ᐯ

"You've barely spoken to me in a week, and now you want me to pilot your sub?"

"David, I'm sorry if I misled you. I honestly like you. It was just getting too hot and heavy."

"Yeah ... I'm not feeling it. Maybe tomorrow."

She chases after him. "You want me to beg?"

"Might help."

"Then I'm begging."

"Still not feeling it."

She balls her fists, grinding her teeth. "What is it you want from me? Sex?"

He turns to face her. "No, Kaylie. I just don't want to feel like a piece of meat. If you want my help then ask me. As a friend."

She softens. "You're right. I'm sorry. If I came across as one of those shallow women who bat their eyes in order to get favors, then I apologize. So, now I'm asking you, David, as my friend, would you please pilot for me?"

"Yes."

She smiles, tears in her eyes. "Thank you."

"And as a friend, if you still want sex—"

He winces as she punches him on the shoulder.

ᐯ   ᐯ   ᐯ

David adjusts his harness as the cockpit clamps shut in a watertight seal. "How many points are you behind?"

"By my calculations, we need to net two turtles."

"Two turtles in twenty minutes? Geez, I hope you brought bait."

One of the technicians knocks on the acrylic glass above his head. David gives the thumbs-up as the Manta Ray is slid backward on its sled down the stern ramp and into the velvety black sea.

He wastes no time in distancing the sub from the massive trawler, allowing Kaylie to get a clear sonar reading. "Bearing?"

"We lost a green turtle in deep water, about a mile out, bearing zero-zero-six. If you can level out at one hundred seventy feet, I can get a better reading. Just watch the currents."

David surface dives the sub, reaching the desired depth in seconds as he races along the deserted Dubai coastline. Covering fifty square miles, the Jebel Ali Marine Wildlife Sanctuary extends several miles offshore, encompassing a rich coral reef-based ecosystem, home to hawksbill turtles and their larger endangered cousins, the green sea turtle.

The olive-brown underworld races by, the sub's ride level and smooth. David glances at Kaylie, who is smiling. "What?"

"Nothing."

"Come on."

"I was just thinking that it's actually fun being in one of these things when the pilot knows what the hell he's doing. And don't you dare show off." She presses her headphones tighter to her ears. "Got something! Bearing two-two-three, eighty yards ahead, sixty feet and ascending."

David slows the submersible, adjusts his course, then rises at a forty-five-degree angle. "Port or starboard shot?"

"Port." Kaylie leans forward, her hand on the knob of a control labeled N-PORT.

"Eighty feet ... seventy ... there she is—a big fat greenie! Nail her!"

Kaylie pulls the control knob—

—ejecting a series of orange softball-size buoys, the pressurized spheres instantly inflating, scooping the 670-pound turtle up within its net—

—floating it to the surface.

David circles the amphibious reptile as it rises against its will. The four-foot carapace is more dark brown than green, identifying it as a mature adult.

Kaylie grabs the radio. "Sub Two pick-up, on my bearing."

"Pick-up on the way. Nicely done. You still have nine minutes."

David descends again, Kaylie listening on sonar, the Gulf traffic polluting the pinging sounds reflecting off objects in the water. "Ugh! It's no use; I can't hear a thing."

"Hang on, hang on. Where's the bottom?"

"Two hundred eighty feet."

"It's too deep here, too much boat traffic. Let's hit the shallows." David jams both feet to the floor, rocketing the sub to the south at thirty knots.

"One fifty ... ninety-five ... seventy-five ... David, this is good. Can you shutdown the engines, let her drift so I can hear?"

David powers off the sub, the neutrally buoyant craft drifting fifty feet below the surface. An easterly current catches the Manta Ray's wingspan, gently swaying the sub, pulling it parallel to shore.

Kaylie lays her head back in the darkness, the quiet helping soothe her overwrought nerves. This last week of training has been full of twenty-hour days—physically exerting, mentally exhausting. The competition has been fierce, and she has never felt more alone.

She snakes her left hand over the console dividing the cockpit, resting her fingers over David's right hand. "You're a great pilot. Better than Suits. Better than any of us. You should be one of the eight going on this mission."

"Can't. I sort of promised my father that I'd go back to Gainesville. You know, finish up school."

"Well, whatever happens ... thanks."

Several minutes pass in silence.

"Kaylie, say things didn't work out for you in Dubai, would you ever want to work at the Tanaka Institute?"

"I'm flattered. But honestly, those Megs scare the hell out of me."

"Yeah, they're great."

"No. I mean they really scare the hell out of me. I'd rather work with river leeches."

"Oh."

"This is your two-minute warning," Brian Suits announces over the radio. "Nice catch, Szeifert. Nearly seven hundred pounds. Wish you had more time."

Kaylie turns the radio off. "Screw it. I'll go back to Graham Hawkes and the job at the aquarium. It paid the bills, most months. What about you? I mean, after you graduate?"

"I don't know. I'm open to anything, except leeches." He restarts the sub's engines, moving ahead at five knots, in no rush to return to the ship. Though the night glass allows him to see fairly well in the shallows, he turns his exterior lights on—

—catching a burst of movement, a swirl of sand behind a patch of coral.

"Kaylie?"

"I heard it! Just a whisper. It's not big—"

"—there!" He points as the heart-shaped shell rises from the bottom, swimming away from the piercing light.

Kaylie grabs the radio. "Two to base, how much time?"

"Forty seconds."

David accelerates after the turtle—a female hawksbill, weighing just over 150 pounds. The creature is far more elusive than its larger cousin, but David puts the larger Manta Ray beneath it in seconds. "Starboard net ready? Shoot!"

Kaylie pulls the control for the second net—

—nothing happens. She tugs on the knob again and again. "Dammit! They didn't reload!" She smacks both palms across the dashboard in anger.

"Hold on. I have an idea."

Brian Suits finishes tallying his candidates scores—

—looking up from his Blackberry at the sound of the applauding crew. "I'll be a sonuvabitch ..."

The Manta Ray circles the trawler doing ten knots, a 150-pound hawksbill turtle pinned to the forward edge of the cockpit's acrylic bubble, surfing the swell as the submersible's hood ornament.

20

Amazing really. He lost so much blood. Did you call his wife?
Yes. She's flying in with his daughter. Will Carlos be okay?
They have him in a recompression chamber; he's being treated for the bends and shock.

▽ ▽ ▽

THE PAIN OF consciousness pushes Ed Hendricks above the dark surf. He attempts to spit out his regulator, but it's wedged too tightly in his mouth and throat. Unable to yank the annoying object free, he grunts in frustration, shaking his head to and fro.

"He's awake. Mac, call the nurse! Ed, it's Jonas. Open your eyes. Ed?"

A slit of daylight breaks through an ocean of shadows as Ed Hendricks opens his eyes. Fran Rizzuto leans over him, smiling with relief. "Thank God."

Groggy, he turns to his left and sees Jonas.

"You're in a hospital. Don't try to talk. You're going to be fine."

Fran shoots Jonas a look as the doctor enters the room. "Welcome back, Mr. Hendricks. My name is Daniel Pernini; I'm your attending physician. You've been in shock due to massive blood loss. We had to place a tube down your throat to keep your airway open. Open wide, this may make you gag."

The doctor removes the tube. "How's that?"

Hendricks flinches as he swallows.

Fran places a cup of water to his lips. "Slow sips."

The master diver nods his thanks while Dr. Pernini checks his vitals. "How do you feel?"

"Pain."

"In your throat?"

"Legs. Hurt bad. Sharp pain. Like needles puncturing my bones. Feet are throbbing."

Dr. Pernini glances at Jonas and Fran. "We'll get you something for the pain."

"Doc, there's pressure ... like a weight squeezing them ... like I'm being crushed. I owe you, Doc ... for saving them."

The doctor prepares a hypodermic needle of morphine. "You're a lucky man, Mr. Hendricks. By all rights you should be dead. Your friends refused to give up; they saved your life." He injects the morphine into the I.V. bag then adjusts the drip.

Ed Hendricks drifts back beneath the waves, the pain receding.

Jonas watches the big man's eyes roll up, wondering how he'll tell him that his legs are long gone—devoured by Angel just below the hip.

Dubai Land
Dubai, United Arab Emirates

For the twenty-three recruits vying for six positions and two alternates, "Decision Day" begins with a farewell buffet brunch in the hotel's second floor Devonian galley.

Brian Suits waits until everyone is seated with their food before taking the dais.

"Congratulations. We've put you through hell, and you survived. And for that you are all to be commended. While scores weighed heavily on our final selections, the ability to keep a clear head during stressful situations was more of a determining factor. When you return to your suites from breakfast this morning, each of you will find a manila envelope on your kitchen table. For those candidates selected, there will be a mandatory meeting at seven o'clock tonight in the *Ancient Seas* restaurant on the top floor of the hotel. For those candidates not selected, you will find your airline tickets home, along with a cashier's check in the amount of ten thousand dollars. Departures begin tomorrow morning, so you have the rest of today to enjoy Dubai. Mr. bin Rashidi has generously chartered a tour bus for those of you wishing to visit the local sites. If you choose to remain at the hotel, we ask that you do not leave the hotel grounds because of on-going construction. Okay then ... enjoy your day."

One by one, then in small groups, the recruits leave their dining area and head for the elevators.

David, Kaylie, and Monty are the only ones left at their table. A waitress comes by offering coffee. Kaylie and David wave her off, while Monty heads back to the buffet for thirds. David smiles. "Damn, that guy can eat."

"He knows he's going home. I envy his peace of mind."

He sees the look of anxiety on her face. "Kaylie, go."

"It's okay. I can wait."

"No you can't. Go and see if you made it. I don't mind."

"Thanks." As she stands to leave, her high cheekbones tighten in a sad smile. "No matter what the verdict, will you spend the day with me?"

"Definitely."

He watches her exit the galley. A moment later she's rising up the atrium in one of the glass elevators, offering a discreet finger-wave.

Life often comes down to a decision or moment that sets you on a new path, determining the rest of your life. I guess for Kaylie, this is one of them.

Monty rejoins him, his plate piled high with scrambled eggs, two steaks, and a generous helping of hash browns. "The guy who invented buffets ... frickin' genius." He sees David is distracted. "Last day of camp, huh? Think she made it?"

"I don't know. She didn't have the score. Suits refused to count that last turtle. He said it was my piloting that nailed it, not her sonar abilities."

"Fire escapes, laser printers, and bulletproof vests."

"What?"

"All invented by women. Would you trust a bulletproof vest if you knew a woman had designed it?"

"I don't know. Why not? I wouldn't trust anything unless it was tested."

"Your woman was tested. We'll see how prejudiced the jury is. Me? I'm just happy to collect a paycheck."

"It's only ten grand. What are you going to do now?"

"Finish my meal, rent a few movies—"

"I meant after tomorrow."

Monty shovels a massive forkful of eggs and potatoes into his mouth, spraying bits into the air as he answers, "Tomorrow's tomorrow, Junior. When you're bi-polar, you're lucky if you can focus on the moment. I'm here, and I'm functioning—at least for the moment—and that's not too bad for a guy who's brains look like these eggs. So go, go find your woman. I plan on camping out here for a while."

▽ ▽ ▽

SHE'S WAITING FOR him in the corridor by his suite, leaning against his door, a sad expression on her face. The manila envelope is in her hand, still sealed.

"You didn't open it?"

"If I open it now and somehow I made it, then I'd be afraid of letting myself grow closer to you ... afraid you'd interpret it as some kind of payback. But if I didn't make it, the disappointment would ruin our day together. So I decided to wait."

"You want me to open it?"

"No. I want you to make love to me."

Hand in hand, they enter his suite, David dead-bolting the door behind them.

Thousand Oaks, California

Located twelve miles inland from the Pacific Ocean, set against the backdrop of the Santa Monica mountains, is the city of Thousand Oaks—a planned community that caters to its well-to-do residents.

Sara Toms maneuvers her Jeep Cherokee through the quiet residential neighborhood, guided by her on-board navigator. She pulls over to the curb, verifying the address on a mailbox. "This is it, Jess."

Jessica Jean Tompson stares at the two-story home, shaking her head. "Tell me again about your big donor?"

"Joseph Michael Park. He owns ShockNetVideo.com. I showed him the raw footage taken in the Meg Pen, and he loved it. He's willing to make a seven-figure donation, but only if we give him the exclusive footage of the juvenile Megs' release … and a celebrity figure head."

"But, Lana Wood? Who is she? I never even heard of Lana Wood."

"She's Natalie Wood's younger sister. Lana was an actress, too. In fact, she was a Bond Girl. Remember Plenty O'Toole in *Diamonds Are Forever?* Lana's probably the only Playboy centerfold who's also a published author. Her book hit number three on the New York Times Best Seller list."

"Come on, Sara, how many decades ago was that? What about Pamela Anderson?"

"She wasn't interested. Every PETA spokesperson I asked backed off once they heard we were rallying to release Belle and Lizzy. Lana was the highest ranked person on Mr. Park's list who even agreed to consider it. And even then, only if we donate a percentage of our proceeds back to the American Cancer Society. Something about her daughter—"

"Fine. Let's just meet this Bond chick and get back to San Francisco. You know how I hate anything Hollywood." She grabs the portable DVD player and exits the Jeep.

▼ ▼ ▼

Now in her sixties, Lana Wood spends most of her time caring for her daughter and three grandchildren while raising money for cancer organizations. The former sex symbol greets the two animal rights activists at her front door in jeans and a white turtleneck sweater that barely contains the signature breasts that made her famous back in the 1970s and 80s. A gold Russian cross hangs around her neck.

"You're the group my agent told me about. Let's talk out back." She leads them through the house, the two women swarmed upon by seven dogs and ten cats. They exit to the backyard garden and pool where Lana's daughter, Evan, is watching her four-year-old son swim.

Though sick, Evan is gorgeous, resembling a young Liz Taylor, her eyes bright green, her hair dark and wavy like her mother's. She is not happy about the meeting.

"For the record, I told my mother not to get involved with you people. We may be animal lovers, but we both think PETA goes too far. And we don't like zealots of any sort."

"We're not zealots," Sara responds. "We believe that every animal has the right to be free. Including sharks. The Tanaka Institute is reaping millions of dollars in profit while these majestic beasts are being tortured."

"How are they being tortured?" Lana asks.

Jessica starts the DVD. The edited underwater sequences, taken inside the Meg Pen, show Belle and Lizzy being shocked by steel rods protruding from a spherical acrylic sub.

"Those rods pack five thousand volts of electricity. Can you imagine the pain?"

"Why are they doing that?"

"Keeps the animals aggressive," Sara lies. "Would you pay sixty to a hundred dollars to see two young sharks swimming peacefully in their tank?"

"I would!" Evan's son, Max, climbs out of the pool, dripping water everywhere.

Lana wraps him in a towel. "My grandson loves sharks."

"We love sharks, too," Sara says. "That's why we want to save them. Two of Angel's pups have already died, thanks to the recklessness of Jonas Taylor and the Tanaka Institute."

"What happens if you release these two Megs?" Evan asks. "Isn't it dangerous?"

"Not really. As your grandson probably knows, Megalodon isn't interested in hunting humans; we're far too small and lean to be part of their diet. The Monterey Bay Sanctuary offers a protected environment where Lizzy and Belle can live out their lives, feeding off of sea elephants and whales."

"It's the way nature intended," Jessica adds.

"What about that college student who … you know—" Lana covers her grandson's ears, "—was eaten."

"Lana, these accidents are always a result of humans foolishly trying to domesticate wild animals, in this case for greed." Sara motions to the R.A.W. decal on the DVD player. "Returning Animals to the Wild. That's what we do. And we need your help."

"What would this involve?"

"Personal appearances, interviews. We want you to become the face of our organization, sort of like Pamela Anderson has done with our sister organization, PETA."

"I don't want to be associated with radicals, Ms. Toms. If I do this, you have to agree to tone things down. No more goons picketing the Tanaka Institute or pelting their employees with eggs. My road's the high road, ladies. Take it or leave it."

"We'll take it," Sara says. "The truth is, we've been wanting to humanize our image for quite a while now. And we hope you'll be there the day we succeed in finally setting these wonderful animals free." She looks at Jessica. "Anything you want to add?"

"Just a quick question, Ms. Wood. When you were making that Bond movie … did you ever have sleep with Sean Connery?"

Dubai Land
Dubai, United Arab Emirates

A brilliant speck of sun drops beneath the veil of purple clouds on the distant horizon, swathing the heavens in its fading orange glow.

David watches the sunset from his bed. He is alone, but Kaylie is everywhere—her scent on his skin, her taste on his lips—

—her absence in his heart.

Their first sexual encounter had been quick and filled with lust, but when it was over, they had simply lain in bed and held one another, their passion evolving into something far deeper.

For the rest of the afternoon they had made love.

When they had finished, Kaylie curled herself naked against his body, and they slept on into the evening. When David awoke, he was alone, Kaylie in the living room, holding the opened manila envelope.

"Well?"

She looked up at him, a bit shocked. "I made it. I made the cut."

"That's ... great," he muttered, feeling empty inside. "You okay? You don't seem that excited."

She wiped away a tear, forcing a smile. "No. This is ... it's good. It's what I wanted ... I have to shower. We have a meeting in an hour."

"The mission. Does it say where you'll be going?"

"No. Only that we leave tomorrow morning at five."

"How long will you be gone?"

"I'm not sure. Six months? David—"

"It's okay. I'm happy for you."

"When I get back to the States, I'll come visit you in Gainesville."

"Yeah, that would be great. I was thinking ... I only need twenty credits to graduate. I can load up on courses in the fall, maybe get out early."

"What about football?"

"Forget football. I'd rather be with you."

They had held one another as if slow dancing, not wanting to let go, knowing their paths had crossed in one exquisite moment. But the moment was over, their destinies leading them in different directions.

"David, come with me. At least for the summer. Or until school starts. I can talk to Captain Suits; he'd add you to the team in a heartbeat."

"I can't. They hired me to teach the staff about caring for the Meg."

"She's doing fine. You're more valuable to them as a pilot."

"It's not just that. My father ... I promised him I'd stay in Dubai until school started. What if you stayed here with me? Dr. Becker lost one of her staff. What if I spoke to her about hiring you? You worked in the Scripps Aquarium—"

"David, I can't. As much as I want to be with you, passing up an opportunity to stock the aquarium with rare species ... the experience ... the money—"

"No, I understand. I wouldn't want you to give that up."

She touched his cheek, kissing him. "It's not the end. Finish school, I'll do my thing, then we'll find a way to be together."

▼ ▼ ▼

THE SUN DIPS below the Persian Gulf, bleeding the horizon red. David remains in bed, watching dusk yield to another Arabian night. The emptiness

176

the twenty-year-old feels is palpable, a pain he has never experienced before. In the past four years he has dated no fewer than a dozen girls, two having turned into relationships—one in high school, the last in college. He had used the "love word" freely, the phrase uttered mostly because it was expected of him. Sure, he had felt something—

—but nothing like this. These feelings actually hurt. They were making him crazy! It was as if he were experiencing every hokey love song he had ever despised, like he was trapped in his own skin. How could he expect to get through the rest of the night, let alone the entire summer feeling like this? It felt as if his soul was being ripped out of him, and all he wanted to do was wallow in the pain.

"Geez, snap out of it! You're whining like a little bitch."

He checks the clock by his bed: 7:18.

She's at the meeting. Probably won't be through until ten, maybe midnight. Figure four more hours. Do something! Don't just sit around and wait for her. Have some pride!

Rolling out of bed, he pulls on his jeans and tee-shirt, deciding to head over to the aquarium.

THE *ANCIENT SEAS* restaurant occupies the Devonian hotel's entire sixtieth floor. The circular chamber rotates counterclockwise on its floorplate, one full rotation an hour, offering its diners a 360-degree view of Dubai Land.

Kaylie Szeifert leans forward against a padded guardrail, sipping the remains of a diet soda as she gazes out the scenic bay windows. The park is dark, save for patches of construction lights and the twelve illuminated, gold-plated shark fins surrounding the aquarium.

As she watches, a solitary figure crosses over one of the bridges.

David ...

Her eyes follow him as he reaches the third floor pavilion. He tries several doors until he gains entry into the facility.

Maybe I shouldn't see him tonight ... it'll just make things worse. He's so young ... where did you think this could go? You knew better ... the last thing you needed was to complicate things. These kind of relationships rarely ever work ... eventually he'd give up his dreams to pursue yours or you'd give in to follow his. Career first ... that was the deal.

She turns to face the room, taking in the other seven candidates.

Six men, one other woman. Smile, Kaylie, you beat the odds. You made the cut.
So why am I feeling so lost?

Brian Suits saunters over, carrying two cold bottles of beer. He offers her one.

"No, thank you, sir."

"Sir is for when we're in training. Call me Brian." He takes a quick swig. "What's wrong? I expected you to be all smiles."

"Just a little tired, sir—er, Brian. Will you be debriefing us tonight?"

"No. Tonight is more of a social event. I want the team to get to know one another." He hands her the beer and clinks her bottle with his. "May you work like you don't need the money, love like you've never been hurt, dance like no one is watching, screw like it's being filmed, and drink like a true Irishman. Cheers."

She smiles. "Cheers." And drains the bottle.

"Alright, everyone, gather around and have a seat. Come on, all of you."

The group joins Brian Suits and Kaylie at the banquet table. "Big day tomorrow, the first of many. I'm sure you're excited, confused, maybe a little fearful. Good. Fear has its place. You conquer fear by being prepared. Preparation breeds success—success, confidence. That's why you were selected: because we liked your swagger.

"I remember the night before I was to ship out on my first tour of duty. My C.O., a crafty Navy vet by the name of Michael John Selby, got us all quite inebriated. Under the haze of alcohol I heard him utter these famous words: 'Some Guinness was spilt on the barroom floor when the pub was shut for the night. When out of his hole crept a wee brown mouse who stood in the pale moonlight. He lapped up the frothy foam from the floor, then back on his haunches he sat. And all night long, you could hear the mouse roar ... bring on the goddamn cat!'"

"Hell yes!" The group raises their glasses and drinks.

Brian drains his beer. "The cat, or cats, as the case may be, await us in the depths of the briny deep, where it will be our job to flush them out. Make no mistake. It's dangerous work; for we are to be the mouse. Do your jobs, and you'll return safely with plenty of cheese. How much, you ask? If your team's among the best, upwards of a million dollars a piece. Maybe more."

Smiles and whistles. Several of the men high-five.

"Bring on the goddam cat, Captain!"

"Easy now. As I said, it's dangerous work, and you're not the only crew. Two other teams have been out there fishing over the last five months. They're ahead of you in experience, but they haven't been using anything like our Manta Rays. Plus, they don't have yours truly as their trainer."

The group applauds and whoops, Kaylie among them.

"We'll kick their asses, Captain!"

"Damn straight. Especially for a million bucks."

"This isn't a game!" Brian Suits slams both palms to the table, his sudden change in demeanor silencing the room. "Cockiness leads to mistakes. Make a mistake out there, and you can die real fast. We've lost three pilots already, and they logged more dive hours than all of you combined!"

Eight pairs of eyes lock on to Brian Suits.

"That's right. Three dead pilots. Or did you think Mr. bin Rashidi has so much money he just gives it away? No, children, this money you'll earn. Each of you had better bring your A-game, because these depths are unforgiving, and some of these cats have sharp claws. Of course—" he grins, "—the nastier the cat, the bigger the bonus."

Kaylie feels her legs trembling. *They already have a Meg, what else could be out there?*

Brian grabs another beer from a waiter then points to the man seated to his right. "You, Mr. Slabine, stand and tell us about yourself."

The slender, dark-haired man with the scar slicing through his right eyebrow stands. "Marcus Joseph Slabine, U.S. Navy, retired. I served two years aboard the *USS Seawolf* as a sonar tech. If these 'cats' are out there, you can bet your ass I'll find 'em. Oh, and I also do a killer impression of Jerry Seinfeld." He clears his throat. "Neuman ..."

The others laugh and applaud, the tension easing for the moment.

"Mr. Hoch."

A short, lean man with a marathon runner's physique stands. "Jeffrey Arthur Hoch, but most people call me Minister. I'm actually an ordained minister, though I had a falling out with my denomination several years ago; they were becoming a bit too radical for me, ranting about evolution and such. Like Marcus, I served aboard a submarine, the *USS Wyoming,* one of the Ohio Class subs that carry nuclear ballistic missiles. I've spent the last five years as a firefighter, completing over a thousand calls; pressure doesn't bother me. In fact, I enjoy it. I'm married with five daughters, so you can imagine why I need the money."

"Five girls ... you should get a medal for bravery. Mr. Shiffman?"

"David Samuel Shiffman. My friends call me Shiff. Duke University. Degree's in marine biology. I'm into experiences. Been to six continents, lived out in the wild, climbed mountains, piloted private mini-subs, and I'm just beginning. I keep a running list of things I want to do before I die. The list totals four thousand."

"Name a few!"

"Name a few? Okay." He reaches into his pocket, pulling out a Blackberry. "I wanted to eat an endangered species. I had a green sea turtle caesar salad in the Caymans once. The way I figure, a lot of these endangered species won't be around much longer, so I owe it to my future grandchildren to tell them what they tasted like."

Kaylie covers her half-drunk giggle.

"Another goal was to lick something Donald Trump recently touched."

Laughter.

"My freshman year at Duke, I saw the Donald at the Duke-UNC basketball game. When he got up to get a snack at halftime, I ran over and licked his chair."

More laughter.

"Thank you, Mr. Shiff. Remind me to keep you away from any specimens we capture; I wouldn't want you licking one. Mr. Magers."

The senior-most member of the group stands, a tattoo of a dancing pig in a sailor suit on his upper right arm. Kaylie is not sure if he is in his sixties or seventies. "Rick Magers. Ex-lobsterman, ex-smuggler, ex-husband, ex-smoker, ex-druggy. Current submersible pilot, bullshitter, dog whisperer, and great grandfather. Wait … let me show you something."

The gray-haired man drops his trousers, showing his bare buttocks and two long scars on his left cheek.

"Got this first scar in 1952 when a drunken bridge leaped in front of my drunker 1940 deluxe coup doing eighty-two miles an hour. Got the second one when I was attacked by a masked Canadian wielding a scalpel in one hand and a titanium hip in the other. Bastard screamed, 'hey, Magers, I'm gonna shove this up your ass!' By God he did. But damned if I haven't learned to walk with it."

Brian Suits waits for the laughter to die down. "Kaylie? Would you like to show the group your ass as well?"

She blushes as the men egg her on. "Kaylie Szeifert. Guess I'm the youngest in the group. Nothing new there. I was born a preemie—weighed only two pounds—and I've been fighting mountains ever since. I'm a quick study, so whatever I lack in experience, I'll make up with hard work."

"Thank you, Kaylie. And our other sister, Ms. Umel?"

A short, stout woman in her mid-thirties stands. "Debbie Umel, and it's actually Missus. I'm happily married with two children, Noah and Mandie. I joined the Navy at nineteen, and I'm a damn good pilot. Give me Kaylie at sonar and watch out. Us ladies will kick your male butts!"

"Ewww!" The guys whoop it up.

"Mr. Geier?"

A cherub-faced man in his thirties, seated in a wheelchair, acknowledges the group. "Forgive me for not standing. I'm Peter Geier. I met most of you during training. I graduated with a degree in marine biology from the University of West Florida. Muscular Dystrophy may have stricken my body, but God gave me hearing that would put a bat to shame. I graded out tops in my class as a sonar tech with the Navy and served aboard a Trident Class submarine until my legs became too weak to get around the ship. If one of these 'cats' gets near our subs, I'll find 'im before he finds us."

"Thank you, Mr. Geier. Mr. Geier graded out highest in sonar in our class as well. Last, but not least, Dr. Gotto. Tell us about yourself."

The short, stocky Italian gentleman stands. "Antonio Gotto, Jr. Besides being a cardiologist, I was a professor of medicine at Cornell University and began the first American medical school in Qatar. It was there that I met several members of the Dubai Royal Family, including Mr. bin Rashidi. You're probably wondering what I'm doing here; I know my family is. Call it a mid-life crisis. Anyway, I'm here and honored to be part of the team."

Brian Suits waits for the applause to end. "I'm leaving you for now—I have some final details to go over with our host—but the staff will treat you well. The monorail leaves for the airport at five a.m., so don't stay out late. By this time tomorrow night, you'll be on board a Dubai tanker where you'll meet our support team. Oh, one last thing—"

Reaching into his jacket pocket, he removes eight envelopes, passing them around the table. "Fill these out and bring them with you tomorrow morning. That's it for now. Have a good night."

Kaylie watches him leave as she opens the envelope.

It's a release form ... to be sent to her next of kin.

21

Crimson droplets, as light as rain, disperse as they hit the surface, each molecule of blood sounding an alarm, each red blood cell as brilliant as a star set against a tapestry of midnight sky.

The Megalodon, Zahra, circles, her back arching, her pectoral fins lowering.

"Odd behavior," Barbara Becker remarks. Her face reflects blue in the aquarium's thick acrylic glass as she makes a note on her clipboard.

"It's territorial," David says, his eyes locked on the albino shark, its girth the size of a school bus. "She's spent her entire life competing with four siblings. She's not used to having the tank to herself."

A silent splash, three stories above their heads, as the dolphin enters the water. High pitch clicks and squeals fill their ears, the panicked mammal echo locating its new environment—

—its slit fluke trailing a dark cloud of blood as it swims.

"We use the Indo-Pacific humpbacks; they tend to be a little slower." Dr. Becker starts her stop-watch.

"I'm sure severing the muscles in its fluke doesn't hurt either."

"You disapprove?"

"It's not necessary."

"Zahra's still feeling the effects of being medicated. Chasing prey, even wounded prey, helps to increase her metabolism, allowing her to recover faster. It's like feeding a pet Boa constrictor. You have to cripple the mouse before tossing it in the snake's tank; otherwise the Boa would never catch it."

The five-ton hunter breaks away from the bottom and rises, nearly disappearing from view in a mammoth upswell of bubbles and blood as it bursts clear through the surface—

—splashing down sideways seconds later, the remains of the half-eaten dolphin spinning wildly in the killer's wake, spewing an oily copper ooze.

Dr. Becker ceases the stopwatch's sweeping second hand. "She's doing better."

"Yeah, but you're conditioning her to hunt live food. *Come to the Dubai Aquarium. See Zahra eat Flipper. Two Shows Daily.*"

"She'll be back to her regular diet in no time, with your help."

"Speaking of help, I wanted to talk to you about adding someone to your staff."

"Another marine biologist?"

"More of a laborer. His name's Monty. He was one of the pilot candidates that was cut."

Dr. Becker checks the time on her stopwatch again and records it in her notes. "You're a good trainer, David. You have a real feel for these predators. You want an assistant, you train him. But he lives in the staff quarters, not the hotel."

"Cool."

She looks up as Fiesal bin Rashidi enters the gallery. "Mr. bin Rashidi. I wasn't expecting you tonight, sir."

"Things are going well?"

"Yes, sir. Zahra's eating. She's nearly recovered from the trip."

"Excellent. Give me a moment, please. I'd like to speak with Mr. Taylor alone."

"Of course." She heads for the employee exit.

Bin Rashidi's predator-black eyes watch the Megalodon as it consumes the dolphin's remains, his thick dark goatee twitching in a half-smile. "Captain Suits tells me you performed well since we had our little talk, that he could not have completed the candidate training without you."

"It was a good experience."

"Perhaps I can offer you another. The pilots leave for their mission tomorrow morning. Continue on with them and we'll pay you a handsome bonus."

"Appreciate the offer, but I can't."

"You'd return to the States in time for school."

"It's not that. I promised my father that I'd remain in Dubai."

Bin Rashidi's uni-brow knits. "Why would he ask you to make this promise? What does he fear?"

"I dunno. But it was his one condition, and he was real serious about it."

"With all due respect, my father—he had seven sons—he would never ask any of us to sacrifice our business futures for a condition so foolish."

"Welcome to America. Anyway, why do you need me? You've already got eight pilots."

"The selected candidates are good, David, but piloting the Manta Ray has become second nature to you. There is a specific task we require on-site, one that will allow our crews to complete their mission more efficiently."

"What kind of task?"

"I cannot elaborate, but it would pay you quite well ... say, a quarter of a million dollars upon completion."

"Shit. Who do I have to kill?"

"Kill? No, it's one dive. Nothing more."

"Why can't Suits do it?"

"You're a better pilot. So then, do we have an arrangement?"

"Let me call my father; I'm sure I can persuade him."

"And if you cannot?"

"If I can't, I can't go."

▽ ▽ ▽

"DAD, YOU'RE BEING unreasonable!"

"I'm being unreasonable? David, you have no idea what these Arabs want you to do? You think bin Rashidi's offering that kind of money for a pleasure trip?"

"I can handle it."

"David, it's too dangerous."

"How do you know?"

"I know."

"How?"

"Because they asked me first!" Jonas remains silent for a long moment, weighing what to tell his son. "I turned them down, David, because it's a suicide mission."

David sits down on the king-size bed, feeling numb. "A suicide mission? What does that mean exactly?"

"I can't elaborate. Mac and I signed non-disclosure agreements."

"The Mariana Trench?"

"Worse."

"Worse? What's worse?"

"David, listen to me. Finish your job at the aquarium, but don't trust these people."

David swallows the lump in his throat. "Dad, I have a friend. She was selected to go."

"She? You mean a *girl*friend. Christ ..."

"What do I do?"

"Talk her out of it."

"That won't be easy." David removes the receiver from his ear—

—someone knocking at his suite door. "Dad, I have to go. I'll call you later."

"David—" The connection is severed.

David hurries to the front door and opens it.

Kaylie steps into his arms. Her lips press against his, her tongue tasting like beer. "Miss me?"

"Yeah." He kicks the door closed behind her, leading her to the couch. "What happened tonight? Did they tell you where you were heading?"

"No, but they told us about the money. Lots of money, honey." She pulls off his tee-shirt then sets to work on his pants.

"Wait, I need to talk to you about something. I met with bin Rashidi; he's trying to convince me to go with you."

"Really?" Her eyes widen. "Wow, David, that would be amazing—"

"I turned him down. I just got off the phone with my father. He told me this is a suicide mission, that bin Rashidi tried to recruit him for it, and he turned him down."

"Why? What's the mission?"

"He couldn't tell me. Some kind of legal agreement. Kaylie, you can't go."

"Can't? David, I am going. And it's not just about the money, which is very good, by the way. I really want to go."

"Didn't you hear what I just said? My father's dived the Mariana Trench, and he calls it suicide."

"No offense, sweetie, but your father's like a hundred. At his age, going to the bathroom in the middle of the night's a suicide mission."

"Nice. Real nice."

"You know I'm just kidding. Listen, every one of us knew there was an element of danger when we signed on, but hasn't that always been part of the deal as a field scientist?"

"I suppose."

"Think about it, David. Whatever bin Rashidi has lined up for us ... it's got to be an incredible opportunity, maybe even a scientific break-through. I mean, look at this facility. The money they've spent. They must have discovered some new exotic species to invest so much into this aquarium. Don't you want to be a part of it?"

"*Kronosaurus.*"

"What?"

"*Kronosaurus.* An ancient marine reptile."

"I know what they are. What about them?"

"Twenty years ago, a powerful businessman, Benedict Singer, began exploring the Mariana Trench in search of a rare manganese nodule he believed would lead to a breakthrough in cold fusion. What he discovered, instead, was a sub-species of *Kronosaurus*, no doubt part of the Megalodon's food chain. My parents were involved; they nearly died down there. My father didn't say, but I'm guessing that's the species bin Rashidi's after."

"Kronosaurs ... wow." She lies back on the leather sofa, trying to recall what the forty-foot pliosaurs looked like.

"Kaylie, you can't tell anyone about this. No one knows—"

"No, of course not."

"Then you'll tell Captain Suits you're resigning, right?"

"No."

"Kaylie—"

"David, what if you had been selected as one of the scientists to be aboard the *Alvin* back in 1977, when they discovered hydrothermal vents? Would you have turned them down because it was dangerous?"

"This is different."

"Not to me. I never wanted to be one of those eggheads who spend twenty hours a day working in a lab. My goal was always to work in the field. You can't have the rewards without the risks. You know that."

"You told me the Megs frighten you."

"They do. But this isn't aquarium work. This is cutting edge science. I can deal with the fear by being prepared. Come with me. I know you want to." She nuzzles his neck. "Think about it ... the two of us on a research vessel, netting deep sea creatures by day, bunking together at night—"

"I can't. I gave my word."

"So did I. I'm going."

"I love you." The words are blurted out, surprising even David.

She stares at him, caught off guard.

"I know, I know. We barely know each other, but I really mean it. And I'm not pussy-whipped! All night long I've been feeling like—like somebody's ripping my heart out. I know it's against your rule, but I really do love you, Kaylie."

She lays her head against his chest. "I feel the same way."

"You do?"

"Shh."

They hold one another, the moment chasing away the dilemma at hand, until exhaustion takes over, and they doze off in each other's arms.

∇ ∇ ∇

KAYLIE AWAKENS WITH a start. She checks her watch. "David? David, wake up."

"What time is it?"

"Just after four. I have to pack. We leave in less than an hour."

"You're still going?"

"Yes, and I think you should too."

"Kaylie—"

"I'll make you a deal. If we get out to wherever we're going and we see it really is a suicide mission, then we leave. No argument. But I just can't blow this off because your father decided it's crazy—not without checking things out for myself. You understand?"

"Yes."

She stands. "What you said earlier ... I want you to know, it means the world to me."

She kisses him softly on the lips then heads for the door. "I'll see you when I get back."

David remains on the sofa, feeling helpless as he watches her go.

PART 2

'TIS BETTER TO BUY A SMALL BOUQUET
AND GIVE TO YOUR FRIEND THIS VERY DAY,
THAN A BUSHEL OF ROSES WHITE AND RED
TO LAY ON HIS COFFIN AFTER HE'S DEAD.
—AN IRISH TOAST

22

Tanaka Oceanographic Institute
Monterey, California

Two weeks later …

A cool westerly breeze blows in from the Pacific, the sun high in a cloudless blue sky.

James "Mac" Mackreides watches from the main deck as the capacity crowd files into the arena. Two CBS film crews are posted at either end of the lagoon, shooting B-role for the *60 Minutes* segment that will air later this month. Seagulls circle overhead, the scavengers alerted by a potpourri of aromas wafting from concession stands, back after a forty-one-day reprieve.

A few of the birds stand sentry atop the new plexiglass wave wall, a barrier which shields the first twenty-two rows in the south end's lower bowl.

Mac touches the radio strapped to his left shoulder. "Deck to Princess—"

A moment's static, then Danielle Taylor's voice comes through. "Don't call me that."

"You've been in make-up for three days."

"Shut up."

"Capacity crowd, lots of film crews. Try not to fall on your head this time. It's bad for business."

"Isn't there an early bird special somewhere that we could drop you off?"

Mac smiles. "Have a good show, kiddo." He clicks over to another setting. "Deck to Base. J.T., you coming up?"

From the lab three stories below, Jonas speaks into his radio. "Be there in five. How's the crowd?"

"Dry, so far."

"Let's keep 'em that way." Jonas turns his attention to Dr. Nichols, who is seated before two computer screens and a bank of closed circuit video monitors revealing various views of the lagoon.

OVER THE LAST several weeks, Jonas and his team have been testing the neurotransmitter they had surgically implanted in Angel's brain, cataloguing different combinations of impulses with the Megalodon's responses. By stimulating the right distal area of the Meg's olfactory center, Dr. Nichols was able to create an alluring phantom odor powerful enough to coax the big female from the canal into the lagoon, thirty percent of the time. When the odor was combined with half of a steer carcass tossed into the southern end of the tank, positive responses increased to fifty-five percent.

When the two were combined with Bobby Baitman, Angel responded every time.

Bobby Baitman was the brainchild of Misty Walker, one of Dr. Stelzer's environmental techs. Having just rebounded from a bad divorce, Misty had been involved in an ongoing debate with several of her female colleagues on what qualities they looked for in the perfect man. Two weeks later, Misty showed up at work with her new boyfriend, a well-endowed, life-like sex doll that she had rigged with robotic appendages.

Inspired by the gag, Jonas approached Misty about making specific modifications to the doll to simulate the erratic movements of a swimmer. The final product was an anthropomorphic robot with limbs that could kick and paddle, and a "beating heart" that generated electrical impulses when submerged in water.

V V V

THE SELLOUT CROWD of fifteen thousand rises to its feet, applauding Danielle Taylor as she makes her way to the podium at the southern end of the tank. Acknowledging the crowd, Dani takes the wireless microphone. "Ladies and gentleman, welcome back to the all new Tanaka Institute and the most frightening show on Earth."

As she speaks, Teddy Badaut and his crew of three—among them a petite woman with dark blonde hair—wheel in a skinned steer carcass placed on a spring-loaded, steel catapult. The small platform is maneuvered into its pre-set location on the south deck, the ancient weapon aimed at the center of the lagoon.

"Today, one lucky audience member will be given a chance to win a million dollars!" Dani approaches one of the patrons seated in the first row. "Sir, what's the craziest thing you'd be willing to do to win a million dollars?"

"Me? I don't know ... feed Angel?"

"Feed Angel? Do you think that's worth a million dollars?"

The audience boos.

"Ma'am, how about you? A million dollars. What would you do?"

"Oh, gosh. I'd strip naked and run around the lagoon in my birthday suit."

Her husband covers his head as the crowd boos.

"I don't think they liked that. You sir, how about you? What would you be willing to do for a million in cash?"

Seated in the fourth row, twenty-eight-year-old Nathan Lee Tolbert stands to address the crowd, a beer in hand. "For a million bucks, I'd swim across the lagoon! How's that?"

The audience goes crazy.

"Wow. What's your name?"

"Bobby Baitman. From Bayonne, New Jersey."

"Let me get this straight, Bobby. For a million in cash, you'd actually swim across the lagoon—"

"—the width, only the width."

"Are you a good swimmer?"

"Pretty damn good. But I'm a little drunk." He flops an arm around Dani's shoulder.

She fends him off. "And you'd be willing to swim the width of the lagoon, right now, for a million dollars?"

"Right now?" He turns to the cheering crowd egging him on. "Sure! Let's do it!"

"Well, Bobby, come on down!" The crowd goes wild as Nathan Torbert follows Dani to the A-frame. "Teddy, can one of your men get Bobby a wetsuit. Make it an extra large."

One of Teddy's men enters a supply closet, returning moments later with a wetsuit, and hands it to Dani—

—who hands it to Nathan. "Bobby, go get changed. You can use that port-o-potty." She points to the enclosed bathroom near the southern bleachers. A security guard keys the unit open.

Nathan waves to the crowd then ducks inside.

"Hold it! Hold it right there!" Jonas appears on deck, yelling through a wireless mike pinned to his shirt, the battery pack stowed in his back pocket.

"Dad, please. I'm in the middle of a show."

"Young lady, maybe your concussion caused brain damage. You cannot allow one of our audience members to risk his life. Even for a million dollars!"

"Why not?"

"Why not? For one thing, if something terrible were to happen—a slipped disk, for instance, or an accidental drowning, or something even worse—the trauma of witnessing such an event might cause members of our audience to sue the Institute."

"Dad, they wouldn't do that. Would you?"

A chorus of *nos* fills the stadium.

"See? Hey, Bobby, how you doing in there?"

"I'm ready. Just a little nervous."

Jonas opens the port-o-potty, and—

—Nathan passes him Bobby Baitman, the robotic dummy dressed in a full wetsuit and hood, along with a flotation jacket, rigged with clear piano wire to the pulley atop the A-frame.

Misty activates a remote control device concealed behind the hunk of beef, signaling the robot's legs to walk. Jonas and Dani guide the mobile dummy to the edge of the southern sea wall, while inside the port-o-potty, Nathan continues speaking through his wireless microphone, carrying on his part of the conversation between the dummy and Dani. "I'm a little nervous. Where's Angel?"

Cheers rise from the crowd.

"Angel's in the canal. Bobby, if you're going to do this, you'd better do it now."

"Any last minute advice?"

"Swim really fast, and try not to splash."

"Just have the cash ready."

They walk Bobby past the newly installed guardrails to the edge of the sea wall. "Okay, then, on the count of three. One ... two ..."

The crowd yells three, but the dummy remains seated on the sea wall, its robotic arms seemingly clutching Jonas.

"Bobby, what happened?"

"Just nervous. Can we try it again?"

"Okay, one more time. One ... two ..."

On "three" Jonas releases the robot, which appears to dive into the water. The flotation device keeps it prone and buoyant along the surface. The crowd screams and cheers as Misty Walker signals the life-like mannequin's limbs to kick and paddle, while the invisible cable wires, fastened atop the A-frame, discreetly pull the dummy across the width of the lagoon as if it were really swimming.

The crowd goes crazy.

Mac speaks into his radio. "Deck to Base. Bobby's in the water. Cue Angel."

Dr. Nichols activates the neuro-implant, stimulating the olfactory bulb in Angel's brain.

∀ ∀ ∀

THE BIG FEMALE remains in seventy feet of water, her snout pressing against the canal's steel doors, her mouth slack-jawed as she filters a current of seawater through her gills. Atop her skull is a rectangular-shaped, blood-red scar—all that remains of the surgical suite which the animal had bashed off shortly after awakening from its anesthesia.

Suddenly she is alert, her ampullae of Lorenzini homing in on Bobby Baitman's electrical impulses, her lateral line registering the robotic doll's vibrations along the surface, her nostrils inhaling an artificially generated, pungent scent.

Leaving the barrier, Angel moves through the canal into the brilliant azure bathtub, her rising dorsal fin announcing her presence.

∀ ∀ ∀

A CRESCENDO OF screams fills the arena as Angel enters the lagoon, the albino creature turning right, heading for the oblivious swimmer now halfway across the tank.

Dani, safe behind the rail with her father, yells into her microphone, "Bobby! Bobby, get out of there! Ted, somebody, get a rope!"

Uncertain of what is actually happening, the crowd is on its feet—screaming, ranting, going crazy—as the dorsal fin circles the swimmer, and goes deep!

Mac cues Teddy by radio. "Wait ... wait ... now!"

Teddy activates the A-frame's pulley—

—retracting the clear spool of cable, jerking Bobby Baitman straight out of the water—

—Angel launching out of the lagoon after him like a Polaris missile.

The Meg snaps her jaws beneath the rising dummy, twisting as she defies gravity for a heart-stopping, camera-snapping moment before plunging back into the water with a thunderous splash.

Dani and Jonas take cover behind the wave wall as the barrier is pelted by the torrential burst, the crowd in the first few rows instinctively ducking.

Dani steps out from behind the clear barrier, speaking excitedly into her microphone, "Let's give our stuntman, Bobby Baitman, a well-deserved round of applause!"

The mechanized sex doll waves to the cheering crowd from high atop the A-frame, most of the audience believing he is real.

"And how about a little treat for Angel ... the Angel of Death!"

Teddy fires the catapult, sending the 150-pound side of beef launching high into the air, before falling gracefully into the center of the lagoon—

—where its perturbed diner snaps its jaws around the offering in one tremendous bite!

Teddy's team uses the distraction to quickly lower Bobby Baitman to the deck, where the lifelike doll is loaded onto an awaiting Gurney, still waving as he's wheeled away.

Dani waits until Angel has returned to the canal before addressing the crowd. "And that's our show for this afternoon! Thank you for coming. Please exit the arena carefully using the nearest gate, and be sure to visit the Meg Pen gallery. Belle and Lizzy's next feeding is at three p.m."

Jonas slips his arm around his daughter's waist as they cross the soaked deck to the staff corridor, listening to comments from the bleachers.

"That Baitman guy's crazy! Whatever they're paying him, it ain't enough!"

"For a million bucks, I'd do it!"

"Sure you would."

"When that fin started circling, my heart was beating so fast, I thought I was having a heart attack."

Jonas winks at Dani. "You were great. How do you feel?"

"A dull headache, nothing too bad. Dad, this new show ... it's brilliant. It puts the audience right there, like they're in the water with Bobby."

Looking up, Jonas sees Tom Cubit waiting for them inside the corridor, the attorney shaking his head, grimacing.

"Tommy. What? Nobody died, did they?"

"Not yet. The paramedics are still treating half a dozen fainting-related injuries and a potential heart attack, which I think may have been your insurance guy. At this rate, I'll never see the outside of a courtroom."

They gaze at the inert figure covered in a sheet on the Gurney, its groin bulging beneath the wetsuit. "Smile, Tom. Things can always be worse. Look at Bobby ... he's happy."

Dubai Aquarium
Dubai, United Arab Emirates

The enormous man-made lake, more than three miles in circumference, harbors the concrete foundations supporting the twelve two-hundred-foot shark fins.

The setting sun at their backs, David and Monty stand on one of the six acrylic glass and steel walkways overlooking the lake. Staring below at the turtles, they estimate there are now several hundred of them—the bigger specimens green sea turtles, the smaller ones hawksbills—all having been transplanted from the Persian Gulf into the thirty-foot-deep, acrylic bowl.

David watches one of the reptiles' heads poke through the surface of the water bathed in reflecting golden hues. "Think they're happy?"

"The turtles? Hell, yes. They probably have a turtle orgy every night. Of course, only humans and dolphins actually do it for fun, or so I've heard. I once read a pig's orgasm lasts thirty minutes. In my next life, I want to be a pig."

David grins. "What do you mean, in your next life?"

"That's the first time I've seen you smile in weeks."

"What's to smile about? We went from living in a five-star hotel with round-the-clock room service and cable TV to sharing a single-wide trailer with an old Sanyo that only gets local stations in Arabic. And no offense, but having lived with you these last few weeks, calling you a pig is an insult to the pig. Plus the fact that I have to practically drag your smelly ass out of bed every morning—"

"I'm bi-polar. Some days are good, some are bad. You knew the deal when you adopted me." Monty hocks up mucus from the back of his throat and spits it into the turtle pond, tempting up a hawksbill. "It's not too late, you know."

"What's not too late?"

"To go and find your woman. They'd still fly you out if you asked."

"How do you know that?"

"I heard one of bin Rashidi's goons talking to Dr. Becker about you. It was all in Arabic, but I picked it up well enough. Things aren't going well on their little hunting expedition. I'm surprised they didn't mention it to you."

David slams his palms on the aluminum rail. "They won't tell me anything. Not where they went or how she's doing ... or *what* she's doing?"

"Want to find out?"

"How?"

"The tank the Arabs labeled 'bad fish.' Let's see what kind of bad fish they captured."

"Again, how? They keep the T-1 gallery locked at all times. A guard is posted outside when Becker enters to make sure no one else follows her in."

"Main ventilation shaft. It connects with every eighth floor deck."

"How do you know that?"

"I spend six hours a day cutting raw fish. On my breaks I sit in my director's office, playing with his computer. Everything's touch-screen. The aquarium schematics were right there."

"How do we access the shaft?"

"We enter through the air conditioning intake on the deck of T-3. From there, it's a short crawl into T-1."

David checks his watch. "Night shift clocks in at eight. That gives us forty minutes. Let's go!"

They jog over the bridge to the third floor entrance, David using his magnetic access card to gain entry into the facility. The main lobby is deserted, the day shift having left twenty minutes earlier. They follow the east alcove to aquarium's T-1, T-3, and T-5, then use the access card to enter the door marked T-3: RESTRICTED. The interior corridor leads them to a stairwell, which they ascend five flights to Level 8. Passing through another set of security doors marked T-3, they step out onto the upper deck of the empty aquarium.

The pond-size surface and work deck is deserted, the tank void of sea life, the filtration systems running. Low level ultraviolet lights illuminate patches of coral formations growing seventy feet below.

"Here!" Monty pushes a mobile gantry toward the air conditioning intake, situated fifteen feet above the deck along one wall. "Standard bolts. A drill would be nice."

David searches through a tool cabinet. He locates a drill, verifies it's charged, and attaches a flathead screwdriver drill bit. He passes the drill up to Monty, who sets to work on the four-foot by four-foot aluminum grid.

The bolts unscrew easily. "Butter. Let's go."

David climbs up the wheeled scaffolding, following Monty inside the aluminum shaft.

It's cold inside, at least thirty degrees cooler, the air rushing at their faces, howling through the dark tunnel. They creep forward on all fours, the palms of their hands taking the brunt of the work.

"A flashlight would have helped," David whispers.

"Just follow me." Reaching the main junction, Monty turns left, crawling another ninety feet before coming to another short stretch of shaft on their left that dead-ends in a dull patch of light. "See there? That's T-1's intake."

David follows him to the grid then peeks through the grill out to the deck of aquarium T-1. "Looks clear. How do we pop the grill from the inside?"

"I dunno. Did you bring a pair of needle-nose pliers?"

"Did you ask me to bring pliers?"

"I assumed you'd know."

"You assumed? Who am I? Freakin' Tom Cruise in *Mission Impossible*? Wait here!" David hustles back out the vent to the main junction, follows it out to T-3's vent, climbs down the scaffolding, grabs two pairs of needle-nose pliers from the tool cabinet, then hurries back through the air conditioning ducts to Monty—

—who has already managed to loosen three of the four bolts with his fingers. "Guess we didn't need the pliers after all."

"Get out of the way." David unscrews the last bolt and they pop open the intake grill.

It's a fifteen-foot drop to the concrete deck below, the area dark, save for the glowing red exit signs.

"Should I jump?" Monty asks.

"And shatter your ankles so I have to take care of your ass for another eight weeks? Move over!" Backing out feet-first, David shimmies down the wall as far as he can then drops the last eight feet, rolling with the fall. He finds a ladder and sets it in place for Monty, who reattaches the grid, then joins him by the edge of the dark tank.

"I can't see a thing," Monty whispers. "Should I turn on the lights?"

"No. They're keeping it dark for a reason. Could be a nocturnal species." Leaving the edge of the enormous pool, he locates the main fuse box and the switches for the aquarium's red nocturnal lights. He flicks the entire row ON—

—blood-red patches of light blooming in the tank.

Monty scans the hour glass-shaped pool. A dark shadow circles along the bottom. "Something's in there."

"What is it?"

"Dunno. Could be the Loch Ness Monster."

"Let's get down to the gallery. We'll be able to see it better from there."

They head for the exit, following the concrete stairwell five flights down to Level 3. Opening the metal fire door, they step out into the vast public gallery, the empty hall dark except for the red glow coming from the aquarium's towering wall of acrylic glass.

Monty paces before the window, looking in. "I still don't see anything. Here, Nessie! Come on, girl."

A shiver crawls down David's spine. "Monty, freeze."

"Why?"

"Just don't move, it sees you!"

"What sees me?" Monty turns—

—as the creature slowly circles back toward the gallery window, its bulbous nocturnal eyes glowing green in the red light.

"Jesus ... what in the holy hell is that?"

The ocean's first true predator moves majestically past the bay window, the placoderm's thick hide appearing dark brown, a silvery hue along its belly. Its body is as long and wide as a bus, tapering back from its brutish, armor-plated skull to a massive upper-lobed tail fin. The hinged mouth is open, revealing bony plated teeth—cusped and deeply serrated from the shearing action generated by the double upper fangs constantly sliding past the lower incisors.

David's throat tightens as the hunter moves off into the shadows then circles back again, stalking the gallery window. "It's a Dunk," David whispers, his voice cracking.

"What's a Dunk?"

Monty's sudden movements alert the creature. Changing course, it charges the window—

—the glass igniting seconds before the impact in searing purple bolts of electricity, the voltage chasing the beast back into the shadows.

Monty collapses to his knees, sweat pouring down his face. "What just happened?!"

David approaches the tank, pointing to the small octagon-shaped devices, each the size of a man's fist, spaced at ten-foot intervals along the inside of the aquarium's bay windows. "They're impact sensors. Generate quite a charge. Designed to keep the Dunk from shattering the glass."

"The Dunk? You mean that prehistoric fish on display back at the hotel?"

"*Dunkleosteus.* King of the Devonian seas."

"I thought those things went extinct?"

"They did ... about 300 million years ago."

"Three hundred fifty-five million years, to be exact." The crown prince enters the viewing gallery, followed by Barbara Becker and two security guards, the bulges beneath their dark suits revealing automatic weapons. "Mr. Montgomery, when you were reviewing the aquarium's schematics, didn't you notice the array of security cameras hidden in every ceiling?"

"You know, I may have missed that. I speak Arabic; I don't read it all that well."

"I admire resourcefulness, but breaking and entering is still a punishable crime in my country. David, it's good to see you again. What do you think of our first resident species?"

"Honestly, I'm blown away."

"I'm glad you like it. What I enjoy most ... is watching it hunt live prey. So? Which one of you would like to go for a swim?"

The two security guards step forward, causing beads of sweat to burst out across David's flesh.

The crown prince smiles. "Just having some fun. Dr. Becker, if you would?"

Barbara Becker speaks into her radio. "Feed T-1."

A few moments pass, allowing David's pulse to settle. The *Dunkleosteus* lurks in the shadows, moving slowly along the bottom like a caged tiger—

—until something splashes down into the tank, directly above their heads!

The six-hundred-pound green sea turtle rights itself then splays itself against the bay window, the claws of its flipper-like legs scratching the acrylic surface as its paddles along the face of the tank in a panic.

The disturbance alerts the Dunk. Its back arches, its smallish pectoral fins going rigid, pointing downward as it swims in a tight figure-eight pattern.

Monty whispers to David, "So much for saving the turtles."

"Shh."

The Dunk rises away from the bottom and circles past the bay window, offering its human guests a close up view of its armored plating and gill slits. Wary of the electrical shock, it does not attack, but rather coaxes the turtle away from the window.

Seeing the large predator, the turtle darts for a cluster of rocks looming in the shadows along the bottom.

The monster races in from behind its prey, snatching the turtle within its powerful jaws—

—*craaaaaack !*

Even underwater and behind the thick acrylic glass, the sound is unmistakable. The *Dunkleosteus*'s bony blades crush the turtle's thick shell like a nutcracker popping open a walnut. David watches, breathless, as the monster gulps down the dead turtle's remains, its silver belly quivering with the effort.

Dr. Becker grips David's forearm. "Watch."

The agitated Dunk swims back and forth several times then suddenly convulses, regurgitating the sharp fragments of turtle shell in a burst of cloudy brown vomit.

Dr. Becker leans in to David. "Incredible, isn't it?"

"It that all it eats? Turtles?"

"We've tried other fish, but it prefers slower moving prey. Dunks are not the swiftest of hunters, and their senses are lacking compared to sharks. But they'll eat anything that moves and regurgitate the bones later. We attached a force-plate to the underside of one of the turtle's shells a few days ago; the Dunk's jaws registered 8,560 pounds per square inch of force. Pound for pound, that's greater than those of your Megalodon."

"Pretty impressive. Just remember, to Angel, the Dunk's still a single serving meal." David turns back to the crown prince. "The Mariana Trench?"

"No. The Dunk was lured up from the depths at a specific location in the Philippine Sea. While I cannot go into details at this time, suffice it to say there are other sea monsters lurking down there as well—exotic creatures the likes of which man has never seen. Join us, David. Help us capture these amazing animals and I'll make you rich beyond your wildest dreams."

"You have your pilots, you don't need me."

"Our pilots are good, but they've had a few ... challenges."

The *Dunkleosteus* passes slowly before the glass, its lidless nocturnal eyeball cold and soulless, its mouth revealing shards of brown turtle meat caught between its hellish incisors.

David closes his eyes, trying to imagine what it would be like piloting one of the Manta Rays in an enclosed alien sea, surrounded by blackness, squeezed beneath sixteen thousand pounds per square inch of water pressure as he uses his sub to lure history's most frightening creations out of their abyssal purgatory and into a net.

"My father was right. It's a suicide mission."

"Ms. Szeifert would disagree. She's in the Philippine Sea, hunting these creatures even as we speak. I hear she misses you terribly, but is doing her best to persevere. You have good taste; that one is a pearl of great price, something to be treasured. If she'd have me, I'd make her one of my wives."

David's blood pressure soars, every muscle in his body trembling, saturated with adrenaline. "Are you baiting me?"

"I'm offering you a once-in-a-lifetime opportunity. Ms. Szeifert seized the moment. When will you?"

"Alright, Your Highness. I'll stock your aquarium. But you and your goons leave Kaylie alone. Is that clear? From now on, she works strictly with me!"

The crown prince smiles. "As you wish. I've taken the liberty of packing your belongings. My private jet leaves within the hour."

"What about Monty?"

"Mr. Montgomery may accompany you as a deckhand. If he wishes to join you, he must pack his own things. And if he desires to remain on board the ship, he'll learn to clean up his mess, or he'll find himself sleeping in the fish chute."

23

The two juvenile Megalodons circle their rectangular habitat in tandem—Lizzy in the dominant top position, the darker Bela below, her head just behind her sibling's pelvic girdle so that the trough created by her sister's moving mass tows her around the tank effortlessly.

Peter Carlisle, the Institute's twenty-six-year-old director of education, watches the two forty-six-foot hunters circle the tank from behind a concrete pillar in the Meg Pen gallery. Obsessed with sharks from the moment he was traumatized by the movie *JAWS* at the age of four, Peter has made a career of studying them. After completing his bachelor's degree in marine biology, he went on to earn his master's degree at nearby Moss Landing Marine labs while completing an exhaustive research project tracking Leopard Sharks in the Elkhorn Slough, one of the largest tracks of tidal salt marsh in California.

For the Berkeley grad student, the job at the Tanaka Institute is both a summer job and part of his research. Peter's dissertation deals with the trophic interactions of pelagic sharks like the great white—specifically, how the predators interact with other species in their respective food webs and chains.

Observing Belle and Lizzy has been an education unto itself. By virtue of cooperative behavior, the two sisters have eliminated the other three siblings within their food web, as well as any outside intruders entering their habitat.

As noted in Peter's dissertation, the juvenile's bizarre behavior is continuing to evolve into new forms of dominance—this time extending outside of their tank. Over the last several weeks, the sisters have been increasingly engaging in a behavior known as spy-hopping, the act of keeping their heads vertically above the surface to observe activity outside of their liquid domain. Four days ago, Lizzy had put the fear of God into several maintenance men who were working on the outer deck when they turned to discover the twenty-one-ton albino staring at them from the edge of the Meg Pen pool. From that moment on, if a staff member ventured too close to the tank's guardrail, the two Megalodons would work themselves into a frenzy, splashing the intruder with great swaths of their tails. After witnessing the behavior, Dr. Stelzer had instituted a new rule: No one was allowed within twenty feet of the aquarium's surface area.

An extension of that rule now applied to the gallery crowd. The heavily layered acrylic bay window was two-way, allowing the Megs to observe the thousands of visitors peering at them on a daily basis. The maturing juveniles were clearly growing agitated by the presence of the humans, leading Dr. Stelzer to stretch police tape from one end of the gallery to the other, preventing guests from coming within fifteen feet of the towering acrylic glass. As an added precaution, the lights in the gallery were extinguished, the rows of seats kept in the shadows.

Peter checks his watch as the gallery's ushers open the corridor doors for the next show. "Good evening, folks, welcome to the Meg Pen viewing gallery. Please fill in every seat as the show is sold out. No one is permitted near the bay windows or beyond the police tape, and flash photography is strictly forbidden."

Fifteen-year-old Connor Booth files in with his youth group buddies, his heart pounding in his throat. This is the teen's fourth trip to the Meg Pen. His first visit eight months ago was so frightening that he had decided to give up surfing altogether.

It is the presence of the police tape that has Connor so nervous, the barrier adding an additional risk to the wager he has made with his friends. Turning to his right he sees Dave Lounsbury take his place only three seats away, the youth director's attention momentarily occupied with his four-year-old son.

"So? You going to do it?" Chessa Manion, the "decided" red-head with the big green eyes and "Chessa-cat" smile, nudges him from the seat to his left.

"Can't. Lounsbury's too close."

"Switch seats with me. Hurry up!" She climbs over him, allowing him to slide into her chair. "Let me know when you're ready, and I'll block his view."

Connor's rival, Ryan Wrightsman, smacks the back of his head from his seat one row back. "No balls."

"Ignore him," Chessa whispers, resting one hand on his knee, using the other to ready her cell phone camera. "All you need is one good shot."

"I can't do it when they pass the window. If I do it so close I'm busted. I have to do it on the approach."

"As long as I get it on my camera phone, you win."

Connor removes his key chain and a small cylinder—a diode-pumped solid-state green laser pointer. He tests the pointer on the floor as the two truck-size behemoths pass by the three-story window before him, eliciting *oohs* and *aahs* from the crowd.

Peter Carlisle begins his presentation, the gallery's speakers positioned along the back wall, away from the tank. "Born in captivity with three smaller siblings, Belle and Lizzy weighed twenty-seven hundred pounds at birth, making them larger as newborns than ninety percent of the world's adult great white sharks, their modern-day cousins. The sisters are now five years old and still considered juveniles. They won't reach adulthood for another four to six years, at which point they'll be as long as their seventy-four-foot mother, Angel, though nowhere near as heavy."

Connor watches the two Megs disappear into the far end of the tank. He has memorized their swimming pattern, knows exactly when and where the two predators will cross the aquarium again before circling into view. Readying the laser pen, he nudges Chessa. The girl leans forward, concealing the device from their youth leader, her own heart beating rapidly—

—as first Lizzy, then Belle, appear in the distance, zagging across the center of the tank along the bottom, ninety feet behind the glass.

Connor activates the pointer, shooting a pencil-thin, lime-green 300 mW laser beam through the bay window and into the aquarium's depths—

—the light striking Belle harmlessly by her left nostril, the Meg oblivious—

—until she continues swimming through the infrared beam and the bright laser pierces her sensitive left eye, damaging her retina while igniting every predatory reflex in the animal's nervous system!

His back to the tank, it is not the laser that alerts Peter Carlisle but the crowd's sudden reaction. Turning, he sees Belle race away from her sibling, gathering speed as she alters her course—

—charging the bay window!

"Oh, Jesus—"

The crowd screams, most of the patrons frozen on their feet as the enraged 42,000-pound goliath rams the glass with the impact of a sledgehammer meeting a bullet-proof windshield. The force of the blow shatters the first three layers of acrylic and lifts the 150-ton bay window from its frame as the concussion wave spreads outward in every direction!

The resounding wallop crushes the cartilage in the Megalodon's snout with its lower front teeth, the thundering sound wave rumbling through the facility like a magnitude 6.0 earthquake.

"Easy! Stay calm! Exit in an orderly manner! You, stop pushing! Security, grab that guy!"

Peter Carlisle turns his back on the chaos and places his hand against the aquarium's damaged window, feeling its dying reverberations through his skin. The impact zone is a twelve foot crater of shattered acrylic, radiating outward into a network of tributaries that create a latticework of cracks across the entire gallery window.

A five-inch lower tooth remains embedded in the glass, its point buried an inch deep, a finger-like piece of pink gum flapping from its severed root.

The window is damaged beyond repair, but intact. For the moment. All that separates the lower level of the Tanaka Institute from being invaded by sixty million gallons of seawater is a scant four-inch-thin, circular section of acrylic.

The last of the panicked crowd pushes its way out of the exits, leaving Peter and two security guards alone in the gallery. "Seal all doors. The gallery is officially closed ... forever."

Western Pacific Ocean
227 nautical miles from Guam

The Antonov An-124 Ruslan aircraft soars 42,000 feet above the Pacific, the ocean below obscured by heavy thunderstorms that rock the immense transport plane.

David Taylor, strapped in one of the eighty-eight seats situated behind the open cockpit, feels air sick. "This blows. I assumed we'd at least be flying out on the prince's private luxury jet, not the Arabian version of a C-5."

"Russian version, actually," says Monty, feeding from a bag of peanuts. "Bigger, too. A gift to the king. Speaking of kings, did you know in ancient England a commoner couldn't have sex or make a baby unless he had consent from the king. Once you had consent, you had to hang a sign from your door that said *Fornication Under Consent of the King*. Get it? F.U.C.K. So now you know where that noun came from. Or is it a verb?"

"I'm about to use it as an adjective. Where do you come up with all this trivial bullshit?"

"It's trivia, actually, and before I enlisted, it was sort of my thing. I used to compete in high school and college. No one in our squadron could touch me. Ever since I had my brains scrambled, it just pops out sometimes. Like hurricanes."

"What about them?" David holds on as the plane drops and rises again.

"Did you know that in ten minutes a hurricane releases more energy than all the nuclear weapons stockpiled in the world. Don't mess with Mother Nature. When it comes to an arms race, the bitch has us beat."

"That's ... great. I've gotta walk around before I puke."

Monty unhooks his seat belt and follows David back to the immense cargo area. "Interesting that I'm perfectly fine up here, but in the depths—"

"What is all this stuff?" David is dwarfed by a dozen cargo containers marked in Arabic.

Monty reads the invoice. "Whale meat—3,150 kilograms of it—about seven thousand pounds. Plus seventeen barrels of innards. Everything frozen. Either this is bait, or bin Rashidi's got his crew on the worst sushi diet I've ever seen."

David heads aft, one hand staying close to the row of containers as the big plane sways beneath his feet. "Look at that!"

Occupying the last 124 feet of the cargo hold is a single container nineteen feet high, twenty-two feet wide.

"What the hell are we hunting?"

"We? What's this 'we' stuff? You got a mouse in your pocket or something? Did you know it's illegal to catch mice in Cleveland without a hunting license?"

"Tell me again why you're here?"

"I'm your conscience, Pinocchio. I'm the guy who gets to call your father after you and Princess Kaylie fail to surface. 'Hello, Dr. Taylor? You don't know me but I used to share a trailer with your son ... yes, sir, fine boy ... good head on his shoulders. Too bad the little head got in the way. Had a perfectly fine job in Dubai, only he decided he had to save Princess Kaylie from the clutches of the bad crown prince and his evil dragon, which he intended to capture for the Dubai Aquarium, by the way ... until it ate him."

"Oh yeah? Well, did you know there's no 'I' in the word team!"

David heads back to his seat, leaving Monty laughing in hysterics.

24

The Boeing CH-47 Chinook twin-engine heavy-lift helicopter slows to sixty knots as the expedition's two ships come into view on the horizon.

The larger of the two vessels is a Malacca-max VLCC (very large crude carrier) designed with a draft shallow enough for it to navigate the Straits of Malacca, the preferred route between the Persian Gulf and Asia. Refitted and renamed the *Tonga*, the Japanese supertanker is crimson-red below the waterline and gray with red trim above, a floating steel island that spans 1,100 feet in length and 196 feet wide, displacing 300,000 tons. The deck, flat and open, is so large it could hold three football fields; the superstructure rising out of the stern is twelve stories high. Despite ten-foot seas, the *Tonga* sits low in the water, undisturbed.

Dwarfed by the supertanker is the expedition's second vessel, the *Dubai Land I*, sister ship to the 196-foot, 280-ton fishing trawler David had worked on weeks earlier. Maneuvering back and forth along the *Tonga's* port-side flank, the trawler is using the tanker's hulking presence as a wave barrier, lessening the effects of the hostile sea.

The Chinook descends, its twin rotors beating a path through the storm. Hovering above the *Tonga's* deck, the chopper's winches lower its payload—the first of a dozen containers to be transported from the crown prince's cargo plane. Steel kisses steel, creating an electrical discharge that momentarily scatters the tanker's crew. Regaining their nerve, they quickly release the container's clamps, freeing the chopper, which lands thirty yards astern.

David and Monty exit the aircraft, each man carrying a duffle bag. They instinctively duck as the helicopter takes off, heading back to Guam's Air Force base for another load.

A cold, driving rain beats against David's face, drenching his clothes. He waves at the Asian crew securing the container, but gets no response. "Now what?" he yells above the wind.

Monty points to the stern.

Fighting the weather, they head for the shelter of the towering superstructure.

▽ ▽ ▽

THEY ARE GREETED by an American in his early forties, his bulbous head bearing a receding brown hairline, his neck, back, and arms matted with hair. The accent is pure New York. "Welcome aboard the *Tonga*, gentlemen. We've been expecting you. Nick Cato, Deck Officer. Rough weather coming out of Guam?"

David nods. "And I thought the plane ride over was bad."

"We get hit by a typhoon and this'll seem like a day on the lake. I'll speak to the captain about letting you ride out the storm aboard the *Tonga* ... give you fellas a chance to get your sea legs. The rest of the sub pilots are all aboard the trawler."

David glances out the steel hatch's porthole, wondering if Kaylie is on board the trawler—

—or miles below the raging sea.

Nick Cato leads them up five flights of winding stairs to the bridge, a wide expanse of steel surrounded by large bay windows. Computerized instrument panels set on evergreen counter tops frame the command center.

Seated in his command chair, sipping a mug of hot coffee is the ship's captain.

Timon Singh is just under six feet, with short, dark curly hair, bushy brows, and a large Roman nose that matches his rugby player physique. Half white, half Indian, his complexion is bronze, his accent British. He is dressed in khaki trousers and a leather jacket, his expression almost bored as he glances at David, a worn toothpick dangling from his mouth.

"So you're the prized submersible pilot we've all been waiting for?"

"David Taylor." He offers his hand—

—the captain ignores it. "Ever been aboard a supertanker?"

"No. Must be a bitch to drive."

"Drive?" Captain Singh snorts a laugh. "Everything's run by computers. We plot our course and set our speed based on sea conditions. Takes us two hours just to reach our top cruising speed of sixteen knots. If you want to make a turn, you plan it hours ahead. If you want to stop you need a good five kilometers of sea in front of your bow, maybe half that as we're presently loaded down with ballast."

"And what ballast is that?"

"Who are you?"

"Jason Montgomery, part-time pilot, full-time dishwasher. What ballast are you hauling?"

"Seawater. The Arabs had the Japs sterilize the crude holds and re-divide 'em into rubber-lined saltwater tanks, each area rigged with saline and temperature controls. All for a bunch of sea creatures that have yet to make an appearance."

"Not true, Captain." A short, heavily-muscled Filipino enters the bridge, dressed in a yellow oil slicker. "Richard Hibpshman, marine biologist, University of Washington. I run the gut shop."

"Gut shop?"

"The lab. But gut shop is more accurate. My job is to analyze the stomach content of anything hauled out of the depths that dies, hoping for clues that tell us what else is down there. And the captain's wrong; the Japanese lured up a *Dunkleosteus* last month—"

"—which was shipped straight to Dubai," responds Timon Singh, spitting out his toothpick. "The only fish that made it onboard have been those big ray fins, and they croak within hours."

"Ray fins?"

"Leeds' fish. *Leedsichthys*. Giant filter feeders, about the size of a blue whale. We've netted four so far, the last one early this morning. It lasted almost twelve hours, twice as long as any of the others, so that's encouraging. I'm about to start the necropsy. Care to join me?"

"Hell, yes!"

"Not me," Monty says, waving them off. "Captain, is there someplace aboard this floating continent where a man can stretch out with a cold Heineken?"

"Mr. Cato, take our friend down to the rec room and see that he's properly inebriated."

"Yes, sir."

∇ ∇ ∇

DAVID FOLLOWS THE Filipino scientist down the infrastructure's stairwell, two levels below the main deck.

"Glad you're aboard, David. I'm a big fan of the Institute. Drove down the coast to see a few shows back when you first reopened. Not too many people to talk to aboard the tanker. Deck officers stay to themselves. Rest of the crew's Japanese and I don't speak the language."

Richard unlatches a sealed watertight door. "Through here."

A blast of noise and steam greets David as they enter the engine room. Richard leads him around a maze of heavy machinery to another watertight door marked

RESTRICTED in English and Japanese. "Ready?"

David nods.

The hatch opens, releasing a blast of cold salty air. David follows the scientist out onto a catwalk that leads them into the very bowels of the ship. The immense space, originally designed to hold three million barrels of crude oil, has been divided into five large holding pens situated four stories beneath the main deck, each containing a simplified filtration system. The tanks are accessible from the main catwalk by a circular stairwell that leads down to a porous steel deck.

"Our specimen's in Pen 4."

Richard leads him to the next stairwell then down two flights to Pen 4's deck, a reinforced grating that extends over one-third of the tank's eight-hundred-square-foot surface area. A series of steel cables attached to pulleys along the underside of the main deck drop down from the ceiling and disappear underwater. Richard opens a control panel situated along a vertical support beam and activates a switch.

The cable retracts, hauling a cargo net from out of the water, dragging with it an enormous fish.

The dead *Leedsichthys* rises tail-first, its half-moon-shaped caudal fin mottled brownish gray. It flops to one side as its long streamlined body follows.

Forty feet ... fifty ... and still the behemoth continues to rise, huge, flipper-like pectoral fins appearing. Then, finally, the grouper-like head, as big as a garbage truck, comes into view. The eighty-seven-foot fish sways in the dripping net just above the deck.

"Mind your feet." Richard presses another button, activating a motor that rolls the deck upon which they are standing forward on tracts, repositioning Pen 5's deck so that Pen 4's tank is almost completely covered.

"That should give us some work space." David stands back as Richard lowers the pulley cables, allowing the cargo net to unfurl, depositing the dead Leeds' fish onto the porous floor before them.

"Leeds-ick-thees is right. This thing stinks!" David covers his mouth against the overpowering stench.

"We'll need breathers and tools. And you'll need a slicker and boots. Come with me."

David follows him down another catwalk to the gut shop. The room is a community shower room converted into a lab. Two steel tables have been anchored to the tile floor, rows of lockers holding various cutting tools, equipment, rubber aprons and clothing.

Ten minutes later, dressed in a slicker, boots, gloves, and air mask, David begins gutting the fifty-ton bony fish with a chainsaw.

▽　▽　▽

IT IS AFTER seven o'clock at night by the time they have finished, two hours of steady work yielding access to a stomach bladder the size of a stretch limousine. Richard uses a seventeen-inch hemostat clamp to cut off the esophagus, preventing the remains of the Leeds' digested prey from being jettisoned out of its stomach. The scientist repeats the procedure with the lower intestines then uses a pair of pruning shears to slice open the immense stomach.

A wave of putrid brown muck flows out of the incision, the concentrated organic soup dripping through the porous decking. Richard adjusts his air mask then shocks his young protégé by climbing inside the stomach lining, sifting through the five-foot-deep organ with his body. "Shrimp ... jellyfish ... same plankton content as the other ones. Rich in hydrogen sulfide and methane ... all coming from cold seeps originating beneath the Philippine Sea Plate. Strange ... there's not much here for an eighty-five footer. Wait a second ... what's this? Feels like—"

Suddenly Richard's head disappears, his entire body yanked into the brown slime!

David rushes over as a gloved hand reaches out of the stomach. He grabs it before it disappears and pulls hard, dragging Richard's body out of the slit-open organ—

—along with a seven-foot, 225-pound shark, its snout embedded into the bloody remains of the marine biologist's stomach!

"—aahhh! Ahhh! Get it off!" Blood pours out of Richard's mouth, pooling in his mask.

David grabs the scientist and drags him away from the creature, the shark's upper jaw still clenching Richard's intestines, clamping them to its bizarre lower jaw—a spiral configuration outfitted with a whorl of teeth resembling the vertical blades of a circular saw!

The primitive shark flops and flounders in the muck. Primitive gill slits gasp for air, forcing it to release Richard. Innards gush out of his open wound, the eviscerated man bleeding out over the deck.

Trembling, David grabs the prehistoric beast by its tail and drags it to the edge of the deck, pushing it over the grated metal floor. The prehistoric shark falls twenty feet into the tank of seawater below and disappears.

Heart in his throat, David kneels by the dying Filipino, supporting his head as he gently pulls off his air mask.

Richard Hibpshmans looks up at him, opens his mouth to speak, and gurgles on his own blood. A moment later his eyes glaze over ... dead.

David leans back against a steel support beam, breathing deeply, fighting shock—

—while below, a spiked dorsal fin skewers the surface, the *Helicoprion* shark feeding off the dripping muck and blood falling through the porous steel deck of pen number four.

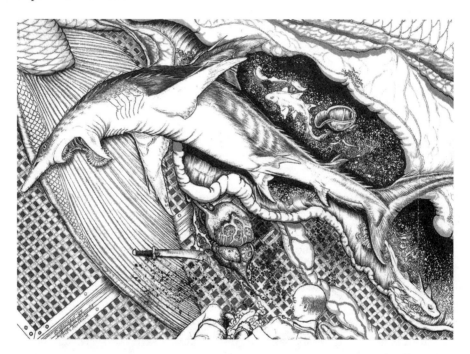

Aboard the Dubai Land I
Philippine Sea

Ibrahim Al Hashemi enters the skipper's cabin, the Dubai Aquarium director shaking as he delivers the news to Fiesal bin Rashidi. "The biologist's remains have been placed in refrigerated storage, as requested."

"I don't care about him. Tell me about the shark!"

"The shark ... is incredible. A female *Helicoprion*, and in excellent condition!"

"How did it get there? You told me these Leeds' fish were filter feeders."

"Yes, sir. I completed the autopsy of the *Leedsichthys*. It seems the fish had recently shed its giant mesh plates in the back of the throat. This probably happens annually. With the filtering organ temporarily gone, the consumption of the shark was purely accidental and probably led to its death by choking. As for the *Helicoprion*, though it will only grow to be ten feet long, its capture is a major prize. The lower jaw contains over one hundred seventy razor-sharp teeth set it in a spiral. The species itself dates back to the late Jurassic Period, over 150 million years ago. Maren's journal made no mention of the shark, so I never imagined such a find existed."

"And what of the species Maren did document? When will we find them, let alone capture one? I'm growing exceedingly impatient, Hashemi. And so is my cousin!"

"Sir, we'll find them—"

"Not today we won't." Brian Suits enters the cabin, wearing greasy overalls and a slicker. He peels off the wet jacket, hangs it on a hook, then flops down on a cushioned chair. "My teams are ascending. No casualties. No captures."

The Aquarium director can feel bin Rashidi's rage. "How far into the Panthalassa Sea did they venture today?"

"Beta team went nearly a mile before the pilot lost his nerve. Part of that has to do with all the bait in the water."

"Then remove the bait! Find a better way!" Bin Rashidi grows angrier, causing his thick uni-brow to knit upward like an inch worm. "What about Taylor?"

"He'll need to be challenged. Leave that to me." Brian reaches into a small cooler and fishes out a beer. "I heard about Richard. Unbelievable. Anyone contact the family?"

"Technically, he was part of your crew," bin Rashidi spats. "You handle it."

"Yeah, sure. Pretty quick thinking by the kid to save the shark. How's he holding up?"

"He's sleeping in sickbay aboard the *Tonga*," says Ibrahim Al Hashemi. "We need to discuss the *Helicoprion*. Who gets credit for its capture? Technically, Delta team captured the Leeds' fish; they will insist on receiving the points."

"No," states bin Rashidi. "Delta team's species died. Give the catch to Taylor. Bring him aboard. I want to speak with him tonight."

▽ ▽ ▽

THE DARK OLIVE ocean is barely visible through the night glass. David can feel the sea's weight squeezing in upon the powerless sub's thin acrylic shell. He can hear the wings buckling beneath timeless pressure, the invisible vise causing the straining microscopic fibers to sing—

—as the long shadow circles closer in the distance, drawn by the disturbance ... the creature's eyes iridescent-green in the glass, its black pupil locked in on him, revealing a godless soul ...

"Huh!" David sits up in bed, his pulse racing. The room is dimly lit, and it takes him several unnerving moments before he can place the memory.

Tanker. Sickbay. He lies back, remembering everything. *I shouldn't be here ...*

He squints as the lights turn on and someone enters. Nick Cato offers him a bottled water. "Feeling better?"

"Yeah."

"Storm's let up. The submersible crews are returning. Captain says they want you on board the trawler."

▽ ▽ ▽

A WAXING THREE-quarter moon illuminates a haze of clouds directly overhead, the night cool but not uncomfortable. David moves to the supertanker's port-side rail and looks down. Thirty feet below, the *Dubai Land I* maneuvers close by, its crew positioning heavy rubber truck tires over the starboard side to prevent the two boats' metal skins from colliding.

Nick Cato lowers a rope ladder from the tanker rail. "It's the only way down, unless you feel like getting wet."

"Think I'll pass." David swings his left leg over the rail, balances his foot on a wooden plank, then follows with the right leg, very deliberate as he descends the unstable ladder one rung at a time. Reaching bottom, he steps out onto a tire, and is helped onto the swaying trawler by an older gentlemen bundled in a heavy sweat suit.

"Welcome aboard, hotshot."

David searches his memory for the former smuggler's name. "Rick? How's it going?"

Rick Magers grunts and spits. "Like herding squirrels. Bunch of pansy-ass pilots—still too afraid to explore the bottom. Take me down with you, kid. We'll show 'em what for."

David looks aft. Beneath the powerful floodlights an object is being hauled out of the sea and up the slanted stern ramp by way of a heavy cargo net. The trawl winches retract more netting, revealing the object to be a submersible—one of the Manta Rays!

The cockpit is unsealed. A short woman in her mid-thirties climbs stiffly out of the pilot's seat, giving an earful to one of the crewmen.

The sonar operator climbs out from the co-pilot's position, wearing a hooded jacket. The hood is drawn back, releasing a mop of long brunette hair.

Kaylie ...

David's heart pounds in his chest as he crosses the deck, waving. Kaylie's pilot, Debbie Umel, spots David first and points.

Kaylie stares at him, expressionless. Leaving the sub, she crosses the upper deck to meet him.

David waits for her by the trawler's big net drum, watching her as she approaches, her head down. In his mind's eye he had imagined their reunion a hundred times, now her offish demeanor is keeping him at bay.

"You shouldn't be here, David."

"I shouldn't be here? I guess I'm crazy, because I thought you asked me to be here."

Rick Magers saunters over to eavesdrop.

Kaylie looks up at the old man. "Rick, do you mind?"

"Hell, no, I don't mind."

Kaylie rolls her eyes then grabs David by the crook of his arm. "Come on." She leads him forward to the trawler's twin bow gantries then down an aluminum ladder to the mid-deck. David follows her through a tight corridor past the crew's galley, turning right at a short hallway bordered on either side by cabins.

She keys open Cabin 5, holding the door so he can enter. The room is small, with bunk beds, two sets of drawers, and a private bathroom. Women's underwear occupy every square inch of available hanging space.

"Nice room. I think your roommate would get along with Monty."

"Debbie's married. There's no laundry service aboard, so you make do."

"Kaylie, for two weeks, you're all I've thought about. I thought you'd be happy to see me."

"I am. My mind's just in a different place than it was back in Dubai. I'm into the job."

"And me being aboard screws that up?"

216

"No. Well, yes. Maybe a little. It's like having your girlfriend show up unexpectedly at football camp. You want to be together, but you need to maintain your focus. Your presence also changes the dynamic of our group."

"From what I hear, your group hasn't been so dynamic."

"We've had our challenges, but we're getting better every day. Nothing—no amount of training—prepares you for what we've had to do. David Shiffman quit after one dive. Guess he crossed that item off his personal to-do list. And Peter, the guy in the wheelchair, he left last week. He was having too difficult a time getting around the trawler. Peter was our best sonar op, so everything got reshuffled."

"Now I'm here. Maybe I can help."

"Maybe. The real problem is the extreme depth and our total lack of knowledge of the Panthalassa—that's what they're calling the subterranean sea."

"Wait ... there's a subterranean sea?"

"I thought you knew. I'm sure they'll brief you, now that you're here. It's located beneath the Parece Vela Basin. We've been told it covers five thousand square miles of sea floor. Somehow we're expected to explore it using this one access hole. Bin Rashidi's losing patience fast. There's no charts to guide us, just a big hole in the sea floor that leads into an even bigger ocean of black water, everything sealed up under a claustrophobic ceiling of rock that just unnerves the hell out of you after a while. Our job is to search the abyss for life forms. The Manta Rays are essentially bait. If we locate something we lure it out of the hole where a Japanese submersible is waiting with the nets. The problem is, everyone's still too freaked out about venturing far from the hole's entrance."

"How deep are we talking?"

"The access point begins at 8,726 feet. The hole drops another 125 feet straight down through volcanic rock before emptying into the Panthalassa."

"And how far down is the Panthalassa's sea floor?"

"Sonar fixes the bottom right around 31,500 feet. None of us have gone deeper than 14,000 feet."

"Who captured the Dunk?"

"The Japanese. They lowered a bait box down through the hole, kept it along the bottom for weeks before the Dunk swam by. Took them six hours to tease it out. Have you seen it?"

"It's incredible."

"I heard about what happened earlier. I didn't know the lab guy; they've kept us pilots away from the tanker for the most part. His death—it must have been horrible."

"As shark attacks go this one was about as freaky as it gets."

"Did you know the Leeds' fish was ours? Debbie and I lured it out late last night. It was our first catch. Had it lived we would have split a bonus of a hundred grand."

"It was an amazing catch. A fish as big as a whale."

There's a knock on the door, then someone keys in.

Debbie Umel enters. "Sorry to interrupt, guys, but David's wanted in the skipper's cabin."

▽ ▽ ▽

BRIAN SUITS GREETS him like an old friend. "David! So we finally got you out here. Come inside. You know Mr. bin Rashidi. Have you met Dr. Al Hashemi? He's the director of the aquarium."

"Hey." David shakes the offered hand then turns to the petite brunette in her early thirties, seated next to bin Rashidi. "David Taylor."

"Yes, I know."

Brian introduces her. "This is Allison Petrucci, a former colleague of Dr. Maren. You know the name?"

"Yeah. He was the asshole who tried to kill my father."

Allison forces a smile, though her eyes shoot daggers. "A brilliant asshole, actually. And it was your father who killed Michael; though, he probably deserved it. His ego had been running unchecked for years. He thought he was infallible. And what about you? Do you also think you're Teflon ... like your father?"

Brian steps in between them. "Easy now, kids, we're all after the same thing. David, have a seat. There's a few things we'd like to discuss."

Ibrahim Al Hashemi unrolls a chart, spreading it out over a desktop before David. It's a bathymetric map of the Philippine Sea plate, the Parece Vela Basin to the southeast heavily detailed in Arabic. "Fifteen years ago, Dr. Maren initiated a comprehensive study of the Parece Vela Basin, after discovering basalt dredges dating back to the Early Cretaceous period, approximately 150 million years ago. While most of Dr. Maren's work was destroyed—"

"—after your father sunk his yacht," Allison injects.

Bin Rashidi grabs her wrist, applying a vise-like grip. "I'm not paying you for commentary."

The intensity of her expression melts to fear. She swallows hard.

Al Hashemi continues. "As I was saying, most of Dr. Maren's work was lost;

however, the surviving journals clearly identify the existence of prehistoric life forms that have survived two hundred feet beneath the Parece Vela Basin, inhabiting an ancient sea that has been isolated from the Pacific for hundreds of millions of years."

David studies the chart. "I saw the Dunk. What other species are we talking about?"

"*Kronosaurus. Thalassomedon. Shonisaurus sikanniensis. Mososaurus.* And the biggest prize—*Liopleurodon.* There are others, of course, all part of a deepwater food web, but these are the specific species we've targeted for this expedition."

"What's the water temperature like down there?"

"Six degrees Celsius. About forty-two degrees Fahrenheit."

"It's too cold. You're in the wrong place."

Bin Rashidi's black eyes meet Al Hashemi's. "As I have been stating."

"David, what is your reasoning—"

"Hot versus cold. Hydrothermal vents versus cold seeps. The entire Philippine Sea Plate's loaded with vents and seeps, which means the food chain in this ancient sea of yours must be thriving off of them, too. Fish prefer cold seeps. *Dunkleosteus* and *Leedsichthys* are both fish; so is that *Helicoprion* shark. *Shonisaurus sikanniensis* was a massive *Ichthyosaurus*—I suppose you might find them down there as well—but these other monsters were all marine reptiles at one time, which means they'd need warmer waters to maintain their body temperatures."

"Your father found Megalodons in the Mariana Trench, inhabiting warm waters created by hydrothermal plumes."

"The Megs were an exception; they may be fish but their enormous size makes them warm blooded. Like I said, find the hydrothermal vent fields and you'll find the rest of your critters. Of course, that's easier said than done when you're working with a five-thousand-square-mile subterranean sea."

Bin Rashidi tugs at his goatee, looking at Allison. "Tell him."

"There's another way." Allison leans forward. "Michael spent sixteen years and most of his family's fortune exploring the Panthalassa. The hole beneath us is only one of nearly a dozen he had drilled at great expense. Most of these access points yielded nothing. Three, however, tapped into thriving food chains, including the one below us. Michael equipped each of the three with a small abyssal lab that was anchored to the bottom by cables and weights. He called them his 'creature blinds.'"

"Show him the schematics."

Brian Suits hands her a poster tube from which she removes a set of plans.

"The lab is a forty-seven-ton sphere, approximately thirty feet in diameter, situated on a four-legged, oval-shaped platform. The sphere is the actual habitat, its titanium hull designed to withstand pressures far exceeding those of the Mariana Trench. The platform situated below the sphere is what makes the design so unique. It contains a series of pressurized locks which function as a deepwater docking station."

David's eyebrows rise. "What kind of sub was Maren deepwater docking?"

"It was a one-man sub, but one of your Manta Rays should be able to squeeze inside the hangar without a problem."

"Whoa. You want me to deepwater dock a Manta Ray in this hunk of metal? At 31,000 feet!"

"It's perfectly safe," Ibrahim Al Hashemi assures him. "Maren used the blind on many occasions."

"Yeah, maybe a decade ago. That tin ball's probably a barnacle-laden rust bucket by now."

"Not true," Brian Suits replies. "We sent the barracuda, one of Maren's remotely operated submersibles, down to inspect the sphere months ago. The hull's intact. We've spent the last six weeks using the barracuda to remove barnacles from the hangar doors. The system's completely operational: the ROV was able to enter, dock, and depart without a hitch."

"So why do you need me?"

"Inside the lab are Maren's charts of the Panthalassa, including the coordinates for the other blinds—the two access holes that will lead us to the other inhabited sections of the sea," Ibrahim replies. "That information is priceless."

"Define priceless."

"A quarter of a million dollars," bin Rashidi answers, "with more coming as these sea monsters are captured. Add another fifty thousand for your capture of the *Helicoprion* shark."

"Wasn't my capture. Besides, that money should go to the biologist's family. As for the dive, the risk is enormous. My life's worth a shit-load more than $250,000."

Brian rolls up the plans. "There's risk, and there's calculated risk. Your father's firm designed the Manta Rays to exceed these depths. You either trust in the design or you don't. The deepwater dock works. You're being paid extraordinarily well to make one dive in depths your father exceeded with an even smaller submersible."

"If it's so easy, Captain, then you do it. Or don't you have the balls?"

"What I don't have, hotshot, is your experience. You're our best pilot. But if you pass up the offer, rest assured I'll take it."

"What else is down there, besides enough pressure to implode a walnut?"

Ibrahim Al Hashemi answers for Brian. "The bottom currents are admittedly swift. We had trouble maneuvering the ROV below twenty-two thousand feet. Of course, the Manta Ray is much heavier than the barracuda."

"Handling the Manta Ray in bad currents is like flying a kite in a tropical storm," David says. "If I did decide to go, I'd need a good co-pilot ... someone who can handle the stress."

"We lost Peter," Brian says. "Kaylie's the next best sonar tech on the team."

"I don't want Kaylie. Give me the old fart."

"Rick? He's not half the sonar operator Kaylie is."

"I don't care about sonar. I care about my co-pilot losing it six miles down. Rick used to be a smuggler; he's used to working under pressure. Now tell me what else is down there. You're not offering me this much money to deal with currents."

Ibrahim turns to bin Rashidi, who nods. "We suspect there may be sea creatures present in the deeper waters. Large ones."

"By large ones, I assume you mean bigger than the Dunk?"

"We can't be sure. It could be more Leeds' fish. Or something else. We attempted to lure them up with bait boxes, but failed. It seems they prefer their food ... alive."

"Enough." Bin Rashidi leans in close. "We're offering you a small ransom to perform a deepwater dive that six months ago you would have done for free. You're ten years younger than your father was when he first conquered the Mariana Trench for the Navy. Still, at your age, you probably have more experience, not to mention a better sub. The question is whether you possess your father's guts."

The Arab leans back. "Or perhaps the prodigal son prefers to remain in his famous father's shadow forever?"

25

Endless night. Endless worries.

The dimly lit tarmac races beneath the Lexus's front bumper, its right headlamp inches from the Pacific Coast Highway's galvanized steel beam. The guardrail is all that separates the twisting, two-lane mountain passage from a thousand-foot plunge into the unforgiving ocean, lashing its perpetual fury upon the rocky escarpments below.

Slow down, Jonas. Life's too precious ...

But he doesn't slow down, even when the fog thickens, concealing the yellow road sign ahead.

Slow down, J.T., you're moving too fast ...

He sees the break in the guardrail up ahead, knows it to be an open shoulder designed to allow southbound tourists an area to pull over and photograph the scenic Santa Lucia view below.

He takes the hairpin left turn too fast—

—the Lexus's right front bumper striking the continuing guardrail doing seventy miles an hour—

—his life moving in surreal motion ...

The vehicle flips and becomes airborne and suddenly he is upside-down, his world frighteningly silent as the retreating highway is replaced by a view of the cliff he has never seen before, nor will he ever see again, the car hurtling in slow motion toward the pounding surf below—

—the rocks reaching up to snuff out his existence.

One dumb mistake ... one fatal slip ... one momentary lapse and now his life is over.

Way to go, asshole. You really screwed up this time.

The resounding impact shatters the night air like crashing cymbals in his brain ...

ᗐ ᗐ ᗐ

JONAS OPENS HIS eyes. His chest is heaving, his face bathed in sweat. Somehow he has survived the crash, which means he must be lying in a hospital bed, crippled beyond all recognition.

The room is gray with morning, its silence mocking him.

He is in his own bedroom. Intact. But how?

A giddy wave of relief washes over him. *A dream ... it was only a dream.*

Terry reaches out for him. "You okay?"

He sits up in bed, his head actually buzzing from the emotional rush as his mind replays the nightmare over and over again, the images still so vivid. "I dreamt that I was about to die—that I did die. I felt the impact. It was so real."

"Angel?"

"No. I was in a car crash, not far from our house, out on Highway 1. It was a foggy night. I was driving way too fast. My front end hit the guardrail and my car flipped over the ledge."

His wife sits up next to him. "What else?"

"As I was falling, I said to myself, 'you really screwed up this time.' I remember thinking it aloud, as clear as I'm speaking with you. What does it mean?"

"Jonas, you went to bed last night worried sick about the Meg Pen, wondering if the tank would flood before you made the necessary repairs. Your subconscious mind is telling you something."

"That I screwed up?"

"Or a major crash is just around the bend." She touches his cheek. "Maybe it's time to cash in our chips and get out."

"What? Suicide?"

She smacks him playfully in the head. "No, dummy, the Institute! Maybe it's time we retired. You know ... get away from the stress."

"What do you expect me to do? Play golf? I suck at golf. Golf gives me stress."

"Monsters give me stress. After twenty-five years I've had enough. You promised me we'd travel one day, that we'd take a cruise to Alaska."

"So we'll plan a vacation. Doesn't mean we have to retire."

"Your subconscious mind says otherwise."

"Maybe I just need to get the brakes fixed on the Lexus?"

"You think it's a joke? Jonas, last night I was watching *The Tonight Show*; that damn R.A.W. group hired Lana Wood as their spokeswoman."

"Who's Lana Wood?"

"An actress. She was a Bond girl back when your hair was brown. Anyway, she showed footage of the *Jellyfish* shocking Belle and Lizzy the night they attacked the runt."

"What! Why didn't you tell me?"

"You had enough on your mind."

"Where the hell did they get the footage? I've got to call Tommy!" He grabs the phone off his night table—

Terry takes it from him. "Jonas, just listen. We have enough money put away to take care of our children and our grandchildren. The stress of running the Institute, dealing with R.A.W. on a daily basis, with Angel—it's taking away what little time we have left. If one day we're blessed with grand-babies, I'd like to be around to enjoy them. Both of us."

Slow down. Life's too precious.

He hugs her to his chest, stroking her long, silky onyx hair. "Okay, granny, tell me what you want me to do."

⩒ ⩒ ⩒

"RELEASE ANGEL? WERE you standing too close to the microwave or something?" Mac stares at Jonas from across the booth, bits of his partially chewed sandwich spewing from his open mouth. "Seriously, J.T, are you insane?"

"A little louder next time. I don't think the waitress heard you." Jonas leans forward, speaking in a hushed tone. "Think it through. Even if we manage to repair the Meg Pen, Bela and Lizzy are growing way out of control. Now imagine them in five years when they've reached Angel's size."

"But releasing Angel?"

"Think about it. Which poison is more lethal, releasing Angel to the wild or the sisters?"

"That's like asking me if I'd prefer to be hung or shot in the head. Either way I'm still a dead man."

"Hear me out. We don't just open the canal doors and release her with some parting gifts. We transport Angel by boat to the Western Pacific then use the neural implant to send her deep. Once she's back in the Mariana Trench—"

"Gee, that's a real Hallmark moment, except for one thing, dickhead ... what happens if she doesn't stay there?"

"We use the GPS system to track her. If she moves near a coastline, we alert the authorities. But she won't. We can use the implant to keep her away from the shallows and the whale migrations. So she kills an occasional gray or humpback. It's a big ocean—"

"—and she's a big fish ... with big teeth."

"What's the alternative, Mac? If we do nothing, in a day or a week or a month, Bela will crash through the Meg Pen glass and flood the Institute, killing herself and Lizzy in the process while causing God knows how many millions of dollars in damage."

"Or here's another option: I take a harpoon gun and shove it in Angel's neuro-implant, and we turn the lagoon over to the two sisters. After we seal off the canal."

"Yeah, I thought of that, but I don't feel good about it."

"Think of Angel as Old Yeller. Old Yeller was sick, a danger to the family, so Paw went out with the shotgun and *BAM!* Right between the eyes."

"I visited Ed Hendricks a few days ago in the hospital. I asked him if he thought we should kill Angel. Know what he said?"

"Let me guess, he said we should cut off her two pectoral fins and he'd eat them."

"He said she never should have been penned in the first place."

"Wow. Good for Ed. I guess having your legs bitten off makes one more spiritual. Be sure and share his sentiments with the families of the victims Angel devoured in McCovey Cove a few years ago."

"I don't want to kill her, Mac."

"And what if she's pregnant?"

"I'm not God. If Nature intended these creatures to breed, who am I to stop them?"

"Tell you what, you take Terry on a week's vacation and when you come back—"

"Mac ..."

His friend shakes his head, giving in. "By boat, huh?"

"Yes. And this stays between us. Someone is Stelzer's department's been feeding R.A.W. our footage. The last thing we need now is the public getting wind of our little plan."

"About that plan ... what kind of boat can hold a fifty-one-ton, seventy-four-foot monster?"

Jonas smiles. "I'm going to show you."

Aboard the Dubai Land I
Philippine Sea, Western Pacific

Thunder rattles the gray dawn like a noisy upstairs neighbor, the baritone reverberations echoing across the ocean, foretelling another rough day at sea for the ships' two crews.

David Taylor lies in the lower bunk of the cabin formerly occupied by Peter Geier. He has barely slept, his mind restlessly debating bin Rashidi's offer. He mentally rehearses the dive, imagining the disorienting steep-angled descent as he spirals into endless blackness, the remotely operated barracuda leading the way, serving as a visual compass. Even in the swift Manta Ray the voyage to reach purgatory will take almost ninety minutes, assuming conditions are stable. Once they reach the Panthalassa's sea floor, the robot will be used to trigger the docking procedure, leading to the most harrowing part of the mission.

At 31,500 feet, the weight of the ocean approaches an unforgiving fourteen thousand pounds per square inch. Fish do not register the pressures of the abyss because the water moves through them, but anything possessing an air bladder—human, habitat, or sub—will implode instantaneously should its protective hull be compromised.

To avoid this, engineers attempting to reach the ocean's deepest realms have always employed a spherical design so that pressures are distributed evenly across the hull. David has faith in his father's submersible—the cockpit/emergency pod essentially being an acrylic bathyscaphe. What worries him is the deepwater dock. An oval design is far less stable than a sphere, and the thought of the docking station collapsing upon his vessel is causing him serious trepidation.

Incredible water pressure, dangerous currents, faulty docking designs, and potential encounters with nightmarish predators. His father was right; it was a suicide mission, and no amount of money could persuade him to go—

—except there is another factor at play ... he's in love.

David knows that if he doesn't go, Brian Suits will, and the captain will recruit Kaylie as his co-pilot. While David respects Suits as a commander, the war veteran lacks experience piloting submersibles, having logged less than one hundred hours aboard the Manta Ray. More important, the man has never dived beyond the shallows of the Persian Gulf.

David had selected Rick Magers over Kaylie as his co-pilot because of his feelings for the girl. Diving the abyss required complete concentration and he knew their on-again, off-again relationship could be a distraction. As his godfather, Mac, has told him on numerous occasions, "you don't shit where you eat, and you don't face death with a hard pecker."

He could have requested Brian Suits at sonar, but he has seen too many military-types lose it in deepwater dives. And the thought of having to man-handle the former soldier as he's experiencing a claustrophobic meltdown six miles below the surface is too daunting a task to even consider.

David glances at the wall clock: 6:35 a.m.

With or without you, they leave in an hour. Dad dived the Mariana Trench in a one-man Abyss Glider. At least I wouldn't be alone.

He also ran into Angel's mom ...

Asshole. You should've listened to your father and gone to football camp.

Lying in bed, he can hear the Japanese crewmen working on the upper deck above his head, untying the trawler's lines from the tanker. His presence had been a topic of conversation among the men in the galley last night, the deck hands speaking in hushed tones about his Asian/Caucasian features. A few of the men had made loud references in Japanese, baiting him to see if he spoke their language.

He had not let on, taking the lessons his maternal grandfather had taught him about combat to heart.

Masao Tanaka had studied Samurai strategy as written by the legendary Japanese warrior, Miyamoto Musashi. Musashi had written his *Go Rin No Sho* (*The Book of Five Rings*) while living in a cave in the mountains of Kyushu in 1645. The Kendo master had penned the manuscript a few weeks before his death, intending it to be the ultimate guide to sword fighting, but hundreds of years after his death, the book was considered to be the most perceptive psychological guide to strategy, battle, and business ever conceived.

How would Musashi advise me?

He closes his eyes, hearing his grandfather's raspy voice quoting the combat master: *There is timing in the whole life of the warrior, in his thriving and declining, in his harmony and discord. There is also timing in the Void. Before entering in battle, distinguish between gain and loss in worldly manners while perceiving those things which cannot be seen ...*

David opens his eyes, the restlessness gone.

Twenty-four years ago, Masao's son, D.J., had rushed into the Void, cocky and head-strong, only to be devoured by it. David's father had survived the abyss and its terrors four years later because his mission had been pure—to rescue his mother.

If my motive remains pure and I'm prepared, then I can enter the Void and return, triumphant. That means I can't do this for the money. It must only be to prevent Kaylie from making the dive.

His thoughts are dashed by the sudden knock on his cabin door. He rolls out of bed and answers.

It's Kaylie.

"Brian told me everything. Are you actually considering making the dive?"

"Yes."

"Then you're taking me as your co-pilot."

"This isn't about money, Kaylie."

"Then what's it about? I hope it's not some kind of macho way of protecting me."

"Actually, I'm protecting me."

"By taking Rick? I've gone deeper than he has and I'm a better sonar operator on my worst day than he'll ever be."

"I can't dive with you, Kaylie ... not this deep. I need to remain focused."

"You'll focus better with a competent co-pilot."

"Rick's focused."

"Rick's off the wagon. He drinks before every dive. I've smelled it on his breath. As for protecting me, if you can't trust yourself with me when there's really something at stake, then what kind of future do we have together? Unless you're telling me what we have is only sex?"

"I didn't say that—"

"Good. Then I'm going. See you up on deck."

He watches her go, wondering how Miyamoto Musashi would fare against a woman.

No wonder the guy wrote his book in a cave.

▽   ▽   ▽

DAVID EMERGES ON deck forty minutes later, having eaten breakfast and purged his jittery bowels. The wind has picked up with gusts blowing in from the northwest at thirty knots. Six-foot swells rock the trawler, urging him to make haste and get the Manta Ray beneath the waves before he loses what's left of his meal.

Brian Suits climbs down from the wheelhouse to escort him to the sub. "Big day. You ready?"

"I'm getting there. Why did you tell her?"

"Because it's important for all of us that you succeed. Kaylie's selection as co-pilot would never have been an issue if you two weren't involved."

"Maybe you told her because you were afraid I might have chosen you?"

Brian's eyes flash a warning. "Listen, sport, keep it in your pants and you'll be fine."

"You listen, asshole. That deepwater dock had better be as stable as you say, or I'll be bringing back holy hell."

The war vet grins. "So you're a tough guy now?"

"No. I'm just the cocky college student hired to make a dive we both know you don't have the balls to even attempt. But hey, if I'm wrong, you can replace me right now. Am I wrong?"

Brian matches his glare. "We need the charts. You're more qualified than I am. It's your dive."

"Yeah, that's what I thought. All talk, no *Kokoro*—no spirit. No matter what happens to me, just remember which one of us is the hawk and who's the pheasant ... sir."

David stares him down, saying nothing, waiting for a parry he knows won't come.

Brian nods, breaking eye contact. "Make your dive."

David leaves him standing there, smiling to himself as he mentally wipes Brian Suits's blood from his sword. Crossing the deck, he heads aft to the Manta Ray, the sub poised on its dolly just above the stern ramp. Kaylie is already inside the cockpit, dressed in jeans and her heavy cotton hooded sweatshirt. Brian leans in to offer her some last minute instructions while David stretches his quads.

The other pilots join him. Debbie Umel gives him a quick hug, Marcus Slabine a knuckle-punch. "Glad it's you, dude, and not me."

Jeff Hoch offers up a prayer. "Please, Lord, we ask that you escort our companions to the depths and see to their safe return."

"Thanks, Minister."

Dr. Gotto hands him a brown paper bag. "Made this myself. Thought it might come in handy."

David opens the bag, removing a flexible plastic six-inch tube attached to a capped sixteen-ounce bottle.

"It's a portable urinal," Gotto says with a wink. "Hope it's the right size."

"Extra large. Thanks, Doc. This may actually come in handy. Did you make one for my co-pilot?"

"She's already wearing hers. Good luck, kid."

Rick Magers approaches, the old man looking peeved. "I have something for you, too." He holds up his middle finger.

"Yeah, thanks." Dropping to the deck, David does a quick set of push-ups, stretches his lower back, quads, and calves, then climbs inside the open cockpit.

Kaylie smiles at him. "Did you want to get in a quick run? I can wait."

"It's a long dive."

"Ninety-six minutes to the lab, if we stay on schedule." She points to a new relay switch, which has been rigged to her side of the command center. "This device sends a signal from the sub's antenna to the docking station so that we can activate the docking doors from here, just in case we lose the barracuda."

"It better work. Or we could end up stuck in that hangar."

"I brought along plenty of bottled water, plus snacks. Want an Imodium chewable?"

"Already did three of them. My intestine's clean. Sphincter's sealed tight. Ready to go down, baby?"

She pouts her lips. "Focus on your job and you might get lucky later ... maybe."

"I hear that." He seals the cockpit, waits for the green light then gives a thumbs-up to the pit crew, each of the four men tethered to the trawler as they walk the submersible on its dolly and cable down the stern ramp. The incoming swells rise to catch the Manta Ray as they guide it into the chilly Pacific.

Waves wash over the neutrally buoyant submersible. David secures his harness and powers on the twin propulsion units. Dipping the starboard wing, he maneuvers the sub into a shallow dive, moving them beyond the trawler's rudder and dormant pitch propeller, diving them into the blue void.

Circling below in forty feet of water is a five-foot-long, torpedo-shaped drone, its contours and steel fins resembling that of a large barracuda. Armed with sonar and an infrared beacon attached to a small video camera, the vehicle is being remotely operated by Brian Suits, who is stationed in the wheelhouse with Fiesal bin Rashidi and Ibrahim Al Hashemi.

As the Manta Ray moves closer, the barracuda descends, leading them into the depths.

"You don't have to spiral down," Kaylie says. "Just maintain a sixty-degree down angle. I'll tell you when to change course."

"Yes, ma'am."

"Missed me, didn't you?"

"Only the sex."

"You lie."

David accelerates, the added torque aiding his harness in keeping him pinned in his seat as the sub descends at a steep angle. The blue void deepens to violet as the submersible leaves the mesopelagic shallows.

One thousand feet ... sixteen hundred ...

The sun's light fades into curtains of gray, extinguishing into black.

David glances at his gauges. The water temperature had dropped to 52°F, the pressure slipping past 720 psi, increasing 14.7 pounds per square inch for every 33 feet of depth.

▽ ▽ ▽

HE SMILES AS the dark void suddenly comes alive with thousands of twinkling lights.

They have entered another universe—the bathypelagic zone, or mid-water region—home to the largest ecosystem on the planet. Encompassing upwards of ten million species, these bathypelagic life forms have adapted to an eternity of living in darkness by evolving large, bulbous eyes that can pick up slivers of light. And by creating their own.

Bioluminescence in living organisms is generated through a chemical reaction, in this case a light-producing luciferin and its catalyst, a luciferase. Fueled by the release of adenosine triphosphate (ATP), the luciferase causes the luciferin to oxidize, creating a bioluminescent light.

Luminous lights zap on and off as the sub and its two passengers race toward the abyss, each color as brilliant as the LED lights on the command center.

David switches on his exterior lights and is immediately blinded by a blizzard of marine snow—organic particles floating from the shallows on their way to the bottom. He douses the lights, relying on the cockpit's night glass and gauges.

His eyes return to the depth gauge as it passes 5,300 feet. *One mile down. Only five to go ...*

The Manta Ray's wingspan creaks beneath 2,400 pounds per square inch of pressure. David tries to be casual as he wipes a bead of sweat from his brow. "Angel's mother's skin was bioluminescent at night. Angel too, but it faded over the years. Must be related to diet, don't you think?"

"I think you're nervous. When's the last time you went this deep?"

"High School. I snuck the sub out into Monterey Bay while my parents were in Hawaii and my sister was making out with her boyfriend."

"Be honest. What would you do if you saw something big glowing in the Panthalassa?"

"If I saw something that big, you wouldn't be doing your job."

"Speaking of which, it's time to change course. Come to two-seven-zero and flatten your angle of descent to fifty-five degrees. In about ten minutes we'll be coming to the spider web."

"What's that?"

"Fishing nets. An array of them. They're anchored along the bottom around the access hole, splayed at different angles using buoys. Each net is rigged to the tanker by cable. This is important, so don't forget it: You can only get in and out of the access hole by following course two-seven-zero along a fifty-five-degree plane. If we get chased out of the Panthalassa you have to follow that escape route or we'll get netted like a tuna."

"Ever happen to you and Debbie?"

"Our first week, on my fourth dive. We were circling in twelve thousand feet of water, and suddenly this huge object pops up on sonar about two hundred yards behind us. I freaked, thinking it was a Meg, and Debbie–she nearly sent us flying bow-first into the ceiling. Finally, she managed to hit the chute—that's what we call the hole—only she headed topside on a straight vertical, completely forgot about the nets. Next thing I know we're being hauled upside-down to the surface in one of the cargo nets. Nothing you can do at that point but wait out the ride."

"What was the object on sonar?"

"Turned out to be a Leeds' fish, as gentle as a lamb. Like I said, it was only my fourth Dive. I can handle things now." She points ahead. "There! See the red warning lights? That's the netting. There's the barracuda. Follow it in. It'll lead us right to the hole."

She flips the radio toggle switch. "Spiderman—Delta team, come in."

"Delta team—Spiderman, we see you. Tell your hotshot pilot to slow to five knots before your wake tangles our nets. I would hate to torpedo you."

"That you, James?"

"None other, sweet pants."

"James Vidal, meet David Taylor, my pilot for the day. David, James is our point man, an extra pair of eyes and ears."

"The bonus baby. About time. Maybe now we'll finally see some action down here."

David adjusts his headset. "James, where are you?"

"Sea floor, two o'clock."

David powers on his exterior lights, illuminating the gray-brown loops of the cargo nets, which are suspended 150 feet off the silty bottom by partially inflated, orange flotation buoys. Hovering along the bottom, barely visible through an entanglement of cargo nets, is the Shinkai 6500 submersible. The twenty-five-ton vessel's rectangular shell is situated around a protective, pressurized titanium sphere with an internal diameter of six and a half feet. Owned and operated by JAMSTEC (Japanese Marine Science Technology Center), the submersible is stark-white with yellow fins, and is equipped with two manipulator arms, thrusters, search lights, digital video and still cameras, sample baskets, and an observational sonar.

"I've got a visual on you, James. Nice sub ... if you like turtles."

"Hey, I'm just the combat engineer. Been doing it for Uncle Sam since '98. Suits recruited me for his hunting expedition after my second tour of duty in Iraq's lovely Al Anbar Province with the 3rd Infantry out of Fort Stewart, Georgia. And I thought those Bradley's were tight. Love to trade these mechanical arms for a 25mm cannon; though, I'm not sure I need one. Been here ten days, and all I've seen so far are a bunch of over-grown tuna. So get your bonus baby ass down in that hole and net us some real monsters, pronto. My boys and I need the extra money."

Following the barracuda, David guides the Manta Ray through the labyrinth of nets—

—as the chute comes into view.

It is the diameter of a cul-de-sac in a residential neighborhood—a black, seemingly bottomless pit set along the flat, barren sea floor. Silt is being sucked down the hole's throat, softening its rocky edges, giving it the appearance of being perfectly round.

"Jee ... zus. How did Maren find this thing? Did he just drill it himself?"

"No one knows." Kaylie switches her headset back to sonar, her expression suddenly more serious. "There's a strong downward current. Take it slow."

David enters the passage dead-center, the sub's exterior beacons showing faint hints of jagged escarpments. The beams barely illuminate the darkness, as if the aperture was a celestial black hole, its gravitational density inhaling all light. Through the claustrophobic funnel of volcanic rock they descend, moving through the vertical on a spiraling downward plane, their speed steady at five knots, the heavy darkness enveloping them from behind, until the hole reopens to an ancient void—

—the Panthalassa Sea.

26

Panthalassa Sea

The Manta Ray moves out from the hole, hovering beneath a vast, endless ceiling of ancient rock, its geology dating back more than 225 million years. An influx of current sweeps nutrients down from the chute and across the ceiling in all directions, feeding an inverted sea floor crawling with tens of thousands of trilobites, the albino arthropods gathered en masse around their abyssal Mecca to feed.

David powers on the sub's exterior high beams, his light casting a spectral radiance across the subterranean roof, illuminating the solid crystalline eyes of crabs and lobsters, snails and sea scorpions, their alabaster exoskeletons covered in spikes and spindly claws, the largest of the horde crawling over the smallest, the oldest as long as seven feet from front pincers to barbed, poisonous tails.

A chill creeps through the cockpit, the water temperature outside barely registering above freezing. Kaylie adjusts the thermostat then leans over and kisses David softly on the lips. "That's for luck."

"Check the time. I want to be back in this very spot in two hours." Pushing down on both joysticks and pedals, he sends the sub accelerating downward in a steep dive, the depth gauge spinning past 9,000 feet.

They ride in silence, the bantering gone, the quiet essential now for Kaylie to listen to the surrounding sea through her sonar headphones. The water is crystal clear and bone-chilling cold, the sub's wings moaning every so often, protesting the increasing weight of the ocean.

Two miles ...

Three.

Particles appear in the water—more marine snow, only different. Composed of hydrogen sulfide and methane, the debris is blowing upward from the bottom, originating from countless cold seeps purging their life-giving emissions from beneath the planet's crust.

The marine snow grows heavier, forcing David to extinguish his exterior lights. They pass 20,000 feet, the water pressure approaching 9,000 pounds per square inch.

Stay focused ... you're breathing fine ... everything's fine. Don't think about how much ocean is above you ... everything's good.

The sudden jolt causes his heart to flutter, sweat breaking out across his body—

—as red lights bloom across his command center!

Kaylie grips his right arm. "What was that?"

"I'm not sure." The sub shudders and shakes beneath them, the turbulence unnerving. David eases back on the left pedal, then the right, isolating the problem. "It's the starboard prop, feels like something's caught on the shaft. I've got to shut it down before I lose my boss nut." He slows the sub, decreasing his angle of descent as he glances at Kaylie, who's gripping her seat as if paralyzed, her face deathly pale in the LED's glow, her eyes filled with terror.

Oh, shit, she's bugging out ... "Kaylie? Hey—" He shakes her by the shoulder, inducing hyperventilation.

"Take me back! Take me back, David, please!"

"You're okay. Just breathe."

"I can't! I can't breathe! Just get me back to the chute! Just a few minutes back at the hole—"

"Kaylie, calm down!" Reaching behind her seat, he grabs a bottled water. "Here, drink this. Slow sips. Wet your face."

She struggles to unseal the cap. Takes a sloppy swig, her quivering hands spilling water down her sweatshirt—

—her eyes locking on to the depth gauge as it flips past 21,500 feet. "Oh God, oh my God, oh God ... ten thousand more feet ... that's nearly two miles! David, I can't go down another two miles. What was I thinking!" She clutches his right arm in both hands, her fingernails digging into his flesh. "Take me back, now! Now, David, take me—

—ahhhhhhhh!"

With a vertigo-inducing lurch, the sub is flung sideways, flipping wing over bow!

David's squeezes his eyes shut as his limbs pump at the controls, his stomach queasy, the propellers useless against a force of nature too powerful to challenge.

G-forces drive Kaylie's body into the contours of her bucket seat, the burning vomit rising in her throat, her eyes squeezed shut, her fingers knotted around the edges of her seat, her mind drowning in fear, blotting out all rational thoughts, time reduced to a final few precious particles of sand in the hourglass of time as she holds her breath and waits to die ... waits for that final moment, the moment the cockpit implodes, the moment her brain matter splatters inside her skull, the anticipation of the moment far worse than the actual event.

Her body coils, her lungs ready to deliver one final scream as the moment arrives ... only it never does. Just as suddenly as it came, the turbulence is gone, the ride level and smooth, as if they've entered the hurricane's eye.

Still hyperventilating, she opens her eyes, her mind fighting to resurface from the panic, a seed of thought telling her the sub has indeed stopped spinning, that she's still alive!

The sensation of relief comes with a price. Fumbling for an air-sick bag, she leans forward and pukes, her blood pressure blasting through every vessel in her head like a cleansing wave.

When she's done she seals the bag and lays her head back, adjusting the air vent so it blows on her sweaty, pale face.

David hands her the water bottle. "You okay?"

She nods. "What ... happened?"

"Bad current. Must have been a half mile wide, running like a flooding river through this entire depth. Real bitch."

"How—"

"My father taught me to treat currents like riptides. Best thing to do when you're caught is to ride it out—swim parallel to shore."

"Where are we?"

"About a mile east of where we need to be."

"David?"

"Shh. Close your eyes and rest."

▼ ▼ ▼

SHE AWAKENS WITH a start. David has changed course, dropping them once more into a vertical descent, his almond eyes harsh as he focuses on piloting the sub while listening in on sonar.

She glances at the depth gauge: 29,265 feet. A hot flash of panic shoots through her, but she forces it aside, too exhausted to deal with it again.

"Kaylie, listen to me. Forget those numbers; they mean nothing. You want to be topside? Get your headphones on and find the bottom so we can finish the job and get the hell out of here."

She nods. Wiping away her tears, she traces the missing headgear by its wire then repositions it over her ears. "I'm going active." Before he can object, she releases the loud, echoing sound wave—

Ping!

The reverberation races outward in all directions, reflecting off every inanimate, and organic, object in the surrounding sea.

"Got it. Four hundred seventy feet. Found the barracuda, too. Come to course zero-eight-five, thirty-five-degree down angle."

He adjusts his course, reducing their forward speed to fifteen knots. "Kaylie, next time ask me before you ping. The sound travels—"

"Shh! I've got a fix on the lab. Five degrees to starboard, then two hundred twenty yards due west."

David adjusts his course. The Manta Ray moves ahead slowly, coming to within forty feet of the volatile sea floor. Clouds of methane gas disburse like steam from a city sewer grate in winter, releasing a timeless outpouring of cold, sulfurous chemicals that seep from countless crevice-like vents.

"I'm activating the docking station." Kaylie presses the green button on the newly installed control switch by her right knee. Seconds later, she hears a low rumble over her headphones—

—as a dull yellow sliver of light appears out of the darkness ahead, growing larger, illuminating the silty bottom.

"I see it." David aims for the rectangular shape and slows the sub, allowing it to hover fifty feet away.

"David, what are you waiting for?"

"We have a guest."

Silhouetted between the Manta Ray and the luminous artificial yellow hue is a dark shadow—a morphing organic blob nearly as large as the lab. A pair of sinister bioluminescent-blue, demonic eyes stare back at them in the darkness, unblinking.

David dims the control console's LED lights to see better. "What the hell is that?"

Kaylie whispers, "It's watching us."

"Something's not right." David feels for the exterior light control switch. Dialing from standard white lights to red, he powers on the external beacons—

—illuminating a puffy gelatinous mass, possessing tentacles covered in seven-inch, needle-like spikes.

"Wow. It's *Vampyroteuthis infernalis*—the 'vampire squid from hell.'"

"It can't be a vampire squid. Vampire squids are less than a foot long. This thing must be twenty-five feet across."

"And great whites only grow to twenty-feet; only my family owns one that's as big as two tractor trailers. It's probably some prehistoric cousin. And those blue lights—they aren't even eyes; they're light organs—photophores. It turned itself inside-out. It's a defense mechanism."

"God, if we could only capture it."

"Thirty minutes ago you couldn't wait to leave, now you want to capture it? I just want to move it out of the way. Let's see how it likes bright light." David switches the red lights back to white.

Blinded by the strange creature, the squid turns itself right-side out, its deep reddish-brown tentacles instantaneously pursing together as it propels away into the darkness.

"They got the 'hell' part right when they named that thing. Let's take a look at this lab." David flies the Manta Ray toward the lab's spherical hull, the sub's lights revealing a titanium shell covered in crusty barnacles and silt. Beneath the nearly unrecognizable habitat is an oval structure, its flat bottom hidden beneath four titanium legs, the docking station yawning open like an alien two-car garage.

The barracuda hovers close by—a robotic sentry.

Now it is David who registers waves of panic as he positions the Manta Ray directly beneath the lab's flooded docking chamber. Peering up through the sub's cockpit, he inspects the interior of the illuminated hanger, his eyes searching for any telltale signs of problems.

"David?"

"Shh. Headphones. Listen!"

"What am I listening for?"

"Metal fatigue. Instability."

She presses her headphones to her ears. "Some groaning and creaks, nothing worse than the sub. David, if we're going in let's go. Hovering along the bottom's freaking me out."

THIRTY-ONE THOUSAND feet above the submersible, Brian Suits operates the ROV from its laptop inside the *Dubai Land I's* wheelhouse. He can see the Manta Ray on the barracuda's night vision camera, the sub hovering below the flooded docking station, refusing to enter. "Come on, Taylor! What the hell are you waiting for?"

The other pilots huddle close by and watch, Jason Montgomery among them. Monty came aboard an hour after David and Kaylie had departed. The Iraqi war vet wonders if he will ever see his naive young friend again.

Brian yells over to the pilot manning the trawler radio. "Marcus, call down to Spiderman. Tell him to relay a message: The longer Taylor waits—"

"—THE BIGGER THE strain on the open dock hangar."

"Roger that, James." Kaylie stares at David, her pulse pounding in her slender neck. "David ... yes or no?"

"I'm not sure."

"Then go with your gut. I trust you."

"I was afraid you'd say that." David increases the air pressure within the sub's cockpit, adding enough positive buoyancy to cause the Manta Ray to float straight up into the hangar.

Surrounded by thick titanium oval walls, they stare at their bizarre surroundings, praying it's not their tomb.

Kaylie presses the red switch on the docking station controls, holding her breath.

Rusty metal grinds against barnacle traces scattered along the docking station's titanium tracks as the horizontal doors seal shut beneath the submersible.

The internal lights flicker, then extinguish.

Darkness.

Silence, save for their heavy breathing.

David and Kaylie hold hands in the claustrophobic pitch, waiting for something, anything to happen. David's skin tingles, beads of sweat trickling down his face, the tiny hairs along the back of his neck standing on end.

Come on ... come on!

A heavy generator jumps to life ... then dies.

A yellow warning light flashes on the docking station's remote control.

Kaylie flicks it with her index finger. Presses the green button. No response. Presses the red button ... nothing. "Shit! It's jammed!"

The blood rushes from David's face. "The system's stuck in the middle of its cycle."

"Then how do we get out of here?"

We don't. We're going to die down here, trapped in this titanium coffin. "Give the generator a chance," he rasps.

Long minutes pass.

Sweat pours down David's face, his pounding heart shaking his entire body. *Was it a set-up? Allison Petrucci's revenge against dad for killing Maren? Why the hell did you trust them? Dad said not to go, he said it was a suicide mission. Why didn't you fucking listen!*

Clunky mechanical noises echo all around them as the backup generator kicks in. The lights return, the walls humming with life as powerful pumps activate, causing the titanium oval walls to shudder.

Water drains from the chamber.

The Manta Ray comes to rest on a porous secondary floor.

David is about to begin the process of unsealing the cockpit when Kaylie grabs his arm. "Not yet." She points to a red warning light in the hangar, indicating the docking station has not pressurized.

They unhook their harnesses and stretch, the two of them shaken from the harrowing descent and what may lie ahead.

"No telling if the life support systems in Maren's lab are functioning. Kaylie, reach under your seat. You'll find a pony bottle and breather."

A loud humming sound fills their ears as pressurized air is pumped inside the chamber.

The docking station's warning lights turn green.

David holds his breath, his hand trembling over the cockpit release control. *Please God, don't splatter our brains across the windshield.*

The hatch pops open twenty seconds later with a suction-like hiss.

David lies back in his seat. "Let's make this fast."

Gently, they climb out of the cockpit, sliding down the sub's wings to the wet floor. Situated overhead and welded to the oval hangar is the lab's immense titanium sphere, its rounded bottom serving as the docking station's ceiling.

A ladder leads up to a hatch.

Kaylie ascends the ladder and begins turning the hand wheel to open the watertight door—

—while David inspects the damaged starboard propulsion unit, surprised to find the deflector tunnel protecting the drive shaft and prop has cracked, wedging a section of the four-inch shattered acrylic against the prop blades.

Kaylie loosens the hand wheel and tugs open the hatch—

—the pressure differential between the docking station and the interior of the lab causing the chamber's titanium oval walls to shudder.

David and Kaylie stare at one another as if caught in an earthquake. "Go! Do what you have to do. I'm needed here!"

She nods. Then, fixing the pony bottle's mask over her face, she crawls up into the lab, sealing the hatch behind her.

The docking station stops trembling.

David sets to work on the propeller.

ᗄ　ᗄ　ᗄ

MOTION SENSORS ACTIVATE the lab's interior lights and life support system. A *whoosh* of stale air pushes out from dozens of vents, filling the habitat.

Kaylie peels off her mask and looks around.

The sphere is divided into two floors, the lower level containing two bunk beds, a port-o-potty and shower, kitchen area, water heater and cooling system, and a life support system plumbed into a large water tank and two generators, the lights on the backup unit indicating it is functioning.

Living quarters. Keep going. She climbs an aluminum ladder to the upper deck.

Work stations divide the area into a lab, sonar station, radio, and a computer. Shelves are lined with books, the walls covered in maps and drawings of assorted prehistoric sea creatures. She glances at a few then pauses to look out the dark viewport.

Come on, you're wasting precious time!

Opening a file cabinet, she searches for Maren's charts of the Panthalassa Sea.

ᗄ　ᗄ　ᗄ

DAVID SQUATS BY the starboard prop, using a monkey wrench to pry loose the damaged acrylic housing—

—pausing as he feels a low, rumbling tremor. Standing, he reaches out to touch the oval wall, his bones registering the thick double layers of titanium as they buckle within their structural frame.

"Jesus."

He rushes back to the prop, tearing and twisting the hunk of shrapnel with every ounce of strength. *Two minutes ... three tops ... or maybe seconds! Make it a minute ... finish in one minute before these walls crush you like a beer can!*

ᗄ　ᗄ　ᗄ

KAYLIE LOCATES TWO charts in a bottom filing cabinet. She rolls them up, turns to leave, then feels the low rumble coming from inside the docking station, building like an approaching tsunami.

David tears off the loosened debris then climbs the ladder, banging on the lab's hull with his wrench. "Kaylie! Now!"

The hatch pops open, causing the chamber floor to rumble, the porous secondary floor twisting beneath the sub. Kaylie tosses him the charts and slides down the ladder.

David hurtles over the Manta Ray's wing, falling feet-first into the cockpit. He shoves the charts behind Kaylie's seat as she flops inside, pressing the green switch on the docking station control. Nothing happens.

The infuriating yellow warning light blinks.

Metal groans. The oval wall before them indents for a frightening second then pops back into place, the depths demanding entry!

"David, we need to get inside the lab!"

He turns to look at the sphere, his mind debating—

—his eyes spotting the open hatch. *A trip switch?*

"Wait here!" He leaps out of the cockpit, races up the ladder and slams the hatch shut, spinning its hand wheel tight—

—causing the yellow light to cease blinking.

Kaylie presses the green button, sending fountains of seawater shooting up from the floor, soaking David as he leaps back inside the cockpit. She seals the hatch and they wait, the process taking a good twenty seconds—

—the titanium walls bowing inward, then out again, the battle tenuous, the chamber lights blinking, the water level rising fast over the Manta Ray.

David powers up the submersible, the two of them quickly strapping in as the chamber goes dark and the water level kisses the ceiling—

—opening the horizontal doors, offering the sea's 14,031 pounds per square inch of pressure a toe-hold that crushes the titanium docking station as if it were made of aluminum!

The flooded chamber minimizes the pressure differential between the abyss and the hangar, staving off the implosion—

—the temperature differential inhaling ocean like a vacuum!

David jams both feet to the pedals, empowering the Manta Ray's twin propellers. For a frozen moment technology battles Nature to a draw, the sub held in place against the incoming torrent—

—the propulsion units cavitating, creating its own vacuum!

The stressed titanium buckles, the chamber walls collapsing around them—

—the sudden shift in volume equalizing the pressure, releasing the sub!

The revving propellers catch the sea, hurtling the vessel down into the darkness! The sea floor leaps at them. David pulls back hard on both joysticks too late—

—the uncontrollable thrust burying the submersible bow-first in the silty bottom.

27

The hopper dredger, *McFarland*, is a 319-foot-long monstrosity of steel, its rusted hull painted red below the waterline, black trim above, its white superstructure towering five stories in the stern. Built by the Bethlehem Steel Shipbuilding Corporation back in 1967, the boat was originally owned and operated by the U.S. Army Corps of Engineers as part of their hopper dredger fleet—ships designed to clear sand from the bottom of the main shipping channels.

Operating like a giant vacuum cleaner, the *McFarland* incorporates two large, trailing suction drag arms that inhale slurry—a water and sand mixture. In turn, the slurry passes through a drag head and pipelines on its way to the hopper. The hopper is a massive hold that runs through the middle of the ship like a giant Olympic-size pool. So large is the *McFarland's* hopper that, at full capacity, it can hold more than six thousand tons of slurry. Once the ship reaches its designated dump site, the slurry is released through giant steel doors located along the bottom of the keel.

Despite its prodigious size and ten-thousand-ton displacement, the hopper dredger is a fast, maneuverable ship, powered by two 3,000-horsepower screws, and a 500-horsepower bow-thruster.

After four decades of service, the *McFarland* had been decommissioned following cutbacks by the GAO to the Federal Government's hopper fleet. For years the ship had sat, slowly rotting in a Philadelphia shipyard, until a private entrepreneur rescued it from the scrap heap.

ᐁ ᐁ ᐁ

JONAS AND MAC stand on the *McFarland's* bridge, a red-tiled command center equipped with banks of new computer consoles and GPS electronics, surrounded on all four sides by large bay windows. Stretched out before them are the main deck and mammoth hopper, the open hold occupying the deck space between the bridge superstructure and the ship's bow. The 175-foot-long, 45-foot-wide, 55-foot-deep tub is filled with seawater, all of the machinery designed to stir the captured slurry long-since removed. The port and starboard drag arms

244

have been fixed at shallow depths so that they now channel seawater into the hopper, not sand.

Mac shakes his head in amazement. "When did you do all this?"

"Four years ago, about three months after Angel birthed her pups. I knew the Institute couldn't house six full-grown Megs. I figured we'd eventually need something large enough to transport a few of them to buyers. The Feds practically gave her away. Cost us about two hundred grand to gut the hopper and refurbish her. Not too bad for a tax write-off."

"Brilliant. Where was I during all this?"

"On your honeymoon. I told you about it when you got back."

"When you said a dredger, I assumed you just wanted to keep the canal clear." Mac walks across the control room's wide expanse to gaze out the aft bay windows and the stern, the back end of the ship situated less than one hundred feet from the Tanaka Lagoon's canal doors.

"How far is it from the canal doors to the hopper's hull doors?"

"The skipper approximated 225 feet. Clearance between the bottom of the hull and the sea floor's only sixty feet, which helps. We'll drop heavy cargo nets along either side of the ship, as well as the bow, forcing Angel inside the open hopper."

"What if she doesn't want to go in?"

"We're baiting the hopper. Plus Dr. Nichols will be enticing her, using the neurotransmitter. And hopefully the anesthetic will take the fight out of her. Once she's secured in the hopper, Dr. Nichols will put her in sleep-mode for the duration of the trip, and off we go. Figure a five day voyage to the Mariana Trench."

Mac smiles. "I like it. And you know what part I like best?"

"That you don't have to get wet?"

"Exactly. Wait ... you said anesthetic. Who's administering that? You?"

"It's not a big deal. I'm not entering the canal. I'm just directing the feed tube through one of the pores."

"J.T., not to overuse a cliché, but you're getting too old for this shit. Let one of our divers handle it."

"After what happened to Hendricks, no way. Besides, we still don't know who's been leaking the Meg Pen footage to that animal rights group; and Terry and I want to keep Angel's release quiet. Everyone thinks the dredger's simply cleaning out the canal entrance. Terry's doing a live televised debate with R.A.W.'s new spokesman this afternoon at the Monterey Aquarium. By the time the staff and the rest of the world figures out Angel's gone, we'll be far out to sea."

"Nice."

"Trish okay with you being gone?"

"She's cool with it." Mac stares at the canal, grinning from ear to ear.

"What?"

"Trish found out the sex of the baby. It's a boy."

"Yeah?" Jonas slaps his friend on the back. "Mac Junior, huh? Man, that's great. I can't wait."

"The way I figure, I'll be teaching him how to play baseball using my walker. You know we should be documenting this whole thing."

"Your son's birth?"

"Angel's release. I bet it'd make a great documentary. I'd love to stick it right in those R.A.W. a-holes' faces."

"It's already in the works. Dani's handling it. She just hired a film crew." Jonas points below to the stern deck where a tall man with a receding, dirty-blonde hairline and matching goatee is directing a shorter Italian gentleman with slicked-back, dark hair.

Mac's eyes go wide. "Erik Hollander and James Gelet? You hired Maren's stooges?"

"Hollander didn't know what Maren was up to. Besides, they do nice work. You saw that *JAWS* documentary: *The Shark Is Still Working?* That was theirs."

"I don't know ... Is Hollander getting in the water with you?"

"Hell, no."

Mac offers a wicked smile. "He is now."

Monterey Bay Aquarium
Monterey, California

The Monterey Bay Aquarium is located seven miles up the coast from the Tanaka Institute in downtown Monterey, close to Cannery Row. Considered one of the top aquariums in the world, the facility features two hundred galleries and exhibits, including a living kelp forest, and was the first to house and keep a great white shark alive.

The debate between the Tanaka Institute and the celebrity spokeswoman for R.A.W. is set to take place on the first floor of the aquarium's Portola Café, its open deck facing the ocean. Security and local police have cordoned off the café's seating area, isolating the two panelist and Channel-5's camera crews from the invited public.

Lana Wood closes her eyes, allowing the make-up artist to powder her eyelids. The former film star, excited to be back in front of the camera again, feels the old adrenaline pumping, even if it is only to represent an animal rights group.

Terry Taylor refuses make-up, her almond eyes fixed on the horizon and the large ship anchored in the distance, just outside the Tanaka Lagoon. Her pulse is racing too, only with fear, knowing that her husband must once more place himself in harm's way.

Keep him safe, God. Let this be the end of it, once and for all ...

Barbara Raby, president of California's League of Women Voters, takes her place at the podium. She welcomes her two guests and begins the debate.

"Ms. Wood—"

"Please, call me Lana."

"Lana, R.A.W. has spent the last four years pushing the Tanaka Institute to release their captive Megalodons back into the wild. Why do you support this position, given that public sentiment clearly favors keeping these dangerous predators secured in their pens?"

"Barbara, I believe in the mission of aquariums and zoos—to educate and inform the public by exhibiting wild animals. That support ends when an animal is abused by its keepers. Our organization has clearly shown that overcrowding in the Meg Pen has led to the death of one pup, the drowning death of trainer Steven Moretti, and a near catastrophe only days ago when one of the juvenile Megs struck, and nearly shattered, the main gallery glass. The two remaining Megalodon pups are far too large to share one tank. As such, we're asking the Tanaka Institute to do the right thing and release the remaining pups back into the wild where they belong."

"Mrs. Taylor."

"The Institute recognizes that something must be done in the near future to afford Belle and Lizzy more living space; however, releasing these two juveniles into the wild is extremely dangerous."

"And why is that?" asks Lana. "You've said yourself on several occasions that humans are not part of the Megalodon diet. Monterey Bay is part of the Red Triangle, home to hundreds of great white sharks and the seal and sea lion populations they feed off of. Why can't these creatures exist in Nature's harmony like their modern-day cousins?"

"Belle and Lizzy are adolescent Megalodons, not great whites. They possess far different dispositions, including a fearlessness that drives them to attack anything and everything that provokes them."

"Yes, we saw just how your trainers provoked them, using five-thousand-volt bang sticks."

"Lizzy and Belle have never been abused, Ms. Wood," Terry retorts. "Shocking them with a five-thousand-volt bang stick is the equivalent of using a Taser on a charging elephant. As for Belle striking the gallery window, video footage taken on the day of the incident clearly shows a teenager in the crowd using a laser pointer to agitate her. That's why she went berserk."

"That's horrible," Lana says. "Still, it's no reason to keep the two pups captive."

"There's another reason. The sisters, as we call them, have formed a symbiotic predatory relationship when it comes to territoriality. We believe releasing them into Monterey Bay could potentially play havoc with the food chain while endangering boaters and divers as well. In many ways it's far safer to release Angel than her two siblings."

The statement draws a shocked response from the crowd.

Barbara Raby signals for quiet. "Mrs. Taylor, I don't think the members of R.A.W. or any other animal rights group is suggesting Angel be released ... are they, Lana?"

Lana Wood searches the audience where Jesse Thompson is emphatically shaking her head "No."

"Of course not. Angel seems perfectly content in her lagoon. Our concern is only in doing what's best for her abused pups."

Terry smirks. "Those pups, as you call them, will one day be as large and just as ferocious as their mother. We're not talking about clubbing fur seals or harpooning whales, Ms. Wood; we're dealing with very large, very dangerous predators."

Tanaka Oceanographic Institute
Monterey Bay, California

"I changed my mind. I am not getting into the water with that monster!" Erik Hollander pushes James Gelet and the air tank away, unzipping his wetsuit.

"Erik, I know you're scared, but you heard Taylor; it's perfectly safe."

"Then you do it!"

"Hey, I'm only the producer. You're the director. Besides, I'm not a very good swimmer."

"Neither am I! Especially when my limbs are paralyzed in fear."

"Erik, think of the movie. You're about to film something no one's ever seen. Remember when we got the Spielberg interview? This is just like that. It's the footage that makes or breaks the documentary."

Erik pauses from removing the BCD vest.

"Look, you heard Mackreides. If one of us doesn't make the dive, he'll call Kreg Lauterbach over at 1080 Productions. Next thing you know, *The History Channel* will be airing this seven times a month, and we'll lose out on an Emmy."

"I don't care about any of that."

"What about the DVDs? Do this and we'll split sixty-forty."

"Seventy-thirty."

"Sixty-five, thirty-five, and you get top billing."

Erik leans back against the rail. "I hate you."

"Yes, but you'll love me in an hour." Gelet hurriedly secures the air tank to the back of his partner's BCD vest. "Just remember, get as close to those openings in the door as you can, or else all we'll see on film is a white blur."

"Define close."

"I don't know ... coupl'a feet. What's the difference? As long as you stay on your side of the canal doors Angel can't touch you."

The blood rushes from Erik Hollander's face. He leans over the stern rail and pukes.

Mac walks by, slapping the gagging director on the back. "That's it, son, let it out. Beats hurling in your face mask."

▼ ▼ ▼

THE TWO DIVERS sink feet-first behind the *McFarland*, Jonas dragging the eight-inch-wide rubber feed hose into the depths, Erik Hollander holding his underwater HD video camera. The thirty-eight-year-old's pulse is throbbing so hard in his head he feels like he's about to have an aneurism.

"Jonas. I can't do this."

"Sure you can. Look behind you. You're missing some great stuff."

He turns as they slowly descend past the hopper dredger's keel, the two divers dwarfed by the ship's starboard twin screw and rudder assembly. "Geez, Louise ..." He fumbles with the lens cap then shoots a wide-angle shot of the *McFarland's* immense bottom. Midway to the bow, sunlight streams down from the hopper's open bay doors. Turning to his right, he catches a veil of cargo nets as they plunge over the side, anchoring in the silt ninety feet down.

"Incredible. I feel so … insignificant."

"That's only the appetizer. The main course is this way." Leveling out at sixty feet, Jonas swims toward the canal doors, the towering gray fortification looming ahead.

"Must you put everything in those terms?" Erik swims hard to keep up, the adrenaline and effort quickly exhausting him.

Jonas moves to within fifty feet of the door and stops. *Something doesn't feel right …*

Erik hovers beside him. Directly ahead, two blue portals reveal the sea on the other side of the wall, but nothing resembling a white blur. "Where is she, Jonas?"

"Close enough to smell you. Wait here." Jonas swims over to the algae and barnacle-encrusted barrier, his breathing rapid, his eyes wide as he waits for the penned creature to show itself.

Nothing.

Moving to one of the two-foot-wide pores, he steals a quick peek inside, checking below and above, then both sides.

The canal is empty.

Jonas fixes his gaze down the corridor of concrete, sunlight streaming in curtains between the rolling waves, the walls thick with algae, the incoming current causing the heavy growth along the vertical enclosures to dance.

After several moments he speaks into his face mask transmitter. "Mac, she's not in the canal. Can you see her in the lagoon?"

▼ ▼ ▼

Standing in the bridge, facing the stern, Mac aims his binoculars at the lagoon—

—catching site of the white blur moving beneath the azure water. "Looks like she's staying deep, circling." He turns to Brent Nichols. The biologist is seated at a work station with his laptop. "Hey, Doc, you think the *McFarland's* size and proximity to her lair is intimidating our fish?"

"Could be." Dr. Nichols scans his monitor, the computer program linked to Angel's nervous system. "Her pulse rate is a bit higher, respiration rate's climbing, too. I suppose she could perceive the ship to be a larger challenger."

250

▽   ▽   ▽

"SOME MONEY SHOT." Erik swims over to Jonas, his fear replaced by anger. "What am I supposed to do now? Rename the documentary *Chicken of the Sea?*"

Erik aims his camera down the throat of one of the canal door pores, filming the blue-green void. "Nothing but B-roll. What a waste of time."

Jonas scans the outer door, his mind slipping back to a bad memory—the first time he had ever observed Angel from the canal doors. He was a different person back then, forty-one and just married, weighed down by the death of his stillborn child and the financial burden of the Institute. He had set out that day to inspect the canal door hinges and had nearly died in this very spot.

Where had the years gone? What would he change if he could go back?

God saved you that day, gave you a second chance ... and here you are, back in the same place more than twenty years later. Did I earn that second chance ... or have I wasted it?

The urgency in Dr. Nichol's voice snaps him from his thoughts. "Jonas, Angel's pulse rate is soaring. I don't think she's intimidated by the *McFarland*, I think she's enraged by its presence."

"Jonas, it's Mac. She's leaving the lagoon. Can you see her?"

He moves to another pore, staring into the aqua-blue waters, waiting ... waiting—

—and then he sees his fish.

Jonas's heart skips a beat, the déjà vu hitting him like his worst nightmare as he registers Angel's speed, body position, and demeanor in one life-and-death split second.

His first instinct is to swim away. Instead, he lunges for Erik Hollander, grabbing him by his elbow.

The young director twists his arm free. "Are you crazy? You're ruining my shot!"

"She's charging the door! Move!" Jonas attempts to drag him away, gives up, then swims past the steel barricade, seeking cover behind the canal's southern concrete wall.

The director turns back to the pore—

—his mind reassuring him that the thick steel King Kong-size doors will remain sealed against the albino creation now filling his vision—

BAMMM!

The deafening roar of rolling thunder assaults his eardrums, blotting out all sound as force-equals-mass-times-weight, releasing an explosion of energy which propels him through the water faster than a human can swim. The sea floor soars by, filling his vision as the concussion wave pile-drives him face-first into the sand, his ragged body flipping end over end, the ringing sensation in his skull unresponsive to the long, shearing scream of weathered steel as the canal doors' hinges are forcibly wrenched from their rusted frame—the brain-piercing sound the last sensation Erik Hollander experiences before his mind says *enough* and shuts everything down.

Angel wiggles her way past the two unhinged barriers, shaking her head like a mad bull. Her proximity to the larger challenger in open water causes primordial defensive mechanisms to take control, her back arching in spasms, her pectoral fins pointing down, her caudal fin stiffening as it beats the sea and she attacks. She gnaws at the starboard rudder then propels herself along the bottom, homing in on the blood seeping out from her challenger's open belly.

▽   ▽   ▽

DECK OFFICER CHRISTOPHER Shane Long had been assisting a deck hand with lowering a chum bucket into the hopper when his bones had registered the massive underwater impact. The Tennessee native leans out over the starboard gangway's rail, glancing back at the canal.

"Oh, shit!"

Barbed wire and buoys, marking the canal entrance only seconds ago, are now floating away like tiny islands.

Long turns back to the hopper, his shouts of warning obliterated—

—as the hold erupts in an upheaval of white water and an ivory-white triangular head that is longer and wider than his brother-in-law's cement mixer!

Christopher grips the rail and hangs on as the monster bashes its skull against the steel contours of the hopper, each wallop shaking the ship and sending small tidal waves from the flooded hold across the open deck.

▽   ▽   ▽

MAC CROSSES THE bridge to the forward-facing bay windows. "She's in! Captain, seal the hopper! Doc, put her to sleep!"

"I can't!" Dr. Nichols is working furiously at his computer. "Her testosterone levels are overwhelming her sensory array. She's too riled up!"

Robert E. Nealis, Jr. joins Mac by the window. The *McFarland* captain stares at the chaos below, the creature's mouth gnashing on pipes, its tail whipping the hopper into a white-water frenzy. "Good God, Mackreides, do something before that monster sinks us!"

Mac exits the bridge and bounds down the catwalk's exterior stairwell to the main deck—

—barely hanging on to the rail as the ship rolls beneath him. Fumbling for his radio, he yells into the receiver, "Rosenfeld, retract the hose and prepare to pump!"

▼　▼　▼

Deck Officer Robin Rosenfeld and her three-man detail are stationed on the stern deck, manning three hundred feet of rubber hose harnessed to a winch. The free end of the hose feeds into a hydraulic pump and whirlpool-size slurry bucket filled with a milky-white mixture of tricaine methanesulfonate and seawater.

James Gelet is filming with his steady-cam, dodging splashes and stepping over hoses as he attempts to stay out of the fiery fifty-four-year-old redhead's way.

"Gelet, get that damn camera off me!" She is about to shove the producer aside when she spots Mac hurrying toward them. "Mackreides, we're retracting the hose. What the hell's happening?"

"Angel's in the hopper! Give me enough line to reach her. On my signal, start pumping the anesthetic."

"You got it!"

"Hold it," Gelet stops filming. "The Meg's on board? Where's Erik and Taylor?"

"Still below. Look for them to surface."

The nozzle end of the hose dances up the side of the ship and across the main deck. Rosenfeld slams the winch into neutral, then reverse, feeding out slack to Mac, who grabs the end of the hose and drags the wet length of flexible tubing past a labyrinth of thirty-six-inch pipes and onto the main deck's gangway.

Gelet looks over the stern rail and sees only empty sea. *Erik's fine, go after the money shot!* Heading forward, he chases after Mac.

A dozen crewmen are caught on the hopper's starboard and port-side gangways, holding on as the twisting, flailing white leviathan batters the inside of the hold just below their perch, the enraged Meg sending six-foot swells rolling across the main deck.

Mac drags the hose across the starboard gangway. Grabbing the slack, the crewmen help him re-position the feed-line, allowing him a clear shot into the hopper. James Gelet crosses the starboard gangway. Anchoring his legs around a rail post, he begins filming—

—as Mac yells over the radio, "Now, Rosenfeld, now!"

Angel lunges for him and misses. Her head surfaces ten feet below him, her teeth gnawing marks into the steel plates as Mac aims the milky-white jet stream down her throat.

The Meg slides back inside the pool of water then rises again to spy-hop—

—Mac nailing her again, spraying the elixir into her open mouth.

Angel's gills process the powerful anesthetic into her nervous system as she flails her head in protest, her movements gradually calming as the drugs gain a foothold. After another minute, her monstrous head slips beneath the water and she levels out, attempting to swim in order to breathe.

Mac yells over his radio, "Captain, start the dredgers!"

The two massive suction pipes trailing along either side of the ship jump to life, pumping a river of water into the front of the hopper, providing a steady current for the Meg to swim against.

With Angel's nervous system finally calming, Brent Nichols is able to alter the Megalodon's brain wave pattern, moving her to "sleep," a shutdown mode that permits the shark to rest while the organ that controls her swim muscles, located in the spinal cord, continues to function, perpetually propelling her forward to breathe.

James Gelet continues to film. Only the tip of Angel's caudal fin is visible above the hopper's water level. The tail flicks back and forth in slow, deliberate strokes, the Meg matching the pace of the dredger pumps' current.

Mac and Gelet turn to see Jonas bounding across the starboard gangway, still in his wetsuit. "She's in the hopper? Thank God."

Gelet smiles. "Looks like you guys missed all the action. No worries—" the producer pats his camera "—I managed to get it all on film. Guess Erik will have to renegotiate his split on the DVD. Where is he?"

"He's in sickbay. Dislocated his shoulder and broke three ribs." Jonas shoves Hollander's HD video camera into Gelet's chest. "You may want to check out his footage before you decide to renege on your deal."

28

The timeless, primordial cold envelopes the wounded animal, seeping into its wings, shrinking its appendages at the molecular level, causing its dense skin to crack. Aided by the ocean's ungodly weight, it presses its advantage, dousing the dying creature's warmth within.

David Taylor opens his eyes. Death has taken his vessel, stealing its life-giving heat, rendering it dark and powerless. The Manta Ray's acrylic shell creaks and crackles, the ocean laying claim to its remains—the submersible buried nose-first at a thirty-degree angle, all but the back of the cockpit and tail section covered in silt.

Hypothermia has taken David's body, dropping his internal thermostat two degrees, setting his limbs to shake, his teeth to chatter. He can see his breath in the dim olive hue coming from above and behind his head, the night glass revealing a final sliver of ocean, the sandy sea floor gradually snuffing out the last of his light.

The girl is somewhere next to him, cloaked in darkness, silenced by sleep. David rasps, "Kay ... lie," and reaches for her, his blood thick and curled, his muscles slow to respond. He shakes her four times hard before she awakens.

"So ... cold."

He tries the engine. The dying backup battery has just enough charge to power up the twin propulsion units, but they quickly choke and die.

Sand's clogging the intakes ... shutting down the props. Without the props I can't recharge the batteries. Emergency pod's no good either ... it's a five hour ascent just to make it to the hole ... at this rate we'll both be dead within thirty minutes.

Can't think ... too cold!

He tugs Kaylie's arm, dragging her, protesting, onto his lap facing him. He pulls off her sweatshirt and tee-shirt then guides her headfirst inside his own sweater so that they are chest to chest, belly to belly, the kiss of their cold bare skin the kindling necessary to generate body heat.

David tosses her discarded garments around her shoulders as they huddle together in the darkness of their coffin.

Her teeth chatter as she whispers in his ear, "Get us home."

"Backup battery's dying. Engine's clogged with sand. Need the props to generate power. Can't use the props while we're buried in sand. Radio's dead, too."

"Find ... a way."

He grinds his teeth, tears of frustration welling in his eyes. *Find a way? How? Should I get out and push? Call for a tow? Why couldn't you have stayed in Dubai with me like I begged you to do?*

He feels her tears roll down her cheeks onto his neck and hugs her tighter, rubbing her back, his mind inebriated with the cold. Amnesia sets in when core temperature drops to 94°F, unconsciousness at 86°F, death at 79°.

Rational thought is abandoning him minute by minute, along with the will to survive.

Laying his head back, he stares out the open neck of his sweater into the olive sea above. A shadow of movement passes overhead, followed by another.

Hell's vultures ... waiting to feed. Freezing to death ... I suppose there are worse ways to go. The two of us will just go to sleep and that will be that. So stupid ... for the first time in my life I had it all ... money, a great job, my own gig, and the most beautiful woman that ever smiled my way. My first honest-to-God true love and I blew it ... threw it all away 'cause of my damn ego. I should have never entered that lab--I knew better—but I didn't listen to my gut. Hell, I should have never made the dive. Brian would have chickened out at twenty thousand feet. He would have turned back ... done the right thing. Not you, Jonas Junior. So many plans ... all wasted.

He bangs his head against the seat in anger. *I would have been twenty-one years old this week. Twenty-one ... barely had fun—*

"Twenty-one?" Masao Tanaka's voice responds in his head with a reprimand. "I was half that age when my father died and I was forced to go to work in the sweatshops to support my family. Miyamoto Musashi was only thirteen when he fought his first duel. By the age of twenty-one he was fighting four men, one after the next!"

How did he achieve victory against such odds?

"By adhering to Bushido, the Way of the Warrior. The Way of the Warrior is death. Death is where solutions lie."

I don't understand.

"When faced with the choice of life and death, most men choose to live. The warrior chooses death, thus he passes through life without the possibility of failure."

Grandpa, how will this help me?

"By remembering there is strategy in all things. Musashi illustrated this in the *Go Rin No Sho*—five rings, five elements."

Ground ... water ... fire ... wind ... and the void.

"You're battle is with water. What was Musashi's strategy in dealing with this element?"

Water conforms to the shape of its receptacle. Musashi used the length of the long sword in the Book of Water to control the battle, to bring the enemy to him.

"And how can you apply this strategy?"

I don't know.

"Think about the creatures of the abyss, living in total darkness. How do they manage to survive the element of water?"

David's eyes snap open. *They bring their prey to them!* "Kaylie, wake up! I have an idea."

She mumbles something incoherent in his ear.

"Kaylie, stay with me! Wake up!" He rubs her limbs.

He searches through a glove box. Locates a flashlight, the batteries still strong. Slipping out of his sweater, he presses his face to the rear of the cockpit glass, aiming the flashlight's beacon at the rear portion of the port-side wing, causing the light to dance.

Angler fish use a bioluminescent lure to bring their prey to them, we'll do the same! Come on, whatever it is that's out there ... take a bite, a big juicy bite—

—anything but a Meg or a Dunk.

A shadow passes overhead, then another, then two more!

A five-foot *Helicoprion* swoops in, circles twice, then takes a quick bite and release of the starboard wing before racing off. Two more sharks follow, one a twelve foot *Edestus giganteus*—a prehistoric species possessing a set of jaws that protrude from its mouth like a pair of scissors, the teeth splaying outward like blades.

Within minutes, the Manta Ray becomes the center of a feeding frenzy for dozens of ferocious, medium-size sharks.

This is no good ... I need something bigger, something with some mass behind it.

He works the light some more, his bare chest shivering uncontrollably.

Another shadow passes overhead, this one causing the other sharks to scatter.

David's heart flutters as the seventeen-foot bony fish, *Xiphactinus audax*, moves in, its tarpon-like head hovering just above the dancing light. The predator's hinged mouth gapes open, revealing four-inch, piranha-sharp teeth, along with four upper front incisors that resemble six-inch spikes.

David stares at the prehistoric fish, keeping the light beam stationary along the starboard wing. *You want this, big guy? You really want it? Well, come and get it!*

He jumps the light—

—the predatory fish jumping with it, snapping its terrifying trapdoor mouth upon the Manta Ray's starboard wing, the creature's tail wiggling violently back and forth—

—as it forcibly drags its meal out of the sand!

David grabs Kaylie and hangs on as the fish whips its head back and forth, tossing them about like a bad carnival ride. "Buckle in!"

Acrylic screeches in protest, sand flying in all directions. David pumps his foot pedals, whispers a quick prayer, and hits the power switch as the fish shakes them again, nearly separating the escape pod from the chassis.

The port-side screw turns twice and jams, the starboard propeller grinding and jamming before spinning awkwardly, the shaft spewing sand as it slowly generates speed.

"Come on, baby. Come on!" David works the right pedal, feeling the prop gaining torque as the propeller shaft sheds more debris.

The fish shakes them again—

—causing the interior LED lights to flicker as the backup battery fights to recharge. The ventilation system's blower fans suddenly blasts them with frigid air as the starboard propeller's RPMs pick up, the screw reviving with power!

David pulls back on both joysticks to loop the sub free of the fish—

—but the fish will have none of it, its clenched jaws and stiletto-sharp front teeth puncturing the starboard wing as it hangs on and shakes its head once more, attempting to swim off with its still-thrashing prey.

Kaylie, barely manages to buckle herself in the co-pilot's seat. Reaching for her sonar array, she presses the ACTIVE switch—

PING! PING ... PING ... PING ... PING...

The stunned fish's jaws snap open, releasing its meal.

David jams his right foot to the floor and takes off. An exhilarating wave of adrenaline pumps his muscles, focusing his mind like a laser.

"David, it's right behind us!"

"Hold on, baby. I own this bitch!" David barrel rolls into a steep climb then cuts hard to port—

—his port-side propeller shaft spewing sand as it grinds back to life.

"Yeah, yeah! That's my girl!" Registering the sudden burst of speed, David pushes his machine to the max, distancing his sub from his swift pursuer before looping back and blasting it head-on with his exterior lights.

The startled fish darts off into the darkness.

The sub's engines warm, pumping out life-giving heat from its ventilation system.

Kaylie hugs David, smothering him with awkward kisses and tears. She removes his sweater and pulls it over his head while he drives before locating her own clothing and dresses, the two of them smiling so hard their frozen cheekbones hurt, their toes burning as the circulation gradually returns to their numbed feet.

Kaylie retrieves her headphones. Positioning them over her ears, she activates the sonar array and listens—

—her expression dropping. "Oh, no. They're right in front of us! Turn around! Go the other way!"

He executes a tight 180-degree loop and accelerates to thirty knots, dousing his exterior lights so he can see better through the night glass. "What is it? What do you hear?"

"Something big, really big. And lots of them!"

"Leeds' fish?"

"Just as big, only a lot faster. Two hundred yards behind us and closing fast!"

David pushes the submersible to its limits, streaking through the abyss doing thirty-two knots. No longer hydrodynamic, the chewed-up starboard wing shudders behind his controls.

"One hundred yards ... seventy yards! Can't you go any faster?"

"This is as fast as she goes! Can I loop around them?"

"No room, too many! David, there's one coming up along your side!"

He glances to his left, his heart still reviving from the cold, straining as it pounds in his chest.

The massive dolphin-like beak appears first—eighteen feet long from snout to tapered-back skull. He sees the pointy orca teeth, then an enormous eye—nocturnal and glowing silver in the night glass—as large as a beach ball.

"An ichthyosaur! A goddam ichthyosaur! Gotta be the big ones—*Shonisaurus sikanniensis*—seventy ... eighty feet long. Bet it weighs as much as a blue whale."

"David—"

"What a monster! Look. You can see gill slits behind its head. Gill slits, Kaylie!"

"David, drive! Swerve! There's one right behind us, snapping at out tail antenna!"

"Hold on!" David yanks back on both joysticks, sending them into a steep seventy-degree climb—

—the school of icthyosaurs—three female hunters, two females, and two juveniles—ascending right behind them.

"Kaylie, call out our depth."

"We just passed 29,850 feet. David, what are you doing? We'll never make it to the chute!"

"I'm not going for the chute." He checks his compass then adjusts his angle of ascent so he's heading east.

"Twenty-seven thousand … " Kaylie screams, holding on as one of the big females snaps at the starboard wing—

—just missing as another hunter nudges them from behind, inadvertently pushing them clear of the attacker's chomping jaws.

"Twenty-five thousand feet ... David, look out!" Two of the hunters have driven them toward a third, the seventy-five-foot, dolphin-like giant launching its attack from above!

David barrel rolls beneath its snapping jaws, looping around the forward pectoral fins, barely avoiding one of the rear fins, which grazes the cockpit glass as he shoots past the flailing tail and ascends at a ninety-degree angle straight up, searching for—

"The current! Hold on!" He executes a reverse loop, slicing into the fast-moving river of water, the torque nearly shearing off his torn-up starboard wing. Leveling out, he slingshots into the darkness.

The Manta Ray bucks and rattles in the current. David compensates on the fly, adjusting his pitch and yaw until the ride smoothes out. The sub races east along the swift conveyor belt of water, leaving the pack of giant ichthyosaurs behind.

"Whoa!" Kaylie unbuckles her harness and kisses him hard on the lips. "I love you! If I wasn't half-frozen with frostbite I'd climb on your lap and start our own mile-deep club!"

David aw-shucks a half grin. "We're not out of this hell-hole yet. Buckle in. I need to get us out of this current before we end up under Guam."

She climbs back into her harness, securing the headphones over her ears.

David throttles back, easing the Manta Ray into a gradual ascent, keeping the sub's damaged wings as level as possible as he attempts to slip out from the raging cold-water current.

▽ ▽ ▽

SEVERAL NAUTICAL MILES to the west, the Alpha team Manta Ray descends to sixteen thousand feet, marking the deepest dive yet for its nervous pilot, Jeffrey Hoch. The former Ohio Class submarine helmsman and ordained minister levels out and circles, his co-pilot, Marcus Slabine, listening intently on sonar.

"Well?"

"Shh!" Slabine hunches over, pressing his headphones tighter to his ears. "I've got something ... ambient sounds."

"Delta team?"

"Could be. Only one way to be sure."

Three sonar pings reverberate through the sea, the sound waves racing out into the darkness, bouncing off of any object in their path—

—alerting every life form in the area to their presence.

"Got 'em. Oh, shit. It's not Delta team. They're biologics! Five ... six ... seven of them! Nineteen thousand feet. They're changing course and rising fast! Jeff, get us the hell out of here!"

Jeffrey Hoch jams both feet to the floor and yanks back on the joysticks, launching their sub into a steep, vertigo-inducing ascent.

"Spiderman, this is Alpha team! We've got company!"

The sub soars past fourteen thousand, its pilot straining to maintain the vertical climb.

"Alpha team, how big?"

"Plenty goddam big!" Slabine yells.

"Don't blaspheme!"

"Shut up and drive!" Slabine rechecks his sonar grid. "Seven bogeys, three at least seventy to eighty feet long. They're right behind us—"

"Stay calm, Marcus. You probably just attracted a school of Leeds' fish."

"Bullshit, James. These aren't slow-moving filter feeders. They're fast and they're coming after us!"

"Passing eleven thousand feet."

Marcus marks the depth and time with his stopwatch, tracking the creatures' pursuit. "We've got less than thirty seconds on them! Jeff, once you reach the hole you can't slow down, you've got to hit that mother doing thirty knots! Minister, are you hearing me?"

Beads of sweat pour down Jeffrey Hoch's face, pooling behind his neck. "Too fast. We can't pull out of the hole at that speed. We'll get caught in the nets!"

"Screw the nets. You'd rather be fish food?"

"Alpha team, we've got a fix on your position. Jeffrey, you're trajectory's off-target! Come to course zero-six-zero on my mark. Three ... two ... one—"

"Mark!" Hoch adjusts his angle of ascent, the Manta Ray rearing back vertically like a ballistic missile.

The Minister's arms tremble, his breathing short and erratic. His exit from hell lies somewhere in the darkness up ahead, only his craft is moving far faster than his skill level allows, his faith in man—and God—being pushed to its limits.

"Maintain your heading, Minister. You're back on course. Mr. Slabine, activate exterior lights."

The sub's exterior lights flash on, illuminating a ceiling of rock and a black recess of water, growing larger.

"Here we go, gentlemen. Access hole on my mark. Three ... two ... one!"

The submersible shoots through the vertical shaft of rock doing twenty-two knots—

—followed seconds later by forty tons of monster!

Spiderman's voice grows excited. "You're luring them up. Don't let up! *Tonga*, stand ready with the nets!"

Disorienting outcrops of rock reach for them. Hoch swerves left, veering back right, every move requiring a deft counter-move, his reflexes falling behind, forcing him to—

"Don't slow down!"

"I have to! I can see the red warning lights!" Easing back on both pedals, Jeffrey Hoch regains control of the sub—

—allowing the nearest ichthyosaur to close the gap. The prehistoric hunter whips its tail into a frenzy as it lurches forward, its carnivorous mouth snapping down upon its elusive prey—

—its conical teeth crushing the starboard wing.

Jeffrey Hoch and Marcus Slabine utter a short-lived scream as their craft careens sideways in a sickening spin, the Manta Ray smashing bow-first into unforgiving volcanic rock, the impact causing a two-inch-long hairline fracture along the cockpit ...

WA—VOOM!

Thirty-five hundred pounds per square inch of pressure implodes the acrylic escape pod, folding it in upon itself, splattering blood and innards a split second before the ocean engulfs the debris field in a vacuous burp.

The alpha female swallows morsels of plastic and human flesh as it soars out of the chute into the Philippine Sea—

—swimming snout-first into one of the cargo nets! Spinning as it rises, it quickly becomes encumbered in the heavy binding as the other two members of its hunting party charge out of the hole, the first becoming hopelessly entangled in two of the nets, the second managing to avoid the chaos as it leads the rest of the pod of giant ichthyosaurs into open water!

▽ ▽ ▽

WARNING SIRENS BLAST across the tanker's main deck, ordering all hands to their stations. Cables strain against winches as a life-and-death tug-of-war begins seven thousand feet below the surface, the hunters now the hunted—

—the exiled species suddenly free as Nature's 210-million-year-old purgatory comes to an abrupt end.

▽ ▽ ▽

IT TAKES DAVID Taylor twenty long minutes before he can ease the damaged Manta Ray into the upper reaches of the Panthalassa current's vast embrace. Exiting the torrent, he slows the submersible, allowing it to drift. The low roaring *whoosh* of water continues to move beneath them, the torrent raging into endless black sea.

Kaylie listens over her headphones. "Sonar's clear. How far from the chute are we now?"

He checks their position twice. "Wow. The exit hole's forty-seven-point-seven miles due west, and that's not counting the four mile ascent. Try the radio."

"Delta to Spiderman, come in please. Delta team to Spiderman? It's no good. I'm getting nothing but static. I think one of those creatures bit off our antenna assembly."

Exhausted from the near-death encounters, David lays his head back and closes his eyes to think, the soothing sound of the Panthalassa current combining with the heat blowing in from the ventilation system to relax his body, sinking him deeper in his seat. His eyelids grow heavy, his body shutting down—

"David!"

"Sorry. I'm wiped out."

"Here, eat something." She opens a glove box, removing sealed bags of trail-mix snacks. She tosses him one, keeping the other for herself.

David shovels a handful of peanuts, dark chocolate, and raisins into his mouth, the sudden rise in blood sugar momentarily staving off sleep. "Where's Maren's charts?"

Kaylie reaches behind her seat, grabbing the two charts. She unravels the first. "This is a bathymetric chart of the Panthalassa Sea. I count twelve exit holes, including these three Maren highlighted in red."

David points to one of the highlighted markings. "This is the hole we descended through." He removes a slide rule from a storage compartment then checks their present location. "That puts us right about ... here, along the eastern half of the Panthalassa."

Kaylie scans Maren's chart. "Looks like we have a few choices. The nearest exit is here, twenty-two miles to the northeast."

"That runs right into the Mariana Trench. No way am I going into that Megalodon nursery."

She scans the chart again, measuring distances with the slide rule. "What about this exit? Granted, it's eighty-five miles from here, but it's due east. We could probably ride the current most of the way out, making it in half the time. Plus Maren highlighted it. I'm assuming that's a good thing."

"Or we could go back."

She looks up at him, her eyes full of fear. "The ichthyosaurs are back there. Do you really want to go that way?"

"Right. East it is. Hold on!" David pushes down on his foot pedals, accelerating to twenty knots, building speed as he eases down on the joysticks—

—immersing the Manta Ray belly-first inside the roaring Panthalassa current.

Aboard the McFarland
Pacific Ocean

A tapestry of stars blankets a moonless night sky, the ocean, lead-gray and velvet, melting into its endless horizon.

Jonas is seated on the starboard catwalk's steel grating, his chest and elbows leaning against the guardrail's lower rung, his legs dangling twenty feet above the hopper.

Below, the dark pool of seawater glows softly from its submerged occupant's snowy-white hide, the only movement coming from the upper lobe of Angel's caudal fin, each east-west stroke of its tail as effortless and steady as a metronome.

The scene takes Jonas back twenty-six years when Masao Tanaka's ship, the *Kiku*, had drugged and netted Angel's mother. On a night similar to this, Jonas and Terry had stood by the stern rail, contemplating whether to drag the captured Megalodon into the Institute's lagoon, or drown it.

Terry was livid. All she wanted was revenge for her brother's death. But I wanted the Meg kept alive, if only to prove to the world that it was still alive, that I was right.

That was a crossroad—a decision that ultimately affected a lot of innocent people. How many victims might still be alive today if I had killed Angel's mother when we had the chance? How many families would have been spared their grief? I could have ended this whole affair back then ... no Meg, no Angel, no Belle and Lizzy.

Ten years from now, assuming I'm still around, will I look back at this night as a crossroad as well? What if my decision to free this monstrous pet of mine leads to my own death ... or worse, the death of a loved one? What if she is pregnant again? How can I allow the resurrection of a species that was never intended to share the oceans with modern man?

Kill her! Do it now! Gut her remains and sink the evidence, then fly home in a week and announce she's been successfully returned to the abyss. Seal the lagoon for good. Seal it so her evil brood never tastes open water.

Jonas smells the smoke from the meerschaum pipe a moment before he turns to see Captain Neal is watching him from the forward deck. "Your friend seems upset."

"Mac? What happened?"

"Don't know. He's in the bridge, speaking with someone on the radio."

🦷 🦷 🦷

WITH A HEAVY heart, Jonas enters the command center. He finds Mac outside, standing on the catwalk balcony overlooking the forward deck. There are tears in his friend's eyes.

"Mac, what happened? Was it Trish? The baby?"

"No."

Relief and panic hit him at once. "What, then?"

"I didn't trust bin Rashidi, so I arranged to get someone on the inside—someone to keep an eye on David for me."

Jonas's skin tingles, sweat breaking out across his body.

"I just heard from my guy. David took bin Rashidi's offer. He made the dive into that isolated sea. He's missing."

Jonas grabs Mac by the shoulders, his blood pressure soaring. "What happened? Tell me everything!"

"They sent David and another pilot down in one of the *Rays* to access a deepwater lab. They docked—"

"Where? How deep?!"

"Deep. Thirty-one thousand feet."

"Oh, Jesus ..."

"They made it inside. A short time later the docking station imploded. The detonation destroyed the barracuda. There's no way of knowing if they made it out alive."

The world spins in Jonas's head. He collapses to his knees and covers his face, his rage blunting his sorrow, his body shaking with emotion.

"The radio's not working. It could just be interference—"

"Get me there."

"I already called for a chopper. You're on a flight out of San Francisco to Hawaii, catching a connecting flight to Guam. I'll have another chopper ready when you arrive that will fly you out to bin Rashidi's ship."

"Contact the Institute—someone you trust. I want the *AG-III* prototype crated and loaded on board my planes."

"An Abyss Glider? Jonas, bin Rashidi has Manta Rays—"

"This is a rescue mission. I need something with a grappler arm."

"Okay." Mac stares at the Pacific. Swallows hard. "Jonas, David's a good pilot ..."

Jonas nods, choking on his words. "I'll find him."

29

Panthalassa Sea

Our planet is an interactive biomass, possessing a self-regulating homeostatic system that stabilizes global temperatures and chemical compositions—conditions necessary to sustain life.

Earth's womb is its oceans, its vast currents the circulatory system that regulates global temperatures and provides nourishment to every living creature. While these currents are affected by wind and tides, the moon's gravitational pull and the planet's rotation, the real power train that keeps these planetary rivers of water flowing is thermohaline circulation. Warm water has a tendency to rise, while colder, saltier water, being denser, will sink. Density differentials in water, created by temperature (*thermo*) and salinity (*haline*) move large rivers of water just as the jet stream moves great volumes of air—

—a prime example being the Gulf Stream.

Part of the oceans' global circulatory system, the Gulf Stream is a shallow, warm current that moves more water than five hundred Amazon rivers. Heated by the equatorial sun, the Gulf Stream rises, releasing enough heat to power the world a hundred times over. As it flows north past Florida, it is chilled by the wind, accelerating evaporation. Now saltier and cooler, the current sinks into the North Atlantic depths, replaced in turn by warm water, which follows its downward flow.

Reaching sub-polar temperatures around Greenland, the current descends to depths of six thousand to ten thousand feet, where it begins its southerly flow into the Western Atlantic Basin. Influenced by the contours of the deep ocean floor, this submarine river winds past Antarctica before flowing into the Pacific and Indian Oceans, looping into other currents before upwelling back to the surface to begin its planetary journey back in the Gulf Stream. So vast is this oceanic conveyor belt that it can take over a thousand years just to complete one lap around the globe.

The Panthalassa submarine current circulates nutrients in a similar way. Cold seeps rising from the ancient sea floor create a massive upwelling of dense, frigid water which is drawn in a clockwise easterly flow by the planet's rotation. As this current continues east it collides with a warm influx of water created by a seismically active sea floor dominated by thousands of active hydrothermal vents. These vents, or black smokers, excrete superheated, seven-hundred degree

Fahrenheit water, heavily laden with chemicals and minerals. As the heated water rises, it meets the freezing cold layer, forming a hydrothermal plume.

This swirling ceiling of dense mineralized water effectively traps and seals in the heat, creating a tropical layer below. The density differential between the upper cold layer and the tropical abyss drives the Panthalassa current like a raging river, increasing its flow rate over the next six hundred miles. As the current reaches the eastern-most point of the subterranean sea, the vents become sparse, the ocean temperatures cooling rapidly. The cooled current sinks as it flows to the south, then west, where it eventually meets the cool water seeps and begins the process all over again.

In the isolated depths of the Panthalassa Sea, the extreme differences in heat and cold that fuel the thermohaline submarine river also provides a perpetual supply of food for its prehistoric inhabitants for more than 250 million years. But the cold seeps and hot vents do far more than circulate nutrients; their vastly different temperate zones also serve to segregate its population into two very distinct food chains.

▼ ▼ ▼

David Taylor closes his eyes as he urinates into the flexible plastic, six-inch tube attached to the sixteen-ounce bottle. "Oh, baby, that feels good. My back teeth were floating."

Kaylie ignores him, too focused on piloting the sub through the Panthalassa submarine current.

"All done here. Sure I can't interest you?"

"I told you, I'm covered."

"With what? Is it some kind of diaper or something?"

"When we get out of this mess I'll let you try it on, okay. Now hurry up and finish, the current's getting rougher."

"You can't rush a guy when he's peeing. Cut it off mid-stream and you're liable to blow out your prostate." He moans for effect then feels the sub rising and glances at the depth gauge.

... 19,175 feet ... 18,840 feet ...

"Kaylie, keep us level. You're ascending too fast."

"It's not me. It's the current!"

As if in response, the sub's bow suddenly heaves upward, causing David to spill urine all over his pants before Kaylie can level them out again.

"That's not funny!"

"I didn't do it! I told you, it's getting too rough for me!"

He caps the bottle and zips up, setting his hands and feet at the port-side master controls. "Switching over ... now." The two joysticks instantly animate in his palms, the current's torque on the sub's two wings registering throughout his upper torso. "What the hell? The current's upwelling."

"No shit. Take a look at the sea temperature."

The gauge reads fifty-seven degrees Fahrenheit and rising.

"We must be entering a hydrothermal vent field."

"Is that good?"

"Not while we're still traveling in the current. The temperature differential could—"

Kaylie screams as a column of rushing water catches the Manta Ray's wing expanse like hurricane winds peeling away a tile roof. The submersible's bow flips straight up, continuing into a 360-degree somersault as the swirling vortex catches the wings like a sail, tossing the craft sideways, punishing the tiny submersible and its two helpless passengers.

Mercifully, the current spits them free.

The damaged sub stalls. Neutrally buoyant, its hovers upside-down in the water, its shaken occupants struggling to regain their equilibrium.

David massages his throbbing head, his brain rattling like it did after his football concussion.

Kaylie moans, "Can you at least right us before I puke?"

He fumbles at the inverted controls, managing to restart the engines. The starboard shaft grinds metal against metal, forcing him to ease off before he tears up the housing. Using only his left pedal, he rights the sub, moving them ahead at a cautious three knots. "You okay?"

"My head's pounding, I'm seasick, my diaper's full, and I'm scared shitless. Would you describe that as being okay?"

"Beats being dead. And if I remember correctly, I practically begged you not to come."

"Remind me later to pat you on the back." She searches a medicine bag for aspirin. Swallows four with a swig of icy water. "Any idea where we are?"

He checks their position. "About four miles southwest of Maren's access hole and two miles beneath the Panthalassa crust. Can you hear anything on sonar?"

She listens over her headphones. "Only that current. It's blotting out every ambient sound in the sea."

"I'll move us farther away." David is engage the port-side propeller when he sees something looming in the darkness up ahead. Adjusting the cockpit's night glass contrast, he stares into the olive-green abyss—

—then shuts down the engine, allowing them to drift.

"What are you doing?"

"Shh! Overhead and up ahead." He points.

She looks up, gazing at swirling shadows of movement converging on a whale-size mass two hundred feet above their present location. Kaylie's eyes adjust, allowing her to identify the ancient participants of the eastern Panthalassa food chain.

Hadopelagic krill swarm through the sea like hordes of locusts, rising up from the depths to feed on microscopic particles of food. Spiraling around a twinkling, albino cloud of shrimp are schools of anglerfish, their bioluminescent orbs swirling through the darkness like a million fireflies caught in a tornado. Dive bombing into the maelstrom are sharks, the predators moving too fast to identify.

At the heart of the abyssal smorgasbord is an 83,000-pound Leeds' fish.

Wounded, gushing blood from dozens of gaping wounds, the eighty-five-foot behemoth is literally being eaten alive as it attempts to distance itself from the Panthalassa's true warm water predators.

A twelve-foot halosaur attacks one of the creature's enormous ray-shaped pectoral fins. Paddling with its four limbs, the small mososaur snaps its crocodile-like jaws upon the lashing fin and holds on, its double row of pterygoid teeth, located along the roof of its mouth, puncturing flesh and bone. Gill adaptions flap behind the ancient marine reptile's powerful neck as it whips its head to and fro until the sixty-pound morsel rips free.

Drawn to the fresh wound is a pair of six-foot *Hybodus* sharks. Bearing a heavy upper-lobed caudal fin like the modern-day thresher shark, this denizen of the Triassic-Cretaceous period possesses a pair of devil's horns protruding from behind their eyes and a spine on the frontal tip of its split dorsal fin, the built-in weapon allowing it to ward off attacks from above. The sharks—both females—swoop in upon the Leeds' fish, burying their blunt jaws nose-deep into a bleeding patch of pink flesh. Wiggling their entire bodies back and forth in a vicious frenzy of movement, they use their serrated teeth to chew through tissue and bone.

Moving out of the darkness to trail alongside the Leeds' fish is the elasmosaur. Forty-five feet long, possessing a thin neck that spans half its body length, the heavy-bellied plesiosaur has targeted a gaping wound located just above the Leeds' fish's left pectoral fin, attracting several dozen piranha-like angler fish. Using its four six-foot-long flippers to propel itself closer to the frenzy, the elasmosaur suddenly lunges laterally with its head, its needle-sharp interlocking teeth spearing three of the angler fish from behind, scattering the rest. Retracting its head, it chomps down the mouthful of food, allowing the anglers time to regroup before it moves in to dine again.

David's peripheral vision catches movement. Turning to his left he comes face to face with the reptilian eye of *Hainosaurus*. The giant mososaur glides by, revealing a terrifying up-close view of its fifty-seven-foot girth. Crocodile-shaped jaws that could swallow a grown man whole yield to a thick neck and stout four-flippered body, ending with a powerful twenty-foot-long, eel-like tail.

Ignoring the dormant Manta Ray, the thirty-two-ton brute circles effortlessly beneath the Leeds' fish as it sizes up its next meal ... and its competition—

—which arrives from above. For a heart-stopping moment David mistakes the huge bodied creature as an adult Megalodon, but as it circles the periphery he can make out not one, but two of the monsters, swimming in formation.

The female kronosaurs are smaller than the giant mososaur, but just as dangerous. Possessing seven-foot skulls, with jaws filled with nine-inch conical teeth, the creatures' bodies are densely muscled, from their powerful necks down to its stubby, triangular tails.

The kronosaurs are swimming in a synchronized fashion, the second pliosaur being towed within the wake of the first—

—*just like Lizzy and Bela!*

And in that fleeting moment of clarity David understands: Among the big predators, size—or perceived size—is everything.

The lagoon's water supply flows into the Meg Pen. Even though the tanks are physically separated by a sealed passage, the sisters can still sense Angel's presence ... and they fear her.

Detecting the kronosaur's arrival, the mososaur launches upward to claim its place at the dinner table, its mouth stretching open like a python's—

—its jaws slamming home upon the Leeds' fish's exposed belly. The dying giant convulses within its attacker's grip as the halosaur lashes its head and body back and forth until its rows of pterygoid teeth excise an eight-hundred-pound mouthful of flesh and innards.

Blood gushes from the mortal wound, bathing the mososaur as it feeds. The creature remains close by the dead Leeds' fish, safeguarding its kill. Heavy jowls chomp the meat into pulp, the brute's gill slits and thick belly quivering with the effort.

And then suddenly the mososaur swims off, abandoning the kill.

The kronosaurs are moving off, too. So are the sharks, the elasmosaur, even the angler fish—every creature vacating the kill zone.

An eerie quiet pervades.

Kaylie's limbs tremble, the blood draining from her face. Squeezing David's arm, she points to her sonar array.

The enormous *blip* is moving seventy feet below them, gliding in from the east.

David presses his face to the cockpit glass by his head, peering down past the portside wing, his eyes focusing on movement, his pulse pounding in his neck.

The creature's dorsal surface is lead-brown, camouflaging it in the sea, its dark skin mottled in patches of ivory that turn stark-white along the underside of its lower jaw and belly. The head, from the tip of its smooth, crocodilian mouth to its short, muscular neck, is as long as the juvenile sisters' entire bodies and spans a full third of its gargantuan torso. Its jaw line alone is thirty-two feet, its mouth filled with ten- to twelve-inch, dagger-like teeth. The fangs located at the tip of its snout are so long and sharp that Nature has aligned them to jut outside of the mouth at crisscrossing angles.

Rippling along either side of the monster's neck are gill slits, each evolutionary adaptation twenty feet tall, enabling the ancient species of plesiosaur to breathe like a fish. The creature's mid-section is as thick and long as a train car, possessing a reinforced ribcage that supports a muscular shoulder girdle, powering a pair of forward flippers twice the size and girth of a humpback whale's pectoral fins. The abdomen tapers back to a pair of rear limbs and a short, thick tail, the sleek design providing the monster with grace and speed.

"*Liopleurodon* ..." David's flesh tingles as he whispers the name, his eyes wide as they take in the largest marine predator ever to have existed in the planet's four billion year history.

The monster passes beneath the Manta Ray then rises majestically from below, its yellow reptilian eyes appearing luminous in the night glass, its 122-foot-long body dwarfing even that of the deceased *Leedsichthys*. Moving almost surreally, the creature wraps its open jaws around the girth of the dead Leeds' fish, bites down, and swims off with its prize, its powerful forelimbs propelling it into the darkness.

David releases his breath. Kaylie whispers a prayer of thanks—

—as the giant mososaur's head suddenly blooms out of the darkness before them, its outstretched jaws clamping down upon their sub!

Only the dense cockpit colliding with the roof of the sea monster's mouth prevents its teeth from meeting and crushing the tiny submersible.

Kaylie cannot muster the breath to scream.

David fumbles to restart the sub, somehow managing to power on the exterior lights—

—turning the blackness into a pink throat and dark gullet, the periphery into brown-stained, banana-size, ivory teeth. External pressure briefly soars past 19,000 psi, sending red warning lights flashing across the command center, the cockpit a mere up-tick of structural stress from being violated by sea and monster, the two terrified pilots seconds away from death.

Unable to bite down or swallow its prey, the mososaur reopens its jaws in order to reset its grip—

—as Kaylie punches the ACTIVE switch on sonar, blasting sound waves at the beast—

—and David slams his left foot to the floor pedal, revving the port-side propeller. The Manta Ray slingshots out of the right side of the monster's mouth, racing into the darkness!

Kaylie tears at her brunette hair, hyperventilating, her exhausted mind overwhelmed by fear. "This isn't happening, it isn't happening—"

David zigs and zags, plunging them into a steep descent. "Kaylie, I need your help!"

"... this isn't happening—"

"Kaylie, get a grip! It's chasing us to the bottom; I need to know what the hell's down there!"

"Huh?" She turns around and sees the mososaur racing after them, its jaws snapping at the sub with every lunge! Grabbing her headphones, she actively pings the Panthalassa, searching for its ancient sea floor.

The depth gauge passes 28,000 feet, the water temperature elevating above sixty-five degrees Fahrenheit. Water pressure continues to build as they race toward the bottom, the ocean's sheer weight crushing the Manta Ray's underlying carriage. The damaged starboard wing's acrylic seams pop, the decrease in hydrodynamics causing the entire submersible to buck like a bronco.

"David, too fast, too deep!"

"Just get me a fix!"

"Bottom's at 31,877, but there's black smokers everywhere. You have to level out!"

"Tell that to Godzilla!" David switches on his exterior lights—

—revealing a petrified forest of hydrothermal vents below, each chimney stack one hundred to four hundred feet high, spewing thick black clouds of super-heated mineral water into the abyss.

The mososaur lunges again, its front teeth snapping off the starboard propeller!

The submersible spins as it descends in a near vertical drop. David targets one of the taller towers of volcanic rock, their bodies squeezed into their seats as he pulls a full G, looping the sub around the black smoker's thirty-foot-wide shaft straight into a dizzying barrel roll before leveling out at 31,470 feet.

The infuriated mososaur smashes through the vent, scorching its belly and tail in the scalding water as it continues the chase.

David zigs and zags around black smokers and clusters of tube worms, the Manta Ray swaying violently in the steamy water, each reverberation shaking the submersible with teeth-rattling jerks.

Kaylie's feet are braced against the dashboard, her eyes squeezed tight as she continues to send and receive sound waves through the chaos, yelling out instructions. "Starboard ten degrees! You're clear for another two hundred feet. Approaching a steep ridge! On my mark you'll climb. Steady, steady ... three ... two ... one ... climb!"

The Manta Ray soars over the sea mount then drops back into the valley.

The mososaur follows them over the ridge then slows. Instead of pursuing its prey into the basin, it circles left, then right—

—then disappears into the darkness.

David eases back on the port-side propeller. "Is it gone?"

"No, it's still out there, circling four hundred feet off our starboard wing, keeping its distance. Something must have spooked it."

David kills the exterior lights, employing the night glass.

The five-hundred-foot monster slowly materializes out of the olive darkness, looming up ahead.

30

Virgil Wade Carmen leans back on the uncomfortable couch, staring at the *Free Willy* poster.

Make them put up cash. Sara's okay, but I don't trust that other woman as far as I can throw her. Anyone who dyes their hair purple can't be—

He stops fidgeting as the two women reenter the loft.

Sara forces a smile. "Virgil, you're not telling us everything, are you?"

"I told you what I know. Angel's gone. Jonas and Mac released her and—"

"—released her where?" The veins in Jean Thompson's neck are bulging, the woman's face a mask of rage. "Taylor wouldn't have just released her, not into the Monterey Sanctuary."

"No one knows. Terry's keeping it all hush-hush, but I found out. I found out how they did it, where they're taking her, and all sorts of other information you'll want to know. But it'll cost you."

Sara looks at Jean, then back to Virgil. "How much?"

"A hundred grand. In cash. And don't tell me you can't afford it. I know you just landed two more sponsors, and it was all because of my footage. Face it, ladies, I'm the one who got you the media, the *YouTube* videos, the sponsors. Hell, I even got you Lana Wood. Now, I want a taste."

Jean is ready to spew a string of expletives, but Sara cuts her off. "Virgil, we appreciate you coming to us with this information, but this isn't exactly something the Institute can keep a secret very long. Of what possible value—"

"—Jonas beat you to the punch, Sara. He's releasing Angel at a remote place far away from humans—essentially stealing your thunder. And just for good measure, he's documenting everything, which means he'll be putting it right in your faces. I can tell you their present location, where they're headed, and—"

"Christ, he's taking her back to the Mariana Trench."

"How?" Jean asks.

"Boat, no doubt." Sara swears, "Son of a bitch! There was a hopper dredger docked outside the canal during the debate."

Sweat breaks out across Virgil's face.

"Sneaky bastards! With Angel gone, Taylor can seal up the lagoon. He'll put Lizzy in one aquarium, Bela in the other—"

"—and we're out of business!" Jean kicks her ergometric chair across the loft.

"Sara, I just signed a contract with the *YouTube Channel*. We promised them footage of Bela and Lizzy's release. Do you have any idea how much money's at stake?"

"I can do that," Virgil states.

Sara ignores him. "Maybe we can still get Angel on tape. What's the status of our sister organization in Japan?"

"Forget it. They're strictly out to protect the whales."

"That could work. With Angel in the Western Pacific—"

"Are you deaf?" Virgil tosses a throw pillow at Sara. "I said I can free Belle and Lizzy!"

"How?"

"The canal's stuck in the open position. The doors must have jammed when they moved Angel. Terry's not bothering to fix it since they're sealing up the lagoon, anyway. Construction starts in three days, which gives you plenty of time to set up a film crew outside the canal entrance while I release the sisters."

Sara looks at Jean, her eyebrows raised. She sits next to Virgil. "How do we do that, Virge?"

"*We?* We don't do anything. I'm the only one who can open the channel."

"What channel?"

"The channel that connects the lagoon to the Meg Pen—it's situated below the main deck about fifty feet beneath the bridge. There are two doors, one on either side, with a foot of free board allowing for pressure differentials between the two aquariums. The engineer designed it that way, just in case we ever needed to move the pups into the lagoon. Only time we ever used it was when Angel gave birth."

Jean sits on the sofa's arm rest on the other side Virgil. "And you have access to the channel's controls?"

Virgil nods. "A hundred grand in cash delivers the two sisters to your film crews while beating Jonas Taylor to the punch. My offer's good until midnight tonight. After that, I'm off to interview at the Miami Sea Aquarium."

"A hundred grand, my ass," Jean shoots back. "I'd rather go belly-up than pay you that."

"No worries, then." Virgil stands to leave. "I'm sure the two of you can always land jobs with PETA, tossing buckets of blood at millionaire athletes in their mink coats."

Philippine Sea
Western Pacific

The Sikorsky S61N helicopter soars high over the Pacific, cruising southwest at 120 knots. The two pilots converse in the cockpit—

—while their lone passenger stretches out in the cargo area next to a twelve-foot-long shipping crate marked: T.O.I. ABYSS GLIDER III HANDLE WITH CARE.

Jonas is lying on an old Army mattress and blanket, his body desperate for sleep, his mind in turmoil. There isn't any worse feeling for a parent than knowing their child is in danger; nor is there any greater anxiety than having to wait to learn of their son or daughter's fate. In Jonas's case, he has had to endure two torturous days of flying from the hopper dredger's helicopter flight pad back to San Francisco, to the flight from California to Hawaii, followed by another long connecting flight taking him to Guam. And now this, the final leg of his five-thousand-mile journey, a chopper ride across the Philippine Sea in search of the supertanker, *Tonga*. Only it is not the final leg—

—it's only the beginning. The final leg is a six-mile journey into the abyss—an endurance test he last accomplished twenty-three years ago—its success already jeopardized by his age, his anxiety, and his overwhelming physical and mental fatigue.

Must sleep ... for David's sake.

He adjusts his head on the make-shift pillow and closes his eyes again, his mind refusing to give in to reason.

Mac's inside guy said David had succeeded in deepwater docking the Manta Ray. *That means he either left the lab and got lost, he left the lab and became trapped, or the deepwater dock imploded and he's trapped inside the lab ...*

His bloodshot eyes pool with tears as darker thoughts once more attempt to pierce his resolve.

No! Don't go there! Focus on the other options. Organize your rescue efforts.

If he's trapped in the lab then you'll need enough cable to reach bottom, plus at least an extra mile of slack. Figure 37,000 feet, just to be safe. The lab weighs forty-seven tons, which means you'll need an industrial winch powerful enough to haul the lab topside. The tanker should have something like that on board.

But if he's lost down there, or his sub is crippled, it won't be easy to find him. Best strategy is to ping an expanding radius along the bottom. Of course, there's a danger in doing that, too.

Memories of his encounters with *Carcharodon megalodon* in the Mariana

Trench slip through his defenses.

Screw it! It doesn't matter what's down there. Besides, if David's sub was damaged, he would have ejected the escape pod. The pod floats free, but the chances of hitting that access hole are a million to one, which means he could be pinned to the Panthalassa *ceiling ... that's probably where you need to begin your search.*

He rolls over again.

No, Jonas, first you need to sleep ... for David's sake.

Panthalassa Sea

The creature is standing upright along the bottom, towering five hundred feet above a sea floor long since decimated by its arrival. Weighing upwards of ten thousand tons, the monstrosity of rusted steel is buried bow-first, surrounded by a debris field highlighted with the remains of its raised upper deck and tripod mainmast, eight boilers and four sets of turbines that had once powered its four out-turning propellers.

David activates the sub's exterior lights as he maneuvers the Manta Ray slowly around the Portland Class heavy cruiser's ancient keel. The silenced propellers are caked with barnacles, the steel plates rusted but intact—

—save for two massive holes located aft of midship, created by the impact of the two Japanese torpedoes that sank the American warship more than six decades earlier.

David guides the Manta Ray around the starboard flank, circling the destroyer's sixty-six-foot-wide beam where he is confronted by the three main battery turrets, now aimed at the sea floor. Encrusted almost beyond recognition by barnacles, the weapons have become a refuge for some of the smaller inhabitants of the abyss.

The Manta Ray's lights settle on an insignia: CA-35.

"Jesus, Kaylie ... it's the *Indianapolis!*"

▼ ▼ ▼

COMMISSIONED IN NOVEMBER of 1932, the *USS Indianapolis* saw its first combat in the South Pacific two months after the Japanese attacked Pearl Harbor. As the flag ship for the 5th Fleet, the destroyer earned ten battle stars for combat in Iwo Jima, the U.S. assault on the Mariana Islands, and the pre-invasion bombardment of Okinawa.

In July of 1945, the cruiser returned to the Mare Island Navy Yard in California to transport a top-secret cargo to the South Pacific—the uranium needed to complete the atomic bombs designated for Hiroshima and Nagasaki. On July 16, the ship arrived at Tinian Island in the Marianas to deliver its payload.

Two weeks later, on July 30, 1945, at 12:14 a.m., the *Indianapolis* was torpedoed in the Philippine Sea by a Japanese submarine. The ship sank in twelve minutes, taking with it three hundred of its crew. The remaining nine hundred men would spend four harrowing days at sea without food or water, floating in shark-infested waters, devoured from below while waiting to be rescued.

Of the 1,196 men who were on board the *Indianapolis* that fateful morning, only three hundred sixteen would survive.

▼ ▼ ▼

DAVID STARES IN awe at the ghostly wreck. "I read about the *Indianapolis* back in high school. The survivors say she went down bow-first. She probably weighed twenty million pounds when she struck the Philippine Sea floor doing thirty to forty knots. Her bow must have punched a hole right through the bottom like a giant anvil, only she kept on going ... straight through to the Panthalassa Sea until she finally struck bottom one last time. No wonder they never found her."

"Maren obviously did," Kaylie says. "Maybe he was searching for the wreckage when he stumbled across that hole. His discovery of the Panthalassa was probably just an accident."

"Makes sense."

The blood rushes from Kaylie's face as she presses the headphones tighter to her ears. "The mososaur, it's heading straight for us!"

David stamps both feet down on the propeller pedals—

—the starboard shaft long gone, the port-side propeller sending them hurtling toward the *Indianapolis's* upright deck—

—and a dark passage that once served as the ship's aircraft hangar.

David regains control, but instead of veering away he slips the Manta Ray inside the barnacle-encrusted rectangular opening.

Wa—boom!

Just missing the sub, the mososaur massive skull collides with the steel housing, sending thunderous sound waves reverberating through the hull. Too large to follow, the predator swims back and forth in front of the opening as it waits impatiently for its quarry to emerge.

From inside the hangar, David and Kaylie watch their would-be killer standing sentry.

"David, if we make a run for it—"

"We'll never make it. The starboard prop is shot, and the wings are no longer hydrodynamic. Best speed we could muster ... maybe fifteen knots."

"What about the escape pod?"

"Bad idea. There's too many things out there that want to eat us, and we've already gotten lucky once. Besides, even if we managed to make it to the access hole alive, there's no way to steer the pod. We could pin ourselves against the Panthalassa's rocky ceiling and be stuck there until our air ran out, a commodity that's already getting thin." He points to a CO_2 gauge. "The scrubbers are shot."

She stares at the gauge, her limbs trembling. "How long?"

"Maybe twenty minutes, another ten if you add the pony bottles." He forces a teary-eyed smile. "I didn't want to say anything. I just thought we'd sort of fall asleep."

"No! This isn't over yet." She fumbles for Maren's charts and scans the map. "If the hole's directly above this ship, then wouldn't Maren's lab be close by as well?"

"I suppose. I hadn't thought of that."

"You could use the deepwater dock to repair the prop! Maybe we can load up on air, or clean out the scrubbers!"

"Give me that map." David checks their coordinates against the highlighted insignia that marks the lab's location. "It's close ... about two hundred yards to the north." He looks up as the dark shadow swims by the narrow aircraft hangar opening. "Next problem: How do we get past our hungry friend?"

"Let's look around. Maybe there's another way we can slip out?"

David rotates the Manta Ray, using its exterior lights to explore the interior of the Indianapolis.

The chamber is a dark, its rusted confines covered in mineral rock, teeming with colonies of albino mussels and ghostly-white, foot-long clams, blind eelpout fish, spindly sea scorpions, and an uncountable number of crustaceans and trilobites, all feeding off a sheer vertical face of steel, coated in three generations of hardened minerals spewed from hydrothermal vents.

Rising up from the ship's buried bow is a perpetual stream of heated mineral water, clouded with heavy doses of methane and salt.

"Kaylie, this is a brine pool."

"How do you know?"

He releases his hands from the joysticks, the Manta Ray rising. "See? The water's so salty it's floating the sub."

"David—" She points to something massive, moving along one of the far walls.

He turns the sub, aiming its lights.

It's a turtle—the biggest turtle he has ever seen! Sixteen feet from its small, narrow head to its pointy tail, with a shell as large as a Volkswagen Beetle, the creature easily weighs over twelve thousand pounds. Moving along the wall, it is casually plucking lobsters from their rocky perches using its sharp, hooked beak.

"*Archelon ischyros* breathing like a fish. Look! There's two more!" Pushing the left foot pedal down, he maneuvers the submersible forward, aiming for the nearest turtle—

—bumping into it, chasing it across the chamber.

"What the hell are you doing?"

"Offering the mososaur an alternative meal." David swerves after the turtle, prodding it toward the exit.

Spooked by the sub's bright lights, the turtle swims toward the hangar opening—

—only to execute a quick about-face as it detects the mososaur.

David rams the turtle again along its soft, leather-like underbelly, driving it back outside the aircraft hangar.

The mososaur snaps at the turtle, which paddles away quickly using its flipper-like limbs, escaping into the darkness.

The mososaur swims after it.

David waits thirty seconds then guides the crippled submersible out of the *Indianapolis*, keeping it close to the sea floor as he heads north.

"One hundred fifty yards ... one hundred ... David, slow down or you'll pass it!"

"I haven't passed anything! Are you activating the docking doors?"

"Do you see me pushing this thing?" She listens on sonar. "It's working. I can hear the doors opening!"

"Are you sure? Where's the hangar lights?"

"I don't know. Maybe Maren's saving on bulbs. Come about! Make your course one-seven-zero, and slow down!"

David whips the submersible around, heading south—

—the silhouette of the spherical lab situated between several hydrothermal chimneys thirty yards ahead.

The cockpit spins in his head, the carbon dioxide levels approaching critical levels. Shaking off the dizzy spell, he guides the Manta Ray beneath the lab and up into the dark recesses of its open deepwater dock.

Kaylie activates the controls once more, closing the doors—

—as something else shoots up inside the chamber with them, bashing the tiny submersible sideways!

The cockpit spins, the chamber walls shaking, the sub's exterior lights spinning—

—the twin beams catching glimpses of the giant archelon turtle, the beast in panic mode as it attempts to swim within the tight confines of the deepwater dock!

The titanium doors seal beneath them.

The generators kick in, slowly draining the chamber.

Trapped, the prehistoric turtle goes berserk, flipping the Manta Ray onto its side, bashing its head against the spherical bottom of the sealed lab. Clawing at the walls, it slashes deep gashes across the polished titanium alloy—

—alerting the mososaur, the enraged creature now circling outside the lab!

WHOMP!

The ovoid chamber dents inward as the monster strikes the docking station's elevated flat bottom.

Seawater continues to drain, the interior pressure equalizing, causing the turtle's limbs and head to swell—

—until they burst like ripe melons! Innards splatter across the oval walls. The docking station rumbles, the intense water pressure threatening its structural integrity.

Wasting no time, David activates the cockpit, starting the excruciating process of unsealing the dome. He and Kaylie gather up pony bottles of air, bottled water, and food, shoving the supplies inside a canvas backpack. As the cockpit pops open, the pressure throttles their ear drums and sinus passages, causing their noses to bleed—an ironic defense against the assault waged by the dead turtle's overwhelming stench.

Kaylie rolls out of the cockpit, sliding down the damaged starboard wing. She slips in turtle slime then drags herself up the titanium ladder, David right behind her. His eyes are bulging, the walls wobbling in and out as if he's on a bad acid trip, the pressure in his head threatening to implode his skull. Climbing the ladder behind Kaylie, he reaches up and helps her crank open the hatch's rusted hand wheel as the entire chamber shakes.

With every last ounce of strength, David bears down on the hatch, wrenching it open. The pressure differential inside vacuums Kaylie head-first into the lab, David grabbing hold of her ankle with one hand and the inside of the hatch with the other, slamming the titanium lid shut behind them milliseconds before the screeching titanium walls buckle and bow inward beneath fourteen thousand pounds per square inch of water pressure—

Wa ... BOOM!

The air space inside the chamber is inhaled in an instantaneous, voluminous gulp, collapsing the chamber's thick titanium shell.

No longer supported from below, the 94,000-pound spherical laboratory drops through the wreckage—

—crushing the mososaur's skull, pinning the dead monster against the sea floor like a bowling ball dropped on the head of a python.

31

Jason Montgomery crosses the vast deck of the supertanker, heading for the contingent of Japanese crewmen that have gathered around the opening in the deck, where a fifty-foot crane is lowering a two-ton hunk of thawed whale blubber into the bowels of the tanker, releasing it above one of the holding pens below.

The water froths as the two captured ichthyosaurs tear apart the offering.

Monty watches a few minutes longer then heads for the tanker's infrastructure. He ascends the stairwell to the bridge, greeted by Deck Officer Nick Cato, who is working at a computer station, his thick brown eyebrows knitted in concentration.

"Mr. Montgomery. Back again to use the radio?"

"My cousin ... she's been ill."

Cato looks up from the terminal. "I thought it was your grandmother?"

"My cousin, Patty, she's been like a grandmother to me. Worried sick about her." He looks around, the bridge deserted. "Heard a rumor the *Tonga's* leaving for Dubai."

"You heard right. Bin Rashidi wants his new fish delivered while they're fresh. We'll be replaced by our sister ship, the *Mogamigawa*. She's even larger than the *Tonga*. Bin Rashidi says he needs her to capture his biggest prize, assuming he ever finds it."

"I've got a suggestion," offers Captain Singh, entering the bridge. "Tell him to drive the *Mogamigawa* back and forth over his hole until he sucks his monster out."

Monty smiles, misinterpreting the skipper's meaning. "Yeah, he's got something big crammed up his ass, that's for sure."

The British-Indian captain shoots the American a harsh look. "You have a problem with Mr. bin Rashidi?"

"Me? No. Of course, not."

Nick Cato steps in. "The captain meant his statement literally. Back in 2007, the *Mogamigawa* was cruising through the Persian Gulf at top speed when she sucked an American attack sub right off the bottom. The *USS Newport News*, wasn't it?"

The captain nods. "The *Mogamigawa's* a big girl, displacing over 300,000 tons. Once she's moving fast in the water she makes a hole that can vacuum everything into her keel. The American sub only displaces about seven thousand tons. Bigger always wins."

"It's called the venturi effect," the deck officer says, returning to his work. "Something about the acceleration of water through a constricted area relating to a rise in pressure."

"Venturi effect ... sure." Monty rubs his head, suddenly lost. "Did you know the planet's termites outweigh the human population by a ratio of ten to one? I mean, so I've heard."

The captain and Nick Cato exchange looks.

"Sorry. I'm just worried about my friend. Everyone's assuming the worst, that he would have radioed in by now. The Japanese sub's heading back down to lower a relay transmitter into the hole to try and pick up a signal, but if Delta team's radio's out, then that idea's fucked."

"What about a rescue mission?"

"We're down to one Manta Ray, and no one wants to pilot it ... not after what happened to Alpha team."

A red light flashes across Nick Cato's control board. "We've got company, skipper. Another cargo chopper." The deck officer takes his place at the radio station, slipping a set of headphones over his ears.

Timon Singh moves to the aft bay windows, the captain's eyes locked in on the approaching helicopter. "Too small to be another delivery. Have they identified themselves?"

Nick Cato listens to the transmitted message, his eyes going wide. "It's a military transport out of Guam. They're delivering a rescue pilot—

—it's Jonas Taylor."

Panthalassa Sea

The sea floor growls like thunder, its anger reverberating through the thick titanium sphere.

Lying prone in the suffocating darkness, David Taylor collapses next to the girl, his body exhausted, his mind falling into sleep's heavenly void ...

∇ ∇ ∇

"Yo, David. wake up, man!"

He opens his eyes, shocked to find himself lying face down on an old, familiar beer-stained sofa. Daylight is streaming in from the open balcony of his off-campus apartment at the University of Florida, winter in the Gainesville air.

His roommate, Chad "Stone Cold" True, the football team's backup center and long-snapper, is seated on the floor using a laptop. "Dude, you were moaning in your sleep."

David sits up, nearly passing out again from the hangover. "What happened?"

"You went a little ballistic last night at the Delta's keg party."

"Delta? I don't remember a thing. Did I have a good time?"

"Looked like it to me. You and that brunette with the sweet hooters were goin' at it pretty good."

"Kaylie?"

"Whatever."

The phone rings. Chad ignores it. "Probably your old man. He's been calling all morning."

David grabs the receiver. "Hello?"

"David, thank God."

"Dad?"

"David, you've got to get out of there. The air's running out, you don't have much time."

David looks around the room, confused. "Dad, what are you talking about? It's a beautiful day. There's a nice cool breeze—"

"Wake up, David—"

∇ ∇ ∇

"—open your eyes."

David opens his eyes, his body bathed in sweat. Kaylie is kneeling next to him. She looks pale in the dim emergency lighting, her eyes filled with fear.

"How long was I asleep?"

"I don't know. I passed out, too. Sorry to wake you, but I'm on the verge of really freaking out."

He sits up, his head pounding. "The Manta Ray?"

"Gone. Along with the entire docking chamber. We're stuck on the bottom. Trapped."

He stands, looking around, his legs and arms aching from piloting the sub for so long. "Where's the life support system?"

"Over here." She leads him to an alcove harboring two generators rigged to a series of fuel cells and a five-hundred-gallon water tank. "Any idea how this thing works?"

The lab's proximity to the hydrothermal vents turning the interior of the metal lab into a sauna. He wipes sweat from his eyes, scanning the life support system. "This is pretty high-tech stuff. It's used aboard naval subs." He points to a toggle switch. "Basically, it has two modes: life support and electricity. When it's in life support mode, which it's in now, it uses this fuel cell to electrolyze potable water and metabolize carbon dioxide to produce oxygen and methane. In fuel cell mode, it uses the stored oxygen and methane as fuel for the solid oxide cell, which generates a direct current."

"Whatever that means. Just tell me how much air we have left."

He checks the water tank meter. "Shit. Less than seven gallons."

"Which means?"

"Which means if you have to use the toilet, don't flush."

"David, don't bullshit me. How many hours?"

"I don't know! I'm guessing not many. I'm not a freakin' engineer." Head pounding, angry at himself for being in this predicament, he pushes past her and climbs the aluminum ladder leading to the upper deck.

Michael Maren's lab is a mess, the work stations littered with charts and drawings, the shelves with books, video camera equipment, and a computer—

—everything having been tossed into one big pile when the sphere had collapsed upon the remains of the deepwater dock.

"Kaylie, come up and help me look for a radio."

"No."

"No?" He looks down the ladder at her. "Are you for real?"

"I don't like the way you're speaking to me."

David slaps himself across the forehead. "Kaylie, we're trapped in a titanium ball at the bottom of some godforsaken sea, monsters everywhere, six miles of ocean above our heads, and we're probably down to our last five hours of air ... and you want to get into a fight?"

"I know our situation! I told you I'm freaking out, and you're making it worse by yelling at me!"

"Okay. Okay, I'm sorry. I'm a little freaked out myself. Now, would you please help me find Maren's radio."

She climbs the ladder. Points to a stainless steel receiver and transmitter lying atop a collapsed desk two feet from where David is standing. "Right in front of your face, Mister Engineer."

Grinding his teeth, he rights the desk and places the two devices on its table, plugging in the power cord. "It's dead. Go back down and flip that switch from LIFE SUPPORT to D/C ... please."

"This is a waste of time. How can a radio possibly work this deep?"

"I don't know. Fiber optic cable, rigged to a set of relay buoys and antennae? Maren was a bit twisted, but he was also pretty clever. He must've devised a way to contact the surface, just in case of a malfunction. When we were circling that first lab, I saw eye-bolts rigged to the titanium hull. At some point, they probably lowered these labs by cable."

"Then we can be rescued! They can send another sub down with a tow cable—"

"—if we can get this radio to work."

She slides down the ladder, flipping the toggle switch atop the fuel cell, powering up the exterior floodlights, bathing the surrounding abyss in red light.

David presses his face to a three-foot-thick funnel of acrylic glass, peering out the porthole. A steady cloud of blood is rising from somewhere beneath the lab. A shadow of movement darts by, then another.

Then he sees the kronosaurs. Moving in slowly from the dark periphery, the two thirty-six-foot pliosaurs circle the lab, their presence chasing away sharks and other life forms as they zero in on an unseen object located somewhere beneath the sphere.

The first creature lunges out of view then reappears several moments later, paddling backward, back into David's sight-line. Hanging out the sides of its hideous mouth is a section of the mososaur's thick tail.

"Does it work?"

"Huh?"

"The radio! Is it working?"

David pulls himself away from the feeding frenzy to check the transmitter.

The green power light is on.

Aboard the Tonga
Philippine Sea, Western Pacific

A cold wind whips across the supertanker's deck, whistling beneath pipes and steel housings, churning up whitecaps along the Pacific's six-foot seas.

Jonas Taylor steps down from the Sikorsky, greeted by a man in his late twenties. He's built like a wrestler, a baseball cap covering his shaved head, a six-inch devil's goatee cloaking his chin.

"I'm Jonas Taylor. I'm guessing you're Mac's inside guy?"

"Jason Montgomery. Call me Monty. Patricia Pedrazzoli's my aunt. Only now, I guess her last name's Mackreides."

Jonas heads for the *Tonga's* infrastructure. "Where's my son?"

"No one knows. We lost contact twelve hours ago ... give or take. But hey, if you need a co-pilot, I'm volunteering. Granted, I'm not very good; in fact, I pretty much suck. But if this is a rescue mission, then I'm your man."

"Thanks, but I prefer to solo. Where's bin Rashidi?"

"Waiting for you on the bridge."

▽   ▽   ▽

FIESAL BIN RASHIDI looks nervous, despite the presence of Brian Suits, Captain Singh, the deck officer, and his armed bodyguard. "Dr. Taylor, no one coerced your son into making this dive. We offered him the mission, and he accepted it."

"He's a kid!"

"He's twenty years old," states Brian Suits. "Legally, he's an adult."

"You took advantage of him, asshole. You bribed my son to take on your suicide mission! You recruited him to make that dive, just like you tried to recruit me. Now I want to know why. What's down there that you needed David to bring back for you?"

"We needed the Panthalassa charts." Allison Petrucci enters the bridge from the captain's quarters. "Michael kept them in his abyssal labs."

Jonas stares at the petite brunette. "Do I know you?"

"We met once, about five years ago, aboard Michael's yacht."

"Maren's yacht? Wait ... you were his assistant."

"And his lover."

"His lover?" Jonas smirks. "I can only imagine which part of him you loved."

She reaches out to slap him—

—Jonas catching her hand. He twists her wrist, forcing her arm behind her back. The guard raises his 9mm, aiming it at Jonas's chest.

"Whoa, let's everybody settle down." Brian Suits pulls Allison free from Jonas, motioning for the guard to lower his weapon. "We all want the same thing here, Dr. Taylor. Tell us what you need to rescue David, and we'll provide it."

Jonas looks from Brian to bin Rashidi, sizing up the situation. "I need seven miles of cable and a winch strong enough to haul Maren's lab out of the sea."

"How will you attach the cable?" Brian asks. "The Manta Ray's aren't equipped with robotic appendages."

"I brought my own ride with me."

Nick Cato glances down at his radio board as the call comes through from the trawler. "*D.L. I* to *Tonga*, come in please."

"This is the *Tonga*, go ahead."

"We're receiving a radio transmission from Delta team."

"Put it through!"

Jonas and the others gather around the radio receiver to listen.

"... eighty-seven point two miles east of your location. Repeat, this is Delta team. We are trapped in Maren's second lab, located 13.84 degrees North latitude, 140.33 degrees East longitude, eighty-seven point two miles east of your location. Repeat, this is Delta team—"

Jonas grabs the radio transmitter. "David, it's Dad! We read you! David, we're on the way!"

The trawler's radio operator interrupts, "*Tonga*, Delta team is unable to receive incoming messages. They can only transmit. We have a fix on their location and have recalled Spiderman. We should be ready to make way in less than an hour."

32

Mac stands at the very tip of the *McFarland's* bow, the morning sun's warmth beating down on his skin, compensating for the brisk Pacific wind.

To the eye of the observer, the hopper dredger's bow appears nothing out of the ordinary—a V-shaped structure designed to slice through waves—but the waterline is deceptive, concealing the ship's true keel—a rounded, bulbous affair that extends another thirty feet beyond the tip of the bow, providing additional stability to the craft, its crew, and the sleeping monster occupying a third of the *McFarland's* girth.

Mac stares at the ocean's surface, his mind's eye penetrating the deep blue surface. Just as the waterline conceals the ship's true keel, so, too, the sea obscures its volatile crusty bottom where a territorial battle has been raging since time immemorial.

ᐁ ᐁ ᐁ

SEVEN MILES BELOW the *McFarland's* keel, two oceanic crusts—the monstrous Pacific Plate and the smaller Philippine Plate—are colliding in an epic battle of tectonic forces, their meeting leaving a geological imprint on the entire planet.

Born along the mid-ocean ridge where molten rock rises from the mantle, cools, and solidifies, the Pacific Plate is far more massive than its tiny counterpart. As its western boundary strikes the Philippine Sea Plate's eastern face, the denser giant is driven beneath the lighter tectonic crust like a giant wedge, creating the Mariana Trench, the deepest gorge in the world. Sinking deeper into the mantle, the Pacific Plate releases hot fluids, causing the overlying mantle to melt. New molten magma rises in its place, erupting along the sea floor in the form of hydrothermal vents and underwater volcanoes.

Twenty-five to fifty million years ago, approximately the same time a new shark species, *Carcharodon megalodon,* evolved to become the ocean's most dominant predator, the Mariana Trench's convergent boundary birthed a volcanic island chain collectively known as the Mariana Islands. Composed of fifteen small land masses, the southern islands consist of level terraces of limestone, while the northern islands rise as towering active volcanoes.

More than fifty volcanoes dot the Mariana Arc, all part of the larger Ring of Fire, a 21,600-mile, horseshoe-shaped series of volcanic islands, arcs, and oceanic trenches that outline the Pacific Plate—home to ninety percent of the world's most destructive earthquakes.

∇ ∇ ∇

STARING OUT TO sea, Mac's eyes wander to the coastline of Guam, the southernmost island in the Mariana chain. Jonas is aboard the *Tonga*, the supertanker racing to the deeper waters southwest of the Western Mariana Ridge, Michael Maren's secret access point into the Panthalassa Sea. Mac's orders are to stand pat and wait until Jonas completes his rescue mission before releasing Angel to the Mariana Trench.

Turning to face the hopper, he gazes at the ten-foot-high upper lobe of the Megalodon's caudal fin, the powerful tail sweeping slowly from side to side as its owner sleeps. "The Panthalassa has enough monsters to contend with; the last thing Jonas needs to worry about is you."

For a long moment, Mac stares at the hopper's drain. He runs his calloused hand over the lever, contemplating ...

I could kill you right now ... put you out of all our misery.

San Francisco Yacht Club
San Francisco, California

Tan and fit, his arms covered in tattoos, his left eye permanently scarred above the brow, Joseph Michael Park does not fit the description of a typical Wall Street tycoon. And yet this is where the *summa cum laude* graduate of Northwestern University School of Law made his millions, taking his Internet company, ShockNet Video, public.

"Welcome aboard. Watch your step." Park greets the R.A.W. guests as they come aboard the *Cleveland Rocks*, his sixty-eight-foot sports yacht. "There's a buffet in the main salon. Help yourself." He applauds as Lana Wood and her four-year-old grandson make their way up the gang plank. "Plenty O-Toole! I am such a huge fan. *Diamonds Are Forever* was the very first Bond film I actually remember seeing in the movie theater. Bet I wasn't much older than this little guy."

Lana forces a smile for the documentary camera. "This is my grandson, Max. Max is a shark fanatic. He practically begged me to bring him along. Isn't that right?"

"Where's Belle and Lizzy?"

Park kneels down to the boy, trying his best not to look at the camera. "Belle and Lizzy are still stuck in their cage, Max, but if we're lucky, we'll get to see them swim free for the first time."

Lana waves and helps her grandson onto the yacht. Crossing the main deck, she leads him inside the salon, a plush, cherry-wood paneled living area packed with present and former members of the local chapter of the Hell's Angels.

Lana's expression drops. "Come on, Max. We're leaving."

"Lana, wait!" Sara Toms quickly intercepts. "I know you're upset—"

"I told you I didn't want to be associated with thugs."

"The Lost Boys aren't thugs; they're just bikers who helped bring national attention to our cause. Why don't you take Max up to the flybridge, where it's more private, and the two of you will have a birds-eye view of Belle and Lizzy when we set them free."

Lana glares at the activist. "You're on thin ice with me. If things get out of hand I'll demand to be taken ashore. If you don't comply, my next public appearance will be my resignation. Come on, Max."

Taking her grandson by the hand, she pushes her way through the inebriated crowd to the spiral staircase leading up to the flybridge.

The sport yacht's twin engines rumble to life, belching white clouds of exhaust and carbon monoxide fumes. Minutes later, the ship pushes away from the pier and into San Francisco Bay, on its way to Monterey.

Aboard the Tonga
Philippine Sea

Tipping the scales at three hundred sixty-three pounds, John LeBlanc, Jr. is, by far, the biggest member of the *Tonga's* crew, his size offering him a sumo stature among the Japanese deck hands. A scruffy beard now converges with what had been a clean-shaven, black goatee at the start of the voyage, around-the-clock shifts over the last three days leaving little time for sleep, let alone shaving.

Seated on a heap of wet cargo netting by the starboard mooring winch, the former Air Force brat and naval engineer fights to stay awake as his team splices lengths of steel cable together to create a single seven-mile-long cord. He forces himself to his feet as Brian Suits approaches. Fiesal bin Rashidi is with him, an armed bodyguard trailing close by.

Brian inspects the coupling. "How much longer, Mr. LeBlanc?"

"This is the last section. Once we add the hook we'll retract the line and we're ready to go."

The *Tonga* shudders beneath them, the supertanker's captain shutting down the engines before putting them into reverse, beginning the three-mile braking process that will ease the supertanker to the drop-off point.

"Sir, this lab we're expected to haul off the bottom ... how heavy is it?"

"Forty-seven tons."

"Then, with all due respect, we're pissing in the wind. She'll never handle that kind of load."

"The winch is not strong enough?"

"The winch is fine. Cable's the problem. These magna splices are strong, but the couplings weren't designed to hold anything over 65,000 pounds."

"Do the best you can, Mr. LeBlanc. That's all we can ask."

The engineer points aft to where Jonas Taylor is preparing his submersible for its dive. "What if he asks?"

Bin Rashidi's black eyes stare coldly across the deck. "Finish splicing the line, engineer. I'll handle Dr. Taylor."

▽   ▽   ▽

JONAS TAYLOR LIES on his back, inspecting the underside of the *Abyss Glider III*. The stiletto-shaped vessel, an untested prototype mounted atop its four-wheeled sled, is nine feet long from its pointed nose to its rear afterburner, with stubby wings located two-thirds back at what would be the dagger's hilt. Each wing holds a propulsion unit, the sphere-shaped cockpit, large enough for one pilot, situated between the wings. The acrylic escape pod's night glass is midnight-green, matching the rest of the sub's dark hull. The aft third of the sleek craft is a four-finned tail assembly that houses a tank of liquid hydrogen—an underwater afterburner designed for short bursts of speed.

Running the length of the sub, situated beneath its keel, is a telescopic robotic arm. Jonas is working on the gripper's claw, which is stubbornly refusing to open.

Brian Suits clears his voice. "Dr. Taylor, a word, please."

"I don't have time. The hydraulic claw's not functioning and I—"

"Make the time, Dr. Taylor," bin Rashidi says, "or you'll have no need for the claw, or your vessel."

Jonas wiggles his way out from beneath the *AG III*, staring the Arab down. "You have something to say, say it."

"Your son has managed to bring us to the very place we've spent three years and countless dollars in search of. Still, what good is an access point if none of my divers are willing to go down and lure up the monsters that I seek."

"That's not my problem."

"Actually, it just became your problem," says Brian Suits. "In exchange for providing you with the means to rescue your son, we expect something in return."

Fatigue and anxiety fuel an anger already seething in the pit of Jonas's gut. "You want a monster for your exhibit? Fine. After I rescue David—"

"After you rescue David, I'll have lost my leverage," bin Rashidi states. "You'll bring me back the creature I seek now, or Maren's lab will never see the light of day."

Jonas takes two steps toward bin Rashidi before the bodyguard steps between them. "All right, you bastard. I'll lure something up for your nets ... after I attach the cable to the lab."

"Not just anything. I want *Liopleurodon*!"

Panthalassa Sea

"... this is Delta team. We are trapped in Maren's second lab, located 13.84 degrees North latitude, 140.33 degrees East longitude. Repeat, this is Delta team—"

"David, enough! We've been at it six straight hours. If they haven't heard us by now, they never will."

David drops the radio transmitter, his voice hoarse. "What are you reading?"

"Maren's theories on how this isolated sea came into being. Say what you will but the guy was pretty damn smart. Did you know bin Rashidi funded his whole expedition twelve years ago?"

"No, and I don't care." He moves to the porthole. The perimeter of the lab is bathed in red light, revealing thousands of twelve- to fifteen-foot albino hagfish. The slimy, eel-like creatures are feeding off the remains of the crushed mososaur. "Look at the size of them. Is it just me, or does everything seem bigger down here?"

"Maren had a theory about that. He compares the conditions of the Panthalassa Sea to those on Earth when species like *Brachiosaurus* grew to be eighty feet long and eighty tons, and *Seismosaurus* over 120 feet and one hundred tons. With so many predators around, benign animals like these sauropods had to grow larger as a defense mechanism. These giants were able to adapt to their sudden increases in size by dwelling in swamps, the water reducing the weight on their frames. Living in the ancient seas, marine reptiles could grow even more enormous. Maren claims there's also evidence indicating the planet's gravitational forces were not as great during the Jurassic Period."

"Ever hear of Bergmann's Rule? It states that body size is larger in colder regions than in more temperate ones. Greater body mass conserves heat better. When it comes to survival, size matters most. The larger an animal's stomach, the more it can consume. Super giants store greater quantities of food as fat and muscle, which helps in times of famine." David wipes sweat from his brow. "I'm still amazed at the size of that liopleurodon. The monster had to be over 120 feet long. That's a lot bigger than any previous skeleton ever found on land."

"According to Maren's journal, the fossilized bones found along the Panthalassa's sea floor indicate *Liopleurodon* only achieved its massive size over the last twenty-six million years. Maren claims the increase coincides with the arrival of *Carcharodon megalodon*."

"We haven't seen any Megs, at least not—" David pauses, his heart suddenly pounding in his chest. "Listen!"

"What? I don't hear anything."

"That's just it. The life support system shut down." He slides down the ladder and hurries over to the two generators. "Fuel cells are working … we're getting power. What about the water level?"

Kaylie stares at the meter. "We're out. Red-lined."

They look at one another, the blood draining from their faces. David tears open the lid of the five-hundred-gallon tank and peers inside. "Empty. How much bottled water do we have left?"

She searches through the backpack. "Two sixteen ounce bottles."

"Pour it in." He pulls back the bathroom curtain and checks the commode. "Maybe a gallon in the toilet. We need to suction it out."

"David—"

"Kaylie, without water the system can't create oxygen. Even with what's left in the toilet, we're down to our last hour of air."

33

Two Japanese crewmen secure the canvass harness around the long nose and tail section of the *Abyss Glider III*. Jonas inspects the mechanical claw now gripping the titanium hook fastened at the end of a seven-mile-long spool of steel cable. Satisfied, he climbs inside the cockpit of the one-man submersible, strapping himself in.

Jason Montgomery hands him a canvass bag, filled with supplies. "I'll stay in the *Tonga* bridge by the radio. If you need something, just holler."

"Contact your uncle aboard the *McFarland*. Set up a relay so I can speak with him directly."

"Did you know the most popular name for boats is *Obsession*?"

"Try to stay focused." Jonas activates the cockpit, sealing the dark acrylic dome above his head.

John LeBlanc operates the winch, raising the sleek, midnight-green sub off the deck—

—and lowering it into the Pacific.

The pilot controls of the *AG III* mirror those of the Manta Ray, with the left and right floor pedals operating the wing propulsion units, the joysticks the sub's pitch and yaw. A third joystick operates the hydrogen burn, a hand control fitted with finger-hole sleeves operates the sub's robotic arm and claw.

The real difference between the two vessels lies in their hull shape and performance. The Manta Ray is a hydrodynamic winged craft designed to maneuver, while the *AG III* is essentially a one-man, underwater missile built for speed.

Jonas glances at the digital clock: 10:37 a.m. *Gotta watch the cable. Don't descend faster than the slack.* He speaks into the radio as divers release the sub from its harness. "Engineer, what's the fastest your winch can release cable?"

"Twenty feet per second."

"On my mark, set it on max. Three ... two ... one ..."

The massive spool of cable located in the starboard bow of the tanker rolls to life, each revolution releasing fifty feet of cable into the sea.

Jonas allows the heavy nosecone of his abyssal racer to sink then starts the twin propellers. The *AG III* plunges through the depths on a straight, ninety-degree vertical like a falling dart. The sea turns black within the first minute, forcing him to rely strictly on his gauges to determine his path through the void. He can feel the cable's tug on his robotic claw, the appendage tucked into its telescopic casing along his keel. Fearing he'll tear the cable loose, he slows his descent, allowing the line to slacken.

Two minutes ... two thousand feet ... all sense of direction lost. Abyssal snow races past his cockpit glass like a midnight blizzard.

Three thousand feet ... four thousand ...

"*AG III*, this is Spiderman. You need to slow your approach to the access hole. You'll tangle our nets."

"Negative, Spiderman. You can reset your nets after I pass through."

Jonas checks his trajectory on sonar, verifying he's still on course.

Five thousand feet ... six thousand ... *Damn cable's feeding out too slowly. The current's dragging the slack.* He slows his descent once more, the pull on the robotic appendage becoming too great.

He sees the lights below; then he sees the hole.

It's far larger than what he expected, a circular aperture, four hundred feet across. As Jonas moves closer he can see the raised geology around the hole's immense rim.

Maren didn't drill this! This is a crater, created long ago. Whatever made this impact must have been huge.

Activating the exterior lights mounted to his wings, he aims the nose of his vessel into the void, racing into hell to find his son.

Panthalassa Sea

David uses the empty plastic bottle to drain the last of the water from the toilet. Although the system is again producing oxygen, the water meter remains on red.

He tosses the bottle and lies down next to Kaylie on the cot. "That's the last of it."

"How long do we have? And don't lie."

"I closed the vents in the upper level and reset the system on its lowest output. At the most ... maybe two hours."

She slides her hand on top of his, tears mixing with the perspiration on her cheeks. "I am so sorry I pushed you into this. It's all my fault."

"It was my choice."

"I love you, David. Do you believe me?"

"Yes."

"There's something I have to tell you, something I should have confessed long ago." She sits up, brushing back a strand of brunette hair matted to her neck. "Bin Rashidi didn't just recruit me as a pilot; he specifically asked me to get close to you."

David closes his eyes, sealing away his tears. "Why?"

"He needed you to make the dive."

"So all that flirting on the ride over ... the morning in the pool?"

"Yes. But things changed once I got to know you. I told him I couldn't go through with it. I told him I either made the team on my own merits or I'd leave."

"And the night I spoke with my father? The night I pleaded with you to stay in Dubai?"

"That was my own doing. I wanted us to be together—"

"—but you got greedy. You didn't trust me."

"My family's not rich like yours. My parents are struggling. They needed the money. Bin Rashidi offered me a hundred grand to make the dive; so, of course, I jumped at the chance. I actually believed I could do it, too ... right up until my first descent. Once Debbie Umel and I entered the Panthalassa, we both knew we could never dive this deep. None of us could."

David sits up in bed, his back to her.

"You hate me, don't you. I don't blame you."

"I don't hate you. You were trying to help your family. I was trying to protect you."

She hugs him from behind, sobbing against his back. "I am so sorry. And I'm so scared."

He turns around and holds her. "It's okay."

"Aren't you scared?"

"Hell, yes. But I made the dive because I was more scared of losing you. I was afraid you'd end up making the dive with Brian."

"Brian wouldn't have made it through the current." She presses her tear-drenched face to his, kissing him on the lips. "You always make me feel safe. Make me feel safe again."

He hugs her tightly, feeling her tremble. "You know how we entered that chute to access the Panthalassa? In a little while we're going to access another chute, a chute with a bright, heavenly light. We're just going to lay down here next to each other and go to sleep, and then, hand in hand, we'll pass through the light into another place—a place where we can be together forever."

He pulls her down onto the bed, Kaylie lying on his chest, the two of them holding one another on their diminishing island of air at the bottom of the sea.

∇ ∇ ∇

THE ABYSS GLIDER drags the steel cable down through the access hole and into the Panthalassa Sea. The water, now registering a balmy fifty-six degrees Fahrenheit, teems with rising particles of hydrothermal flakes.

Swarms of hungry squid attack clear, gelatinous jellyfish, the creatures obliviously blinking their bioluminescent mating lures like fireflies in estrus. The jellyfish hover close to the Panthalassa's subterranean ceiling, crawling with albino mussels and shrimp, crabs and clams, and snake-like creatures with bulging eyes. The crustaceans move through a jungle of tube worms, which grow upside down from the geology in clusters. Mixed within the inverted patches of riftia are dark red palm worms and accordion-like Jericho worms, the communities all feeding upon bacteria and other micro-organisms. The bacteria, in turn, are feasting off chemosynthetic layers of carbon dioxide and hydrogen sulfide that has been adhering to the Panthalassa ceiling for the last 250 million years.

Ignoring the abyssal food chain, Jonas powers off his exterior lights and continues his frenetic descent.

Ten thousand feet. The cable feeds cleanly down the chute, the water warming noticeably.

Fifteen thousand feet. Still only halfway there.

"Jonas, can you hear me?" The familiar voice emerges in pieces against the static.

"Mac?"

"I'm ... pal. Where ... hell are you?"

"Approaching twenty thousand feet. Mac, can you hear me? Mac?" Jonas reaches for the radio—

—as the objects appear on sonar right alongside his sub! He turns on his exterior lights, the peripheral beams illuminating the creatures. There are three of them descending with him off his starboard wing, the largest in excess of twenty-five feet. Incredibly, they resemble his sub, their long, pointy mollusk shells shaped almost exactly like the *AG III*, only ending in the thick tentacles and crushing beak of an enormous cephalopod.

Cameroceras ... giant orthocones. Are they to be my abyssal escorts, or are they perversely attracted to the sub?

He hears the rushing tide a moment before he enters the Panthalassa Sea current, the Abyss Glider's cylindrical, dart-shaped girth plunging straight down through the raging river, Jonas adjusting his pitch so that the angle of his sub's wings offers the least resistance.

The giant orthocones refuse to enter the current, retreating back toward the ceiling to feed.

Below, the predators gather, attracted by the loud reverberations of his engines.

The pack of nothosaurs strike before he even emerges from the current, their dragon-like mouths suddenly appearing in his beams. Rows of interlocking, needle-sharp teeth strike at his wings, the creatures darting in and out of the lights like ravenous thirteen-foot seals.

Jonas shuts off the lights, bashing his way past the reptilian fish, nearly lancing one with the bow of his sub as he emerges from the swirling hydrothermal maelstrom into prehistoric hell.

The tropical sea swarms with a gauntlet of Mother Nature's worst nightmares. The plesiosaurs are the aggressors. Thirty to sixty feet long, their crocodilian bodies are propelled by four immense flippers, their jaws the stuff of drug-induced hallucinations.

A kronosaur soars past his starboard wing, Jonas barely able to lurch the sub away—

—as a giant mososaur bears down on him from above, chasing him into a swarm of forty-foot *Xiphactinus,* the giant, piranha-like fish, lightning quick, converging on his submersible as if it were an injured porpoise!

Desperate, Jonas grabs the joystick controlling his hydrogen engine. Pressing the top button, he ignites his tank, the combusting liquid scorching the mososaur snout, the *AG III* rocketing away—

—ripping the cable from his robotic claw's tenuous grip!

"Damn!"

Within seconds he is approaching the bottom. Shutting down the hydrogen burn, he levels out, his sonar searching for Maren's lab as he approaches the living reef that was once the *USS Indianapolis.*

For several moments he stares at the ghost ship, transfixed. *So that's how Maren discovered this hell hole.* He grabs the radio, praying his proximity to the lab's fiber optic cables will allow him to communicate with his son. "David, it's Dad! David, can you hear me?"

▼ ▼ ▼

EACH BREATH IS a panicked rasp, the lab now a steamy vacuum of space, the pony bottle strapped around his nose and mouth long expired of its compressed air.

In his delirium, David hears a voice. *Dad?*

His scorched lungs ache as he heaves himself over Kaylie, who is curled in a ball, hyperventilating. His eyes bulge, the room spinning loop-de-loops as he claws his way up the ladder and locates the discarded radio transmitter.

"Hhhadd!"

"David? Thank God—"

"Air ... no air!"

▼ ▼ ▼

JONAS'S MIND RACES as he tries to recall the schematics of Maren's lab. *Radio's on, so he's got power. The life support system converts water to oxygen ... he's probably out of water!* "David, listen to me! The life support system needs water—"

"Gone!"

Gone? "David, use anything ... the toilet water, the water heater overflow! Piss in the damn tank if you have to!"

▼ ▼ ▼

WATER HEATER OVERFLOW? Barely conscious, David stumbles down the ladder then crawls to the water heater. He can barely control his limbs as he unhinges the side panel—

—revealing a two-gallon, calcium-encrusted drip pan overflowing with water!

Careful! Don't spill it! He eases the container out of the heating unit, wheezing as he staggers toward the open water tank. Gently, he pours the life-giving fluid into the cache.

Seconds pass. Nothing happens.

No longer able to feel his feet, he drops to his knees and crawls to Kaylie. Grabbing her wrist, he pulls her convulsing body on top of his, then drags them both to the closest air duct—

—as the life support system kicks in, pumping out a wave of cool, stale air.

Pressing their faces to the grating, they gasp each breath like feeding baby birds.

"David? David, answer me when you can. Kiddo, don't give up!"

A few more lungfuls and his head clears. He climbs halfway up the ladder and reaches for the radio. "The water heater ... it worked. But there's ... not enough ... to last."

"Look out your porthole."

David hauls his trembling form onto the upper level and gazes out the dense, cylindrical window.

The *AG III*'s cockpit hovers three feet away.

The sight of his father causes David to weep. "Dad, I'm sorry—"

"I love you, kid. Now listen to me. Shut down all the vents except one. Find a way to encapsulate a smaller breathing space, so that you're not ventilating the entire lab. A little air can go a long way. I lost the tow cable, but I'll be back real soon. You keep it together. Okay?"

"Okay."

Fighting to maintain his composure, Jonas banks the sub away from the lab and the remains of an unrecognizable carcass caught beneath the titanium sphere. Pulling back on the joysticks, he aims the Abyss Glider's long nose on a ninety-degree vertical plane then reignites the hydrogen tank, launching himself toward the volcanic rock ceiling like a Tomahawk cruise missile.

The *AG III* shudders as it climbs one hundred feet per second.

Dark shadows appear ahead, the stunned creatures snapping wildly as they whip past his cockpit. He veers past the swarm and up through the swirling hydrothermal plume, his mind focusing only on the problem at hand.

He debates whether to attempt to locate and retrieve the lost cable.

Realizes it's an impossible task.

Accepts the reality that he must return to the surface to begin anew.

Keep the cable slack, that'll allow you to increase your rate of descent. But how the hell do I keep these monsters off of me long enough to attach the cable? Can't kill them, can't out-maneuver them in the Glider, and the lights only attract them. What can I use to scare these creatures away?

"Oh, hell." He grabs the radio. "Mac, can you read me? Mac!"

"... read you."

"Bring the *McFarland* to me as fast as you can. Monty will give you the coordinates. Then have Nichols wake up sleeping beauty.

"I need our girl to escort me through hell."

34

Virgil Carmen remains at his computer, waiting for the last person to leave the lab.

By 10:15, he is alone.

Heart racing, he shuts off the lights and heads down the deserted basement corridor to the control room. Using his access card he keys in. Looking around, he locates the instrument panel labeled MEG PEN CORRIDOR.

Fishing in his pocket, he locates Dr. Stelzer's keys, finds the panel key, and pushes it into the keyhole, turning the switch clockwise.

The instrument panel's small monitor blooms to life, the touch-screen offering a user menu. He presses OPEN CORRIDOR, enters Stelzer's access code, and waits.

Several moments pass.

ACCESS ACCEPTED. A time code appears, indicating the Meg Pen doors are opening.

A STARRY NIGHT greets Virgil as he steps out onto the deserted Meg Pen deck. Along the western horizon he can see the lights and silhouette of the yacht, anchored just outside the canal entrance.

Virgil takes out his cell phone and speed dials a number. "So? How'd it go? Did you get the footage?"

Sara Toms's voice snaps him back to reality. "The cameras are all in place. Where the hell are our guests of honor?"

"What? They didn't leave? Wait, stand by."

He crosses the arena to the Meg Pen, the water dark. Moving to a fuse box, he flips on a bank of underwater lights, illuminating the tank.

Virgil leans out over the rail, spotting Lizzy and Belle, the two juvenile Megs circling slowly, moving in their usual formation. *Damn! Didn't the channel open?*

He crosses the bridge and hurries to Angel's lagoon. Climbing over the northern sea wall, he looks down.

The lights from the Meg Pen appear below, the channel clearly open.

"Sara, the pen's open. They just haven't left yet."

"Then coax them out! We don't have all night!"

"Okay, okay. Just be ready." He hangs up the cell phone, his mind racing. *Why the hell aren't they leaving? Angel ... they can still smell her presence in the lagoon. How do I lure them out?*

Bobby Baitman!

Virgil sprints across the deserted deck to the equipment room to locate the robotic mannequin—

—never noticing Danielle Taylor, seated alone in the eastern bleachers, listening to music on her iPod.

Aboard the Tonga
Philippine Sea

Word of Angel's impending arrival and release has sent ripples of chaos running through the ships' crews. Working in eight thousand feet of water, Spiderman and his two-man team aboard the Shinkai 6500 submersible quickly decided that being underwater with an adult Megalodon on the prowl was not a good idea. Abandoning the array of nets, the twenty-five-ton vessel executed an emergency ascent, the crew refusing to return to their posts despite Fiesal bin Rashidi's financial incentives.

Roger Gober has his own resistance to being so close to the monster he had seen twice in captivity back in Monterey. The captain of the *Dubai Land I* has lashed the trawler to the side of the supertanker with all non-essential personnel ordered aboard the *Tonga*. Only Gober and Ibrahim Al Hashemi remain behind, while Jonas Taylor prepares his Abyss Glider prototype for its second launch in as many hours.

Jason Montgomery stands by the starboard rail of the *Tonga,* watching the sea. The hopper dredger, *McFarland,* is clearly visible on the eastern horizon, the big ship approaching fast. *Using a monster to scare off other monsters ... and I'm the one who's supposed to be bi-polar.*

Aboard the McFarland
Philippine Sea

Brent Nichols paces the *McFarland's* bridge, the marine biologist quickly losing patience. "The neuro-implant's not designed for this, Mackriedes. The only way Angel will follow Jonas into that hell hole is if she's convinced the

Glider is food."

"Then do it. Scramble her senses."

"No! This was intended to be my experiment—tag and release research designed to monitor Angel's behavior, not a dog and pony show where the variables can't be controlled. I'm sorry, but I'm a scientist, not a cowboy. I won't do it."

"You'll do it, or I'll toss your fat scientist ass into that hopper!"

"You just don't get it, do you? Once I trick the Meg's brain into perceiving the sub as bait, I can't undo it. As soon as Angel follows Taylor into that subterranean sea we'll lose the signal, and I can't call Angel off. For Taylor, it's suicide."

"*You* don't get it. He doesn't care. His kid's dying down there. Now start typing keys on that laptop and wake Angel up!"

Aboard the Tonga
Philippine Sea

John LeBlanc stands by the starboard winch as mile after mile of dripping steel cable winds itself around a spool the size of small school bus. One of his men watching from the rail signals as the end of the line and its titanium hook rise out of the sea. The engineer stops the winch, allowing Jonas Taylor enough slack to haul the free end of the tow cable aboard the trawler.

▼ ▼ ▼

JONAS STANDS ON the upper deck of the trawler, using a grappling pole to retrieve the end of the rescue cable. He drags the line aft, where the Abyss Glider sits poised before the trawler's slanted stern. Crawling under the sub's narrow bow, he re-secures the titanium hook to the claw of the Glider's robotic appendage then tests the grip several times. Satisfied, he signals to the crewman standing by the supertanker's bow rail. Climbing inside the *AG III*'s cockpit, he seals the hatch, his heart pounding.

The crewman signals to John LeBlanc, who restarts the winch, allowing the spool to unravel its length of cable, feeding the slack into the sea.

The weight of the falling cable pulls the Glider bow-first down the stern ramp.

Jonas powers up the sub, careful to avoid the plunging steel cable. He descends quickly to two hundred feet then heads east to intercept the hopper dredger. The big ship has moved to within a half-mile of the *Tonga*, its twin propellers shut down, allowing the boat to drift.

307

The Abyss Glider circles beneath the hopper dredger's ominous set of steel doors. Jonas activates his radio. "Mac, I'm in position. Are you ready?"

∀ ∀ ∀

JAMES MACKREIDES STANDS on the *McFarland's* bow deck, seeking cover from a torrent of waves and high arcing splashes blasting out of the ship's flooded hold. "Your girl just woke up, and she's mighty pissed. Nichols wants you to circle beneath the keel until Angel locks on to you. He'll take it from there."

"Thanks. And Mac ... thanks for being there for me all these years. I love you like a brother. Just wanted you to know that."

"What the hell does that mean?"

Jonas can hear the deep booming reverberations in the water. "You'd better release Angel before she tears apart the hopper."

"Jonas—"

"Let her go, Mac. Please."

Cursing aloud, Mac swaps his radio transmitter for the walkie-talkie. "Open the hopper doors. Let her go."

With a groan of metal, the two steel doors located along the ship's keel slowly swing open, venting the hopper to the sea.

∀ ∀ ∀

FOR THE LAST eighty-six hours, Angel has been kept in sleep mode, an autonomous state that has allowed the Meg to swim and breathe while her senses have remained in hibernation. Having been forcibly awakened, the seventy-four-foot, fifty-one-ton predator becomes disoriented and enraged, her steel confines emitting electrical impulses that scramble her senses. Unable to acquire her bearings, she flips over and over, slapping at the walls of her cage with her caudal fin, ramming the hopper with her head—even after the doors have been opened.

She finally manages to swim free, more by accident than intent. Dazed, she moves away from the boat's keel, circling in tight figure-eights as she attempts to reorient herself. Functioning like a built-in GPS system, the Meg's ampullae of Lorenzini registers the Earth's geomagnetic field, lifting the veil of fog from her brain—

—engaging the rest of her sensory array.

It has been nearly two weeks since the Megalodon last fed. Suddenly obsessed with hunger, Angel's senses lock in on the closest prey in her new territory. Her olfactory center inhales what her brain translates to be the pungent taste of blood. Her lateral line registers the animal's wounded vibrations. Her eyes adjust to the light as they catch movement somewhere below ...

🦷 🦷 🦷

His head laid back on the pilot seat, Jonas stares up through the cockpit glass, watching and waiting while the Meg's senses scan her new environment. *Come on down, Angel. I'm right here ... find me!*

As if she can hear him, the predator suddenly breaks off her pattern and descends, launching her attack.

Jonas dives the *AG III*, accelerating to twenty-five knots as he adjusts his course to the west, angling his steep descent toward the access hole. His heart is racing, but it is not from a primordial fear of being eaten.

I've been gone too long ... almost an hour. At this speed, it'll take me another twenty minutes at best to get back to David, and that's assuming everything goes perfect. He turns around to check on Angel, the monster closing the gap to just under two hundred feet. *That a girl, stay with me!*

The blue water turns black, the depths cloaking the sunlight, forcing Jonas to rely on his instruments. Down he soars, passing the first mile, the pale beast in his wake keeping pace, her senses locked onto him now, refusing to allow him to escape.

Another two minutes and the Philippine Sea floor blooms on sonar, the crater-like hole revealing itself in his night glass.

Jonas circles the aperture once, allowing Angel to move to within a hundred feet of his vessel before he jams both pedals to the floor, plunging the Abyss Glider down the crater's throat.

Come on, Alice ... follow me down the rabbit's hole, and I'll treat you to some crumpets.

🦷 🦷 🦷

Angel slows, suddenly wary. Her back arches as she circles the crater's perimeter, her senses awash in the stream of minerals flowing out of the aperture. The warmth entices, the scent of prey teases her appetite, yet still she will not enter the void—put off by a distant memory.

▽ ▽ ▽

JONAS DESCENDS THROUGH the tunnel of volcanic rock, his exterior lights illuminating outcrops of basalt carpeted with colorful sponges. It is not until he emerges from the chute into the Panthalassa Sea that he realizes Angel is no longer behind him. For several moments he hovers by the subterranean ceiling, watching his sonar ... waiting.

"Aw, hell."

Maneuvering the two joysticks, he guides the sub slowly back up the chute. He slows two hundred feet below the exit point, dousing his lights. Through the night glass he can see the Meg circling the crater, waiting in ambush.

She won't enter the hole ... she's waiting for me to emerge. How do I entice her down?

He flashes his exterior lights on and off repeatedly, but gets no response.

An albino sea scorpion the size of a small child propels itself from its rocky perch, landing on his cockpit, nearly giving him a heart attack. Reflexively, he jams his right hand against the control panel, striking the switch that changes the *AG III*'s sonar from passive to active.

PING! PING ... PING ... PING ... PING...

The reverberations echo up through the funnel of rock, causing the Megalodon's lateral line to buzz like a tuning fork. Shaking her mammoth head to and fro, Angel enters the hole, charging like a mad bull.

Caught off-guard, Jonas executes a hasty 180-degree turn. The point of his lance-shaped bow scrapes the rocky cliff face—

—wedging him in!

He steels a quick glance above his head. Angel's jaws are already widening, the Meg nearly on top of him!

Jonas jams his left foot down on the pedal and holds it there, sending his sub spinning clockwise until the torque wrenches him free. He dives the sub—

—as Angel's jaws slam shut inches from his port-side wing! Her right jowl presses against his cockpit, her gray-blue pupil rolled back, revealing a bloodshot sclera.

The Glider strikes the far wall. Pinned in by the Meg's enormous head, Jonas can only accelerate down the chute, Angel's mouth opening and closing as she blindly searches for him. Jonas adjusts his speed on the fly, fighting to keep his vessel behind the crook of that wicked smile, rolling and maneuvering the sub's angle of descent to keep his wings free of her jaws as the shark drives him laterally, inching him toward the far wall—

—and then they're free!

Monster and machine shoot out of the hole into the Panthalassa Sea, the open water allowing Jonas to veer ahead and out of harm's way. He distances himself from the Meg—

—leading his abusive escort into the depths to rescue his son.

35

Virgil Carmen drags the lifelike anthropomorphic doll, known as Bobby Baitman, across the arena to the western bleachers and the ocean-access canal. Running alongside the canal's southern wall is a twenty-two-foot-high chain link fence. He keys open the gate, gaining access to a rusted catwalk that dates back to Masao Tanaka's original whale lagoon design.

The catwalk runs the length of the southern canal wall, situated six feet above the top of the concrete barrier. The tide is high, submerging the catwalk about a hundred yards past the short stretch of private beach. Two hundred yards beyond that point is the yacht.

The opening chords of a Metallica's *To Live Is To Die* reverberate from his pants pocket. He pulls out his cell phone. "I'm on the catwalk, Sara. Start rolling your cameras."

Virgil drags Bobby Baitman to its feet by the doll's life vest then feels beneath its pants along its left pelvis, activating the power switch. The doll's chest pulsates rapidly, simulating a human heart beat.

"Okay, Bobby, this is for the down payment on a house." Leaning out over the catwalk, he releases the doll, which belly flops into the canal, floating face-down.

"What are you doing?"

Virgil spins around, his pulse racing as the woman's flashlight blinds him. "Dani? That you? Can you lower the light so I can see?"

"Answer my question."

"What am I doing? What does it look like I'm doing? I'm working."

Dani shines her light on Bobby then sees the yacht, poised at the end of the canal. "You bastard. You're the one who's been feeding R.A.W. our footage."

"Now, hold on. Just hold on, Dani. You're jumping to conclusions."

"Tell it to the judge." She reaches for her walkie-talkie. "Security, western bleachers—"

Virgil lunges for her, grabbing the radio. Dani fights him off, kneeing him in the groin—

—as the rusty, twenty-eight-year-old catwalk heaves upward beneath their feet, the steel grating ripped free from its support beam as Bela strikes it from below by!

312

Dani and Virgil flail in mid-air, tumbling sideways down the back of the juvenile Megalodon before plunging six feet into the dark, frigid waters of the canal.

Panthalassa Sea

Fourteen ... fifteen ... sixteen thousand feet ...

Beads of perspiration pour down Jonas's face, dripping onto the control console beneath him like rain.

Eighteen thousand feet.

The active sonar continues pinging the sea, providing him with precise readings on Angel's position. With every passing minute his Megalodon escort continues to lose interest, forcing Jonas to slow, and on one occasion to circle back and bait her again.

A loud *hissing* sound builds in his headphones as he approaches the deep sea current. This is the moment of truth, the moment he has dreaded. He slows the sub's descent, allowing Angel to close the gap between them once more, knowing it's the only way to entice the Meg to follow him through the hydrothermal plume.

The bow of the *AG III* pierces the current. Jonas zigs and zags against the heavy easterly flow, hoping the floundering movements will keep Angel interested.

At 21,000 feet he loses her acoustic signature.

The first nothosaur appears five hundred feet later, swooping past his portside beam before the bright light turns the ancient predator away. Two more of the creatures cross his path moments later, one of the thirteen-foot sea dragons body slamming him sideways. The current catches the starboard wing like a foil, tossing the Abyss Glider into its stream. Jonas fights to regain control, riding the flow a quarter mile to the east before he can angle his descent and emerge from the raging torrent.

The blips appear on his sonar monitor within seconds, the hunters drawn to his sub's high pitched acoustics. Jonas debates whether to shut down the pings, but fears being blind more than he fears being bait.

A solitary blip separates itself from the dizzying swirl of bogeys on his screen, rising from the depths to meet him. The female hainosaur is well over fifty feet long, her snake-like movements propelling her thickly muscled body gracefully through the sea. The giant mososaur is not alone, her two hunting partners, also females, are circling below, waiting in ambush.

One hundred feet and still he cannot shake her. *Hit the hydrogen burn, it's your only chance.* Jonas feels for the joystick, but refuses to hit the afterburner, knowing the sudden jolt of speed will most likely tear loose the rescue cable from his robotic claw, dooming his son.

Seventy feet ... sixty!

He veers to the west, altering the angle of his descent, praying he can shoot past the first creature and make his way through the rest of the gauntlet to reach David.

The giant mososaur locks in on its prey—thirty-six tons of horror charging up from the depths. The massive triangular mouth suddenly appears in the sub's twin beams, the enraged monster intent on swallowing the Abyss Glider whole!

In a sudden déjà vu, Jonas knows he is dead, that he has failed his son, that his life has been rendered meaningless. He closes his eyes, never seeing the white blur streak in from the west.

Angel's hyperextended jaws catch the stunned hainosaur mid-chest. The punishing blow drives the giant mososaur's rib cage through its internal organs even as the Megalodon sinks its teeth deeper.

Jonas opens his eyes, once more amazed to find himself alive.

Angel swims around him in a slow, sweeping figure-eight pattern, her back arched, her pelvic fins rigid and turned down. The mososaur is held sideways in her open jaws, still twitching in death. The Meg shakes her prize like a dog tearing up a ragged towel, stifling the convulsions.

The remaining blips on his sonar screen have scattered along the periphery, giving him a clear path to the sea floor. Re-plotting his course, Jonas accelerates into the depths to rescue his son.

Tanaka Oceanographic Institute
Monterey, California

Virgil Carmen surfaces in a state of fear, his frenzied mind unable to rein in his greatest nightmare. *Where's Bela? Where's Lizzy? Get the hell out of the water! Find the canal wall! Climb to safety!*

He never sees the soft white glow rising majestically beneath him, Lizzy's out-stretched jaws plucking him from the surface, dragging him under.

Virgil's shouts become a groan of air bubbles as he thrashes back and forth, the flesh along his right ankle—caught between two serrated teeth being stripped down to the bone. The biologist's last rational thought: *It's okay, it's okay! Lose the foot and swim to safety!*

He never sees Lizzy's darker sibling sweep in from behind, mercifully engulfing him in one savage bite.

Danielle Taylor, desperate to stay afloat, has grasped onto Bobby Baitman. Despite the danger, her mind is calm. Feeling her way beneath the sex doll's clothing, she deactivates the battery pack, then hoists herself atop the dummy's broad back, sitting on top of it like a surfboard. Her rationale is simple: *Remove all vibrations and electrical impulses from the water and the sisters can't find me.*

Dani remains perfectly still, barely breathing. Incoming swells push her toward the collapsed section of catwalk, but she makes no effort to paddle.

The white dorsal fin slices slowly past her, so close she could reach out and touch it. For a heart-stopping moment, the powerful current created by the two sisters' moving girths tugs on Bobby Baitman, spinning the dummy sideways into a swell. Nearly tossed into the sea, she barely manages to maintain her balance.

She waits until the dorsal fin moves off. Then, very carefully, she stands atop the floating doll and grabs onto a section of bent steel frame above her head. She hoists herself out of the water and makes her way along a narrow steel beam that only moments ago had held the catwalk.

Exhilarated, she climbs to safety on an intact section of walkway.

Dani turns, catching sight of Lizzy's albino dorsal fin as it heads for open water. Somewhere below is Belle, moving in formation, riding in her wake.

The sisters leave the canal, heading straight for the yacht ... and open water.

Panthalassa Sea

They are huddled on the floor together next to a solitary air vent, their bodies enveloped beneath a plastic tarp, the radio receiver close by.

"Kaylie, are you sure you don't have to pee?"

"You asked me that ten minutes ago. I promise, I'll urinate in the water tank the moment I feel the urge." She squeezes his hand. "Don't worry. He'll be here soon. He made it down safely the first time; he'll make it down again."

He kisses her hand then lays his head back, trying to slow his breathing. When he last checked, there was less than a gallon of water remaining in the tank, equating to no more than thirty minutes of air. Even at an accelerated rate of ascent, he can't imagine the lab being towed to the surface in under an hour.

"Kaylie, what day is it?"

"I don't know. Thursday?"

"I meant the date."

"August fifth, I think. Why?"

He smiles sadly. "It's my birthday."

She leans over him, kissing him softly on the lips. "Happy birthday. So, David Taylor, now that you're officially of age, what can I do to make your day a little better?"

"Marry me."

She chokes on a nervous laugh, tears welling in her eyes. "That's kind of sudden, don't you think?"

"I'm serious. I want to be with you for the rest of my life."

"Baby, be careful what you wish for."

"We're getting out of this alive, Kaylie. I promise. And after all we've been through, I don't think a weekend visit at the University of Florida is going to suffice. Somehow, I'm guessing you won't be diving the Panthalassa anytime soon."

"True enough. But marriage ... that's a big step. We're both kind of young."

"So we'll make it a long engagement. At least think about it."

"Shh. We're wasting air." She lays her head on his chest, hugging him tightly.

"David? Son, can you hear me?"

"Dad!" David rolls out from beneath Kaylie and grabs the radio. "Dad, where are you?"

▽   ▽   ▽

"OUTSIDE THE LAB." Slipping his hand inside a glove-like control device, Jonas extends the telescopic appendage from beneath the Abyss Glider's bow, praying the collision with the chute's wall has not damaged the mechanical claw.

The claw appears, still clenching the titanium hook and steel cable. Locating an eye-bolt along the benthic lab's outer casing, Jonas threads the hook into place, the eye bolt barely large enough to accommodate the thick clasp.

"The line's connected! Stand by while I signal the *Tonga*." Activating the claw, Jonas releases the hook and clamps the grappling device onto the steel cable. Twisting in his seat, he reaches behind him to a series of car batteries powering the mechanical appendage. Slipping on a pair of heavy rubber insulated gloves, he connects a black wire running from the claw's hydraulic system to one of the battery's negative terminal, then strikes the red wire to the positive terminal over and over—

—sending an electrical signal through the claw and up the steel cable to the *Tonga's* engineer.

Long, excruciating minutes pass. And then, slowly, the slack tightens on the rescue cable, the taut line straining to lift the forty-seven-ton lab away from the sea floor.

Come on ... come on! Jonas's eyes move from the cable to the bottom of the lab, which refuses to budge. *Christ, it's too heavy, the line's going to snap!*

Retracting his claw and appendage, he circles the *AG III* behind the lab. His lights reveal the flesh-stripped carcass of the giant mososaur, along with the crushed remains of the titanium docking station.

The docking station ... it's still attached. Looks like its legs are welded to the sea floor by a dozen years of mineral growth.

Maneuvering the Abyss Glider so that the outer front edge of the cockpit is pressing beneath the lab's spherical hull, he attempts to provide thrust from behind the massive object, hoping to help free it from the bottom.

Gently, Jonas presses down on both propeller pedals, gradually increasing the torque. He hears the screech of titanium against his windshield, imagining the water pressure squeezing against his escape pod's thick acrylic surface. Still, he continues on, the pressure building. Clouds of sand and mososaur remains billow out from behind his sub as he revs both propellers to their maximum RPMs.

The lab refuses to budge.

Reaching for the hydrogen tank's controls, he ignites the fuel in a powerful blast. Titanium bolts along the crushed docking station screech in protest, twisting and snapping, the *AG III*'s exhaust scorching the ancient sea floor.

With a final jolt, the lab wrenches free from the docking station and begins to rise!

36

Master dive instructor and underwater videographer Scott Jenkins has been collecting Megalodon teeth for the last thirty-five years, ever since he opened Poseidon Adventures, his four-thousand-square-foot PADI 5-star diving training center in Wilmington, Delaware. Each year, the former officer in the U.S. Army Signal Corp leads deep sea diving expeditions along the continental shelf—an area that served as the United States coastline during the last ice age. In this secret diving spot, Jenkins and his clients haul up thousands of fossilized Megalodon teeth, many over six and a half inches from root to tip. While most fossil-tooth collectors prefer to search the river beds in South Carolina and Georgia for Meg teeth, it is Jenkins's contention that the largest teeth lie in the deeper waters because that is where the mature Megalodons, like Angel, were more likely to hunt.

Of course, everything had changed twenty-eight years ago when Angel's mother had surfaced from the Mariana Trench.

Two days ago, the dive instructor had been contacted by Joseph Michael Park. The shock video guru was interested in setting up an underwater video sequence at night and needed an experienced man he could trust. Jenkins passed … until he was told the location would be outside of Angel's Lagoon.

Scott Jenkins owns nearly eight thousand Megalodon teeth, but none of them are of the white, unfossilized variety. Logic tells him that Angel must have shed dozens of teeth over the last five years, teeth that can be easily dug up from the sea floor within the canal. With the big female long gone and the siblings on the way out, Jenkins will have a few hours to explore the bottom to locate teeth, each pearly white fetching $250,000 to upwards of a million dollars from private collectors.

∇ ∇ ∇

With the assistance of his daughters, Shannon and Shauna, it had taken Jenkins less than an hour to set up underwater cameras along the periphery of the canal. The sight of the devastated steel doors had unnerved him, giving him second thoughts about making the dive.

318

One quick dive at dawn. The first tooth I keep for myself, the rest we sell.

He changes his mind yet again as the two creatures appear on his undersea monitor.

Up on deck, a buzz takes the yacht as Lizzy's albino fin is sighted.

Sara Toms calls out from the pilot house, "Here they come!" The R.A.W. leader forces herself not to look at Shauna Jenkins's camera as she delivers the news.

Off camera, one deck below, two members of the Lost Boys biker gang carry the carcass of a 220-pound Pacific white-sided dolphin out to the transom, the dead mammal wrapped in a bed sheet. Their leader, a shaved-headed roughneck named Blair Bates, ties one end of a long nylon rope to a ten-inch hook. Reaching under the sheet, Bates shoves the barbed end of the hook into the dolphin's mouth and out its blow-hole, piercing the thick skin.

Lana Wood stands by the starboard rail of the yacht's open flybridge, her grandson, Max by her side. She looks away in disgust as the dolphin is tossed overboard, attached to a three-foot orange buoy.

"Nana, look! Here they come!" Climbing the flybridge rail, Max points to the canal where a six-foot, white dorsal fin cuts the dark waters, circling the yacht to resounding applause.

"Nana, it's Lizzy! It's Lizzy! Where's Belle?"

"I don't know, but I don't want you climbing the rail like that."

Two decks below in the V.I.P. stateroom, Scott Jenkins continues monitoring the images displayed on his six viewing screens. Three of his underwater cameras transmit night vision images taken from the canal doors, two from the yacht's keel, the last from a handheld unit attached to a reach pole, held over the side by his daughter, Shannon.

Annoyed that he cannot locate the dark-backed Meg, Jenkins yells over his headset to his daughter carrying the reach pole and camera, "Shannon, she's still circling, and all I have is a forbidden shot of Flipper twisting on a hook. Where's my port-side view?"

"The walkway's too narrow, and there must be twenty bikers on the bow. I can't—"

"Can't? Sorry, never heard of the word." He switches channels. "Sara, we can't give you documentary footage if your bikers are in our way. Tell the Lost Boys to get lost before we lose our subjects."

Jenkins focuses in on Lizzy, the albino Meg circling the bait, remaining cautious. "Peek-a-boo, I see you. Now where's your nasty sister?"

The dive master scans his monitors then he sees her, the dark-backed creature's stark-white triangular head filling the screen—

—on his daughter's remote!

"Shannon, get back! Bela's charging the yacht!"

Panthalassa Sea

Twenty-four thousand feet.

Particles of silt and bits of mososaur continue to flake away from the bottom of the titanium lab like a comet's tail. Steel cable creaks, the sound violating primordial silence as the line strains to support the object's forty-seven-ton mass.

Escorting the lab on its ascension through the seemingly endless pitch is the Abyss Glider. The submersible's pilot is cramped within the confines of his cockpit, sweating every square foot of pressure and every tick of the digital clock, knowing that precious drops of water are emptying from his son's life support system, dispersing with it the last molecules of air.

Twenty-three thousand feet.

For the umpteenth time Jonas recalculates the lab's rate of ascent. *Eighty-five hundred feet divided by sixteen minutes ... that's four hundred seventy-two feet per minute. Figure four hundred seventy feet, with another 23,000 feet to go ... that's another forty-eight minutes to the surface ... assuming everything goes without a hitch.*

He hesitates then grabs the radio. "David, how much air do you have left?"

"Stand by."

Jonas can hear David checking the water tank's capacity meter. He hears the strain in his son's voice as he reports, "Eighteen minutes."

Beads of sweat burst from every pore of Jonas's body. *Thirty minutes short!* He swallows hard, forcing himself to sound calm, refusing to peek inside his mind's eye and the image of Steven Moretti's dead body being pulled from a similar underwater sphere.

"David, you're rising fast, but it's still going to be tight. Is there any more water?"

"None. And both our bladders are empty. How much farther do we have to go? ... Dad? ... Dad, are you there?"

Jonas shuts off his radio. For days he has been running on adrenaline and fear—fear for his son's life. Despite making repeated trips into the crushing depths of the Panthalassa Sea, despite barely having survived attacks from Angel and an assortment of creatures that would give Mother Nature nightmares, he has never given a thought to his own well-being—

—until now.

The monster's presence had resonated on sonar seconds before it appeared from out of the darkness. Jonas stares at the beast as it effortlessly ascends with his sub, gawking at its incredible size, trembling at his own sudden insignificance. The creature's head is larger than a school bus, its crocodilian jaw line overflowing with crisscrossing, needle-like teeth, some as long as his own forearm. The left eye, yellow and luminous in the night glass, is clearly sizing him up, the creature's cold, reptilian mind debating whether to taste him, kill him, or if the energy expended is even worth the effort.

An upheaval of muscles jump to life beneath the liopleurodon's massive shoulder girdle as its forelimbs execute a single, graceful forward thrust, moving a river of water as it circumnavigates, almost lazily, around the Abyss Glider to take a closer look at the lab. An ancient ocean predator that hunted with its nose, the gargantuan pliosaur now uses its two nostrils to taste the surrounding sea—

—locking in on the scraps of mososaur meat still clinging to the bottom of the titanium sphere!

The strange creature is not only edible, but wounded. The big female opens her mouth, the action that causes the edges of her upper fangs to slide against the lowers—sharpening her own teeth as the 200,000-pound liopleurodon reaches for its prey.

"No!"

Terrified the leviathan's interaction with the lab will snap the cable and send his son careening to his grave, Jonas powers on his lights and charges the beast head-on!

Momentarily blinded, the monster twists its head sideways, veering away from the lab. A rear flipper, as large as a house, blooms in Jonas's view, its tidal wave of current flipping him bow over stern—

—directly into the path of the creature's tail, which whips sideways, snapping off his port-side wing assembly and propeller! The force of the blow nearly knocks Jonas unconscious. Suspended upside-down in his harness, his bearings shot, he gropes for the hydrogen burn, igniting the fuel—

—the pink flame scorching the liopleurodon's snout as its teeth clench down upon the *AG III*'s starboard wing, shearing the remaining engine assembly like husk from an ear of corn.

Having lost both its propellers, the crippled Abyss Glider becomes a twisting, rudderless rocket, its hydrogen burn dying rapidly as it soars past the lab, out of control. His controls rendered useless, his life again teetering on the brink, Jonas reaches for the sub's robotic appendage controls with his left hand, unbuckling his harness with the right. Estimating the trajectory of the titanium sphere rising beneath him, he slams his body back and forth against his seat while pumping hydrogen blasts in a desperate attempt to guide the rocketing hunk of acrylic in the direction of the steel cable before he loses what little power remains.

After several attempts, the *AG III's* bow strikes the rescue line. Jonas extends the sub's hydraulic claw and grasps hold of the steel cable as the rising titanium sphere plows upward into his aft burner assembly, giving the crippled sub and its distraught pilot a ride to the surface.

The liopleurodon rises with them, the enraged predator all business now as it snaps its charred jaws at its fleeing prey. It lunges for the Glider and misses then attempts to bite hold of the lab, the titanium hull splintering two of its front teeth on contact.

Changing tactics, the predator soars past its prey and disappears into the darkness—

—only to reappear moments later, bull-rushing the lab!

She'll tear the lab from the tow line!

Powerless and out of options, Jonas clenches the radio in his trembling hand. *You failed, old man. You're best wasn't good enough and you failed.*

The crocodilian mouth widens, the creature bearing down on the pod—

—veering off at the last possible moment!

The wake causes the Abyss Glider to spin, the ten-inch steel claw all that adheres the submersible to the rising lab's platform. After a long moment the cockpit resettles, offering Jonas a far different view—

—this one of Angel. The Megalodon is circling the remains of its mososaur meal. The shark's broad back is arched, its pelvic fins pointed down, the Meg's posture revealing its intent to defend its kill against the liopleurodon.

37

Agitated by the presence of what it perceives as yet another territorial challenger, Bela attacks the yacht's keel with 42,000 pounds of testosterone-laced fury.

Camerawoman Shannon Jenkins, balancing on a narrow slice of deck running along the outside of the main salon, manages two strides before the Megalodon strikes the boat, the titanic impact launching her sideways over the rail and into the water.

The bone-jarring jolt rolls the ship a dizzying thirty degrees to port, pitching the ship's passengers into chaos.

Standing on the flybridge, Lana Wood nearly flips head-first over the rail as the boat suddenly tilts, the sea reaching up for her. Clutching the rail, she hangs on, managing to maintain her balance while lunging for Max—

—her young grandson already airborne, flung into the night.

"Max!" The former Bond actress lands on her back as the yacht rights itself. On hands and knees she crawls to the circular stairwell, then bounds down the steps to the main salon, pushing her way through an entanglement of bodies and out onto the aft deck, her eyes frantically searching the dark water.

"Max!" Lana is bordering on hysterics. "Help me, somebody help! I can't see him!" She drags Blair Bates to his feet, the biker's shaved head trickling blood. "My grandson fell overboard. I can't find him!"

Bates scans the surface—

—as Lizzy breaches sideways out of the surf, a gushing object clenched within the albino's chomping jaws.

"Max!" Lana collapses to her knees, her blood-curdling wail eliciting screams from the other passengers.

Bates grabs her by the arm. "No, lady. That was the dolphin! Look, there's your kid!" He points to where the boy has surfaced thirty feet off the port-side bow.

Max treads water, wide-eyed and terrified, barely able to muster the strength to keep his head above the five-foot swells, let alone call out in the darkness for help.

Spotting her grandson, Lana kicks off her high heels and leaps into the Pacific! One deck below in the V.I.P. stateroom, Scott Jenkins retrieves a monitor from a pile of equipment, an underwater image appearing sideways on the screen, a pair of woman's legs suddenly plunging into the frame. "Jesus, there's someone in the water." He adjusts his headset. "Shannon, did you lose the camera overboard? Shannon?" He switches channels. "Shauna, where's your sister?"

"I don't know? Wait ... I see her camera and reach pole floating overboard. Dad, that actress is in the water!"

"Find your sister!" Scott's eyes are locked onto the monitor as a lead-gray dorsal fin moves vertically down the frame, gliding just beneath Lana Wood's churning feet. "Dear God."

Swimming with the current, Lana closes on her grandson—

—oblivious of Bela, who glides ten feet beneath her, homing in on Max's fluttering heartbeat. Interpreting Lana's presence as a rival competing for her meal, the agitated predator banks away from the boy and rises to the surface—

—engulfing Lana Wood whole!

Disoriented, suddenly cloaked in darkness, yet still very much alive, Lana fights to swim back to what she believes is the surface against a steady flow of water streaming in from Bela's partially open jaws. She flails, prone in the suffocating pitch, slicing her hands against a sharp object, her bare feet pressing against something that feels like rubbery sandpaper. Convinced she has stepped on one of the Megalodon's backs, she kicks wildly, her lungs on fire—

—only to be driven chest-first against the Meg's tongue by the roof of Bela's mouth. Pinned down, the Meg's tongue heaves Lana sideways in the muted blackness—

—the unseen daggers puncturing her flesh! Her cries are stifled by an ungodly embrace that crushes her existence into pulp and releases her soul to a heavenly light, even as Bela's tongue guides her physical remains into hell.

Unable to see over the dark swells, Max never witnesses his grandmother's demise. Caught within Bela's undertow, the boy is dragged back toward the yacht then snatched from the sea by Blair Bates. He releases the child to the deck, fighting to catch his own breath.

"You okay, kid?"

Max nods, still in shock. "Where's Nana?"

"Help! Somebody help me!"

Bates and several crewmen hurry forward to the yacht's bow. Shannon Jenkins is treading water by the anchor windlass, the boat's freeboard far too high for her to reach up and grab onto the rail. "What is wrong with you people? Didn't anyone hear me screaming?"

The camerawoman is helped on board as a Coast Guard cutter appears from the south, its lights flashing. Danielle Taylor is in the bridge, wrapped in a wool blanket, her livid mother, Terry, by her side.

ᗢ   ᗢ   ᗢ

A THREE-HOUR search for Lana Wood will yield nothing. By daylight, the news is everywhere, the incident shockingly reminiscent of the tragic drowning of her beloved sister, Natalie, decades earlier.

By noon Pacific Time, the developing story will continue with the arrests of Sara Toms and Jessica Tompson. Within hours, manslaughter will be added to the R.A.W. founders' growing list of charges as the remains of Virgil Carmen are pulled from the Tanaka Lagoon's main drain.

A small craft advisory is issued. Surfing beaches are closed, all diving ceased until further notice. Boat captains and fishermen are asked to report any shark sightings immediately to the Coast Guard, with helicopters added to patrol the shoreline.

None of these precautions will prove necessary. Freed from the confines of their birthplace, the two Megalodon siblings have gone deep, following the abyssal terrain of the Monterey Bay Canyon to open water, far away from the lingering scent of their dominant mother.

38

Panthalassa Sea

Angel stops feeding, her back muscles and pectoral fins rigid as she assumes a defensive posture. Remaining close to the kill, her senses lock on to the larger challenger moving along the periphery.

The liopleurodon's forelimbs turn downward, her back muscles taut as she sizes up the Megalodon. Apex predators rarely cross paths, but when they do it becomes a battle for supremacy; and there can be only one survivor.

Angel is first to act, feigning a direct strike, her sudden charge meant to put forth the challenge and evaluate her opponent's response.

More maneuverable than the shark, the liopleurodon easily circles out of harm's way—

—sending the Megalodon rushing back to safeguard her kill.

This dance is repeated three more times until the Meg, bull-rushing the liopleurodon, gauging her enemy's speed, the liopleurodon circling away, only to drift closer to the mososaur remains with each pass—

—she finally snatches it!

Having drawn the liopleurodon into her kill zone, Angel attacks in earnest, her jaws managing to latch onto the pliosaur's short, muscular tail. The bite is neither mortal nor crippling, but it is serious nonetheless and causes the liopleurodon to whip its crocodilian head around, the big female's jaws slamming down upon the Megalodon's left pectoral fin!

For the next twenty seconds the two monsters swim in tights circles, remaining attached to one another. Their mammoth heads shake back and forth, attempting to gain the torque necessary to allow their teeth to sink deeper into their opponent's lacerated flesh—

—until each releases the other, signaling the end of round one.

The liopleurodon glides off to circle once more, her wounded tail trailing blood.

The Meg is bleeding, too, but the wound is superficial, no worse than her mate's assault during her last conception. Like a vigilant yard dog, Angel remains by her kill, refusing to pursue her quicker challenger unless the pliosaur moves closer.

The liopleurodon weighs twice as much as her challenger, but the Megalodon's jaws, better suited for delivering a mortal bite, force the pliosaur to change its tactics.

The liopleurodon moves off into the darkness then descends into a steep dive. The big female will initiate her own attack from below.

∇   ∇   ∇

THE TITANIUM LAB rises through the Panthalassa current, the raging water causing the sphere to spin counterclockwise.

David and Kaylie huddle on the floor within their "air bag," the radio transmitter close by. "Dad? Dad, are you there? Come in, please!"

"I'm here."

"What happened? Are you alright?"

"I'm attached to the rescue cable. Lost both wings when I had a little run in with Maren's monster."

"The liopleurodon?"

"Never seen anything like it. Don't worry, Angel's got its undivided attention."

"Angel? Dad, what's Angel doing down here?"

"Long story, and we need to conserve your air. But I had an idea. What are the interior walls made of? Are they padded, or is the titanium showing?"

"Titanium."

"Good. And the interior temperature?"

"Right now? About sixty-five degrees. Dad, what are you thinking?"

"The higher we ascend, the colder the ocean temperature will get. I want you to turn the thermostat up as high as it can go. Let's see if we can't sweat those metal plates."

"Condensation ... that's brilliant."

"Once the moisture builds up, you'll need to wipe it down with a cloth and squeeze the excess into the water tank. It'll be tight, but it can work, provided you two don't expend too much energy."

"Understood." David pinches tears from his eyes. "Dad—"

"David, I know I can be rough on you at times, but I'm very proud of you. Don't worry about a thing. We're going to get through this little challenge together. Okay?"

"Okay." The lab stops spinning, allowing David to reset the thermostat. He turns the temperature up to one hundred degrees Fahrenheit, the blower fans on high.

"Mr. Taylor, this is Kaylie Szeifert. I just wanted to tell you that your son's amazing. He's already saved us about a dozen times. It's my fault he even made this dive; he was just trying to protect me. I should have listened when you."

"Well, Kaylie, I don't know what it is with us Taylor men, but the women in our lives always seem to get us to do the craziest things. I'm guessing my son must really like you. I'm looking forward to meeting you in person in about thirty-three minutes."

"Me, too."

Aboard the Dubai Land I
Philippine Sea

Fiesal bin Rashidi stares, breathless, at the sonar monitor now tracking the abyssal lab. Moving beneath the steadily rising blip are two larger objects.

Brian Suits points to the blip hovering at 21,890 feet. "This one's Angel. We've been tracking her using the Abyss Glider. This second object is much larger."

"The liopleurodon?"

"Has to be."

"How do we lure it up?"

"There seems to be a territorial battle going on between the two creatures. Angel's been rigged to a neurotransmitter. The control device is aboard the hopper dredger. We tell Taylor's people that we want Angel to surface—"

"—and the liopleurodon will follow."

"Hopefully."

"How far out is the *Mogamigawa*?"

"The supertanker should arrive within the hour."

"We can't wait. Have the *Tonga* prepare their nets, then contact the hopper dredger and tell them what we want."

"And if they refuse?"

Bin Rashidi stares again at the sonar screen. "If they refuse, tell them we'll shutdown the winch."

Aboard the McFarland
Philippine Sea

"Son of a bitch!" Mac slams down the radio receiver. "I knew we couldn't trust these bastards." He turns to Brent Nichols. "Can we bluff them? Convince them the receiver's still working?"

"The receiver is working. The steel cable must be acting like an underwater antenna."

"Then do it. Lure Angel back up the hole."

"And what if the liopleurodon doesn't follow her up? Bin Rashidi's already threatened to leave Taylor and his kid on the bottom of the sea floor."

"You're right. I need to handle this myself ... get on board the Arab's boat, stall them if I can." Mac hovers over the marine biologist's laptop. "Show me how this thing works."

Panthalassa Sea

Ten thousand feet.

Pressed back in his pilot's chair like an astronaut, Jonas stares straight up through the night glass as the Panthalassa's geological ceiling appears out of the olive-green darkness. Moments later, the exit hole looms into view, bringing with it a sense of relief.

"David, we're about to enter the chute. How are you two doing?"

David is in the lab's upper level, Kaylie in the lower, both busy mopping beads of condensation from the titanium walls.

Kaylie grabs the transmitter. "The primary generator gave out a few minutes ago. We're using the backup. David was afraid to put too much strain on it, so he shut down the thermostat. But the walls are still sweating, and so are we. Between the two of us, we must have added another three inches of water to the tank."

"Good, that's good. Soak up as much as you can then lay down and rest. We're almost home." Jonas clicks off the radio, and that's when he feels it—a distinct *twang*—the reverberation coming from the steel line above his head.

Jonas grips the edge of his seat, his pulse pounding in his neck as the Abyss Glider and lab enters the hole. The sub begins to quiver as a thin strand of steel line—one of four woven together to form the cable—tumbles down upon the outside of the cockpit.

No, not now ...

They pass the halfway point, the exit coming into view overhead when a second *snap* sends the lab swaying.

"Dad?"

"The cable's fraying. Hold on. We're nearly out of the hole!"

The lab and its submersible escort continue rising, the steel cable groaning as it drags them out of the crater and into the Philippine Sea. They rise another eighty feet before one of the joints gives out.

Jonas registers a sickening rush of adrenaline in his stomach as the sub, weighed down by the 94,000-pound lab, plunges backwards through the depths—

—landing with a skull-rattling thud on the outer rim of the crater.

The sphere rolls toward the edge of the black hole, the *AG III* flipping around its hull, crashing sideways against the sea floor—

—creating a wedge that prevents the lab from rolling back down the hole.

39

"What do you mean, the cable snapped?"

"It was an accident, Mr. Mackredies, just as Captain Suits reported." Fiesal bin Rashidi's cold, ebony eyes return Mac's accusing glare. "The lab and Glider made it out of the Panthalassa Sea but remain marooned along the Philippine Sea floor in 7,800 feet of water. We will not send a rescue sub down with another line until we get what we want."

"David's running out of air as we speak!"

"Then I advise you to stop speaking and begin instructing your monster. Once the liopleurodon surfaces, we will make the Shinkai available to you to so that you can attach another tow line ... provided you supply your own crew. Those are my terms, Mr. Mackreides. And I won't be adding a luxury box at Pac Bell Field or a peace treaty between the Israelis and Hamas."

Bin Rashidi smiles smugly.

It takes all of Mac's reserves to keep from bashing the man across his uni-brow with the laptop. He storms out of the wheelhouse, pushing past Ibrahim Al Hashemi.

Bin Rashidi turns to the marine biologist. "The harpoon gun loaded with the tagging device ... it is operational?"

"Yes. Mounted in the trawler's bow."

"Be ready, my friend. We may need it."

Panthalassa Sea

The liopleurodon rises from the depths, its 200,000-pound frame slicing through the sea, leaving barely a ripple. It cannot see the Megalodon but it can smell its blood, just as it can taste the mososaur's remains. The monster homes in on both, ascending in a steady, spiraling pattern so as not to reveal her presence.

Equipped with the best sensory array afforded by nature, Angel tracks its challenger as it rises, its ampullae of Lorenzini locked in on the electrical impulses emanating from the pliosaur's beating heart. The liopleurodon's speed and angle of ascent, similar to that of a great white attacking a seal, places the Megalodon in grave danger.

The Meg continues to circle the dead mososaur in short, muscular bursts, its predatory instinct preventing it from abandoning its kill and fleeing.

And then another signal reaches its brain, stimulating its olfactory senses, beckoning it to the surface. The Meg becomes agitated, the danger growing, its challenger streaking toward it from below!

Snatching the mososaur remains in its jaws, Angel launches her girth topside, her caudal fin pumping hard.

Shifting from stealth to speed, the liopleurodon executes a series of quick downward strokes, closing the gap to fifty feet. Opening its jaws, it lunges forward to bite Angel's caudal fin—

—when it's bashed sideways by a roaring river!

The Panthalassa current whips the pliosaur sideways, forcing it to streamline its limbs. By the time it has resumed its ascent, the Megalodon is gone.

Emerging from the current, the giant female once more picks up the Meg's scent. Swimming side to side like a crocodile, it races toward the subterranean ceiling in pursuit.

$$\forall \quad \forall \quad \forall$$

THE LAB IS teetering on its side, the interior a shambles. Equipment lies in heaps, computer monitors smashed, books buried beneath collapsed shelves. Darkness beckons, the lights flickering behind the nearly drained backup generator.

David claws his way up the slanted lower deck floor to the life support system. The unit is bolted to the floor, but the tank is angled sideways, preventing the hard-earned pint of remaining water from draining into the liquid-gas conversion unit, stifling the flow of air.

"David, your father!"

He slides down the floor to the ladder and enters the upper level, now on an equal plane to the lower. Kaylie has cleared a path to the portal and is staring out the thick acrylic window, the sea bathed in the lab's eerie red exterior lights.

David joins her.

The lab is situated on the crater's precipice, the hole looming beneath them. Just visible below the viewport is the bow of the *AG III*, the sphere pinning the sub's cockpit.

"Dad!" David scrambles through the pile of smashed equipment, locating the radio. "Dad? Dad, can you hear me?"

"I'm ... here." Suspended sideways at a painful angle in his seat, Jonas releases his harness, allowing his body to tumble to the top of the inverted escape pod, now wedged under the lab.

"Are you hurt?"

"I've been better. What's your status?"

"Life support's off line. I need to find a way to drain the water into the system."

"Find a way. The good news is that we're out of the Panthalassa. They can send a vessel down with another tow line."

"Dad ... here comes the bad news."

Angel rises from out of the crater, her albino hide glowing behind the night glass, her jaws clenching the remains of what had been a forty-foot mososaur. Emerging into the Philippine Sea, the Meg releases the ragged carcass and circles the hole.

David presses his face to the portal, catching a glimpse of her posture. "She's really agitated. I've never seen her like this."

Unable to see, Jonas's eyes settle on the sonar monitor and the rising blip. "The liopleurodon, it followed her up. David, hold on!"

The pilosaur soars out of the hole—

—as Angel launches her attack, driving her hyperextended jaws into her larger foe.

But the liopleurodon is far too big and is moving way too fast. The Megalodon's jaws miss the creature's forelimb and strike her muscular torso as big around as a C-5 cargo plane. The devastating impact costs Angel two front teeth.

Reacting quickly, the pliosaur rolls its body away from the shark's jaws and snaps at its secondary dorsal fin, its eight-inch needle teeth succeeding in crushing the neurotransmitter's antenna.

The two titans continue to rise, entwined as they bite and gnaw at one another—

—oblivious to the *Tonga's* nets.

Aboard the Tonga
Philippine Sea

Storm clouds roll in from the east, the late afternoon shower soaking the crewmen toiling on the supertanker's main deck.

Monty rests his exhausted body on an expanse of pipe, his mind entering an almost vegetative state as he watches his uncle James chase after the heavyset engineer.

"You have six winches! All I need is one."

"For the last time, Mackreides, two winches per net, three nets in the water, those are Mr. bin Rashidi's orders. He said nothing about lowering the Shinkai back into the drink. And believe me, with those two monsters down there, that slow-moving bucket of bolts is the last place you'd want to be right now." John LeBlanc hustles to the crew manning the bow winches.

Mac gives chase, refusing to back down. "The last place I'd want to be is in that lab. My godson's trapped down there, suffocating! Now I want a tow line and that Japanese sub in the water right now, or—"

"Or what?" LeBlanc turns to face him, backed by three rain-soaked, grease-covered members of his crew. "Listen, friend, the moment we haul bin Rashidi's new pet out of the sea, we'll harness the sub. Until then, stay the hell out of my way."

The rain is coming down in sheets now, forcing Monty to turn away. On the distant horizon he can make out an approaching vessel—the *Mogamigawa*—the *Tonga's* sister ship. Still many miles away, the massive supertanker is preparing to slalom—to commence a braking pattern that veers the ship back and forth from starboard to port while her engines run full astern, the boat's captain attempting to bring his vessel in as close as he can to the *Tonga*.

Monty stares at the distant speck, the idea germinating in his head buried beneath an avalanche of scatterbrain thoughts. *Big ship ... pray for David. Pray for the ship. A praying mantis can't impregnate the female while his head is still attached to his body. The female initiates mating by ripping the male's head off. A headless cockroach can live nine days before it starves to death. Right-handed people live nine years longer than left-handed people. Polar bears are left-handed. I wonder if Jonas Junior is a southpaw.*

Monty slaps himself repeatedly across the forehead, trying hard to focus. *Tanker, tanker, tanker, tanker. How can the tanker help David? Tankers are so big they can't stop. Fleas are small, but they can jump three hundred fifty times their own body length. Ants can pull thirty times their weight. Tankers can pull submarines off the bottom, it's called the Venturi effect ...*

Mac grabs him by the shirt collar. "Come with me. I need your help rigging a tow line and hook to the Manta Ray."

"Tankers can pull submarines off the bottom!"

"I know. But first we need to attach a tow line."

"No, Uncle James. No, we don't!"

❧ ❧ ❧

THE TWO SUPER-predators break away from one another, both bleeding from flesh wounds, neither seriously hurt.

Liopleurodon's rule over the Panthalassa Sea dates back tens of millions of years, the species' evolution, from a marine reptile to a gilled giant, allowing it to establish its dominance. Since reaching maturity, the prodigious female has never been challenged, even by her own kind, but the Megalodon's sheer ferocity, combined with the biting power behind her jaws, make her a formidable opponent and a real threat to her survival.

Opting for a less risky method of winning the battle, the pliosaur descends quickly, veering toward the abandoned mososaur remains. In one motion, the female plucks the discarded carcass off the bottom and banks sharply to retreat down the crater.

But unlike her rival's serrated teeth, the liopleurodon's fangs are narrow and smooth, designed for puncturing, not gripping. Double-clutching the eviscerated mososaur, the pliosaur loses its hold and must loop back to grab it again before the sinking carcass strikes the sea floor.

WHOMP!

With a full head of steam, Angel strikes the liopleurodon flush on its thickly muscled neck, pile-driving the one-hundred-ton goliath sideways into the silty bottom. The pliosaur's neck is too wide even for Angel's hyperextended jaws, but the impact with the sea floor creates a fulcrum that allows the Meg's lower teeth to sink root-deep into the thick hide, her upper teeth buried to the gum line.

The puncture wounds are deep but not mortal. The liopleurodon tries to twist itself free, but its enemy has pinned it awkwardly against the sea floor. Each attempt to free itself provokes the Megalodon into whipping its head to and fro, the frenzied action causing its seven-inch, serrated teeth to saw into the nerve endings within the pliosaur's thick neck muscles.

The pain is paralyzing in its intensity.

The liopleurodon stops struggling, conceding its defeat.

Her challenger immobilized, Angel maintains her death grip. Now, it is just a matter of time.

▽ ▽ ▽

FOR DAVID TAYLOR and Kaylie Szeifert, time is nearly up. The backup generator has died, the air expired, the powerless lab growing colder by the minute. Lying on their backs on the slanted lower-deck floor, the young couple stares into the suffocating darkness, holding hands—awaiting death.

David is first to gasp.

Kaylie squeezes his hand tighter. "I want to marry you, David. But I want a spring wedding. So you'd better hang on. Do you hear me, David Taylor? You're not weaseling out of this!"

He smiles in the darkness, tears rolling down his cheeks.

His father's muted voice stirs him from unconsciousness. "... wait until the lab strikes the supertanker's keel, then open the hatch and swim to the surface. David, can you hear me? If you can't speak, at least give me a sign that you understand! David?"

Kaylie crawls to the radio. Taps the microphone twice.

"Good! Hold on to the hatch, kids. I can hear the tanker bearing down on us!"

Kaylie grabs David and shakes him awake. Digging her nails into his wrists, she drags him toward the hatch and holds on—

—as the forty-seven-ton sphere is heaved upwards as if by the hand of God!

∇ ∇ ∇

Cruising at sixteen knots, displacing over 300,000 tons, the eleven-hundred-foot-long supertanker, *Mogamigawa*, races past its dormant sister ship, its titanic wake actually dragging the *Tonga* a quarter of a mile to the east as its vast keel excavates a vacuous channel across the surface of the Pacific—

—plucking the lab, the Abyss Glider, the fishing nets, the mososaur carcass, and the two interlocked predators off the sea bottom with its prodigious suction, inhaling them into its keel.

Centrifugal force pins David and Kaylie to the floor as the lab spins wildly in the darkness, their arms interlocked around the hatch's wheelhouse.

Dong!

The titanium sphere bashes against the supertanker's reinforced steel hull. Kaylie twists open the wheel until a sliver of blue water rushes in and becomes a raging waterfall that tears open the hatch. The sphere bounces against the keel twice more before the flooding lab is spit sideways beyond the propeller shaft and rapidly begins to sink.

Gripping her unconscious companion in a headlock, Kaylie drags David out the open hatch and into the roaring Pacific. The lab falls away beneath them as they are suddenly rocketed to the surface by the drag from the passing tanker.

Kaylie gasps a life-giving lungful of air then shakes David ... no response. Cradling his head, she breathes into his mouth until his blue complexion pales and he coughs up seawater.

She floats on her back, positioning the back of his head between her breasts. Rain beats down upon them, the sky billowing with thunder clouds.

Simply seeing daylight again makes her giddy. "David, lay back and breathe. Just breathe, baby."

He gasps several breaths then opens his eyes against the blinding downpour. The feeling slowly returns to his limbs. "How?"

"A miracle."

"My father?"

"I ... I don't know."

He lifts his head away from her chest and treads water, the two of them searching the surface, unable to see beyond the nearest swells.

The *Tonga's* stern looms a hundred yards away. Something massive is being hauled out of the water alongside the tanker. The creature's body is tangled within a fishing net, its tail free, slapping the side of the ship.

A shiver shoots down David's spine. "Angel ..."

▽   ▽   ▽

FIESAL BIN RASHIDI bounds across the *Tonga* catwalk to confront his engineer, Brian Suits in tow. "Who gave the orders for the *Mogamigawa* to pass us? Answer me!"

"I did." Mac joins them. "Told them I was you. Must've sounded like an asshole on the radio because they believed me."

"Captain, have this man removed from my ship. Let the Taylors rot in the depths—"

"There!" Monty is at the port rail, searching the sea through a powerful pair of binoculars. "Two survivors. Looks like David and Kaylie!"

Brian Suits takes Monty's glasses and confirms the sighting. He activates his walkie-talkie. "Captain Gober, we have two survivors in the water one hundred yards due west. Unhitch the trawler and pick them up."

"Yes, sir."

"No! You will contact the *Mogamigawa* and order their return. Then empty the net of this abomination and find the liopleurodon!"

"Yes, sir ... right after we pick up my two pilots. Mackreides, get to the trawler. See to it that my orders are carried out."

"You got it."

"There it is!" Monty points below, where an immense dark-backed creature is circling beneath the thrashing Megalodon.

337

Fiesal bin Rashidi rushes to the rail, gawking at the beast. "Incredible. Engineer, ready your nets!"

As he watches, the pliosaur disappears underwater.

▽ ▽ ▽

"DAVID, THERE! I see your father's escape pod!" Kaylie points in the direction of the *Tonga*. Forty yards away, a small acrylic escape pod is rising and falling with the swells.

They swim out to the buoyant sphere, Kaylie on one side, David the other, the two of them using the remains of the *AG III*'s shredded wings as a flotation device.

Pressing his face to the night glass, David peers inside.

His father is strapped halfway in his harness. He is not moving.

"Dad!" David bangs his hand repeatedly against the dense cockpit. "Dad, can you hear me?"

"David ..." Kaylie points to the tanker.

He looks up to witness the liopleurodon in mid-leap, the creature's immense head rising thirty feet above the surface as the pliosaur's monstrous jaws slam shut along the base of Angel's flicking tail.

Angel convulses in the net, fountains of blood spraying in all directions. The liopleurodon remains suspended halfway out of the water, her jowls clenched tight, her weight forcing her teeth to tear through the Meg's thick band of muscle and cartilage.

Angel heaves upward in spasms as her entire caudal fin is torn from her body.

The liopleurodon plunges back into the sea with its prize. Blood gushes from the Meg's mortal wound, spraying the side of the tanker, pooling along the surface.

Kaylie looks down at her chest, already covered in oily blood. Amazed that the current could spread Angel's remains so quickly, she turns around, shocked to find the mososaur's shredded carcass floating beside her. In a sudden panic, she kicks both legs, churning up a pink froth as she tries to climb atop the Abyss Glider's escape pod.

David's face is pressed against the cockpit glass, he can see his father stirring inside! Overjoyed, he looks up at Kaylie, a smile on his face—

—his expression turning to horror, fear bursting through every pore of his body as the impossibly large crocodilian mouth rises from below, the jaws opening to snatch the mososaur remains—

—and Kaylie along with it!

Kaylie wheezes as the breath is driven from her chest, the dagger-like teeth impaling her. She looks at David, bewildered, then disappears beneath the crimson-frothed surf.

David bellows a blood-curdling scream, pounding his fists against the escape pod's glass, rousing his father. And then his tortured mind simply shuts down and he passes out.

Lying in the bottom of the cockpit, Jonas opens his eyes and is sickened to witness the girl as she's dragged underwater and devoured alive! He turns away only to see his son's pale face sinking underwater!

Jonas activates the emergency escape hatch, blowing the lid off the cockpit. Lunging over the side, he grabs David by his hair and hauls his inert body into the open sphere.

The pod swirls like a giant teacup, caught within the current generated by the liopleurodon's moving mass. The monster circles just below the surface, gauging the floating object.

The trawler bears down upon them, its growling twin engines scaring the pliosaur away. Standing in the bow, Ibrahim Al Hashemi fires the harpoon gun, the lance and its tracking device shooting through air and sea before burying itself deep within the creature's broad back.

The liopleurodon submerges, returning to the deep with the mososaur's remains.

Mac rushes to the trawler's bow and looks down. Jonas is hugging his unconscious son to his chest, his face pale and distraught.

"J.T.? Is David okay?"

"He's alive, Mac. But I'm not sure if he'll ever be okay again."

Epilogue

Two months later ...

Though he is only forty-six, Tim Schulte's hair is almost completely gray, an occupational hazard common among psychiatrists. He opens the door to his office, ushering his patient in from the waiting room.

David Taylor is wearing a white tee-shirt and faded jeans, a double-wide 49ers sweatband over his right wrist. His brown hair is long and unkempt, hanging below his shoulders. He collapses in the leather easy chair, staring at Schulte's diplomas, his almond eyes vacant, hovering above dark circles.

"So? You've been on the new meds a week. Are you sleeping any better?"

"No."

Schulte scribbles a note on his legal pad. "Let's give them another week. Adjusting one's brain chemistry takes time. And the night terrors ... do you still wake up screaming?"

"Yes."

"Every night?"

"Unless I'm drunk."

"And how often does that happen?"

"Every night."

"A bit excessive, don't you think?"

"Adjusting one's brain chemistry takes time."

"David, therapy means very little unless you're a willing participant."

David says nothing—stares out the window.

"Your mother mentioned to me that you and Monty moved into an apartment together. He's the bi-polar fellow."

"Is that a problem?"

"You tell me."

"He babbles and I scream. We make a nice couple."

"And the two of you get drunk together." The psychiatrist waits for a response, but gets nothing. "I understand your father's been in touch with Kaylie's parents. He said they wanted to meet you. It could be a good thing. Sharing grief can sometimes ease one's sorrow."

David's eyes pan slowly across the room, locking in on Dr. Schulte's. "Sorrow's a funny thing. There's the sorrow one feels when a loved one dies, say, of cancer;

that's a pretty bad sorrow. You feel empty inside. You share that grief with others. Eventually you move on. Then there's a different kind of sorrow ... like, say, I shove a gun in your wife's mouth and blow her head into a million pieces. That sorrow's a little trickier to deal with.

"Basically, you have three options. The first is to take the easy way out." David pulls back the 49ers sweat band, revealing the three red, swollen wounds on the inside of his wrist, the slashes stitched together. "That option only works until you think about the repercussions, that you're pulling your family into the same hell hole you're wallowing in. Then it's not so cool. The second option is to go numb while you talk about shit with professional sorrow sharers like yourself, as if anything said in this room's going to change a thing."

"And the third option?"

He stares at the psychiatrist's blue eyes, his expression stone.

David stands to leave, pausing at the door. "This'll be our last session. Me and Monty, we're going away for a while. Call it a business trip."

"Do you think that's a good idea? You've only been out of the hospital three weeks."

"Yeah, well, it beats the other two options. See you in my dreams."

With a final wave, he walks out the door.

Juan de Fuca Strait
Vancouver Island, British Columbia

The northwest coastline of British Columbia stretches nearly seventeen thousand miles, incorporating countless islands, inlets, and bays. Vancouver Island is British Columbia's largest island, separated from the mainland by the Strait of Juan de Fuca, a narrow waterway that connects Puget Sound and the Georgia Strait to the Pacific Ocean. Marine life is abundant in these nutrient-rich waters, which serve as feeding grounds for both local and migrating populations of humpbacks, orca, grays, and minke whales. For saltwater fishermen, the deep waters off Vancouver Island are home to Chinook and coho salmon, rockfish, lingcod, and the giant halibut—the major carnivore fish of the Pacific Northwest.

Now, a new species of carnivore has made this oceanic waterway its home.

The orca are transients, the resident killer whales having mysteriously vacated the area weeks earlier. There are six whales in the pod: two mature females, two calves, a juvenile male, and a thirty-foot, twelve-thousand-pound bull. They have been moving at a steady pace all day. Now they have slowed with the night to feed.

The big male is uneasy. Vocalizing frequently, it scans the dark sea using its echolocation as it leads the others toward their next meal.

The kill is fresh, the gray whale bleeding badly as it floats in the current. The females feed first, their three-inch conical teeth ravaging great bites from the bloated carcass, their young feeding off the scraps.

Suddenly, the male senses something large moving along the bottom. The creature circling below is longer than the bull and three times its girth. Slapping its fluke against the surface, the male sets the pod back in formation—

—as the second predator appears, closing fast.

One of the females leads the pod to the north, while the other guards the calves. The juvenile male takes up the rear, the bull moving beneath the pod to discourage any attack from below.

Lizzy charges along the surface, baiting the bull.

The big male soars past the lead female to confront the albino—

—as Belle launches her attack from below. Cruising vertically at twenty knots, the Meg strikes the orca between its flippers, lifting the bull clear out of the water, its serrated teeth tearing open the tender belly!

Lizzy moves in quickly, gnawing off the killer whale's dorsal fin in one horrific bite!

The rest of the pod quickly alters its course as the two Megs slaughter their leader.

No other creatures approach the sisters' kill. None will challenge their rule; for, the Strait of Juan de Fuca now belongs to *Carcharodon megalodon*. It is in these waters that Belle and Lizzy will birth their young, the pups protected from their parents within the rocky alcoves and shallows until the day that they, too, become sizable juveniles. Forced to territorialize another body of water, these young females will eventually beget their own kind, their internal fertilization defying extinction—Mother Nature setting a different course for her apex predator.

THE ANGEL OF DEATH IS DEAD—
—LONG LIVE HER QUEENS.

The End of
MEG 4: Hell's Aquarium

The Taylors will return in

MEG 5: Night Stalkers

To receive free sneak peeks or to enter a contest to become a
character in an upcoming Steve Alten novel, go to:

www.SteveAlten.com

and register for FREE UPDATES.

Now Available

KRONOS is the next amazing thriller from Jeremy Robinson, one of the most fast paced and original thriller authors. Kronos will have readers on the edge of their seat and then knock them out of it with a twist that is impossible to see coming.

"JEREMY ROBINSON IS AN ORIGINAL AND EXCITING VOICE."
-- STEVE BERRY, NEW YORK TIMES BESTSELLING AUTHOR OF THE VENETIAN
BETRAYAL AND THE CHARLEMAGNE PURSUIT

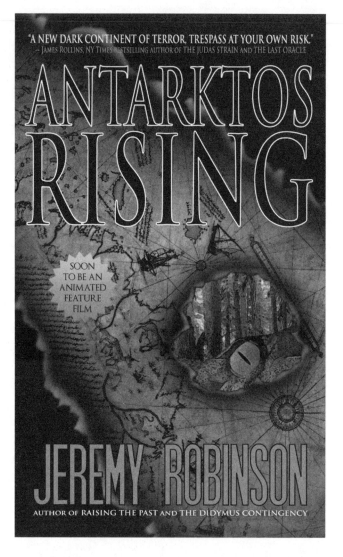

COMING SOON

COMING SOON FROM VARIANCE

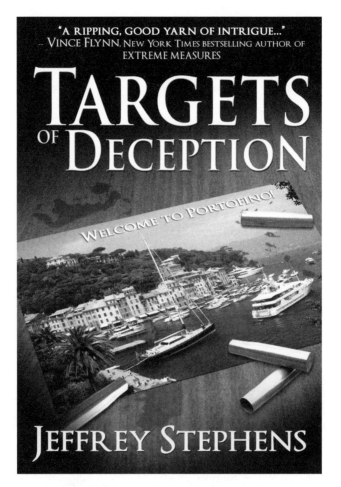

"JEFFREY STEPHENS HAS ARRIVED WITH TARGETS OF DECEPTION; A RIPPING, GOOD YARN OF INTRIGUE THAT WILL KEEP YOU TURNING THE PAGES ALL THE WAY TO ITS EXPLOSIVE ENDING."

-- *VINCE FLYNN #1 NEW YORK TIMES BEST-SELLING AUTHOR OF PROTECT AND DEFEND*

COMING ON AUGUST 25, 2009